THE LAST WARRIOR

THE LAST WARRIOR

W. MICHAEL FARMER

FIVE STAR
A part of Gale, Cengage Learning

GALE
CENGAGE Learning·

Farmington Hills, Mich • San Francisco • New York • Waterville, Maine
Meriden, Conn • Mason, Ohio • Chicago

GALE
CENGAGE Learning·

The publisher bears no responsibility for the quality of information provided through author or third-party Web sites and does not have any control over, nor assume any responsibility for, information contained in these sites. Providing these sites should not be construed as an endorsement or approval by the publisher of these organizations or of the positions they may take on various issues.

LIBRARY OF CONGRESS CATALOGING-IN-PUBLICATION DATA

Names: Farmer, W. Michael, 1944– author.
Title: The last warrior / by W. Michael Farmer.
Description: First edition. | Waterville, Maine : FIVE STAR, [2019] | Series: The life and times of Yellow Boy, Mescalero Apache ; Book 3
Identifiers: LCCN 2018025294 (print) | LCCN 2018027305 (ebook) | ISBN 9781432849979 (ebook) | ISBN 9781432849962 (ebook) | ISBN 9781432849955 (hardcover)
Subjects: LCSH: Apache Indians—History—Fiction. | Mescalero Indians—History—Fiction. | Mescalero Indian Reservation (N.M.)—Fiction. | Bosque Redondo Indian Reservation (N.M.)—Fiction. | GSAFD: Historical fiction.
Classification: LCC PS3606.A725 (ebook) | LCC PS3606.A725 L37 2019 (print) | DDC 813/.6—dc23
LC record available at https://lccn.loc.gov/2018025294

First Edition. First Printing: February 2019
Find us on Facebook—https://www.facebook.com/FiveStarCengage
Visit our website—http://www.gale.cengage.com/fivestar/
Contact Five Star Publishing at FiveStar@cengage.com

Printed in Mexico
1 2 3 4 5 6 7 23 22 21 20 19

For Corky, my best friend and wife.

TABLE OF CONTENTS

ACKNOWLEDGMENTS

I owe a debt of gratitude to many friends and associates who have supported and encouraged me in this work. There are several who deserve special mention.

Melissa Watkins Starr provided editorial reviews and many helpful questions, suggestions, and comments to enhance manuscript quality. Her work is much appreciated.

Bruce Kennedy's knowledge of the southwest and invaluable commentary made many helpful contributions to this story. I thank him for his support.

Lynda A. Sánchez's firsthand knowledge of Apache culture and history provided guiding light and clarity on many details. Her insights and comments on this story were invaluable. I owe her a debt of gratitude.

Pat and Mike Alexander graciously opened their home to me during return visits to New Mexico for research and book tours, and they provided company on long roads across endless deserts and prairies and tall mountains. Friends such as these are rare and much appreciated.

Excellent descriptions of Apache culture, beliefs, and methods of raiding and war in the mid- to late-nineteenth century are provided by anthropologists, linguists, and historians. Some of the ones I found most helpful are provided in Additional Reading at the end of the story. The work by Grenville Goodwin in *Western Apache Raiding and Warfare* and by Eve Ball and her associates Lynda A. Sánchez and Nora Henn in *Indeh* provided especially valuable insights into Apache life because they faithfully recorded the stories Grenville's and Eve's Apache friends remembered of the old days, and they remembered those days very well.

FICTIONAL CHARACTERS

Beela-chezzi (Crooked Fingers)—Friend of Yellow Boy

Bitághaa' Lichoo' (Red Beard)—Yellow Boy's Apache name for Red Tally

Bitl'ól Dáhále (His Fast Rope)—Husband of Red Bird Singing

Blue Flower—Wife to Running Wolf and daughter of Kitsizil Lichoo' and Calico Dove

Calico Dove—Second wife of Kitsizil Lichoo'

Camisa Roja (Red Shirt)—Pancho Villa Dorado, who tried to kill Hombrecito

Carmen Rosario—Mexican wife of Beela-chezzi

Dawahn Dáha (Always Laughs)—Daughter of Yibá and Lucky Star

Deer Woman—Wife of Kah

Falling Water—Knows Horses's second wife, daughter of Sleepy

Hawú dat'éhe (Quiet Dove)—Wife of Hígháh and daughter of Beela-chezzi and Carmen Rosario

Hidloh (He Laughs)—Youngest son of Yellow Boy and Juanita

Hígháh (He Comes)—Oldest son of Yellow Boy and Juanita

Hombrecito (Little Man)—Henry Fountain, aka Henry Grace, Yellow Boy's adopted grandson

Idish'aal (I am singing)—Son of Quiet Dove and Hígháh

Idlaaní (One Who Drinks)—Daughter and first child of Knows Horses and Lola Mes

11

Igod Kah—Shortened Arrow

Ish-kay-neh **(Boy)**—Early name of the first son of Knows Horses and Lola Mes

Juanita—Yellow Boy's first wife

Kah (Arrow)—Lifetime friend of Yellow Boy

Kitsizil Lichoo' (His Hair Red)—Adopted Indah son of Juh and friend of Yellow Boy

Knows Horses—Yellow Boy's younger brother (formerly Little Rabbit)

Lola Mes—*Di-Yen*, daughter of Sangre del Diablo, raised by Ojo Verde, wife to Knows Horses

Lucky Star—Yellow Boy's adopted sister, married to Yibá

Maria—Mother of Juanita and Moon on the Water

Moon on the Water—Yellow Boy's second wife

Na'ilín Súl (Flute Girl)—Name of first child of Knows Horses and Falling Water

Ojo Verde (Green Eye)—Witch, half-sister and lover of Sangre del Diablo

Para-dee-ah-tran (The Contented)—First son of Kah and Deer Woman

Quentin Peach—Reporter for the *El Paso Herald*

Red Bird Singing—Daughter of Kah and Deer Woman

Redondo—Son of Yellow Boy and Moon on the Water

Red Tally (Bitághaa' Lichoo')—Professional assassin paid to murder Albert Fountain

Rufus Pike—Rancher living in Organ Mountains, mentor and guardian for Hombrecito

Running Wolf—Adopted son of Beela-chezzi, son of Carmen Rosario (aka Jesús and *Shiyé*), married to Blue Flower, daughter of Kitsizil Lichoo'

Sábado (Saturday)—Mescalero tribal police sergeant

Sangre del Diablo (Blood of the Devil)—Witch and leader of scalp hunters

Fictional Characters

Shis-Indeh—People of the Woods (the Apache name for themselves)

Sleepy—Camp midwife, mother of Yibá and Falling Water

Sons-ee-ah-ray (Morning Star)—Mother of Yellow Boy and Knows Horses

Steps in Water—First wife of Kitsizil Lichoo'

Yellow Boy—Killer of Witches and the Last Warrior

Yibá (He Waits for Him)—Young Apache warrior (aka *Ish-kay-neh*)

HISTORICAL CHARACTERS

Almer Blazer—Son of Joseph H. Blazer, owner and operator of Blazer's Mill and Store

Joseph H. Blazer—Original owner and operator of Blazer's Mill and Store at Mescalero

Father Albert Braun—Franciscan Priest at Mescalero from 1916–1951

James R. Carroll—Mescalero Agent from 1902–1912

Chato—Chiricahua Apache leader, army scout

Eugene Chihuahua—Son of Chief Chihuahua, educated leader of Chiricahuas

George R. Crook (Major General US Army)—Commander of Sierra Madre Expedition in 1883

Daklugie—Son of Juh, nephew of Geronimo, educated leader of Chiricahuas

Henry Fulton (Major US Army)—1875 World Champion in shooting for Wimbledon Cup

W.H.H. Llewellyn (*Tata* Crooked Nose)—Mescalero agent from 1881–1884

C.R. Jefferis—Mescalero agent from 1912–1920

Kedinchin—Last Mescalero to kill a white man

Oliver Lee—Accused of being one of the killers of Albert Fountain

Dr. Walter M. Luttrell—Mescalero agent 1898–1902

Magoosh—Lipan Apache Chief, leader at Mescalero

Don McLane—Killed by Kedinchin, brother of Roy McLane

15

Roy McLane—Foreman of Flying H Ranch, brother to Don McLane, killed by Kedinchin

Muchacho Negro—Mescalero warrior and tracker

Peso—Mescalero Chief

Sans Peur—Mescalero Chief, brother of Peso

V.E. Stottler (Lieutenant US Army)—Mescalero Agent from 1895–1898

Ted Sutherland—First Superintendent of Livestock at the Mescalero Reservation

Ussen—Creator God of the Apaches

Pancho Villa—General in 1910 Mexican Revolution, major opponent of Venustiano Carranza

APACHE AND SPANISH
WORDS AND PHRASES

Ázhúo—for sure
Ba'ihénsih—I thank you
Be'idest'íné—binoculars
Bitághaa' Lichoo'—Red Beard
Casa—house (Spanish)
D'anté—greetings
Di-yen—medicine woman or man
Enjuh—good
Googé—whip-poor-will
Hacendado—wealthy landowner (Spanish)
Haheh—puberty ceremony
Hoddentin—sacred pollen
Idiists'ag nih—I hear you
ínashood—missionary
ínashood dilhil'n—Catholic priest
Indah—white men
Indeh—Apaches, the People, as also used in Diné by the Navajo
Ish-kay-neh—boy
Ish-tia-neh—woman
Iyah—mesquite bean pods
Llano—dry prairie (Spanish)
Máquina—sawmill (literally "machine") (Spanish)
Nakai-yes—Mexicans
Nakai-yi—Mexican

Nantan Lupan (Chief Gray Wolf)—the Apache name for General George Crook

Nish'ii'—I see you

Pesh—iron

Pesh biyi'kq'i—iron stove

Pesh-klitso—gold (literally "yellow iron")

Pesh-lickoyee—nickel-plated or silver (literally "white iron")

Pesh líí'beshkee'é—iron horseshoes

Qué pasó?—What's happening? (Spanish)

Ranchería—Apache camp, settlement, camp (Spanish)

Reata—rawhide rope (Spanish)

Río Grande—Great River (Spanish)

Shibébé—uncle

Shináá Cho—telescope (literally "Big Eye")

Shis-Indeh—the Apaches' name for their people (literally "People of the Woods")

Shitaa'—father

Shiye'—my son

Teniente—lieutenant (Spanish)

Tsach—cradleboard

Tsélkani—mulberry wood

APACHE RECKONING OF
TIME AND SEASONS

Harvest—used in the context of time, means a year
Handwidth (against the sky)—about an hour
Season of Little Eagles—early spring
Season of Many Leaves—late spring, early summer
Season of Large Leaves—midsummer
Season of Large Fruit—late summer, early fall
Season of Earth Is Reddish Brown—late fall
Season of Ghost Face—lifeless winter

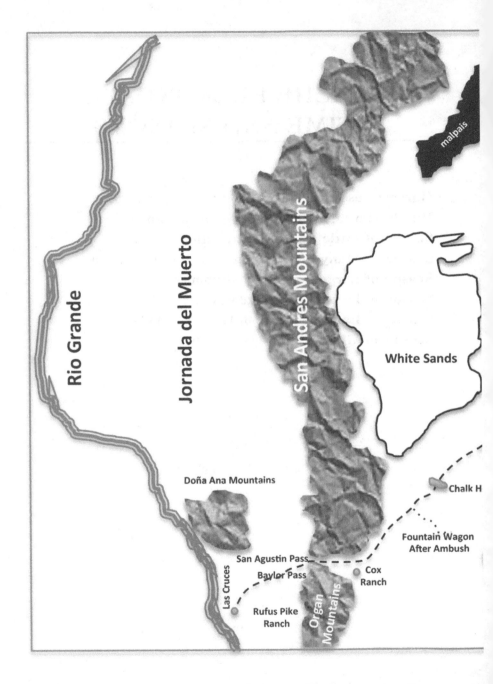

Rio Grande

Jornada del Muerto

San Andres Mountains

malpais

White Sands

Doña Ana Mountains

Chalk H

Fountain Wagon
After Ambush

San Agustin Pass

Baylor Pass

Cox
Ranch

Las Cruces

Rufus Pike
Ranch

Organ
Mountains

Tularosa Basin Country

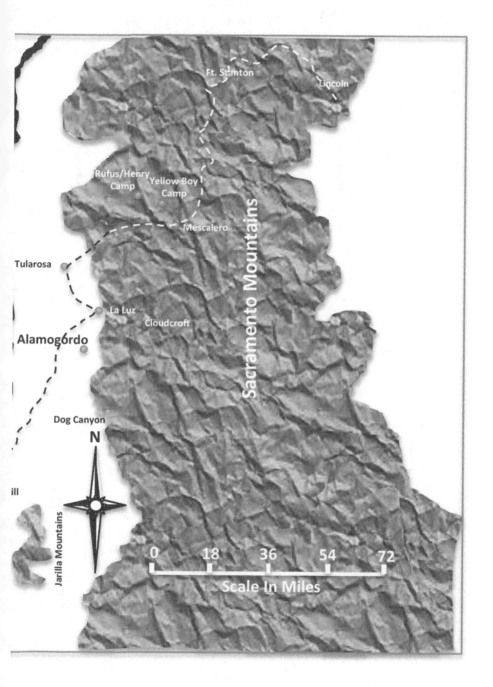

Ft. Stanton

Lincoln

Rufus/Henry Camp

Yellow Boy Camp

Mescalero

Sacramento Mountains

Tularosa

La Luz

Cloudcroft

Alamogordo

Dog Canyon

N

Jarilla Mountains

ill

| 0 | 18 | 36 | 54 | 72 |

Scale In Miles

and the Fountain Ambush

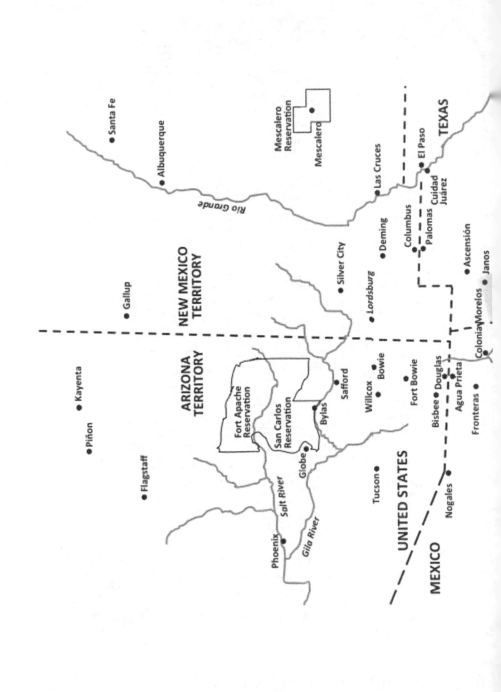

Lipan Apache Country
In Mexico Around 1900

Shaded area was major terrain for the
Apache remnants during the 1886-1940
era

Colonia Oaxaca
Juh Stronghold
Casas Grandes
Colonia Juárez
Buenaventura
Bavispe
Colonia Garcia
Chuhuichupa
Rio Bavispe
Madera
Nácori Chico
Rio Aros
Nacozari
Rio Bavispe
Moctezuma
Rio Yaqui
Hermosillo

Chihuahua
Cuidad Guerrero

Creel

SONORA
CHIHUAHUA

N
W   E
S

0   miles   200

Gulf Of California

Map By W. Michael Farmer 2016

Apache Country Around 1900

PREFACE

The Last Warrior is the third book in an imagined autobiography of a Mescalero Apache warrior, Yellow Boy, who lived from about 1860 to 1951, a span of years that saw his people pushed to the brink of cultural extinction and slowly return. The Mescalero survived to keep the values and beliefs of their life-ways in an ever present, changing, technologically advanced Anglo culture. *The Last Warrior* covers the years 1896 to 1918, a time of many hard changes.

The historical events in the years of *The Last Warrior, The Life and Times of Yellow Boy Mescalero Apache, Book 3* further illustrate what was shown in Books 1 and 2, *Killer of Witches* and *Blood of the Devil,* namely, that while mid-nineteenth-century Apache life-ways were far different from those of the tsunami of Anglo settlers sweeping over them, the Apache people had similar hopes and fears for the survival of their children and the continuation of their life-ways. References for the historical basis and timeline of these stories are in the Additional Reading list provided at the end of the story. A list of historical and fictional characters has been provided to help the reader discern historical fact from fiction and to understand the roles of those who brought an often mixed blessing of great changes to the southwest reservations and how Anglo culture and technology impacted the Apache.

These stories are told through the eyes of Yellow Boy, who, with his gifts of Power, served his people and his family, learned from the whites, and came to an understanding of how to use the white culture to make his own Apache culture survive. The stories of Yellow Boy in the *Life and Times of Yellow Boy Mescalero Apache* series—*Killer of Witches, Blood of the Devil,* and *The Last Warrior*—complement the stories of his relationship with Henry Fountain told in the *Legends of the Desert* series: *Mariana's Knight, Knight's Odyssey,* and *Knight of the Tiger.*

W. Michael Farmer
Smithfield, Virginia
April 2017

★ ★ ★ ★ ★

THE LAST WARRIOR: THE LIFE AND TIMES OF YELLOW BOY, MESCALERO APACHE

★ ★ ★ ★ ★

PROLOGUE

Yellow Boy, my Apache mentor and close friend for over fifty-five years, saved me from certain death in the winter desert when I was eight years old. He helped Rufus Pike raise me, taught me to survive in hard, unforgiving desert and mountain country, and helped me take blood vengeance for my father before I was fifteen years old. In 1950, I persuaded Yellow Boy to tell me his life story while I made "tracks on paper" to keep it for others to read.

Over the course of many afternoons and pots of coffee at his house in a canyon on the reservation, I wrote down his story in English as he told it in a mixture of Mescalero Apache, Spanish, and English in the whispery, rasping voice of a vigorous old man. At the beginning of each session, I read back to him what I had written from the previous session, and after I explained the meaning of some of my fancy words, he usually agreed I had captured the essence of what he had said. When I missed what he meant, I rewrote it until he said it correctly told both the facts and spirit of what had happened.

These journals are his story as he told it and meant it to be heard. The story thus far has been divided into three books. Book 1, *Killer of Witches*, covers the years 1865 to 1880, when Yellow Boy gained his Power and first faced the witch, Sangre del Diablo (Blood of the Devil). Book 2, *Blood of the Devil*, covers the years 1881 to 1896, years when Yellow Boy, in his prime, had some of his greatest victories and hardest defeats. This book, *The Last Warrior,* covers the years 1896 to 1918. These years were a time when the outrageous treatment and willful ignorance of Mescalero culture by agent Lieutenant V.E. Stottler and other agents caused terrific turbulence in Apache lifeways on the reservation, and Ojo Verde, the half-sister and lover of the witch, Sangre del Diablo, appeared for her long-coveted blood revenge against Yellow Boy and his family. During these years, Yellow Boy's family on the reservation grew and adapted to survive in the white man's world until the point where decisions had to be made between life and death in a world his family had no part in creating but in which it now must live.

—Dr. Henry Grace, 1953

CHAPTER 1
A DREAM SPEAKS TRUE

I am Yellow Boy, the last Mescalero warrior, Killer of Witches, man of two women with lodges far apart, and father of children a long time to come and all too quick to die. I'm a survivor of the Apache hard times and disappearance at Bosque Redondo. I escaped the disarming and unhorsing of my People on their own reservation in the time of the Victorio War. I've tracked the great Apache leaders Naiche, Geronimo, Juh, Chihuahua, Loco, Jelikine, and Nana in the Blue Mountains (Sierra Madre) for Nantan Lupan (literally "Chief Gray Wolf," General Crook). I fought the great witch the Nakai-yes (Mexicans) called Blood of the Devil (Sangre del Diablo) three times before I shot out his eyes to send him blind to the Happy Land. I've had dreams and visions and seen the future. Burdened with bitter life on the reservation, my People and I have still endured. Now I'll tell you of the days when a dream I had came to pass and what followed.

In the Season of the Ghost Face, when snow lay in patches across the llano (dry prairie) and the cold wind whistled and moaned, shaking all the brush and pushing gray clouds across a sky scattered with dark spots of blue, an *Indah* (white man) with a great *bitághaa' lichoo'* (red beard), hiding behind a spreading creosote bush, stood and shot a man who drove a wagon. The man had a rifle across his knees and a small boy by his side.

The man fell from the wagon to bleed in the dust. The boy stopped the wagon and ran to hold the man's hand and speak to him. Laughing and watching the man die, Bitághaa' Lichoo' made the boy climb back on the wagon. Soon the boy tried to escape. He yelled and whipped the team and drove the wagon in a hard run up the road toward the Organ Mountain pass the Indah call *San Agustin*. Bitághaa' Lichoo' and his vaqueros (cowboys) laughed when the boy drove the team away. They knew he wouldn't get far before they caught him. The boy saw a vaquero waiting for him on the road ahead and turned the wagon out on to the llano, driving it across patches of snow and little arroyos, past dry weeds and brush, dull green creosote bushes, bare, ragged mesquite, and tall, dry stalks of yucca waving in the wind.

The wagon, bouncing across the rocks and brush of the llano, threw the boy out when it crossed an arroyo no more than a cattle path. The black and the white horses pulling the wagon charged on, leaving him far behind. The boy lay still, facedown in the rocks and sand. I thought he might be dead, but he soon staggered to his feet, his face cut and bloody on one side, his right arm dangling and unmoving. Holding his arm close to his body, he ran up the cattle trail toward the mountains until he found a hiding place under gray tumbleweeds caught in mesquite thorns.

The boy acted more like *un hombrecito*, a little man filled with courage, than *un muchacho*, a child filled with fear. I saw it all through my *Shináá Cho* (telescope, literally "Big Eye") from my hiding place on a little mountain near Baylor Pass. Seeing the evil Bitághaa' Lichoo' and his vaqueros brought to a child of their own kind, I was ready to use the Power Ussen had given me to save the one I would name Hombrecito.

In a dream three harvests earlier, my Power had shown me the ambush and the boy's escape, and it had spoken to me more than thirteen harvests earlier when I, scouting for Nantan Lupan, faced Geronimo on a high ridge in the Blue Mountains in the land of the *Nakai-yes*. Geronimo said, "A time will come for you to help an Indah boy. Do this. He will help our people." Geronimo spoke true. I did not understand his words then, or that they came from his far-seeing Power, but when I saw the ambush, I understood my Power had been telling me to stop the boy from disappearing into the Happy Land of the grandfathers, never to be seen again by human beings.

When the long shadows filled the mountainside canyons and arroyos, I rode down the dark trail from my hiding place and across the llano until I neared the boy's wagon path of mashed weeds and broken bushes. A little light from the setting sun glowing golden on the purple and red mountains gave me just enough light to see. The wind had died, and the clouds had run away, leaving a black sky with a milk river of stars across its great arc, and the icy Ghost Face cold was stronger than during the day. I took care so the vaqueros of Bitághaa' Lichoo' did not see me as they rode the cattle paths looking for *el hombrecito*. I knew I had to get him plenty quick or the Ghost Face would kill him.

The vaqueros couldn't find *el hombrecito* and were angry. They said he was like a rabbit hidden in a hole somewhere and cursed him because they had to ride in the darkness away from the comfort of their fires to find him in places where they could not see. I saw two of them stop by the mesquite where the boy hid, and light their *tobaho* (tobacco). I pulled my bow from its case, strung it, and placed an arrow on the string and held others in my bow hand. I was ready to take them both with the silence of arrows if they found him, but they finished their smokes, one even flipping the cigarette remains into the same mesquite where the boy hid, and rode away down the cattle path. I waited unmoving until I no longer smelled or heard them or their horses.

I threw the big tumbleweed off the boy. Gray, dead grass he had pulled around him to hide and keep warm surrounded his face. He stared at the sky with open eyes. I thought for a heartbeat he had already gone to the grandfathers. Then I saw his chest swell to pull in air. He opened his mouth to speak, but I signaled quiet with the edge of my fingers against my lips and pulled on him to help him up. The pain twisting his face told me he was hurt. I remembered how his right arm dangled when he stood up and how he held it when he ran. I felt a knot below his elbow and knew his forearm was broken. He had a long cut on the side of his face and blood smeared and dried on his shirt, but the cut missed his eyes and mouth, and it didn't look deep. It would be a good warrior scar and make him look fierce to his enemies.

I carried him to my pony and gave him water. He drank too fast, and I had to pull the jug away and make him understand that he had to drink only little swallows, or it could give him a cramping belly that might kill him. Then the Ghost Face cold would surely take him. He began to shake. I felt his bare neck. He was too cold, cold enough to pass soon to the land of the grandfathers. I wrapped him in my blanket and went to cut sticks that would hold his arm straight after I set the broken bone.

He bit down on a stick when I pulled his arm straight. The pain sent him to the land of dreams, but he never whined or moaned. He was brave and strong like an *Indeh* (Apache) boy. Working close to him, I saw that he had much courage, and I admired and liked him even more than when I watched him escape and drive the horses and wagon charging off the road out across the llano.

I tied the sticks in place to hold his arm straight and sat him up on my pony while he was still in the land of dreams. I mounted so I could hold him next to me for warmth while he slept. I tried to think of the best way to keep him alive and return him to his family while I listened to Coyote and his brothers. If I started a fire to warm him, I knew the vaqueros of Bitághaa' Lichoo' would see it and come. It was too far to ride to the Jarilla Mountains to start a fire there on the way back to the tipi of my first wife, Juanita, in the Rinconada Valley. Since the Geronimo War had ended ten harvests ago, Indah still shot Indeh first and then asked what they wanted. I had wives and children to protect and provide with meat. I could not risk going directly to the Indah with the boy.

I thought of Rufus Pike, my Indah teacher and friend over many harvests. He could take the boy back home and say nothing about me. His ranch on the western side of the mountains the Indah called Organ, rising beside me, was the closest, safest shelter. I held the boy close while he stayed in the land of dreams and shook from the cold, even though I wrapped my blanket tight around us and warmed him with my body. In the black night, I rode west over Baylor Pass and then south down the trail away from the lights of Organ village on the west side of the mountains where Rufus's rancho lay.

Rufus's hound howled when he smelled us and heard us coming, but wagged his tail and sat down to watch when I rode up to the lodge Rufus called "shack." Rufus, holding a lantern high, threw open his door and came out wearing the scratchy red pants and shirt in one piece the Indah call long johns. He carried a big shotgun with two barrels, its hammers pulled back and ready to use. He had told me when I had stayed with him the day before that a big cougar was after his stock, and he meant to kill it before it wiped out his little herd.

35

When Rufus saw me, he let down the shotgun's hammers and leaned it against the porch before walking to my horse, still holding his lantern high, his breath in the cold air like steam boiling from a coffee pot. We said nothing as he lifted the blanket to see the boy's face in the lantern light. Rufus lowered the blanket, went to set his lantern on the shack porch, and returned to hold up his arms to take him from me. His face was that of a man who had eaten bad meat and was near to losing his stomach.

Rufus carried *hombrecito* inside to yellow lantern light, medicine, and heat. In the darkness, I led my horse to water and grass in the canyon pasture where Rufus kept his cattle. I planned to camp there and stay out of sight of Rufus's Indah friends. When I knew what we would do with *el hombrecito*, I would leave for the great pleasure and warm comfort of Juanita and our little son, Híghăh (He Comes). Before returning to the shack, I found and pulled some plants Mescalero women use in poultices to heal rashes and cuts.

Rufus was a good *di-yen* (medicine man) for *el hombrecito*. In two suns, after much wandering in the land of evil dreams, Hombrecito came back to us. Rufus planned to carry him back to his mother, but Hombrecito refused to go, and swore by a horsehead fetish she had given him to take blood vengeance for his father before he returned to her. When Hombrecito described the man who had killed his father, Rufus swore like a drunk Indah and said the man was Red Tally, a known assassin. He decided it was best for Hombrecito not to return to his mother until blood vengeance was taken against his father's killers, because Tally and his men might try to kill the boy and his family to keep the truth from coming out.

Hombrecito, eager for blood, asked my help and that of Rufus in taking a son's revenge. Rufus and I agreed to help him, but only after he grew strong and had learned warrior and survival craft from us. This Hombrecito promised, and I agreed to begin training him when his arm healed.

I left Rufus and Hombrecito to return to Juanita and Hígháh as the fourth sun of my stay with Rufus and Hombrecito set behind the mountains the Indah call Florida.

CHAPTER 2
JARILLA VISION

As the stars filled the night sky and the glow from the moon behind the Sacramento Mountains grew brighter, I saw from the top of Baylor Pass the orange, flickering glow from fires scattered across the basin. There were the usual small fires vaqueros with their cattle made for coffee and a little rest, and much bigger fires made by bands of riders who searched for Hombrecito and his father. Some fires were near the Jarilla Mountains, some in the middle of the llano, and still more to the north near the White Sands and the mountains the Indah call San Andres.

I committed to memory where the fires were and decided how I would ride to the little canyon in the Jarillas where I'd rest through the time the sun rode across the sky. There were too many riders in the basin looking for Hombrecito and his father who might see me if I rode when the sun was high. I knew I had to be very careful not to be caught by trackers from Mescalero. They might be tribal policemen, who, if they found me, would ask to see my pass for permission to leave the reservation. Since I didn't have one, my next place to sleep would be the nasty, stinking agency jail.

I rode down Baylor Pass and out on to the llano lighted in white light and deep, black shadows from the rising moon. Swinging wide of all the fire glows, I saw only cattle that raised their heads from grazing to watch me wander through the brush.

Soon after I rode down on to the llano, I sensed being watched. Using every trick I knew, I couldn't find any sign, any track, any moving shadow to suggest someone followed me. After a while, I decided the feeling I had of being watched was from my Power telling me evil searched for me.

Dawn's soft gray light was filling the cold Ghost Face night when I rode into the little hidden canyon my people had used many times in the Jarilla Mountains. I gave my pony some grain and hobbled him near the natural water tank that made this place good for rest while crossing the big basin. I hid my saddle from the coming sun under an overhanging cliff shelf where I often slept and, taking a blanket, a sack of trail food, and my rifle, climbed to the lookout ledge where I had a clear view of the basin all the way back to the Organ Mountains.

As I watched the light slowly drive the mountain shadows from the llano, the fire glows across the basin disappeared to leave thin, vertical columns of gray smoke. I ate the mixture of pounded dry venison, mesquite flour, nuts, and juniper berries my second wife, Moon on the Water, had made for me to eat during my ride back to Mescalero. Moon was the younger sister of Juanita. I lived with her in the Blue Mountains in the camp of Kitsizil Lichoo' because she had evil dreams of what Blue Coats had done to our People during the Victorio War. Those dreams would not let her rest in Mescalero, but they did not come in the Blue Mountains, so my women's lodges were far apart. I tried to stay with each one for a moon or two before returning to the other.

I finished eating and wrapped my blanket around me. My thoughts were many as I yawned and spiraled into a deep sleep. I thought of my little son, Híghàh, and the strength and understanding he would need as he grew into times of great change for our People. I thought of *el hombrecito* and the evil that had come to him and how I would help him make it right. I thought of Juanita, her warm body, and the pleasure we shared by her fire, and I thanked Ussen for blessing me with her and Moon on the Water and our child.

There was no light, only darkness like that found in a cave. I ran my hands over smooth walls searching for a door. I heard breathing, a sound like a great bear snuffling. I turned my back to the wall, sliding my hand to my knife, ready to defend myself. The sound came closer. Out of the darkness came two great, glowing eyes, one bright green like new grass by water in the Season of Little Eagles, the other brown like desert sand. The eyes grew bigger, but the sound of breathing came no closer. The wall turned to vapor, and I ran through it, ran hard, pushing my body to get far away. The eyes followed me, but grew no bigger. I ran for a long time, my lungs bursting, my heart pounding, but the eyes, still the same distance away, stayed with me. I stopped running and stood to face the eyes.

A powerful wind came, a west wind in a great storm with many lightning arrows twisting and moaning around me, and it drove the eyes away. A voice out of the wind said, "A witch comes to destroy you and all your family. Be ready. I will help you. The witch must die. You are Killer of Witches." The dark place shook, and a beam of light came driving away the darkness. The voice said, "Go to the light."

My eyes flicked open, and a beam of sunlight falling through a crack in the ledge where I slept nearly blinded me. The comfort of my rifle was in my hands. I sat up, remembering my dream and committing it to memory. The sun's arc was fast pointing west of the Organs, and the cold air lay still and unmoving in the disappearing light. I saw a small plume of smoke rising from a place near the wagon road passing the north end of the Jarillas. The *Shináá Cho* showed four men squatting around the fire making the plume. It appeared they were eating a meal. At first, I thought they were just vaqueros, but then I noticed they all wore long braids that swung from under their big hats with flat brims. They were not Mescaleros. Mescaleros didn't wear long braids, if braids at all. One, older than the rest, seemed to be their leader. He used the point of a long knife to draw some kind of pattern in the dust. At points in the pattern, he motioned west toward the Organs sometimes, then east toward the Sacramentos and the reservation. I thought the men looked like a people I had seen before. Then I realized they were Comanche vaqueros. *Why would they be here? Maybe they have come to help search for el hombrecito.* I didn't know, but I planned to avoid them until I knew who they were and why they were eight suns' ride from their reservation.

I ate again and then climbed down from the ledge and made ready to travel when the darkness came.

Rested, my pony and I rode on to Juanita and Híghah. I wanted Juanita to find me in her tipi before the morning mountain shadows left our camp and the birds began to call. I wanted to tell her of finding Hombrecito, of my dream about a witch searching for me, the vision the spirit in the wind gave me, and that Moon on the Water was now carrying our first child. As I rode through the night, I thought of that dream. *Something my way comes, something I don't yet know, but something I must fight. My Power says a witch comes that I must kill. Maybe the witch is this evil man with the bitághaa' lichoo', the man Rufus called Red Tally. What can the two eye colors in my dream mean? This I must have a di-yen tell me.*

Soft, gray dawn came as I followed the Rinconada trail to our camp through patches of snow under the tall pine trees whispering in the easy wind above me. I stopped in dark shadows as the light grew stronger. Smoke already curled out of Juanita's tipi flaps, and I heard the thunking sounds of axes used by women to cut wood for their first fires of the day. I looked, but did not see Juanita, and decided she must be in her tipi. As usual, she had already chopped wood for her fire and was cooking a morning meal before other women in camp had stirred. *Ussen blesses me to have such a fine woman.*

I led my pony to the camp's brush corral where other horses and mules grazed and snuffled through hay thrown out for them. I pulled off my saddle, rubbed the pony down with a handful of hay, and fed him grain Rufus had given me to help him recover from the long ride through the last two nights.

Carrying my rifle, saddle, and blanket roll, I walked to the entrance of our tipi and waited by the blanket-covered entry like any guest coming to visit. The morning light, coming fast, shot through the trees and down the cliffs, and struck the camp tipis like golden spear shafts. I made a little cough. The shuffle I heard from inside told me Juanita heard me and saw my shadow by the tipi door. She called out, "Come, Stands by the Door. You're welcome to eat by my fire. We have plenty."

I threw back the blanket over the entranceway and stepped inside. Her fingers flew to her lips, and I saw happy light in the sparkle of her eyes before she modestly looked down. She said in the deep, soft voice that always stirred me, "My man comes! Yellow Boy has returned!" She sprang to her feet and stepped around the fire fast to wrap her arms around me and pull me against her body. Hígháh, age three, jumped up and ran around the fire with his arms out and his small hands clenched in fists as he called in his high, child's voice, *"Shitaa'! Shitaa'!"* (Father! Father!)

He laughed as I lifted him high and swung him in great swooping arcs. "Hígháh! *Shiye'* (my son) flies high. Soon he draws a bow. My eyes are glad to see him in the tipi of his mother."

I sat him down. He looked up at me and said, "*Shitaa'*, *Shibébé* (Uncle) Beela-chezzi has already made me a bow and arrows. I shoot them every day. The arrows fly straight when I point them to the right place. He says I do well and will get better." He ran around to the other side of the fire where he slept at the end of Juanita's blankets and held up the little *tsélkani* (mulberry wood) bow and reed arrows to show me what my friend and warrior companion, Beela-chezzi, had made him while I was gone.

"Ha! *Shiye'* hunts soon and wins arrows in shooting contests. Beela-chezzi is a good friend and *shibébé* for you."

Juanita, humming the women's welcome song for returning warriors, motioned me to sit as she filled a gourd with venison, wild potatoes with sage, slices of dried mescal, and acorn bread she had cooked and steamed by the fire. "Sit by the fire, husband. I know you've ridden all night. Fill your belly."

I eased down on the blanket. Smiling, she handed me the gourd and said, "Eat, husband. Coffee is in the pot when you want it."

CHAPTER 3
A *Di-yen* COMES

Juanita sat across the fire, smiling and watching me eat like a starving wolf, her legs chastely folded under her, as her mother, Maria, had taught her many harvests ago, when we played together as children. When I finished her good meal, my hands wiped the grease from my mouth and rubbed my legs to keep them smooth and flexible. She poured coffee into a blue speckled cup from the old, blackened pot bubbling on the fire and handed it to me as she kneeled down beside me. Híghah, who had sat next to her and watched silently while I ate, came and sat on my other side. We spoke of bows, making straight arrows, and hunting game when he was big enough to draw a hunting bow. When I finished the coffee, I said, "Go and practice with your bow and arrows, *Shiye'*. Now, I speak alone with your mother."

I handed the empty cup back to Juanita, who poured me more hot steaming coffee. Híghah said, "I go, *Shitaa'*. I'll practice a long time." Picking up his little bow and reed arrows from beside his blankets, and wrapping himself in a blanket like a grown man, he darted out to find his friends as he yelled, "Yellow Boy returns! My *shitaa'* comes!"

Juanita handed me my coffee. "What news of my sister?"

I smiled. "Something you've wanted to hear for a long time. She carries our first child."

Juanita laughed. "I know she's happy. I am, too. I knew she carried a child. I dreamed it, and a young *di-yen* (medicine man

44

or woman) told me it was so. But husband, you can't rest. Now I'm ready for another child. My mother says soon the time comes when my body will make no more children."

I grinned and pulled her to me, and there by her little fire, we eagerly pleasured each other to make another child for our family. When I had done all I could do to increase our family and she lay warm and relaxed under the blankets with me, her mention of a new *di-yen* in camp and my need to talk with one about my dream drifted through my mind.

I said, yawning and ready to nap the rest of the day, "*Ish-tia-neh* (Woman), who is this *di-yen* saying your dream was true?"

"She comes from the south, from the land of the *Nakai-yes* (Mexicans), from Chihuahua. She escaped from a hacendado (wealthy landowner) who kept her and others as slaves to work around his *casa grande* (great house)."

"Hmmph. Where in Chihuahua was she a slave?"

"She didn't say. We didn't ask. She said she learned much medicine from the woman who raised her, one whose man taught her many things before he went to the Happy Land. We first saw her when she was running across the ridge above us. Your brother ran up the ridge after her and coaxed her to come to our fires."

Juanita frowned. "She said she ran from hacendados vaqueros following her from the *casa grande*. She looked like she had run a long time. Her toes showed through the end of her moccasins, and her skirt, blouse, and blanket had many tears. The men looked away from her when she tried to cover herself. Her hands, face, and feet were raw and nearly frozen. We gave her a new blanket and something to eat. I'll never forget her wild eyes as she watched us while she gnawed meat like a starving wolf from a deer shank I'd roasted over the fire. She spoke our language well and begged us to hide her for a while so those vaqueros didn't catch and tie her across a horse and take her back to Chihuahua, using her whenever and however they wanted.

"Our women heard her story. We understood her heart, held a council, and then asked the men to let her stay. We said that if she caused trouble, we would run her off ourselves, and the men said, 'All right, she can stay, but you women hold her rope. You're responsible for her.' "

I had no reason not to accept this *di-yen*, but the feeling of shadows falling over my life came again. It was the same sense of warning I'd had from the dream in the Jarillas and on the ride there from Rufus's rancho, the same feeling I'd had on trails when I knew someone or something watched for me.

"Then I, too, agree with the men. Did you see the vaqueros chasing her? If she is a *di-yen*, has she done any ceremonies yet? Has she shown you her Power?"

"Knows Horses looked for the vaqueros following her tracks back from the place where he found her. He stayed up a few nights watching, but never saw them or anyone else. Then Maria had a bad fever. It started a few days after you left for the Blue Mountains and grew worse, despite all we did. I thought she might go to the Happy Land, so I decided to ask for help from a *di-yen* in the camps near the agency, maybe even get Doctor Blazer to come do a ceremony for her. I would have asked him to come with his medicines, but he's a man of many harvests, too old to be riding high, ice-covered ridges in the Ghost Face season.

"The *di-yen* from Chihuahua said she had a ceremony that drove away fever. I asked her to help us. She asked only that we bury a blue stone she gave us on the north side of Maria's tipi."

"Hmmph. What did the *di-yen* do after you buried the blue stone?"

"Before the Sing, she called to Green Moth with Big Eyes on Its Wings. In a dream, it came and told her what plants to use for Maria to overcome her fever. Over a fire in Maria's tipi, the *di-yen* made medicine in a pot of hot water with dried plants she had collected from us. She let the pot boil with the plants as she sang and did her ceremony. Before she finished singing, she let the pot cool and then gave Maria a drink from it four times after pointing it to each of the directions. All the women in camp were there with us, Sons-ee-ah-ray, Lucky Star, Deer Woman, Carmen Rosario, and bringer of babies, old Sleepy, and her widowed daughter, Falling Water. We all watched her Sing."

As she spoke, Juanita and I heard a child's arrow hit the tipi and bounce off. I started up to run the children away, but Juanita pushed me back down on my back and shook her head that it was nothing, just children playing and learning.

She said, "Soon you rest. Let me finish. The body of Maria was hot to touch when the *di-yen* started, but she was much cooler by the end of the Sing, and up doing her work the next day. The other women and I think this *di-yen* has great Power. I had much to thank her for and gave her one of my baskets and all the dried mescal she wanted, but she didn't take much. She said her needs were small, and she was grateful we let her camp with us. She stays with Sleepy and Falling Water and works hard to help them."

I felt better hearing this, but a voice in my mind said, *Be careful with what she tells you.*

I said, "It sounds like she uses her Power in a good way. I'll speak with her soon and learn what my Power tells me about her."

I relaxed and felt Juanita's warmth making me drowsy, when I remembered Stottler.

"Just before I left, the new agent, *Teniente* (Lieutenant) Stottler, came. Blazer told me Stottler said he would make us follow

Indah ways whether we wanted to or not. Has he done anything yet?"

Juanita sighed and stared at the tipi smoke hole. "He brought Navajo women to the reservation. They taught us how to handle wool, make looms, and weave blankets. Blazer says Stottler plans to buy five thousand sheep for us to keep for ourselves and to have wool for weaving. Some of the women who worked with the Navajos learned to make good blankets like they do. I've tried this wool-weaving to make blankets, but I like weaving baskets better. I don't want anything to do with sheep. They're wolf bait and too hard to care for."

"So, he leaves the men alone? It's just the women he tries to break?"

She slowly shook her head, her eyes still on the smoke hole. "The men will tell you what he does. I don't like to hear you roar in anger."

"I won't roar. Tell me!"

"Stottler orders every man on the reservation to cut his hair short and wear clothes like the Indah."

Anger rose from my guts and nearly flew from my lips, but I remembered my promise and kept silent while my ears grew hot with angry blood.

I swallowed my anger and spoke calmly. "My father, *Caballo Negro*, told me once that anyone who leads like Stottler is a fool. He sees no further than his hand and soon walks over a cliff. I know the men don't want to do this. How did Stottler force them? Chase them down like dogs and shear them like his sheep?"

I heard crows flying and calling over the canyon. They seemed to be giving voice to the anger burning inside me.

Juanita shook her head and sighed. "First he told the tribal police that if they wanted to stay policemen and get extra rations, then they must cut their hair. They didn't like this, but nearly every one of them cut his hair. Then Stottler sent them out to arrest and cut the hair of any man who had been to Indah schools and returned to let their hair grow back long. Then Stottler said for them to arrest any man who still had long hair and make them cut it—"

"Our men in camp, they have cut their hair?"

"No one in this camp has done this shameful thing. The tribal police leave us alone. I think they won't cross you. But our men fear that minds change. Perhaps the police will come and shear them. Our men want and need your wisdom. They believe the demands of Stottler will grow worse and take away who they are as Mescaleros."

"They're right. I'll rest and talk with them later in council. Now I tell you of the Indah boy I saved from a vaquero ambush."

Juanita turned to me, her eyes wide. "You saved an Indah boy from being killed? Are the killers after you? Where is he now? How . . . ?"

I sat up and waved the flat of my hand parallel to the ground to show her all was well. "Listen, and I'll tell you."

She nodded and lay back and pulled the blanket up to her neck, her fingers over her mouth as I told her what happened. When I finished my story, she said, "So only Rufus and the Indah boy know you saved him?" I nodded, and she frowned. "And you say this boy, not yet even ready to apprentice as a warrior, won't go back to his mother until he takes blood revenge? And you and Rufus will teach him to become a warrior and help him to avenge his father?" I nodded again. "Husband, your moccasins follow a long, hard path, but I think you did the right thing. Geronimo and your dreams told you this would happen."

"It is what my Power called me to do, and the child called me by my name. I must help him make his world smooth again."

I drew her to me. "*Ish-tia-neh,* I've ridden far to come to you.

49

This day we've begun to make us another child. I've thought of doing this many times with you. Let's enjoy the pleasures of making a child again before I sleep."

She looked at me with warm eyes, and, nodding, pulled the blanket back over us as she whispered, "I'm here, ready, my husband. Come to me."

CHAPTER 4
A TALK WITH SONS-EE-AH-RAY AND KNOWS HORSES

I slept like one who had entered the spirit lands. I never knew when Juanita left my side to work. When I awoke, she was not in the tipi, but the fire burned bright, and I heard the children outside playing Catch Me. I pushed away the blankets, sat up, and yawned and stretched. It was good to be back with my first wife. I poured a cup of Juanita's coffee and, drinking it, decided to visit my mother and brother.

Sons-ee-ah-ray (Morning Star) knew who paused at the tipi entrance. She was quick to say, "Come! My eyes want to see my first son."

Even in the tipi's warmth, she sat wrapped in a blanket by her fire, trying to warm swollen joints that made her fingers look like eagle talons, and her half-blind eyes were mere slits of her once big, deer-like eyes. Most of our women never lived to be her age. They wore out much faster than their men. That was a reason warriors often took a second, younger wife. I wondered if Ussen, the Apache's great creator God, had gifted or cursed her with long age. My younger brother, Knows Horses, sitting near her and cleaning a Winchester rifle I had never seen, looked up smiling when I came in.

Knows Horses said, "My brother returns safe from a long trip of three moons. *Enjuh!* (Good!)"

I nodded and gave the all-is-well swing of my hand parallel to the ground and eased down by Sons-ee-ah-ray so she could hear me without straining.

51

I lighted one of my *Nakai-yi* (Mexican) *cigarros,* smoked to the four directions, and passed it to her. She smoked and passed it to Knows Horses, who smoked and passed it back.

I said, "I've been gone over three moons. Heavy snows in the passes held me two moons longer than I planned to stay. My mother still looks strong, and my brother cleans a new rifle. Juanita tells me much has happened since I left. Stottler makes life hard for the Mescaleros, and a *di-yen* from the south stays in our camp and shows great Power. She brings healing to Maria."

Sons-ee-ah-ray nodded. "Yes, the *di-yen* has great Power. After she holds my hands and rubs them with her special oil, my fingers work again that day. She takes nothing for this gift. I'm grateful to Ussen for her. Tells us, my son, what news from the far Blue Mountains?"

She leaned close to catch every word as I told them that Moon on the Water carried our child, and the camp under Kitsizil Lichoo' continued strong with warriors and families from other camps joining his. I decided not to tell them of saving Hombrecito until I knew more about the shooter who killed his father.

I said, "My brother now has a fine new rifle. How did you get it?"

Sons-ee-ah-ray, missing many teeth, cackled.

Knows Horses smiled as he used an arrow shaft to push a piece of oily rag down the barrel. "I bet a pony worth much more than the rifle in a monte game and won. The dealer wasn't happy, but he gave it to me and said I had won fair."

"Do you still help Yibá with his cattle? Someday you might wear a vaquero's hat."

He nodded, but said with a little anger, "I still help him. It's hard work. But I want to be a warrior and take a woman for my own, not be a child running after cattle. Here on this reservation, I can never be a warrior. How will I become a man ready for a wife when there are no warriors to follow? Yibá was lucky. He went on the last raid to kill the giant witch in your stories, and you and the other warriors recognized him as a new warrior. Where are the raids for Running Wolf, son of Beela-chezzi, and me? Where will the raids be for Kah's son, Para-dee-ah-tran (the Contented), when he is ready? How will we be known as men on this reservation where we are penned up like horses in a corral?"

Sons-ee-ah-ray nodded and squinted at me. "Your brother asks a good question. I cannot answer it. Can you?"

I shook my head. "I've thought on this often, but I don't yet have an answer. Beela-chezzi, Kah, Yibá, and I will smoke together and decide what needs to be done for Knows Horses and Running Wolf to show they are men ready to support a woman and her family. Do you have a woman in mind for a wife when we recognize you as a man?"

"I want the *di-yen* from the south. She has good, strong Power; she works hard with Sleepy and Falling Water; and she stirs me when I look at her."

"Hmmph. Has she had her *Haheh* (puberty ceremony)? Have you spoken to her about your interest in her? Does she want you?"

Sons-ee-ah-ray nodded and smiled. "She has had her *Haheh*. This I know."

Knows Horses raised his eyes and slowly shook his head. "I haven't spoken to her. She has no people here, so I can't speak with them about her, and I won't speak to her until I know I can speak as a man. Help me do this, brother."

I nodded. "This I'll do before I return south to Moon on the Water."

Juanita made a fine night meal to welcome me back from the

Blue Mountains, and even now, I still remember it. She had a cut of beef, acorn bread, mescal softened and mixed with piñon flour, juniper berries mixed with mescal paste, wild potatoes boiled with sage and onions, roasted mesquite-bean flour cakes, and more of the good coffee she had traded for at Blazer's trading post, not the strong, bitter drink she usually made mixed with piñon nuts.

Full and content, I sat and smoked and watched as she put Híghàh under his blankets. Then she came and sat beside me. We watched the fire burn down until she added a little more wood, and then we wrapped in a blanket and lay down together. I drew her to me, and again we held each other.

CHAPTER 5
SÁBADO COMES

Beela-chezzi, Kah, Yibá, myself, and the two grown young men we had not yet recognized as warriors—my brother, Knows Horses, and Beela-chezzi's adopted son, Running Wolf—sat in the tipi of Beela-chezzi's wife, Carmen Rosario. Beela-chezzi was the oldest warrior in the camp, the man with the most wisdom and fighting experience, and the one all of the men went to for wisdom and knowledge on how to best fight and overcome enemies.

My brothers believed the tribal police had left us alone because they feared my rifle and I had been one of them under Tribal Police Chief Tom Branigan. If the tribal police feared my rifle and respected me, then it was a good thing, but we did not know if this was true or how long it might be before they feared Stottler more than me and came to force Indah ways on us. If we did not submit, they would put us in jail as they had others, and our families would starve on reduced rations.

Beela-chezzi made a cigarette with an oak leaf and *tobaho*, lighted it, and we smoked to the four directions sitting wrapped in the thin blankets the agency gave us. We finished and Beela-chezzi threw the last bit of *tobaho* in the fire as he said, "Speak, brothers, and I'll listen." Each man around the circle spoke.

I said, "I've heard Stottler forces the Mescaleros to cut their hair and to wear the same clothes as the Indah. He forces little ones to leave the fires of their mothers and fathers to work in the Indah School so they forget their memories of the words and customs of their fathers and grandfathers, forget they are Mescaleros. Soon he'll try to make us farmers, which we all know is work for women. I'll never do a woman's work." I felt the heat of my words in my face and the anger in my belly, but then I began to cool and speak in a thinking way. "My father once told me that any chief who tries to make his warriors do things that are not needed, as this agent Stottler does, is a fool. I say he's a fool for trying to make men farmers. He's a mad dog that takes our children. If we try to fight him, the Blue Coats will come, and many will die. We're too few for any of us to die, even with honor. Stottler must fail one day, but, before he does, our people will continue to suffer. We must stay out of his way until a new agent who is not so foolish comes. We must avoid him until another *Tata* Crooked Nose (W.H.H. Llewellyn) comes who will work with us and help us. That is all I have to say."

Kah nodded, "Yellow Boy speaks true. I think in a little while Stottler's police will come. If we fight the police, we'll lose, because they have more guns and bullets. But even if we won, killed them all, the Blue Coats would come and slaughter us. We must somehow disappear so Stottler and his police no longer see us."

Yibá frowned and said, "I've taken what little the agents gave us and made it more. You know that whatever is mine is yours also. I know that my strength as a man is not in my hair. It's in my head. I don't fear losing my hair, even if it costs a little of my pride. My hair will grow back after Stottler leaves. The child my wife and I have is now six harvests. She learns much already by helping her mother. Those in other camps tell me Stottler even puts grandmothers who object to schooling their grandchildren in his jail and cuts rations until a child is left at the school. In the school, the Indah teach our children Indah ways, and the children forget where they come from. They no more see their fathers or mothers and respect them. I wouldn't have my child not respect me and her mother and the old ways. If our daughter goes to the agency Indah School, my wife will wail many days. It will be as if our child went to the Happy Land. Somehow, we must stop Stottler. What does the great warrior Beela-chezzi say?"

Beela-chezzi sat smoking a new cigarette with his arms crossed and his face a mask, his eyes narrowed, as he heard us. He stared at the fire and spoke. "I hear you. You all would hide from Stottler, he who makes men cut their hair and wear Indah clothes, he who takes little ones from their families, he who tries to make men farmers. Blazer says Stottler does these hard things to show the Indah chiefs that we can be forced to do as he wills, and that he has a good vision for us. His chiefs think it is a good thing he makes the Mescaleros into Indah, but we say it is a good thing to stay away from Stottler. I ask you, if we hide, where? If we fight, how?"

The only sound in the tipi was the crackle of the fire on the piñon and a kind of sigh from us all as we crossed our arms to think. Beela-chezzi looked around the circle, holding our gazes with his, looking into our spirits to see how strong we were in what we wanted.

Outside, the sounds of children playing and women talking to each other stopped as if someone held up their hand in a signal. We looked at each other, frowning. We all began to stand, and we heard Juanita say in a loud voice, "Ho! What do you want?"

I pulled back the hammer on my Henry rifle, ready to fire, but waved the other men down on their blankets and signaled their silence.

A man's deep voice said, "We're tribal police. Agent Stottler sends us here. We look for our brother, Yellow Boy. Agent Stottler wants him at the agency plenty quick. I see children who should be in school, not playing in the snow. You must bring them to the agency school. You must do this if you want your rations."

I knew the voice. It was Sábado (Saturday), a big, muscular police sergeant who was fearless. I wondered if he had cut his hair like Stottler wanted. I knew from experience he must have at least two other men with him. I turned and stooped to leave the tipi and face the police, but I stopped when Maria, mother of Juanita, croaked, "You won't take our children. You'll face the straight-shooting rifle of my son-in-law if you do. He can shoot out your eyes and send you to the Happy Land blind. I say the children stay. Now, you go. If you value your life, don't come back here again. You go! I say no more."

The word of a grandmother is powerful medicine. Her daughters usually do as she says, and so does her son-in-law, who never sees her. Since I had to avoid seeing her, I paused before going out, to give her enough time to return to her tipi.

"Ho!" said Sábado. "Mother of Yellow Boy's wives shows courage. Where is Yellow Boy? Has he no courage to face his brothers in the tribal police?"

I was out of the tipi with my Henry rifle on my shoulder and fired three times before Sábado and the other two could raise their rifles. The hats of all three policemen sailed off their heads, each one with a bullet hole in the middle of the crown. Their eyes grew as big and round as Spanish *conchos*. Sábado, his teeth clenched under thin, tight lips, started to raise his rifle, but lowered it when he saw me shaking my head. The other two had already lowered their rifles to the pommels of their saddles. Their long hair was gone, cut so their ears showed and none lay on their shoulders. I felt embarrassed for them.

I said, "Be careful who you ask for, Sábado. You might find him. Tell Stottler I'll come before the next moon, but at a place and time I choose. I won't accept any agent forcing our children to be slaves in the agency Indah School. Send no policemen for our children. If we choose to send them to the Indah School, they'll go. If not, they'll stay with us. No one in our camp causes trouble. Don't return. If you come uninvited, more than your hats will have holes, and you'll wander blind in the Happy Land. *Comprenden?*"

They all nodded.

"The man on the right side of Sábado," I said, pointing toward him with my nose, "dismount and get your hats. Your heads need not be cold on your ride back to the agency while you think of a story to tell your chief. Tell your brothers how you got the holes in your hats. Speak true. Say they were gifts from Yellow Boy, gifts of life. All those holes could have been five fingers lower."

The policeman, his face bright red from the cold, climbed off his horse, picked up the hats, and returned them to their owners before he remounted. Sábado pulled his hat down over his brow so its bullet hole showed clear and plain and said, "You're wrong, Yellow Boy. Stottler will have a red face because you treated us this way. If you don't come to see him, he'll cut off the rations of all in your camp. He'll send many policemen back here to put you in jail. Others may die in the shooting to take you. You have to do what Stottler says."

Sábado jerked his pony around and, the other two following, rode off down the canyon to the trail over the ridges while everyone in the camp watched them go. I waited with my rifle in the crook of my arm. When they were out of sight, I returned to Beela-chezzi's council.

After I sat down, all the men, including Beela-chezzi, grinned and nodded. Yibá spoke first. "I'm grown and a warrior. Still, I have not the experience of the rest of you. But I think we ought to leave the reservation and go to the camp of Kitsizil Lichoo', where Yellow Boy keeps his second wife in the Blue Mountains. I don't think we should fight tribal police and Stottler. Even if we win that battle, the Blue Coats will come and wipe us out."

I said, "Yibá speaks good words, but he forgets some things we must consider. If we leave, we'll have to travel fast. Stottler will learn in a day or two we've left the reservation and send the tribal police and maybe even the Blue Coats to bring us back. If they catch us, there will be blood. If not, we can never come back to the reservation. We'll have to live out our lives in the Blue Mountains. Sons-ee-ah-ray, Maria, and Sleepy are old and slow; Hígháh and Dawahn Dáha are young and slow. We won't leave any of them. They can't ride or run fast like a warrior or a good woman or a half-grown child. We can't escape the tribal police by running to the Blue Mountains if the old and little ones come with us, yet we can't leave them."

I looked around the circle of faces, and even Yibá nodded that what I had said was true.

Kah hunched his shoulders, stared at the fire a moment, and then said, "Why don't we just hide in the Rinconada like old Nana did? Give the tribal police an excuse not to find us, and they won't if they think Yellow Boy and his rifle are somewhere up one of those side canyons."

Beela-chezzi, with crossed arms, stared frowning in thought at the little fire. At last, he said, "All the men in this circle speak true. The best thing is to stay out of Stottler's way until a new agent who accepts us comes. We can't go to the Blue Mountains. If we go to Nana's old camp, we risk the tribal police coming for us, but if we go there and camp like we were in the Blue Mountains, keeping quiet and, with their fear of Yellow Boy making them stay back, we might be able to avoid the tribal police when they come to the Rinconada. Like Nana, we'll have to hunt often because there will be no rations from Stottler if we disappear."

All the heads around the circle nodded. Beela-chezzi said, "We should move soon, before the tribal police are driven back here by their angry chief. We must think how best to get our rations, or the children and women will go hungry. Yes, we must hunt more. Will Yellow Boy go to meet with Stottler and his friend Blazer to help us?"

I nodded. "This I will do. I've given my word. Let's find the canyon over in the Rinconada that Nana used for his people, and move quick to be there before more snows come. That way the police will not see our tracks. What do my brothers say?"

They spoke with one voice. *"Enjuh!"*

CHAPTER 6
A VISIT WITH DOCTOR BLAZER

After I met with my brothers in council, I waited until the sun started falling into the west before I rode to the agency to talk with Blazer and face Stottler. By the time I crossed the high ridges to the agency, there would still be enough light to see Río Tularosa Canyon but stay out of sight in the twilight and shadows.

The sky filled with orange, red, and purple clouds as I sat on my pony by the tall trees high above the agency. There weren't many riders around the agency or Blazer's trading post, and golden light from lanterns in the windows was easy to see. The cold wind had stopped earlier in the day, but the deepening darkness made the night's cold come quickly. I pulled open the *Shináá Cho* to study the grounds around the trading post and saw Blazer, wrapped in an ancient, shaggy buffalo coat, leave *La Máquina* (literally "the machine," the Spanish name used for the sawmill) in long, striding steps for his house.

I let my pony pick his way down the slick trail, winding along the ridge through dark shadows and twilight. Splashing across the Río Tularosa out of sight above the agency, I rode down a trail by the wagon road until I came to Blazer's barn, and seeing no one, pulled my pony into a stall, loosened its cinches, and gave it a little hay. I watched Blazer's house until I saw him and his family eating their meal before I cut across the corral and down the hill to creep up the stairs to his office on the second floor. I eased open the door and edged inside to wait in a dark corner for him to come, as he always did, to finish his day's work.

In a while, Blazer came stomping up the steps, blowing and slapping his hands against his arms to drive away the chill. He lighted and turned up a lamp to see the papers on his desk and, out of the corner of his eye, saw me standing like some spirit beside him. His eyes grew big, and his mouth dropped in surprise.

He practically shouted, "Whoa! Yellow Boy! Where'd you come from?"

I nodded at him, but I didn't take time for idle words. "Blazer, we talk?"

He waved toward the chairs by the stove. "Sure, sure. Glad to see you, old friend. Sit down. I don't know if you've heard, but we've had awful news here in the last few days. My friend, Albert Fountain, who you know is a big chief and Indah warrior in the councils at Las Cruces, and his little boy, Henry, have disappeared. Most, me included, think they've been murdered out past the White Sands on the llano. The whole country is in an uproar. Posses are ridin' all over the basin lookin' for 'em. Scouts and tribal police are tryin' to find their tracks, and newspapers are saying Oliver Lee ought to be hung for killing 'em. Folks have kinda lost their minds. I doubt we'll ever know for sure who murdered 'em."

He poured coffee into a couple of clay mugs from a bubbling pot sitting on the stove and handed me one. He groaned from the stiffness of his joints as he dropped into a chair near the hot stove, and I sat down beside him.

Blazer stared off into the darkness beyond the lamp as though watching a spirit. "You picked a good time to come if you want to avoid the tribal police. Most of 'em are out scouting the basin looking for the Fountains. It's mighty bad, mighty bad."

He sighed and took a slurp of the steaming hot coffee in his mug. "I'm just sick about it, and maybe a little to blame. Albert and his little boy stayed the night here with me two days before they disappeared. I tried to talk him into letting me send a couple of men with him, your friends, No Foot and Quick Knife, who drive my lumber wagons over to Las Cruces. Albert and Henry would have had some protection with them along, but he was too full of pride to do it. I sure hate to see him and that little boy of his gone. It just ain't right, the way they disappeared."

I nodded, but said nothing.

After a while, he looked over at me and said, "How's the family?"

"Hmmph. Juanita is good. Wants to make another child. That is good. Moon on the Water carries our first child. That is good. Maria has a fever, but a new *di-yen* comes and helps her. That is good.

"What I hear Stottler does to the People is no good. You tell me before I go to Mexico last time that this new agent, Stottler, is hot to change the People. Make 'em look and work like Indah. I hear bad things he does, but my camp escapes because the tribal police leave us alone until today. I run them off, but we know they'll come again. We know we must move and stay out of their way until new agent comes. What does Stottler want from us? You tell me, Blazer. I must know."

Blazer nodded and frowned, light from the lamp making the shadows of his wrinkles and big bush of white face hair stand out strong, like mountains drawn on a map. "It's simple, my friend. Like I told you before, Stottler believes your People must act and look exactly like Indah to live in this country. He started with men's hair bein' cut short, and now they're gonna be wearing Indah clothes. There're no more G-strings for the men and on their heads hats, not bandannas. He's gonna try to make every child go to Indah School, where they ain't much more than unpaid servants for the school and its teachers. He's already threatened to cut rations and put grandmothers in jail who're against it. He's gonna make the men build log cabins and move out of tipis, and he's gonna make 'em all work for their rations. I tell you straight, I just ain't got much use for that pompous son-of-a-bitch, but the fools he works for thinks he hung the moon."

"I speak truth to him. He listens?"

Blazer smiled and shook his head as he looked at the floor for a time. Then he looked in my eyes and said, "No, he ain't listenin' to nobody, unless the one speakin' is a bigger chief than he is."

"Hmmph. Then when we have talk, I stand tall. Maybe he listens."

Blazer nodded. "Maybe he needs to see your gift of Power in action."

Blazer and I talked a long time. He put many thoughts in my head about the People surviving on the reservation and what would happen to us if Stottler stayed a long time. I told Blazer how I had run the tribal police off and told Sábado to tell Stottler I come when I am ready.

I said, "I'll speak with him early tomorrow and be gone."

Blazer said, "He'll likely let you talk, and then throw you in jail and cut off your family's rations until you agree to wear Indah pants and have your hair cut. Be careful."

"If he tries this with me, there will be blood, and the tribal police know it, even if he does not."

"Maybe so. But if there is blood, especially if you kill him, it will be hard for all the People. Think of what will happen to Juanita and Hígháh. There ain't many soldiers left at Fort Stanton, but the few that come will make many suffer. Think about it, amigo. It'll be your pride against the lives of your

People, and if you're killed, your wives and children will have no one to provide for them."

"I have thought about it, Blazer. There are places a warrior cannot go. His family, his People expect this. To cut an Apache warrior's hair is a sign of disrespect. Warriors respect the agents that come here, and the agents must respect them. They must respect the People. They're fools if they don't. If Stottler tries to cut my hair, there will be blood. Where does this agent work? I wait there for him."

Blazer told me how to get into Stottler's office without waking up the agency after I promised I wouldn't go there to kill him, and I disappeared into the darkness.

CHAPTER 7
LIEUTENANT STOTTLER

I sat on the floor in the dark corner of Stottler's office next to the post he used to hang his hat and coat. Through the ice and frost on Stottler's office windows, I watched the sun throw long, bright arrows of light through the treetops across the eastern ridges as the sky grew bright. Soon I saw lantern lights under the door's bottom edge, heard boots stomping down the hallway toward the tribal police chief's office and two men, one an Indah and the other a *Nakai-yi,* speaking and laughing in muffled voices about how cold it had been during the night. Down the hall, a door creaked open, and I heard the hinges on a stove door squeak and wood tossed inside to bang against the *pesh* (iron) sides. Soon footsteps came back down the hall, and Stottler's door opened.

I sat unmoving in the dark corner as a policeman, his hair cut short like an Indah, came in with an armload of firewood, dumped it in the wood box, flung the stove door open, and, grabbing a stick, stirred and blew the coals to life before adding a handful of kindling. His back was to me, and after the kindling flames grew he added two bigger pieces out of the wood box. He slammed the stove door closed, blew his breath on his hands, and left the room, his footsteps thumping back down the hall. Now the sun seemed to rise faster, bathing the snow-covered ridges in its soft, red light.

Footsteps, not like the others, but measured, fast steps like a soldier marching, came down the hall and stopped at the door.

I stood and cradled my rifle in my left arm, its hammer set to safety, as a man walked in and closed the door behind him. He stepped to his desk and turned up the flame on his lamp before taking off his hat and heavy coat as he turned to hang them where I stood.

His eyes grew wide and his mouth dropped when he saw me. He sucked wind and said with some heat and snarl in his voice, "Haaa! Who are you? What are you doing here?"

I stepped into the light so he saw me clearly. "I am Yellow Boy. Tribal police come to my camp. They say *Teniente* Stottler wants to see me. I tell them go. I come when I am ready. They go. Now, I am here. Who are you?"

Stottler's eyes narrowed. "I'm Agent Stottler. So you're Yellow Boy?" He nodded the answer to his own question. "Yes, I've been looking for you." He motioned to a chair near the stove as he moved to hang up his hat and coat. "It's a little cool in here. Let's sit by the stove and warm up while we talk." Seeing my rifle and that it was half-cocked to safety, he made a coyote grin, showing his teeth under the straggly, brown hair on his upper lip, and nodded toward a chair sitting in front of his desk. I kept my eyes on him as I reached for the chair, dragged it over to the stove, and sat down, still cradling my rifle in the crook of my left arm. From somewhere down the hall, there came a big belly laugh, and then all was quiet.

Stottler rubbed his hands together over the stovetop and then pulled up a chair to sit where he could face me as we talked. He sniffed a couple of times, like he smelled something, fumbled in his vest for his pipe and *tobaho*, filled the pipe, and lighted it from a match he struck on the stove. After taking a few puffs, he blew a long stream of smoke toward the ceiling, all the while watching my face, as if he didn't know that to my People, staring at a person's face was rude. I stared back, pulled one of my cigarros from my coat pocket, lit the match with my thumbnail, and made a nice coal on its end before smoking to the four directions. If he knew anything about the People at all, he would understand I was there for serious business.

I said, "Now we talk. I come to hear you. Speak."

He eyed me for a moment and then, pulling his pipe stem from his teeth, spoke with the same assurance I had heard other Indah use when speaking of the Shis-Indeh (literally "People of the Woods," the Apaches). "What I want is to make your people good, self-supporting citizens who can take care of themselves, who don't need the government to help them, and who are accepted as good neighbors by white people in this country. That means your people have to change. They have to look and dress like white people; they have to bathe and stay clean; they have to learn to support themselves and no longer live on what the government gives them."

The big belly laugh down the hall came again, as if laughing at Stottler's words, but I didn't think his words were funny. He grinned when he heard the laugh and continued. "No matter what you Apaches think and how much you resist, I intend to make all these things happen. First, I'm making all the men cut their hair short like all good white men, and wear clothes like the whites."

He ran his hand over his thinning hair as if touching and smoothing his thoughts. "Next, all children over the age of five years—I think you people would say five harvests—must attend school, not in some far-off place like Albuquerque, but right here on the reservation. They must live at the school, but their parents can visit when permitted. They will learn to read, write, and speak English. They'll forget how to speak Apache, a backward language spoken by backward people. They'll learn to do sums, and they'll learn a skilled trade like carpentry or black-smithing so they can support themselves. They'll learn they can't marry a girl who's twelve or thirteen just because she can have children. They'll learn the ignorance and superstition behind your ceremonies won't do them any good. I'm going to forbid *di-yen* magic and ceremonies for that very reason—they're ignorant, and they lead you in a bad way."

He paused to let me speak, but I was so angry I dared not say anything and felt my jaw muscles rippling with my outrage. His pipe made a couple of more puffs as I sat there silent, unbelieving, and staring.

Then he said, "I plan to continue to teach your women how to work wool like the Navajos by bringing Navajo women down here again to demonstrate how to card and dye wool and then to weave blankets. The men are going to learn to farm and raise sheep. When the snow is gone this spring, your men will start fencing to hold the animals I'll give them in areas they can claim as their places on the reservation. In a year or so, they'll cut logs and get some sawed for flooring and roofing lumber, and with the rest, build cabins for their families so they no longer live in those awful tipis breathing smoke all the time, sweating in summer, and freezing in winter."

As he spoke, he leaned forward, smiling, his eyes flashing at the thought of his vision, and holding up a finger to make his point, he said, his voice rising, "And, I plan to buy ten head of sheep for every man, woman, and child to raise as their own for food and for wool they've been taught to use. I think all this will lift your people up, and it's something they've needed to do for a long time. What do you say? Are you with me to bring your People up to the level of the whites?"

My mind filled with thoughts that ran and hopped in many different directions like antelope in a surround before we kill them. Stottler planned to kill the life-way of my People, make it disappear. I didn't know whether to shoot him or laugh at him.

"What if my people don't want to do this? No Mescalero man wants to cut his hair or wear Indah clothes. It's a sign of weakness. No woman will want him. No man will respect him. Farming is woman's work. No man will do that for long. Maybe the People don't want sheep. Sheep ruin the grass and have no sense. Sheep are wolf bait. Maybe the People just want their rations and a little beef in order to live in peace. We know how to work. We do men's work, and women make baskets to buy things from the agency or Blazer's store that aren't in our rations. Maybe we want to stay in our tipis. They were good enough for our fathers. Maybe children want to stay with their mother and father until they marry. How you make the Shis-Indeh do all you say?"

Stottler narrowed his eyes and leaned forward, his teeth clenched. He reminded me of an angry, snarling dog with his back hair up.

"You don't seem to understand, my friend. You and your people have no power. I represent all the power. It comes from the big chiefs far to the east. There is no other power. You must do as I say, or I will punish you until you do. No work, no rations. That's what I say. You don't cut your hair? I'll put you in jail and cut off your family's rations until you do. Only I can say what you can do on this reservation, and by God, one way or the other, you'll do it, even if I have to get the tribal police to tie you down like a steer for branding and shear you clean like a sheep. Nearly all the men see that I have power over them and they have none. They have yielded to my power."

He took a long draw on his pipe and blew the smoke toward the ceiling and then stared again at me. "I sent the tribal police for you because you were once a policeman and, they say, a good one that Branigan depended on because you shoot well and have sound judgment. I wanted to talk with you so you could understand you have no choice but to do what I say when I say it, and avoid trouble that might come because you don't understand all the good I want to do for your people. Otherwise, the house with bars that stinks from unwashed men and old women awaits you, and while you are there inside, outside your family starves. I'm a hard man. I'll use pressure where I have to." He grinned, showing all his teeth and said gently, as if he spoke to a child, "Do you understand, Yellow Boy?"

My right thumb pulled the hammer on my rifle back to full cock as I stared at him and argued within myself if I should kill him. Stottler's eyes grew large, and he ran his tongue over his lips. He said, "You know if you kill me, the tribal police will never let you leave this building alive. Then the army will come, and many of your people will die. Put that rifle on safety. There's no need for this, no need to spill blood. Surrender now, and I'll forget your threat. Hand over that old rifle, and get your hair cut, and there'll be peace between us."

I shook my head. "No, Stottler. You do this, and there will be blood. You'll be the first to bleed, even if I am the second. This thing you do cannot, will not, stand. You want to make our People and their life-ways disappear. When I was not long off the *tsach* (cradleboard), I escaped with my parents from Carlton's slavery at Bosque Redondo. He, too, said he wanted to teach us to farm and to be just like the Indah so we could get along. My father tells me many times what the chief Cadete said to Captain Cremony about this when they talked before we became like the wind and left Bosque Redondo.

"I remember every word Cadete told Cremony. Cadete said, 'You desire our children to learn from books, and say, that because they have done so, they are able to build all those big houses, and sail over the sea, and talk with each other at any distance, and do many wonderful things; now, let me tell you what we think. You begin when you are little to work hard, and work until you are men in order to begin fresh work. You say that you work hard in order to learn how to work well. After you get to be men then you say, the labor of life commences;

then, too, you build big houses, big ships, big towns, and everything else in proportion. Then, after you have got them all, you die and leave them behind. Now, we call that slavery. You are slaves from the time you begin to talk until you die; but we are free as the air. We never work, but the Mexicans and others work for us. Our wants are few and easily supplied. The river, the woods, and the plains yield all that we require, and we will not be slaves; nor will we send our children to your schools, where they learn to become only like yourselves.'

"Ussen gives me my Power through this rifle. It will not leave my hands. I have killed witches who harm my People. I have hunted Geronimo and his Chiricahuas for Nantan Lupan and Chief of Scouts Al Sieber in the Blue Mountains; and I have killed many bad men, Indah and Indeh (White and Indian). I may be the last warrior on this reservation willing to die for the freedom of his life-way, but these things you say I must do, I will not. I'll kill you first and disappear. Every man must decide the best for him and his family and follow his Power. You decide, Stottler. Is it life or death for you, for me? I will not, my band will not, change. Speak straight, or I'll see the lie in your eyes and kill you where you sit. Speak!"

CHAPTER 8
SHOOTING MATCH

I saw no fear in Stottler's eyes as we stared at each other and he rubbed his chin, thinking. Then his eyes narrowed, and he smiled, looking like Coyote the trickster. He said, with a taunting challenge in his voice, "Are you a gambling man, Yellow Boy?"

I shrugged and said, "I have played monte and raced horses, but not in many harvests. It is a strange question an agent asks when he is close to death."

"How about a bet? You win, and I'll let you wear your hair any length you want." He paused and waited for me to answer, but I stared at him and made no sign I was interested in his bet. He puffed his cheeks with a heavy sigh and said, "And, if members of your band don't want to better themselves, then I won't force them, either, as long as they stay out of sight of the rest of the reservation. You lose, you cut your hair, dress like a white man, get to work clearing land and stringing fence, and you convince the men in your band to do the same."

I saw Stottler's way even as he spoke. If I agreed to this bet, then I wouldn't kill him. If I won, he had a reason why I didn't have to cut my hair and wear Indah clothes or do farm work unless I chose to. If I lost, none of my People would trouble him, he would still be totally in control, and I would have to convince my brothers to do as he said. His smart Coyote grin said he knew he wouldn't lose, and I wondered what he wanted to bet.

"What is your bet?"

He crossed his arms and leaned back in his chair. "Blazer and the tribal police who have seen you shoot say you're a good shot. I don't doubt that you are, for an Apache, although I've never seen an Apache who could shoot worth a damn. There's an army surveyor, Major Fulton, from my home country back east, who's passing through. He's staying a few days at Fort Stanton on the way to California. He won a long-range shooting contest the Americans had against the Irish about twenty years ago at a place called Creedmoor. He's several years older than you, but steady as a rock with his rifle. I'll bet you a haircut and you dressing and working like a white man that Major Fulton, a white man, can outshoot you."

I thought, *I could have killed this evil teniente and been done with him, but now Ussen has given me a good way to keep my hair and bring hope to the People.* I stared at him as though I was thinking hard. I even chewed my lip from the inside as I had seen Indah do when they thought hard. I wanted to make *Teniente* Stottler believe I was thinking hard and that maybe I was a little scared of losing, but Ussen's gift of Power had never failed me. I didn't have to think.

I let the hammer down on my rifle and nodded. "What is the contest?"

"You and my friend shoot four targets each, the size of a man's head, at two hundred yards, free-standing shots, four shots straight. Whoever hits the most targets wins. That ought to be within range of your old Henry and what my friend uses. How about it? I'll send a telegram to Fort Stanton this morning to ask his participation. You come back in three days. When the sun is high, we'll shoot. Who knows? Maybe you're better than the world's best shooter twenty years ago." He made a big Coyote grin and said, "In the meantime, I'll sharpen my scissors."

"In three days, I come. We shoot when sun is high. Target size of man's head. I win, no haircut, no fence, no Indah lodge, and it is so for the warriors in my band."

Stottler nodded and stuck out his hand. I pumped it twice, as Rufus Pike said I should. Stottler said, "It is so. We have a bet."

By the time I returned from facing Stottler, the band had moved our camp into the Rinconada canyon where Nana hid his band seventeen harvests earlier. I sat with our band gathered around a fire and, after the men and I smoked, I told them what *Teniente* Stottler had said he planned for all the People on the reservation.

The People frowned when they heard this, and the children were very still. Beela-chezzi said, "Why does he do this? What have we done?"

I answered, "We don't deserve this. He says the old ways must go. They are no good on Indah land. We must live with the Indah. He says he can make us do this because he has all the power. We have none. We must do as he says or go to the jail and get no rations."

"You didn't kill him? We thought you would and then leave for Mexico, but Juanita said you would come back. Why did he not cut your hair?"

"We made a bet."

"What kind of bet?"

"A bet that I can shoot better than a soldier he knows who stopped at Fort Stanton on the way west to the land the Indah call California. If this soldier beats me, we all have to do as Stottler says. If I win, he won't bother us."

The whole group, as if from one mouth, said, *"Enjuh!"*

Early on the morning of the third day, cloudless with an ice-blue sky and bitterly cold, the band—all except for Maria, Sons-

76

ee-ah-ray, and Sleepy, who were all too old to walk or ride over the icy ridges—mounted their horses and followed me to the agency to watch the shooting match.

Ten army horses stood huddled together, their reins tied to the hitching rack in front of the agency and cinches loosened, their breath making a cloud of steam around their heads even near the middle of the day. We tied our horses in front of Blazer's store. My people went to the store to stand near the big stove or to look at the blankets, cloth, and other supplies until the shooting for the bet started. From the side of my pony, I nodded toward Juanita and Híghái and saw the light in Juanita's eyes when she smiled back before I took my rifle and walked across the road to the agency.

Stepping inside the agency building, I looked down the hall and, through an open door, saw buffalo soldiers crowded around the big, potbellied stoves in the workplace of the tribal police chief. In the other direction, I saw only one soldier in Stottler's workplace. He sat with his back to the door, talking to Stottler, who sat at his desk, intently listening and nodding. Many stacks of white papers lying in a perfect, aligned row covered the front of Stottler's desk. Stottler saw me at the door and, curling the fingers of his right hand, motioned for me to come in.

As the soldier, who wore Indah clothes, turned his head to see who Stottler had motioned to, Stottler said, "Major Fulton, our contestant has arrived. Meet Yellow Boy."

Major Fulton stood and faced me. He was nearly a head taller than me and had a great bush of black, gray-streaked hair covering the bottom part of his face. I wondered how he managed to eat through all that hair around his mouth. His eyes went instantly to my rifle, and he smiled. He looked me over, nodded, and stuck out his hand for the Indah shake. He said in a voice that reminded me of Blazer's, calm and unhurried, "I'm always glad to meet another marksman. I wish you luck, sir."

"Hmmph. My bullets go where Ussen says."

Major Fulton frowned, not seeming to understand what I meant, and Stottler, coming around from behind his desk to get their hats and coats, said, "Just an Apache superstition, Major Fulton. I have targets ready and the range measured over by the road. We'll get the tribal police and the soldiers who came with you to witness this little match, and I'm sure the congregants at Blazer's place will want to watch, too." He handed Fulton his hat and coat and a long leather case that must have held his rifle.

They pulled on their coats, but just as Stottler was about to step out the door, he stopped and went back to his desk, saying, "I guess I ought to carry these binoculars, since my eyes are not as good as yours. I'm sure I'll need my scissors, too." He grinned, every tooth showing, when he looked over at me. I said nothing and walked outside to wait on them. I wished I had killed Stottler when I had the chance, but I knew this was a better way. Winning is always the best revenge.

Up a canyon behind the agency, Stottler had the tribal police erect a frame two hundred yards from where we stood. He had eight pieces of sawed board about two hand-widths on a side wide and blackened with charcoal hanging from a heavy, sawed crosspiece mounted between two poles. Four of the pieces were for Major Fulton, four for me, and against the snow, they all looked like the little black spots that are buzzards so high on the wind you're not even sure anything is there. Light winds blowing down the canyon made the black spots dance and twist a little. A wood bench on the straight path through the snow to the target frame marked where we were to stand when we shot.

A big crowd of Mescaleros and soldiers gathered to watch. Stottler stood on a stump cleared of snow. He yelled, "Gentlemen, your attention!" After the crowd grew quiet, he began to explain the match. "Yellow Boy, Mescalero Apache, bets his haircut and work time I require for rations that he can outshoot the white man's champion, Major Fulton, who a few years ago won the Wimbledon Cup for being the best shot in the world. I hesitated to take advantage of Yellow Boy in this way, but I have agreed to the bet for his own good. Mescaleros say Yellow Boy is the best shot on the reservation. It is good to learn who shoots better and has more power, Mescaleros or white men." He went on to explain the shooting rules we had agreed to and what the targets were, ending with, "Major Fulton will shoot first, and then Yellow Boy. They will stand behind this bench." He smiled his Coyote smile and nodded toward me. "When the match is over, and Yellow Boy loses, he will sit on this bench for his haircut. I have the scissors in my pocket, and I'm sure he'll be ready and willing. If there is a tie, I will move the bench back another hundred paces, and we will shoot again another round of four, and continue moving back when there is a tie until one of them misses, at which time I will declare the winner and cut Yellow Boy's hair."

I stood in a place off to one side of the trail to the targets, and Major Fulton stepped to the bench, in his hands a single-shot rifle, which looked much like Rufus's long gun. I knew that the longer the shooting range, the more advantage Major Fulton had. A murmur passed through the Mescaleros. Looking to my right, I saw Doc Blazer frown and step forward, but I shook my head to keep him from protesting that the proposed tiebreaker wasn't fair. Stottler then turned to us and said, "Gentlemen, you may begin."

Major Fulton loaded his rifle with one of the big .45-70 cartridges the army used, sighted for a long breath on the first target, and then the rifle boomed. Its crack sounded back off the ridges as the first target board on the right went sailing as if some giant, unseen hand snatched it off its strings and flung it into the snow behind the frame. He ejected the spent shell, loaded another, and sighted again. The wind had picked up and made the targets dance in bigger arcs. He sighted on the second target and waited with the ten-pound rifle sighted and ready. As soon as the wind died down and the targets didn't swing wildly, he fired again and hit the second target a little off-center, but it went flying like the first. While the wind stayed low, Major Fulton quickly reloaded and shot his last two targets smoothly. Smiling, Stottler, looking through his field glasses said, "Major Fulton hits all his targets. Yellow Boy, your turn."

I stepped up behind the bench, felt the wind pick back up, and saw my targets swaying back and forth more than Major Fulton's had. I flipped up the rifle's ladder sight, set it to two hundred yards, and then levered a cartridge into place. The target's black dot hovered in my sights only an instant before I fired and knocked the first target high and spinning into the snow behind Stottler's frame. As Rufus had taught me, I continued in an easy rhythm to lever a cartridge, sight, and fire three more times, hitting all my targets. I shot all my targets in less time than Major Fulton had taken to do one. Stottler ran his tongue over his lips and stared at the empty target frame. Frowning, he turned to the chief of tribal police and said in a low voice, "Did he shoot more than four times?" The chief shook his head. Major Fulton stared at the target frame, his lips forming an O.

A collective sigh seemed to come from the Mescaleros, and even the tribal police were smiling. From his perch on the stump, Stottler said to the crowd, "Yellow Boy hits all his targets. It is a tie. Chief, send the men to hang the second set of targets, and we'll move the bench back a hundred paces. Since Major Fulton shot first last time, Yellow Boy will shoot first in the new round."

As the tribal police hung new targets, the afternoon wind

blowing down the canyon grew and made them toss and twist like men staggering home after drinking too much tiswin. While we waited for the targets, I looked over and smiled at Juanita holding Hígháh in her arms. Wrapped in her best heavy blanket, she smiled and nodded. Lucky Star, wife of Yibá, the adopted daughter of Sons-ee-ah-ray, stood behind her. To prove I had Power from Ussen so the great Nednhi chief, Juh, would tell me what he knew of the witch, Sangre del Diablo, I had shot a gourd off the top of Lucky Star's head while she ran screaming in fear through the brush. Lucky Star was then a nameless little child Juh had taken for a slave. When I shot the gourd without hitting her, he gave her to me. Juanita gave her to Sons-ee-ah-ray, who needed help in her tipi. Sons-ee-ah-ray, pleased with her work, adopted her and changed her name from Gourd Girl, what Juh's people called her, to Lucky Star. I thought, *Wind makes the targets move like the gourd on Lucky Star's head. Major Fulton doesn't like Wind. Ussen is with me. I'll keep my hair.* The Mescaleros in their blankets, backs turned to the wind, laughed and joked, waiting for the shooting to begin again. The Fort Stanton soldiers and Major Fulton stood beside their horses, smoked their pipes, and stamped their boots against the cold.

The tribal police finished tying the targets in place and hurried back down the path to the crowd around the shooting bench. Stottler motioned Major Fulton and me over to him. He said, "Gentlemen, you've both shot very well, but we can't resolve the bet until there is a clear winner. A tie won't do. You've already shot targets the wind shook a little. Now the wind is much worse, and the moving targets are farther away. Shall I tie the targets in place so they don't move? With iron sights, they'll be very hard to hit even tied in place, and I know you'll have to correct your shot for the wind drift before you shoot." He looked at Major Fulton and said, "What do you recommend we do, sir?"

Major Fulton frowned. "I would suggest tying the targets in place and giving us a couple of practice shots to correct for the wind before we shoot. Yellow Boy does not have a long-range rifle, so even without the wind I have an advantage. I'll accept his judgment. Let him choose."

Stottler, a smile barely cracking his lips, nodded toward me.

I said, "Shoot now."

Stottler's little smile turned to a deep frown as he looked back to Major Fulton, who shrugged his shoulders and slowly nodded that he agreed.

Stottler found a new stump near the crowd, brushed the snow off the top, climbed up on it, and raised his arms for silence. The crowd quieted and he said, "We will now shoot at a range of three hundred yards and let the wind move the targets as it wills. Whoever hits the most targets in four shots at three hundred yards wins. Yellow Boy shoots first in this round."

Stottler, continuing to stand on his stump, motioned me to the shooting bench and readied his field glasses to see if I hit any of the targets. I moved to the bench, set the sight range to three hundred yards, and looking at the distant target frame, saw the black specks that were our targets dancing in the wind. Time seemed to slow down and the target specks grow larger as I stared at them. I levered a new cartridge into my rifle, aimed a little high and to the right to compensate for the wind, and fired at the first target, which the wind made dance up and to the side. Then, with the same rhythm I used for the first set of targets, I shot the remaining targets, the thunder from my rifle rolling away down the canyon like that from rainstorms in the Season of Large Fruit.

Every soldier in the crowd had his field glasses on the targets. After I fired my last shot, they all lowered their glasses, silently staring at each other. One raised his glass and looked again at the target frame, while the others shook their heads. Stottler continued to stare through his glasses, his face turning red from the cold and wind, before he slowly lowered them, and looked at me walking back to stand with the People. He announced in his loud voice to the crowd, "Yellow Boy hits four targets with four bullets. It is your turn, Major Fulton. Proceed to the bench, sir."

Major Fulton loaded his .45-70 cartridge, brought the big rifle to his shoulder, and waited for his first target to stop swinging in the wind. But, unlike the first round, the target never steadied. He took a deep breath, lowered the rifle, and waited. Soon the wind seemed to slow, and the speck floating in the distance seemed to steady. The rifle came to his shoulder, but he hesitated. The wind began to gust again, and the speck's jitter increased.

From where I stood, I could see his jaw muscles flexing over clenched teeth. I knew he was determined to shoot, and he did, just as a strong puff of wind rolled over us. The boom from his big rifle filled the wind, and a second later, the frame holding the targets shook as his bullet hit the frame crossbeam. Stottler slowly lowered his glasses and shook his head. Fulton reloaded and shot three more times, but only hit his last target, and then only because the wind dropped to almost dead calm.

Before I reached the People, Major Fulton stepped in my path and held out his hand. I took it for two quick pumps, and Major Fulton said, "I was once considered the best long-range shot in the world. Today I've found among the Mescaleros a better shot than I could ever be. Congratulations, sir. I'm proud to have had a match with you."

I nodded, and he turned and walked away. Stottler turned to the crowd gathered around the bench blowing on their mitten-covered hands and stamping their feet in the cold. "For the second round, Yellow Boy has hit four targets, and Major Fulton has hit one. Yellow Boy wins the match and the bet."

My People and I quietly turned and walked away with Blazer to the agency store, where we went inside to warm ourselves before the long ride home. The tribal police walked to the agency building, hands in their coat pockets. Stottler and Major Fulton, their shoulders hunched against the cold, walked behind them. I was glad I had not killed Stottler. It was good to see Juanita laughing with the other women as they ran their hands once more over Blazer's store cloth.

CHAPTER 9
LOLA MES

Before our band returned to the Rinconada, Agent *Teniente* Stottler sent a written note to the agency store that said to give us our supplies that day for the next moon, and that in the future, a tribal policeman would bring them once a moon on pack mules to an agreed place near the Rinconada. However, we were not to show ourselves at the agency until we agreed to dress and work like Anglos as all the other Mescaleros had done. We took our supplies and left.

Agents might come and go, but we remained. If Stottler wanted us to think we were outcasts, he was wrong. We knew the rest of the Mescaleros would welcome us any time we wanted to visit. Stottler had already stopped all the big ceremonial dances and feasts, so we missed nothing in the reservation gatherings. All the people in our camp knew that the shooting bet I won against Stottler had given them a choice, and they had chosen the ways of our grandfathers, not the Indah ones he demanded.

After we returned from the agency, a storm passing over the mountains brought much snow. No storms had blown across the reservation for ten suns before it came. In those times, deer always followed elk to find dry, winter grass in the high, windblown places where most of the snow was gone. Caught in the high places during storms, deer took shelter under tall pine trees, but after the storm passed, heavy snow falling off the

85

branches formed a wall and trapped them until it melted. Taking deer in small herds trapped under the trees made hunting easy. The men in our camp needed to hunt. The camp was short of meat, but we waited until the wind and blowing snow passed. We spent the time telling stories around our fires, making weapons good again, making toy bows and arrows for our sons, and carving dolls for our daughters.

Beela-chezzi came to Juanita's tipi to smoke and talk while the snow fell and the winds howled on the ridges above our canyon. We spoke of the need for the men to hunt often to keep from starving on Stottler's rations, and about when I expected to return to Moon on the Water in the camp of Kitsizil Lichoo'. He wanted to know how to help Juanita and Hígháh while I was away and what to say if Stottler sent word for me to come. We considered what might happen if the band needed a *di-yen's* Power, and the young woman who had come to us couldn't do a cure or had left for other places. I told him he knew how to move around the reservation and find any *di-yen* we wanted. I suspected the tribal police didn't care what we did, as long as we stayed out of sight.

Beela-chezzi said, "I think Yellow Boy speaks true. We shouldn't worry about problems that might be. There are problems we need to fix now, such as how we can know when our sons and brothers are grown men ready to take a woman and start a family. Already Running Wolf and Knows Horses are eager to be men and take a wife. Running Wolf wants to court the young *di-yen* who comes from Mexico. I've told him I'll think on it, but he can do nothing until he's a man and can support a woman and children. Besides, who will speak as the parent of the *di-yen*?" He saw me smile and with a curious frown said, "This problem makes you laugh? Tell me. I will laugh, too."

I shook my head and blew smoke toward the top of the tipi.

"I don't laugh at your son or my younger brother. Knows Horses has asked for the same *di-yen*. I told him I would think on it, as you told Running Wolf. Have you spoken to this woman? Does she want either one? Does she want someone in the camp to adopt her? Maybe Sleepy? I don't know."

Beela-chezzi laughed. "My friend, truly we have the same problem. I haven't spoken with the woman and don't know her interests, but we must learn them soon, or my son and your brother will decide they must leave us and become Indah to find themselves a woman."

"Beela-chezzi speaks true. I'll visit this woman and learn what she thinks about the matter. I haven't spoken with her either. I wish to know and understand how she found her Power."

Beela-chezzi made a little fist shake and said, *"Enjuh!"*

The high wind and snow passed in two days. As the sun, a brilliant gold ball, came over the eastern ridges after the clouds had gone, warriors and boys began looking for a deer-trap tree. Near the middle of the day, we found one. Five whitetails trapped by the snow wall around the tree waited patiently for the sun to help them make their escape. We took them, every one, with bowshots to save ammunition. We carried them back to camp for the women to butcher and to begin tanning the hides. It was too cold to do much with the hides, but the cold made saving the meat easy until we could cure it.

The deer meat and hide preparations finished, I stood outside Sleepy's tipi a day or two later and waited for an invitation to come inside. Her daughter, Falling Water, saw my shadow or heard me cough and called out, "Our fire is warm, and the day is cold. Come. We share what we have."

I pulled back the door cover and stepped inside. The three

women stared through the flickering firelight at the shadow outlined against the bright door and smiled, motioning me in when they saw I was Juanita's man. Falling Water was working leather and, judging by the shapes of the pieces, making a pair of moccasins in the Chiricahua style. Like my mother, she used heavy bull elk hide for the soles. I know she did well trading her moccasins for other things she needed. Sleepy sewed beads on thin, soft leather, which would be used to decorate the moccasins Falling Water made. The *di-yen* from Chihuahua knelt by a small *metate* she used to grind herb mixtures drawn from little individual piles of dried plants lying neatly in a row beside her.

I waved my hand parallel to the floor to show that all was well.

Sleepy said, "Yellow Boy honors us. We're glad to see the one who stopped *Teniente* Stottler from taking our life-ways and our children. Sit by our fire. There is piñon nut coffee. Will you have some?"

I said, "There is generosity in Sleepy's tipi," and sat down cross-legged on a blanket next to the fire between Sleepy and the Chihuahua girl. Falling Water poured a cup of the hot, strong brew, and passed it to me.

While I sipped their coffee and they worked, we spoke of the success of the hunt, how others were doing in the camp, and how Moon prospered in the Blue Mountains in the camp of Kitsizil Lichoo'. When I told them she carried our first child, they all smiled, nodded, and murmured, *"Enjuh. Enjuh."*

At last, Sleepy asked, "How can we honor Yellow Boy for his visit?"

"I would speak with the *di-yen* who lives with you."

Sleepy nodded and, reaching for her blanket, said, "Falling Water and I will visit Juanita while you speak alone with the *di-yen.*"

"I'm grateful to you, Grandmother. I won't be a long time."

She nodded and said, "Leave when you're ready."

I waved my palm parallel to the ground, and they left, carrying some of their work with them.

The young woman, still on her knees using the *metate,* paused and stared at me, waiting for me to speak. I realized as I studied her that she reminded me of someone I knew in the long-ago times, but I couldn't think who it might be. She was pleasing to my eyes with wide-set, intelligent eyes, thin lips, an oval face, long braids that reached to her waist, and hips and breasts made for child-bearing. Her wrists were large, which said she was strong and aggressive, but her fingers were long and graceful, good for sewing and making medicine for wounds. I understood why Knows Horses and Running Wolf wanted her.

She set the *metate* grinding stone aside and modestly sat with her legs folded under her skirt, and bringing her right hand to the middle of her chest, she said, "I am Lola Mes. I traveled far to find the camp of Yellow Boy. I'm glad he speaks with me. Juanita told us you might do this when you returned from visiting your second wife in the Blue Mountains."

I nodded and pulled a cigarro from my vest, lighted it with a yellow-flame splinter I pulled from a piece of firewood, and we smoked. Unlike many women, she didn't cough from the cigarro smoke.

"Do I know you? Your face is in my memory from long-ago times, but I cannot find the time or place."

She bowed her head and looked in the fire. "No, you have never met me to remember me, but you knew my father well. The stories floating on the winds in the Blue Mountains say you killed him. I'm the daughter of Fernando Mes, the man you knew as Sangre del Diablo. You once saved me and my mother from him. Later, when he destroyed those you freed, he might have killed me, too, but he saved me for reasons only the gods of the Comanches know."

Surprised by her reference to my old enemy, I understood why I thought I knew her from the past and how her fine features somehow reminded me of the hard, coarse face of Sangre del Diablo. "I remember learning that a baby survived his destruction of the slaves Beela-chezzi and I freed from his *hacienda*. You're the child he gave to a woman in Casas Grandes?"

"Yes. I'm that child. The woman you saw in Casas Grandes is his half-sister. If you ever saw her up close, you would never forget her. She has a green eye and a brown one. The Mexicans call her Ojo Verde (Green Eye). She was a beautiful woman, but the passing harvests have taken much from her."

The memory of my Jarilla dream flashed in my mind. My heart raced as I understood the image that chased me through my dreams. The voice of Lola Mes drifted back into my hearing. "He trained her to be a *di-yen* and to give him pleasure, and she used his teaching to become a powerful witch, a woman of evil. She said he thought he might teach me how to use his Comanche Power, too. He died—you killed him—a couple of harvests before I was old enough to begin learning his medicine. But the woman he taught and used for his pleasures trained me in the same ceremonies after he died."

The wind came up in the treetops with a low moan and then drifted away. I wondered if it was a sign of good or evil coming as Lola Mes continued. "Ojo Verde believed she might sell me to a house of women in the City of Mules (Chihuahua City) or sell my medicine to those who came to her if she needed this thing the Nakai-yes call money. I learned well. I know many cures. The spirits have given me much Power over many evils, and I know how to give men much pleasure. Do you want me to show you what I can do?"

I lost my manners, stared at her, and crossed my arms. Her

obsidian-black eyes stared back at me with a little prideful lift to her chin.

"No, I don't want you to show me what you can do with your Power or your pleasures. Are you saying, as young as you are, that you have been with many men and learned what women in a house of women know? I don't understand your words."

"Sangre del Diablo's woman taught me preparation of many medicines and to do ceremonies for cures and attacks by evil. I've never attacked anyone with what she showed me. She trained me in men's pleasures. I've been with no man, but I've pleasured many."

"You have never known a man?"

"No."

"Then how have you pleasured many?"

"Sangre del Diablo's woman showed me many things women do to men in the houses of women in the City of Mules. Most Apaches don't know these things, but Comanches do. She showed me how women stir men by what they do before their eyes and with their hands. She showed my Power in pleasures often to men who came to her for more than I would give."

I looked into the fire and away from her eyes, offended that she spoke so plain.

"I'll speak no more of this, and if you're wise, neither will you, or the women in camp will run you off. Now, tell me, why have you come here?"

A blast of wind blowing through the camp shook the trees again, and their limbs rattled like the sound of dried bones shaking in a cloth sack as if evil approached.

"Sangre del Diablo's woman often told me you killed her man, and one time she told me where she thought your camp was. She said that many times she had sent little bands of Comanches to the basin to watch for you and to learn your ways, and that when the time was right, she would find you and use her Power to make you suffer for killing Sangre del Diablo before she destroyed you. She is very evil, like he was, and very patient, like a hunter on a deer trail. For a long time the Comanches came back and told her they had found your camp, but they never saw you. They thought maybe you had Power to disappear when their eyes searched for you. At first, I didn't care what she did. I didn't know you, and I didn't know Sangre del Diablo, except from what she had told me."

I heard wind swishing through the tops of the trees retreating to calm, and children playing with loud squeals and yells in the icy creek water. I thought, *Ussen has blessed me. The Comanches must have come when I was in the Blue Mountains.*

Lola Mes continued, "Hard times, a drought over three harvests, came to Casas Grandes, and Sangre del Diablo's woman, needing gold for food, had to sell me to a hacendado before she was ready to sell me to a house of women. I worked in the kitchen of his *hacienda* for two harvests. It was hard work, but I was strong and grew stronger. Life in the kitchen was easier than life in the fields."

She paused, puffed her cheeks, and seemed to stare inside herself at the memory.

"A few months ago, the hacendado's son tried to take me for his pleasure while his family traveled to the City of Mules. I escaped him and hit him hard enough with a big iron pan to send him to the Land of Dreams. I was afraid of what he would do when he came back to this side and opened his eyes. I took a knife and blanket and ran north toward the only place I knew I might have the eyes to find the warrior who killed Sangre del Diablo and would protect me from the vaqueros they were sure to send after me. I found your camp, and your People let me stay. I've healed your mother's hands now for a while and taken a fever from the mother of your wife's family. I'm ready to use my Power to help anyone here. Others in the camp have accepted me. Will you do the same?"

I held out my cup, and she poured more coffee. Something in her eyes warned me to be careful, but I looked past the danger and saw her strength, courage, and Power. She had come to our camp for safety because I had once tried to save her and her mother and other slaves from Sangre del Diablo. Perhaps she knew more than she should about women pleasuring men, but that was her secret. Having lived a long time, I knew women know many more things about the nature of men than most men would ever believe.

I took a long slurp and said, "I will accept you and your word until I know better."

She folded her hands in her lap and, looking down, murmured, "*Ba'ihénsih* (I thank you)."

"Now I would ask you something else. There are many sources of the question. It's like a blanket design made with many colored threads. My brother, Knows Horses, and Beela-chezzi's son, Running Wolf, are close in age. In the old days before the reservation, they would already be warriors with wives. Now they want recognition as men, but living on the reservation, warrior days are past. Beela-chezzi, Kah, Yibá, and I must decide how we'll test and approve their readiness for respect as men. We meet soon in council to decide this. Knows Horses and Running Wolf both want to court you, but neither yet knows that the other wants you. Are you interested in either one? If you accepted one, would you ask Sleepy or someone else to adopt you so you and your man supported that family?"

She stared at her hands for the span of a few breaths and then looked up into my eyes, never blinking, again with a prideful tilt to her chin. "Sleepy and Falling Water are kind to strangers. They've been kind to me, but they've said nothing about adopting me. If they wanted to adopt me, I would accept them.

Running Wolf and Knows Horses are good boys. I like them both. I think Knows Horses is the one I would choose—if I were asked."

She saw the smile on my lips and shook her head. "Yellow Boy, do not misunderstand what I tell you. I won't take a boy for a husband, no matter how old, good, and strong he is." She looked down at her hands and then into my eyes again and added, "I would rather be a third wife to a warrior who is a man, Yellow Boy, than first wife to a boy."

I stared at her. I was the only warrior in camp with two wives. Thoughts of what she said about knowing how to pleasure a man drifted through my mind, creating a little flash of desire, but then made me tremble inside as I thought of what might happen in the camp if I took her.

I nodded. "I hear you, Lola Mes. Soon we will decide how Running Wolf and Knows Horses can prove they are men. In the Season of Little Eagles, you might find ponies tied in front of your tipi. Choose well. You will speak with Sleepy and Falling Water about making you one of their family if you should take a . . . man?"

"This I will do."

CHAPTER 10
BOYS TO MEN

Before the reservations, a boy became a man by first serving as a novitiate to warriors on four raids. The novitiates took care of the horses, cooked, carried water, and made new camps. If novitiates did well, then warriors accepted them as men, and the new warriors led the next raids to prove their skill and bravery. More important, the camp considered new warriors ready for a man's life, ready to take women, make families, and provide for them and their wives' parents. The age when boys became novitiates usually began five or six harvests earlier than the ages of our boys. Knows Horses had seen nineteen harvests, and Running Wolf twenty-one.

Living on the reservation, our men couldn't go on raids. They hunted, worked livestock, cut and hauled timber, farmed when they had to, played hoops, and gambled. Age or physical maturity now determined when a boy became a man. Knows Horses and Running Wolf wanted recognition as men as in the days before reservations. They wanted to court Lola Mes as men and offer presents to her adopted parents. They wanted the old ways back, and I think Lola Mes did too.

Beela-chezzi, Kah, Yibá, and I smoked in Juanita's tipi before deciding how to give Knows Horses and Running Wolf their recognition as men. Yibá, the youngest among us, the last boy in the camp to be a novitiate and accepted as a warrior, said, "The rest of the camps across the reservation wait until their boys are old enough to make money hunting or working at *La Máquina*

95

or herding cattle. Then they can support themselves and a family. The camps say they're men. Why don't we treat Knows Horses and Running Wolf like that? I already pay Knows Horses to help with my cattle. It's enough for him and a woman to live on. Running Wolf hunts in the Ghost Face and works at *La Máquina* when the snow is gone. He, too, makes enough to support a woman. All the People on the reservation think these boys are men except us."

I saw Beela-chezzi glance my way and then shake his head. He said, "No, we all became warriors the old way. We survived our challenges. The challenges helped us understand who we were. Now *Teniente* Stottler says we must be somebody else. This will not stand. We're Apaches, ready to fight, ready to raid, even though we don't fight much, don't raid at all now. We must challenge these boys in men's bodies to know who they will be as men. I won't say to my son, '*Running Wolf, today you earn Indah money. Today you're a man.*' "

Yibá nodded, and Kah said, "Beela-chezzi speaks true. In the same way a *Haheh* says girls are women, boys must know what their band expects from them in supporting their families like men. Lola Mes says a boy will not live with her? She speaks straight, like a woman should. I say to prove they are men, let them slip off the reservation, take a string of wild horses, and return. This would be hard, truly a man's work. What do you say, Yellow Boy?"

"Beela-chezzi speaks wise, true words. We must challenge these boys who would be warriors. I've thought on this a long time. Hear me. Our boys remember their fathers and brothers raiding in the long-ago days. They know harvest times soon come when they'll make the first generation born on a reservation that has never known raiding for supplies and animals. They'll have to decide when this generation of boys, their sons, are called men." The sounds of women chopping firewood and children playing drifted into our ears. The sounds made stronger what I had to say. "I say for these boys to become men, they must go on a raid and prove they can survive by themselves. They will be the last raiders."

My brothers all looked at each other, frowning, and then at me.

Beela-chezzi said, "What? Are you loco? The first time there is a raid from a band on this reservation, the Blue Coats will come, try to kill us all, take the land, and drive away those who live to starve."

Kah and Yibá nodded, glancing first at me and then at Beela-chezzi.

"My mind is good. Hear me. I'll take these boys to the Blue Mountains when I return to stay with Moon on the Water. They can learn places of water on the trail and to travel at night along the way. At the camp of Kitsizil Lichoo', they can go to high mountains for their visions of Power or have a *di-yen* sing for them in a sweat lodge, and they can serve as novitiates to warriors when they raid hacendado herds along the border. After they have done this, then they must find their way back here alone, traveling at night and unseen by Indah or the tribal police. If they can do this, then we should call them men and warriors and ask them to join us. They can tie their ponies in front of Sleepy's tipi for Lola Mes and send one of us with presents to ask for her. Perhaps she'll choose one of them, but I don't know this. I know only that she will consider them. That is all I have to say."

Beela-chezzi crossed his arms and frowned at me from across the fire. "If the boys run back here from the camp of Kitsizil Lichoo', how many days will it take?"

I thought for a few breaths and said, "Running at night and without trouble, six to eight days."

"And would you follow them in case there is trouble?"

"I would follow a day behind them in case there is trouble."

"Hmmph. I think, Yellow Boy, you have sun behind your eyes. You give us a test that only an Apache warrior could pass. It's a hard one they will tell their grandchildren about. They'll be eager to do it."

Kah and Yibá stared at the fire, and, for a while, it made the only sound in the tipi as the wood cracked and popped under the heat. First Kah smiled, and then Yibá. Both said together, *"Enjuh!"*

Knows Horses and Running Wolf leaned forward, listening, their ears collecting every word Beela-chezzi spoke as he told them in council what we expected them to do in order for us to call them men and warriors. Their faces were unmoving masks in the flickering orange and yellow light of the tipi fire, but their eyes betrayed them, bright, shining, and eager to face whatever we set before them.

Beela-chezzi finished by saying, "You understand, little brothers, if you slip off the reservation and are caught, you could be killed or spend many days in *Teniente* Stottler's house of *pesh* (iron) bars where there is bad light, bad food, bad smells, dirt, and, sometimes, sickness. You understand that if you don't risk it, most of the rest of the reservation already sees you as men ready for women to make you families. That's a good thing. But we in this camp will not call you warriors. You won't have proved yourselves that way. Which path do you choose?"

Running Wolf looked at Knows Horses and then around the fire, pausing to stare in the eyes of every man. He said, "I go to the Blue Mountains with Yellow Boy. I'll be a helper to warriors on cattle raids for the camp of Kitsizil Lichoo'. I'll find my way back to the reservation alone."

Knows Horses also looked around the fire, and then he said, "What Running Wolf has said he'll do to pass your manhood and warrior trial, that I will do also. I ask my brother when he will return to the Blue Mountains. Running Wolf and I will be ready to ride with him."

I answered, "I'll ride early in the Season of Little Eagles when the snow in the passes goes away. I'll tell you three days before I leave. Be ready."

Chapter 11
To the Camp of Kitsizil Lichoo'

Teniente Stottler was a man of his word. The tribal police left our supplies where we agreed on a trail into the Rinconada. The Season of Little Eagles came and, with it, a warm wind the Indah call Chinook that made snow in the passes disappear fast. After that wind blew, I told Knows Horses and Running Wolf to be ready. I planned to leave in three days.

Juanita and I had prepared much meat for her fire so I could go south and stay with Moon on the Water until well into the season of Many Leaves. As the Ghost Face began to leave and the melting snow dripped from high pine branches like falling rain, I worked a long time to straighten or make arrows for my bow, sharpen my knife, and keep my rifle clean and well oiled. I spent many suns with Hígháh teaching him the skills every Apache child learned early. Juanita taught him not to make noise with his mouth, and, although he was still very young, I taught him how to avoid making sounds under the trees, in the canyons, and around the horses and mules. While he was still noisy for an Apache, he practiced what I showed him and grew quieter. Near the yellow and orange flames of Juanita's fire after the evening meal, I told Hígháh Coyote stories to help teach him manners and the value of speaking true and of following customs that had been long with the People.

Every night, I lay with Juanita enjoying our pleasures, hoping we would make another child, and speaking together by the fire about when I should bring Moon back. Juanita had not seen her sister since Híghá had been born, and knowing that Maria did not have many remaining days, she asked that I try to bring Moon, if not to stay, then to visit, when I returned. I agreed to speak with Moon about this in the camp of Kitsizil Lichoo' in the Blue Mountains.

The sun was setting on the western ridges of the Rinconada when Knows Horses, Running Wolf, and I swung up on our ponies and, like warriors in the long-ago times, rode out of our camp's canyon, silent and ready for the business of avoiding enemies and taking their wealth. The People silently watched us go, Lola Mes among them, her arms crossed, her gaze following us. Even in the fading light, when I looked back, I saw her attention on me and a crooked smile on her lips.

I took a way to the camp of Kitsizil Lichoo' that would be the shortest way back for Knows Horses and Running Wolf when they finished their novitiates in the Blue Mountains. We rode in bright moonlight over the ridge above Three Rivers and down into the llano south of the black rock covering the Valley of Fires, and then through a San Andres pass where I had taken the Jicarilla, Red Pony, after he had tried to escape the tribal police. From there, we rode west across the llano the Nakai-yes call *Jornada del Muerto* (Dead Man's Journey) and the great river, then south, until I turned west again across the llano toward the mountains the Indah call Three Sisters. I followed the Animas Valley south past the Animas Mountains toward the great white spaces sometimes covered with water usually not much more than a hand's width deep, the place the Nakai-yes call playas. We were in Chiricahua country, but the Indah, ten harvests earlier, had taken all the Chiricahuas east and kept them there because Geronimo had made war against them too many times.

We rode across the border and up into the high Blue

Mountain canyons and ridges where Kitsizil Lichoo' had his camp. Knows Horses and Running Wolf had ridden looking back most of the trip, seeing the details of the land they must remember in order to return to our camp on the reservation. In the Blue Mountains, they were careful to look for landmarks along the trails by the rushing water we followed up to the high places. Watching them do this, I was glad to see they had learned their early lessons well.

On the morning of the fourth day after leaving the Rinconada, we rode down the wide, slow stream flowing over sand and great, flat stones that gave water to Kitsizil Lichoo's camp. From the water, we rode up on to a bench on the eastern side of the stream. The bench was covered with brush all the way to cliffs over three hundred feet high. Kitsizil Lichoo' had his camp there against the canyon cliffs. A light fog lay over the camp, mixing with thin smoke from cooking fires, and nearly all who saw me nodded an acknowledgment and took care not to stare impolitely in my direction. But they didn't know Running Wolf and Knows Horses. They studied them with frowns of concentration, trying to understand the strange young men who were with me. Even upon seeing new arrivals, they made very little sound, and everyone continued about their business.

I motioned for Running Wolf and Knows Horses to wait while I dismounted and went to the big round lodge of Kitsizil Lichoo' in the middle of the camp, where he sat by the blanket door, warming himself at his wives' morning cooking fire. He saw me and smiled, but, like the others, he stared at the young men. As I approached, he waved his hand parallel to the ground in greeting. "My friend, the great warrior Yellow Boy returns. *Enjuh.* All is well. Moon on the Water has waited a long time while her belly grows with your child. She is eager to see her husband again." He pointed with his nose toward Knows Horses and

Running Wolf. "You bring us more warriors?"

"They're young men from our camp on the reservation. They ask to be novitiates for your warriors, taking hacendado cattle, that they might become warriors. I offer you the strength of my brother, Knows Horses, riding the black pony, and Beela-chezzi's son, Running Wolf, on the red pony. Running Wolf is the child we took from the witch, Sangre del Diablo, many harvests ago. Will your warriors take them as novitiates?"

Kitsizil Lichoo' crossed his arms and looked them over. I had no doubt that he would accept them, but he made a good show of considering them while he rubbed his jawline with his left thumb and forefinger. He stood and walked over to them, inspected them carefully as he walked around their ponies, and then walked back to his fire, staring at the ground in thought, before he nodded to me and said, "Yes, our warriors will accept them as novitiates. There's a small, empty lodge near the corral. They're welcome to stay there. I'll speak with you alone after you visit with Moon on the Water."

I nodded, saying, *"Enjuh,"* and then motioned Knows Horses and Running Wolf to dismount and follow me. At the edge of the village, I stopped at the empty lodge Kitsizil Lichoo' said they could use and told them, "Kitsizil Lichoo' offers you this shelter while you are in his camp. Make your beds, and store your saddles and weapons here. The corral is a little further up the path by the creek. Leave your ponies there until you need them. You'll need to cut some grass for them and for the camp every day from the top of the ridge on the western side of the canyon." Then I pointed toward a lodge similar to and near that of Kitsizil Lichoo' and said, "Now I visit my woman in that lodge. When the sun rides into the western mountains, come and eat with us. Know the people of the camp. They welcome you with smiles. Make them glad you're here."

★ ★ ★ ★ ★

We led our ponies to the corral hidden in the brush. The ponies already in the corral lifted their heads with their ears pricked up to study the newcomers before they returned to their fresh cut grass. We used some of the grass to rub our ponies down and then took our saddles and bridles to our lodges. It had been a long night, and we needed rest.

I stood before the blanket door of Moon on the Water's lodge and cleared my throat. There was silence for the space of a breath before a soft voice from inside said, "Come. You're welcome in this lodge. There's food on my fire."

I pulled back the blanket and stepped into the flickering orange and yellow light of its fire in the center. Moon, standing out of sight beside the door, surprised me. She grabbed my vest and pulled me close to her warm body. In a trembling, excited voice, she said, "Ussen has blessed me. My man returns safe to my lodge." I felt the swell of her belly against me, her arms around me, and the sweet joy of her yucca flower smell filling me.

"All is well?"

Her laugh deep and throaty, she said, "Our child grows strong in my belly. My husband returns in the Season of Little Eagles. All is well."

We sat down by her fire, where she had been making a basket in a style I had not seen her try before. She gave me a cup of piñon nut coffee, a gourd filled with dried fruit, nuts, and juniper berries, acorn bread, slices of mescal, and meat from a *Nakai-yi* cow she grilled over her fire. The big meal's tasty flavors filled me up and made it easy to tell that Moon and Juanita had learned how to cook from the same woman. She told me of her life while I waited out the Ghost Face season at Mescalero before returning to her. The snow in the Blue Mountains that year had been heavy in all the passes. I had tried, but I couldn't get through. Like all good Apache women, she had patiently waited. She told me how she had learned new basket-weaving tricks from the Opata women Beela-chezzi, Rufus, Kah, Yibá, and I rescued and brought to the camp of Kitsizil Lichoo' many harvests earlier, after we finally caught and killed the great witch, Sangre del Diablo, who had wiped out most of our families.

I told her how, after I heard all the evil things Stottler was doing to our People, I had gone to kill him but made a shooting bet instead and won it to stop him from forcing us to live like Indah. I also told her how I had saved an Indah boy from an ambush I had dreamed about three harvests earlier. She held her hand over her mouth, finding it all hard to believe, but she knew that I spoke true.

I also spoke of moving the camp deep into the Rinconada, and of the young *di-yen* named Lola Mes. She laughed when I told her Knows Horses and Running Wolf came with me to serve as novitiates so they might be known as men, and that both wanted to court Lola Mes.

Moon stared at me and slowly shook her head. She said, "I believe you, husband, but a *di-yen*, an older woman, Ojo Verde (Green Eye), has come from Casas Grandes and stays in this camp. She has a green eye and a brown eye and is very powerful. How can it be that a new woman *di-yen* comes to both our camps at the same time and from the same place?"

I felt shadows on my spirit grow darker. I remembered the words of Lola Mes about Ojo Verde: *Ojo Verde often told me you killed her man. She said that when the time was right, she would use her Power to make you suffer before she destroyed you.* Now she was in the camp of Kitsizil Lichoo', like a spider in a hole, waiting for me. I knew that if the people in camp respected her power as a *di-yen*, then I would have to catch her using a witch's power before shooting out her eyes.

"This *di-yen,* why does she come here?"

"She said her Power told her in a vision that the camp of Kitsizil Lichoo' in the Blue Mountains needed her medicine, and her Power and guided her here."

"Have you seen her ceremony for curing a fever?" I knew her answer before she spoke.

"Yes, I've seen her cure the fever of a child. She gave a blue stone to the child's mother and told her to bury it anywhere on the north side of her mother's lodge. In a vision, she called on Green Moth with Big Eyes on Its Wings. It told her what ceremony to use. The ceremony lasted all night. The women in the village all watched. The next day the child was better and up helping her mother. This *di-yen* is very powerful."

"Does this *di-yen* know you are Yellow Boy's woman?"

Moon frowned and cocked her head to one side as she looked at me. "Yes, she knows. Everyone in the village knows this."

I stared into the fire and tried to think how to stop this witch. I saw the brown and green eyes in my dream and trembled inside at the threat we all must be facing. But then, remembering the warning I felt when I spoke with Lola Mes, I thought, *Are Lola Mes and Ojo Verde both witches? How will I know both are not using their Power on me?*

Something flickered in my memory, a few sparks that said I already knew the answers to these questions. I stared at Moon's little fire for a time before it came to me. I remembered Lola Mes had told me Ojo Verde was Sangre del Diablo's half-sister and that he had trained her to pleasure him. *Incest! It's the worst kind of evil.*

The Mescaleros burned those who knowingly committed incest. Sangre del Diablo was the most evil of witches. He would have committed incest with his half-sister, even with his full sister. Ojo Verde was part of that incest. She, too, was a witch. She was the one I had to fear, and now she lived in the same village, waiting to take me with her witchcraft.

I felt Moon's warm hand on my arm. "Husband, your face betrays you. It's black as the clouds before Thunder and Wind Spirits come with lightning arrows. What will you do? Tell me."

"First, I must speak with Kitsizil Lichoo' and tell him I believe Ojo Verde is a witch. Perhaps he has knowledge that will keep us from burning her."

CHAPTER 12
OJO VERDE'S POWER

The shadows were deep, fingers of night spreading over the land, as I sat down beside Kitsizil Lichoo' at the fire in front of his lodge. It was a peaceful time. Women worked at preparing their evening meals, children played in the burbling creek, and small groups of men sat talking and smoking.

Kitsizil Lichoo' saw me approach and motioned toward a sitting place on his left. I sat down, reached in my vest pocket, and pulled out one of my black cigarros. I lit it with a twig from the fire, smoked to the four directions, and then gave it to Kitsizil Lichoo', who also smoked to the four directions and gave it back to me. He knew from our smoke and the anger in my face that I expected to have a serious talk with him.

I said, "Knows Horses and Running Wolf are anxious to learn how your warriors will take the cattle and what they must do as novitiates for these raids. They want to earn the respect of those who will call them men."

Kitsizil Lichoo' smiled and nodded. "They'll learn what will happen tonight. It's a wise thing in this time when raids are few that you let them learn in the old way. It is not as hard as what we did in the long-ago times, but it's enough. I see your face. You think of other things?"

"You will leave our words here?"

He frowned and nodded. "I won't speak to others."

"A woman named Ojo Verde, a *di-yen*, now lives in the camp?"

He slowly nodded.

I said, "She's the half-sister of Sangre del Diablo. She was his woman and raised his baby, a child saved from the slaves he destroyed after Beela-chezzi and I had set them free. Ojo Verde pleasured Sangre del Diablo as a woman does a man, although she was his sister. She's a witch. She's sworn to make me suffer and then kill me in revenge for sending Sangre del Diablo to the land of the grandfathers, but I'll send her to the grandfathers first when I shoot out her eyes and burn her body."

Kitsizil Lichoo' crossed his arms and stared at the fire. "How do you know this? Tell me, and if it's true, I'll burn her now." Crows flew over the canyon, cawing, heading for their night roost, and *googés* (whip-poor-wills) began their night calls.

"The baby, his child, saved from the slaves he destroyed, and raised by Ojo Verde is now a young woman and a *di-yen*. She lives now in my camp in Mescalero. Her name is Lola Mes. She told me this."

Kitsizil Lichoo', his face filled with questions, held up his hand, palm out, to stop me. "How do you know Lola Mes is not a witch also? Maybe she wants to kill you for killing her father."

"This I have considered. All the Power she used in my camp has been for the good of the People. I have looked in her eyes while she told me of her life and of Ojo Verde. I saw no evil or lies there. I do not believe she is a witch. I dreamed of evil with a brown eye and a green eye before I spoke with her. I know Ojo Verde is a witch. She lay with her brother. She must die."

Kitsizil Lichoo' stared at me for a time, his face clouding with dark anger, and then he said, "Come."

We left his fire and walked toward a lodge on the opposite end of the camp from the one Knows Horses and Running Wolf used. A small fire burned in front, providing heat, a place to cook, and yellow light for the coming night. At the lodge's blanket-covered door, Kitsizil Lichoo' said in a deadly flat voice,

109

"Ojo Verde, come out." There was no answer. He threw back the blanket and looked inside. The lodge was empty.

An old woman by her fire at a lodge nearby watched us with her head tilted in curiosity. He called to her, "I look for Ojo Verde. Where is she?"

The old woman, nearly toothless, croaked. "She takes bread to welcome the new ones in camp."

I ran to my lodge, Kitsizil Lichoo' right behind me. Moon worked by her fire, but her left hand had been wrapped with a piece of cloth. A large round piece of mesquite bean flour bread sat on a pan nearby. Our rush out of the dusky gloom startled her. I said, "Where did that bread come from? Why is your hand wrapped?"

"Ojo Verde brought it for you. She said she learned you had traveled far with Knows Horses and Running Wolf and wanted to give us a present. I took the pan she offered. It was still hot and burned my fingers a little. She put herbs she had on them and wrapped this cloth around them to hold them there for a while. My fingers don't sting at all now."

I ground my teeth in fear and fury. "Eat none of that bread! It will make you sick! Clean and change the wrapping on your hand. Use your own herbs on it, and throw that cloth in the fire."

Moon bowed her head and stared at the ground as she said, "I know you think she may be a witch, but I was careful around her. I ate nothing she offered, and the herbs she chewed and put on my fingers made them feel better. But I will do as you say."

"We go to the lodge of Knows Horses and Running Wolf. Maybe we will catch her there."

Knows Horses and Running Wolf sat by their fire, the mesquite-bean bread on a pan between them. Half of it was gone.

Knows Horses said, "Ho! Brother, you come in time to eat a piece of this fine bread the *di-yen,* Ojo Verde, brings to us. You'll like it. Have some. We should have waited to share it with you at Moon's fire, but we were hungry after sleeping all day."

Running Wolf held up a small jug and offered it to me. "She even left us some honey to go with it. I say forget the bread. Just eat the honey. Here, there is plenty left."

I saw Knows Horses had a cloth wrapped around the palm of his hand and asked, "Why is that cloth on your hand?"

He looked at his hand and back to me. "She saw I had a rope burn, the one I got holding the horses when we came up Cañon Bonito yesterday, and she said she happened to have some herbs with her that would make it better. She chewed them, put them on the burned place, and wrapped it with this cloth. My hand already feels better. Why do you ask me this?"

"Wash your hand, now. Throw that cloth in the fire. Moon has something to put on it. Eat no more of this honey or bread. Ojo Verde is a witch, and we're her enemies."

Kitsizil Lichoo' growled, "Where is she?"

Knows Horses and Running Wolf turned pale and trembled as they pointed toward the corral. Knows Horses said, "She told us she was going to check on her pony."

Ojo Verde was not at the corral, and neither was her pony. Down in the canyon, it was too dark to find her trail. Kitsizil Lichoo' said, "If she tries to ride out of here in the dark and with no moon, she will likely be dead at the bottom of a canyon by sunrise. We'll find her at first light."

After Moon's evening meal, Knows Horses and Running Wolf joined me, and we went to the lodge of Kitsizil Lichoo', where the men were to speak of plans for the cattle raid. Kitsizil Lichoo's women, Steps in Water, his first wife; and Calico Dove, his second, sat in front of the lodge working with their three daughters, one very pretty who must be near her *Haheh,* grinding acorns and mesquite beans to make flour for bread. They smiled when they saw us come into the fire's light and motioned us to go inside their lodge. I heard voices talking and laughing inside.

When I pulled back the door blanket, it grew quiet, and the warriors, all my friends, turned to see who entered. They sat in a circle around the lodge's center post used to support the roof poles. A big clay pot next to the center pole held a small fire providing light and warmth to keep us comfortable.

Kitsizil Lichoo' waved us inside and motioned us to sit beside him to his left. After each one smoked to the four directions, he said, "Yellow Boy returns from his band of Mescaleros. He brings with him Knows Horses and Running Wolf, who would ride with us as novitiates when we take hacendado cattle. Will you accept them?"

There were general grunts of approval around the circle. One warrior, Wrestles with Strong Hands, who was short, quick, and very strong, and usually overpowered anyone fool enough to wrestle with him, said, "These two should already be warriors. Why were they not novitiates a few harvests ago?"

Knows Horses started to speak, but I held up my hand, palm out, to answer. "Life on the reservation has ended the old ways you still follow here. The old ways are good ways. A girl knew she was a woman after her *Haheh.* A boy knew he was a warrior ready to take a woman after he served four times as a novitiate with warriors going on raids. Girls can still have their *Haheh.* But living on the reservation, men and boys can only hunt and do the work of Indah. We can raid no more and act as true warriors. It's a hard time for us. These boys, now grown to man size, were children when we first went to the reservation. They are the last ones who lived in the days of raids. Their sons will be born on the reservation, never having a connection with the old ways except through the memories of their grandfathers. Their sons will decide when their sons are men. The men in our camp decided the best way for Knows Horses and Running Wolf to be recognized as men and warriors was to be novitiates in the old way. In the Blue Mountain camps of Kitsizil Lichoo' and others, warriors still raid. I agreed to bring them here and offer them to you as novitiates. The warriors in my camp in Mescalero ask that you accept them."

Wrestles with Strong Hands crossed his arms, studied them, and said, "Have they worked with cattle on the reservation?"

"Yes, they both know cattle as well as any vaquero."

"*Enjuh!* The novitiates can ride in the dust behind the cattle as we drive them up the canyons to slaughter. When the sun rises, I say let them go to those who watch the hacendado herds and learn the trail we use driving them back here through the canyons. Let them be ready when we strike."

There were smiles and nods from all the warriors in the circle. They would test these young outsiders and make sure they were worthy to be called warriors.

I said, "They'll be ready. We thank our friends for taking them."

Kitsizil Lichoo' and the warriors discussed how the raid would be done, who had special responsibilities, and how the novitiates would help. When he was satisfied we all understood the plans, he said, "Now I tell you evil has come to this camp."

The warriors looked at each other, frowning. High on the ridge above us a wolf howled, and a puff of breeze coming down the canyon shook the limbs of trees, making them sound like women moaning.

"The woman who came to us from Casas Grandes, Ojo Verde, is a witch. She plans to witch and kill Yellow Boy for sending her brother, the great witch, Sangre del Diablo, to the Happy Land. We went for her just before dark. I was ready to burn her. But she had left the camp and has perhaps witched Moon on the Water and these young men. Tomorrow, we must find and burn her before her Power works its evil."

The warriors wanted to know how Kitsizil Lichoo' knew this, some protesting that she had done good, not evil, for them with her Power. We spoke long into the night about this. When the council broke up, none had any doubt that Ojo Verde must die.

CHAPTER 13
EVIL COMES

Leaving the council, I noticed Knows Horses's hand that Ojo Verde had made medicine for was starting to swell. I asked him about it, but he said he had no pain. Moon waited for me in our lodge. Reeds of different colors she used to make baskets were laid out around her. Her burned hand looked normal, but her lips were drawn tight across her teeth, and her other hand rested on her belly.

She looked up at me, her eyes filled with pain, "Husband, I burned the cloth and bread as you said. They sounded like gunshots in the fire. Something is not right in my belly. I am bleeding. Don't get any of this blood on you. Ask Calico Dove, Kitsizil Lichoo's second woman, to come and help me."

I hurried to the lodge of Kitsizil Lichoo' and told him Moon was bleeding, looked sick, and had asked that Calico Dove come to help her. Calico Dove grabbed a basket filled with herbs and moss and was out the lodge door ahead of me before I could turn around. Steps in Water called after us, "Soon I come."

When we returned, Moon lay on our blanket, her face twisted with pain and bathed in water, as if she was very hot or had a fever, the blanket dark and wet. Calico Dove gave me a water skin and asked that I fill it from the creek. Moon saw me and said, "I'm sorry, husband. Something tears and rips at me inside. I bleed much. I fear our child tries to escape, and if he does, he will die outside me."

Calico Dove pointed out the door and said, "Hurry. We will need much water. Stay away from her blood. It will make your joints ache and swell."

Hurrying to the creek to fill the water skin, I passed Steps in Water and an old woman running for my lodge carrying baskets of moss and medicines. I made many trips to the creek that night to fill water skins. Each time I returned to the door, I heard Moon groaning in pain. When I tried to go in to her, the women looking after her said it was better if I waited outside by the door. I accepted their judgment. I stirred up the coals, added wood to the outside fire, and waited and smoked, listening to every groan and panting gasp that came through the blanket over the door. Each time I heard the agony of my woman, I swore a thousand more deaths for Ojo Verde, the witch who had done this to her.

As the stars were fading in the gray light of dawn, I heard one last groan of pain and then it was silent inside. Soon Calico Dove brought me a covered basket. "Your son tried to leave Moon before it was his time and has gone to the Happy Land. There is a place for you to hide his body in the cliffs up canyon. Moon has lost much blood, but she will be strong again and live to give you more sons. Go. We will look after her."

In the dim gray light of dawn I made a cairn over the basket on a shelf in the cliffs up the canyon. As I walked back toward the village, the rising sun threw shafts of light through the mists across the top of the canyon. When I returned to my lodge, Moon on the Water was resting, although she looked pale and drawn. I thought perhaps she was dying, but Calico Dove told me she would be better with a few days of rest. Calico Dove said she would stay with her until she gained back some strength. I went to the lodge of Knows Horses and Running Wolf, where they sat by their fire drinking piñon nut coffee.

They offered me a cup, and I sat with them to drink it. A canyon wren was beginning to call, and the camp stirred as the women worked over their fires and sent children to the creek for the day's water.

Knows Horses's hand and arm had grown swollen and red, his fingers so big he could barely bend them. I asked, "What happened when you threw the cloth and bread into the fire?"

Running Wolf, his eyes round with surprise, said, "They popped and flared, sounding like guns going off."

Knows Horses scowled and shook his head. "It'll be all right. I'm ready to ride as soon as we eat. Does Moon have a meal ready?"

I stared at the ground and shook my head, my throat feeling inside like an angry badger clawed at it. "She was witched, too. She lost our child and much blood last night, but the woman with her says she'll grow strong again. If the witch can do that to her, I worry about what she has done to you. Look at your hand and arm. We should wait before we go to the watchers of cattle."

Knows Horses shook his head. "Brother, my heart is heavy for you and Moon, but we should go. That witch can't hurt us as bad as she did Moon, can she? I mean, we carry no child. We're strong. We're men and will soon be warriors."

"I don't know the strength of this witch, but her brother, who taught her, was very powerful. I'll speak with Kitsizil Lichoo' and learn what he thinks."

Light shafts streaming through the mists and trees were moving down the western wall of the canyon when I went to the lodge of Kitsizil Lichoo'. His daughters worked at the fire as he ate. He waved for me to sit down and for his oldest daughter to bring me something to eat, but I shook my head that I wanted nothing. He said, "Steps in Water and Calico Dove told me what happened when they returned from your lodge. I hope Moon is better soon. Wrestles with Strong Hands and Angry He Takes No Prisoners will go after the witch and bring her back. She must be burnt to stop her evil."

"Yes, she must die in fire to destroy her evil. I will shoot out her eyes so she is blind in the Happy Place. She also witched Knows Horses and Running Wolf. Knows Horses's hand and arm are red and swollen, but he says he can ride. Running Wolf doesn't show signs of harm yet. They both want to ride to the cattle watchers and work when the raid begins. What do you think they should do?"

I noticed Kitsizil Lichoo's daughter Blue Flower listened to us with interest. I smiled inside and thought, *She must have an eye for one of those boys.*

Kitsizil Lichoo' said, "Perhaps the hand and arm of Knows Horses gets no worse. If they want to ride to the cattle watchers, go ahead. Steps in Water or Calico Dove will look after Moon while you're gone. They would do this anyway while you are here, and you would just be in their way. A *di-yen* will do a Sing for her, and she will be better when you return. It might be two or three days before Wrestles and Angry return with the witch. If they return before you, we will hang her by her wrists and wait to burn her until you return."

Moon, pale and weak, her face sagging from lack of sleep and much weariness, was lying by a small fire wrapped in a blanket. Seeing me kneel beside her, she rose up on an elbow and pulled her hair back. "I lost our child. Sunlight comes to our door. I'll make you something to eat."

I shook my head. "No, rest. Calico Dove or Steps in Water will return soon. I need you to rest for the next two or three days and get strong while I take Knows Horses and Running Wolf to learn the canyon trails and meet the cattle watchers. You didn't lose the child. The witch took it from us. Soon she will burn. No more will she trouble anyone. When you're ready, we'll make another child."

She lay back and pulled her blanket up and smiled. "I look forward to that, husband. Where is the witch?"

"She tried to witch Knows Horses and Running Wolf after she attacked you. Now she's disappeared. Wrestles with Strong Hands and Angry He Takes No Prisoners will bring her back. Kitsizil Lichoo' says he will hang her by her wrists and wait to burn her until we return from the cattle watchers. Grow strong again, *Ish-tia-neh* (woman). Soon the witch who took our child will burn in fire. I am back in two or three suns."

She nodded. "May we live to see each other again."

We followed a trail through the canyons I had followed many times in Ghost Face seasons to reach Moon when the high passes were blocked with snow, and Kitsizil Lichoo's people used it to hide hacendado cattle they drove back to their camp. Knows Horses wrapped his hand and arm with a long piece of cloth a camp woman gave him to protect it and carried it close to his body in a sling. He managed his pony well with his good hand and arm. Running Wolf rode effortlessly, showing no signs Ojo Verde had witched him. They paid close attention to trail features and the many side canyons they had to avoid driving the cattle west down the canyons toward the camp from the llano.

Late that day, near dark, we came to and scanned the llano from the canyon mouth where warriors would first drive the cattle. The *Shináá Cho* showed the two cattle watchers where Kitsizil Lichoo' said I would find them. They watched the distant cattle using old army *be'idest'iné* (binoculars) while they stretched out on top of a low, rock-covered hill directly in front of the canyon. The hill made the canyon hard to see and find from the llano unless you knew where to look. Rather than spook the watchers and perhaps disturb the cattle, we decided to let them find us. We built a small fire back in the canyon to give just enough smoke for them to smell and come looking for us. While we waited for them, we ate a meal of cactus fruit and dried meat and nuts pounded together.

We didn't have long to wait. The two men, rifles in the crooks of their arms, like the warriors I expected them to be, seemed to rise out of the ground fully formed when they appeared at our fire in the darkness of the night. The wrinkles on the face of one made a map of mountains and valleys framed by his long, nearly white hair. The other man, not nearly so old, looked enough like the old man that he might be his son.

The old one said, "Ho, Yellow Boy! You return again with the passing of the Ghost Face. Who are these young men? I've never seen them. You come to help us with the cattle?"

I waved my hand parallel to the ground and said, "Ho, Hanging Lance and Igod Kah (Shortened Arrow). It is three or four moons when I see you last. These young men are my brother, Knows Horses, and our friend, Running Wolf. They've asked to serve as novitiates for this raid so that my camp will recognize them as warriors and men. They're here to learn the country and to become knowing helpers when you take the cattle. I also will help you but as a warrior."

Hanging Lance and Igod Kah studied Knows Horses and Running Wolf for a moment before Hanging Lance said, "*En-juh*. Cattle come. Follow the new grass this way. We take 'em in five, maybe six days. We have hunger. Use your fire?"

"*Ázhúo* (for sure), use our fire. We offer you what we have, but it is only trail food."

Hanging Lance said, "Igod Kah catches quail. Plenty here. We give you some. What news of the camp?"

While the boys cooked the quail on mesquite sticks over the fire, Igod Kah, Hanging Lance, and I spoke of the plans for taking the cattle and the Ojo Verde trouble. While listening to Hanging Lance tell me about witches in the long-ago days, I saw how Knows Horses's fingers had swollen so badly, he could not bend them at all, and I knew I had to get him back to Kitsizil Lichoo's *di-yen* soon. Hanging Lance pointed with his nose at the arm and said, "Not good. You find Fat Old Woman. She's a good *di-yen* who knows what to do for things like that."

"This I will do, Grandfather. Your wisdom is good."

After we finished eating, Igod Kah showed Knows Horses and Running Wolf the place to wait for the cattle driven into the canyon. The moon had only half its full light, but it was enough. He carried them to the top of the hill where they could see the cattle he and Hanging Lance watched, and he showed them a small spring where they could get water.

The sun was a great, fuzzy, golden ball rising from behind the far mountains. We told Hanging Lance and Igod Kah we would carry to Kitsizil Lichoo' their guess of when the cattle would be close enough to take, and then rode off up the canyons for his camp. Knows Horses and Running Wolf led the way to show me they remembered the trail. There were intersecting canyons back up the trail where it was easy to make a wrong turn and wind up in a box canyon, but they always chose the right path. They had learned their trail lessons well, and I was proud of them.

Well past the easiest places to get lost, we stopped to rest the horses by a slow-moving stream when the sun cast no shadows. Running Wolf watered his pony. He motioned toward the far canyon wall and said, "I'll check the bushes over there." He headed for brush growing close to the canyon cliffs about a hundred yards away. Hobbling the horses so they could graze,

Knows Horses and I found places in the tall golden grass to sit and smoke in the cool air close to the burbling water. It was a peaceful place, but my thoughts were on Wrestles and Angry and whether they had caught Ojo Verde.

A sharp snapping sound of dry wood breaking came from the bushes where Running Wolf had gone. Knows Horses and I rose up on our knees and looked through the grass toward the spot where Running Wolf went. I didn't like it. It was too quiet. Even the birds were silent. I pulled back the hammer on my rifle and waited.

Running Wolf yelled, "Help me! Help me!"

Knows Horses and I kept low and ran, zigzagging across the open grass to the bushes close to the red cliffs, where we heard Running Wolf puffing and groaning. We found him on his back stretched out beside a long-dead fallen tree, a broken branch in his hand and his breechcloth and shirt laid across the tree trunk. He looked unhurt, but his legs trembled and shook as if he had no control over them.

He raised his head when he saw us approaching and said, "Help me. I can't stand, and I'm lying in the dirt I just made."

Knows Horses, concern filling his eyes, looked at Running Wolf and frowned. "What happened?"

The tremor in Running Wolf's legs grew, and he moaned low in his throat. "Ummmm. I finished my business and tried to stand. My knees didn't have enough strength to lift me, so I grabbed hold of this branch to pull myself up. But it broke, and I fell backwards. I can't get up or stand, and I have this stinking dirt all over my back and legs, and my legs shake. I can't stop them. What's happened to me?"

Disgusted, I shook my head. "Ojo Verde happened to you. You ate her bread. She used it to witch you."

He moaned again and said through clenched teeth, "Ummmm. Am I going to die?"

"You won't die. I'll find a *di-yen* with medicine that's stronger than hers."

Knows Horses asked, "What are we going to do?"

"We've got to get him back to the camp of Kitsizil Lichoo'. He'll have a *di-yen* with strong medicine."

I handed his breechcloth, shirt, and my rifle to Knows Horses and pulled Running Wolf up to a sitting position.

"We'll get you back to the creek and clean you up before we leave this place." I squatted with my back to his face, and directly in front of him. "Put your arms around my neck and hold on."

He put his arms over my shoulders, and I grabbed his wrists so he wouldn't slide off. It was like lifting a dead weight to stand, but I managed it and staggered forward out of the brush. It was a long hundred yards to the creek, but we made it. I let him float in a shallow pool where the fast-flowing water could carry his dirt away, and we scrubbed him clean with sand and the small, leafy branches of willows and cottonwoods.

When we finished, we helped him pull on his breechcloth and shirt. Knows Horses helped him stand and pushed him up in front of me on my pony. We pushed hard the rest of the day for Kitsizil Lichoo's camp. Since both men had eaten Ojo Verde's bread, I feared Knows Horses might soon weaken, and would be unable to stay on his pony because his arm, swelled almost to bursting, had turned dark blue. However, he stayed in the saddle until we rode into Kitsizil Lichoo's camp as night shadows began creeping down the canyon.

My shoulder muscles were cramped into knots from holding Running Wolf in front of me during the long ride, and I had to have help getting him down from my pony. Knows Horses had become so weak that he could barely slide off his pony and stumble to their lodge. I felt like a fool for letting inexperienced boys talk me into the ride down the canyon, but they had shown they had the steel inside to be good warriors.

After a couple of young boys took our ponies, I staggered toward Kitsizil Lichoo', who was coming to the lodge, his face wrinkled with concern. As he approached, I said, "We need Fat Old Woman to help Knows Horses with his swollen arm and Running Wolf, whose legs are too weak to stand. How is Moon on the Water?" I looked around the camp to see everyone with their attention on me, including Wrestles with Strong Hands and Angry He Takes No Prisoners, but I didn't see Ojo Verde hanging from a tree.

CHAPTER 14
FAST RIDE TO MESCALERO

Kitsizil Lichoo' motioned to a boy and said, "Bring Fat Old Woman to this lodge. Tell her I need her to come quick. Go." The boy ran for the far end of the camp while Kitsizil Lichoo' offered me a water jug and said, "Moon is weak but grows stronger. Wrestles and Angry returned without Ojo Verde. They followed her south along the high ridges, but her trail disappeared. I think she used her Power to vanish. They have no thought where she might be hiding. What happened with your two?"

"Running Wolf fell in his own dirt because his legs were too weak to stand. They no longer support him. Knows Horses's arm and hand swell like something dead in the sun too long. I'm afraid it might burst. He grew weaker as we rode. I thought I might have to tie him on his pony before we got here, but he was strong and held up all the way. I fear that soon he'll have no more strength than Running Wolf. Can Fat Old Woman help them?"

He shrugged his shoulders. "I can't speak for a *di-yen*. If she thinks her Power is stronger than the witch's, she'll try." I looked through the trees in the fading light and saw a woman, her hair long and gray, her body shaped like a gourd, thin in her chest, very broad in her hips, hurrying across the camp toward us.

Fat Old Woman examined Knows Horses and Running Wolf and said, "These men suffer from a witch's Power. My Power isn't strong enough to save them. I can sing and make their suffering easier and maybe delay what the witch has done, but someone with Power greater than mine must save them from an early journey to the Happy Land."

Kitsizil Lichoo' nodded. "Do what you can as soon as you can. We will find a *di-yen* with stronger Power than Ojo Verde to help them."

Fat Old Woman said, "*Enjuh*. I go to prepare for my ceremonies. I start when the moon rises over the canyon."

Kitsizil Lichoo' turned to me and said, "I'll send runners to other camps to ask *di-yens* with great power to come. We'll defeat the witch's Power here and then find and destroy her. Go now to Moon on the Water. She waits for you. Come back when the moon sends us its light."

I nodded and walked for Moon's lodge, thinking, *Ojo Verde kills us, and we can't stop her. Maybe she'll witch Juanita and Hígháh. What if there are no other* di-yens *with Power greater than Ojo Verde's? These boys will die. They'll never know the pleasures of being a man who hunts or wars or has children. Maybe one of these boys would have taken Lola Mes as his woman and had children who learned much from her, and the other might take Kitsizil Lichoo's daughter.* Then a thought like a flash of lightning striking a mountaintop filled my mind. *Lola Mes was raised by Ojo Verde. She's a* di-yen *and knows how Ojo Verde does her medicine.*

I found Moon in front of our lodge working on a meal by her fire. The flush of color was back in her cheeks, but she moved slower than normal, as though she had been running all day and still felt weary. She smiled when she saw me and said, "*Enjuh*. My man returns from the end of the canyons. My spirit is glad. Are you ready to eat? How are the young men?"

"Seeing you, *Ish-tia-neh*, makes my eyes glad. You are better after I left?"

"I'm better, stronger. I have the evening meal ready for the

126

young men and us."

"Ojo Verde witched them, too. I think they want no food now. Maybe after Fat Old Woman does her ceremony, they will eat. But she thinks she can only ease their suffering and delay their death for a little while. Fix me food I can carry with me. I must leave as soon as the moon gives light."

She cocked her head to one side and frowned. "Where do you go in these mountains with only the moon for light?"

"I go for a *di-yen* who can undo what Ojo Verde has done."

"Ojo Verde has disappeared. Even Wrestles and Angry couldn't find her. Perhaps she pulls you to her, waits to kill you on the trail to this *di-yen* whose Power is stronger than hers. Where is this *di-yen* stronger than Ojo Verde?"

"Mescalero. Ojo Verde raised Lola Mes. Lola Mes knows how Ojo Verde calls and uses her Power. I know Lola Mes can help us. Now get me some food together. I have a long ride coming. I'll be back in six or seven suns with Lola Mes. I go now to tell Kitsizil Lichoo' my plan."

With most of the camp gathered around the lodge of Knows Horses and Running Wolf, Fat Old Woman had just begun her ceremony when I rode past them and crossed the creek to take the trail across the high west ridge into Cañon Bonito. Kitsizil Lichoo' said I should I take two extra horses so I could ride fast and swap out riding the ponies as they tired, and I did. I planned to stop only for water and to let the ponies rest and eat a little before riding on. I wanted to reach the reservation at night, ask Lola Mes to come back with me, and leave before sunrise. The light would much increase our chances of the tribal police catching us leaving the reservation, and we would lose time having to travel slow and careful.

I made good time and saw no one as I crossed the llano, the

great river, and the mountain passes to reach our camp in the Rinconada. Using the extra horses had gained at least a sun, maybe a sun and half a night, over the time it usually took me to return to Mescalero. I was lucky the air was still cool even with the sun high. It meant the horses could go faster and longer over great stretches of llano without breaking down.

Light from inside cooking fires made the camp tipis looked like lanterns scattered among the trees. I stopped by the creek and watered the ponies before putting them in the hidden corral, rubbing them down, and feeding them. I refreshed myself by lying in a cold pool in the dark shadows of the creek. The night air was cold. I ran from the pool to Juanita's tipi, stood before the door blanket, shivering, and cleared my throat. I heard her tell Híghah to crawl under his blanket and be quiet. She said, "You're welcome in my lodge. Come." Her surprised look of joy changed to one of concern as she jumped up to throw her arms around me.

She looked in my face and said, "What has happened?" Before I could answer her, Híghah was out of his blankets and running for me with his arms out, happily yelling in his little voice, *"Shitaa'! Shitaa'!"* I picked him up and held him and Juanita to me. I said, "I come for Lola Mes. Ojo Verde, who was the sister of Sangre del Diablo and raised Lola Mes, has witched Moon on the Water, Knows Horses, and Running Wolf. Lola Mes is the only *di-yen* I know who might have enough Power to overcome Ojo Verde. If I don't return in time, my brother and Beela-chezzi's son will surely die, and Moon will continue to suffer. Make me something to eat while I ask Lola Mes to go back with me."

Juanita took Híghah in her arms and said, "Go! Your meal and trail food will be ready when you are."

★ ★ ★ ★ ★

Standing before the blanket over the door of Sleepy's tipi, I cleared my throat. I heard movement inside, and when the blanket lifted, I looked on the face of Falling Water, Sleepy's widowed daughter. Her eyes widened in surprise. "Yellow Boy? We thought you were with Moon on the Water in the land of the Blue Mountains." She curled her fingers, motioning me inside. I stepped through the door to see Lola Mes and Sleepy staring at me with sewing work in their laps.

"I came on a fast, hard ride out of the Blue Mountain camp where Moon and I live. This is not a polite time to visit, but I must speak with Lola Mes now. Will she speak with me?"

Lola's eyes narrowed, and she slowly nodded her head and said, "I ask my mother and sister to stay as we speak." She motioned to a place by the fire near her left. "Sit there so I can hear every word and see your face. We have coffee?"

"I've had little to eat or drink in the last three days. A cup will warm my belly."

Lola poured some into a battered, tin cup from an old, black pot sitting by the fire and handed it to me. I drank half of it without taking the cup from my lips and felt its fire spreading down my throat to my belly and across my body, giving it life again.

She watched me drink it, and as I lowered the cup, she asked, "Why does the great warrior Yellow Boy need to speak with me?"

"The warning you gave me when we last spoke about the woman the Mexicans call Ojo Verde has come true. She witched my second wife, Moon on the Water, and she lost our first child. Ojo Verde also witched the two young men from this camp who went south with me. They will die soon if a *di-yen* with Power as strong as Ojo Verde's does not help them. Ojo Verde raised you. My People in this camp know you are a great *di-yen*. Will you, can you, save Knows Horses and Running Wolf?"

Lola Mes stared in the fire for a moment, chewing her lower lip, and then she said, "When will you leave?"

"I leave before the moon starts to fall toward the west. Fat Old Woman, the camp's greatest *di-yen,* sang for them, but she says her Power is too weak to overcome that of Ojo Verde. She has only a while to keep them alive. We must hurry."

"Maybe I can overcome Ojo Verde's Power over them, but I won't know until I see them. I'll be ready to ride when you are, if someone can give me a pony."

"I'll give you a pony and saddle. We'll leave after the stars have moved two hands above the horizon (about two hours)." I nodded toward Sleepy and Falling Water. "Don't worry. I'll keep your daughter safe. The coffee was good."

Sleepy shook her head and said, "Ojo Verde is a strong enemy. Bring our sister and the young warriors back to us."

On the way back to Juanita, I stopped at Beela-chezzi's tipi and told him what had happened. His face became a frown filled with fury, and, clenching his teeth, he said, "I'll go with you and Lola Mes to the Blue Mountains. We must stop this witch. If Kitsizil Lichoo's warriors can't find her, we will. I'll be ready when you leave."

Beela-chezzi was a great warrior who knew much. I was glad he wanted to join us.

Juanita gave me a big meal of beef stew, roasted yucca tips, savory wild potatoes, and new berries. She had packed a sack with the trail food she always made for me when I went on a long ride, and she sat by me while I ate and held Hígháh, who, despite his excitement, was nodding off to sleep.

Juanita asked me how Moon held up after she lost the child. From what I told her, she said Moon would be strong and ready to make another child soon. We talked about reservation news.

Since the Fountain killing, most of the tribal police were still trying to find the bodies of father and son, and paid little attention to the reservation. Lieutenant Stottler was still making life miserable for the Mescaleros with his loco ideas. In fact, the Mescaleros had started calling him "Tata Loco."

I said, "When I return, maybe Moon will come with me. Perhaps she'll stay a while before her bad dreams return. I must also see Hombrecito and Rufus Pike. Beela-chezzi says he rides with us to the camp of Kitsizil Lichoo'. He goes to protect or avenge Running Wolf against Ojo Verde. If Stottler causes our camp problems before I return, ask Yibá to bring the news to us. He knows how to find the camp of Kitsizil Lichoo'."

She looked at me with calm eyes. "Híghah and I wait for you. Bring Moon with you when she will come. Stay safe, and send Ojo Verde blind to the Happy Land for all of us."

CHAPTER 15
THE FIRST WITCH WEAPON

We had much ground to cover and a short time to reach the camp of Kitsizil Lichoo'. Even if we returned before Knows Horses and Running Wolf died, they might be so far gone no one could bring them back. I was especially worried that Knows Horses's arm had filled with so much poison that nothing or anyone could save him.

Beela-chezzi, Lola Mes, and I left our People before the moon began falling into the black outline of the southwestern mountains against the stars and followed it toward the mountains of visions, the San Andres. We crossed the llano to the great river, and then pointed southwest toward the Blue Mountains. Instead of stopping at first light, we rode far into the day before taking a long rest. Then we began again early, riding into the sunset before an all-night ride with short stops to water and rest the horses. Beela-chezzi and I didn't know if Lola Mes could ride a fast pony over long times, but she didn't slow us down. Since we didn't have extra ponies to change to when our mounts tired out, we walked them awhile, jogged them awhile, and then loped with them before starting over with a walk. This way of riding ate up the miles, but let the ponies stay strong. Sometimes we got off and ran to rest the ponies. Even running, Lola Mes stayed with us. She was a strong, smart woman, and my appreciation for her increased as the trail we covered grew longer. I hoped that if her medicine saved Knows Horses and Running Wolf, she would choose one for a husband and stay with our band.

It took three days of hard riding and running to reach the camp of Kitsizil Lichoo'. We rode into camp as the shadows grew long at the end of the third day. Moon, her face grim and jaw set, ran up to us and, placing her hand on her chest, said to Lola Mes, "I am Moon on the Water, second wife of Yellow Boy. He has told me you are probably the only one whose Power is greater than Ojo Verde's. Knows Horses and Running Wolf have not eaten for four days. We ask you, Lola Mes, to help them."

Lola Mes nodded and slid off her pony.

"Show them to me."

Moon hurried toward their lodge and said over her shoulder, "Kitsizil Lichoo' and the warriors left to take the cattle that were grazing near the canyons on the llano before the hacendado vaqueros came. Fat Old Woman does what she can, but they are weaker. I can't tell if they sleep or are in a trance. They won't speak, but I fear the Happy Land calls them."

Lola Mes said to Moon, "How do you feel? Does your strength return?"

My fury at Ojo Verde grew as Moon shook her head and said, "No. I can't sleep and grow weaker, but I can eat."

Knows Horses and Running Wolf lay by the fire in front of their lodge, their bodies turned so their heads pointed toward the east. Their eyes were open, but neither seemed awake or understood who was there or what had happened to them. Beela-chezzi knelt beside Running Wolf and stared at the boy's blank face. I heard him whisper under his breath, "Live, my son. I will avenge you."

Moon stood beside me while Lola Mes knelt beside each one, felt their foreheads and necks, ran her hands down their arms and across their chests, and appeared to be searching for something. Neither moved nor seemed to know she was there. She lifted Knows Horses's arm and hand, now stiff and blown up tight like an air bladder, and blue nearly to his shoulder. She looked closely and carefully at it, especially at his palm. She smelled and touched his arm and hand with her lips—not kisses, just swipes to feel them.

She came to Moon on the Water and stared closely at places on her face and then felt her neck and put her palm to her forehead. "I would see you alone in your lodge."

Moon nodded. "I do as you say. What of these men?"

Lola looked at them and, nodding, said, "Yes, I think I can help them. We must start their ceremony after the sun hides for the night. Turn them so they face the east. Be ready with a big fire. My ceremony requires it. There is much evil to find and destroy."

She turned to me, reached in a bag she had tied to her waist, and pulled out a smooth, bright yellow stone the size of a quail's egg, and said, "Put this in the earth between them at their hip joints after they are turned to face the east. After I see Moon on the Water, I will bathe and prepare. Before the moon rises, make the fire ready. I will pray and then sing to find and break the Power of Ojo Verde over them all." After she examined Moon on the Water, Lola Mes told us what things her Power would require for her to do at the ceremony for the three of them, and we promised to provide them.

Everyone in the camp seemed to know that Lola Mes would perform a ceremony for the young men. They gathered around the great fire Beela-chezzi and I made just before the moon floated above the canyon rim. As the moon's soft light began to fill the western side of the canyon, only the snaps, pops, and swooshes of the gold and orange fire broke the silence. Lola Mes suddenly appeared as if out of the air at the feet of Knows

Horses and Running Wolf. She motioned Moon to come forward and told her to stand at the heads of the young men and face her. She asked me to stand by the belly of Knows Horses and asked Beela-chezzi to stand by the belly of Running Wolf and for us to face each other.

She began a long prayer, and when she finished, she said so all could hear, "These boys are witched. Knows Horses suffers from the power of two witch weapons that work together to kill him. Running Wolf suffers from one of the witch weapons, and Moon on the Water suffers from the other. These good people deserve to live. It may kill me to take the witch weapons out of them, but I will risk it." She turned to me and said, "For this ceremony, my Power requires that you give me yellow pollen, two blue stones, four hawk feathers, and three pieces of black flint."

She had told me this earlier, and I already had the hawk feathers. Beela-chezzi gave me the blue stones; Moon, the yellow pollen; and Fat Old Woman, the three pieces of black flint. I had these in a bag tied to my gun belt and handed them to her. She glanced in the bag, nodded, and said, "Now I will sing four songs for these who are witched. Then I will sing again for Knows Horses and Moon on the Water. The witch weapon is in him and has power over him and Moon on the Water, for she is the wife of his brother. It is a hard thing to take out. But I will do this and show it to you so you can believe. Ojo Verde is the witch who has done this evil. Someday the evil she has used will turn against her."

Lola Mes raised her hands and began her first song. She sang each song to a different direction as the fire burned down. When she finished the fourth song, she said, "Make the fire great again. Put a white cloth near it, and watch for this thing called a witch weapon. I'll sing four more songs, and when I'm finished, I'll show you the weapon."

And so she sang until she finished her fourth song. Then she walked four times east to south around the boys, stopping each time by Moon, Beela-chezzi, and me. The first three times around, she touched first our chins, then each cheek with golden pollen. Finally, on the fourth round, she also touched our foreheads with pollen. When she completed the fourth circle, she turned west to south and walked to the head of Knows Horses, knelt, and, placing her hands on his shoulders, put her mouth to his forehead at the top of his hairline. Working her lips, she pulled something out of his head we had never seen before, a sliver of bone about half-a-finger-length long and shaped like an arrow. The head and string notch were painted red and the shaft, blue, and it was wrapped with four strands of human hair, two black and two white, the same colors as the hair of Ojo Verde.

Lola Mes held the little bone arrow up between her thumb and forefinger and slowly turned for all to see. "This is a witch's arrow. It is made from human bone for suffering and killing." She threw it hard into the fire, and there was a big bang like Rufus Pike's big thunder gun going off as evil left it. "Now Knows Horses will stop his journey to the border of the Happy Land, and Moon on the Water will grow strong again and make strong children. Another witch weapon hidden here in the camp still attacks Knows Horses and Running Wolf. Tomorrow when the sun stands at the place of no shadows, I'll search the camp and find its hiding place. Tomorrow night at moonrise, another great fire burns, and I'll do another ceremony to take and destroy this weapon. Knows Horses and Running Wolf will come back to us after I burn this evil. That is all I have to say."

The next day, when the sun stood at the place of no shadows, Lola Mes, her face half-white from white clay and half red from ochre, searched for the hidden witch weapon. She studied the ground around every lodge, beginning with the vacant lodge of Ojo Verde. After she looked around each lodge, she left two crosses of yellow pollen on the lodge entrance post closest to the east, one cross showing it was free of witch weapons, and the other to protect it against future attacks.

Lola Mes found no witch weapon until she came to the last lodge, that of Knows Horses and Running Wolf. Knows Horses was very weak, but he was alert, and his swollen arm had decreased in size enough that he could wiggle his fingers. Beela-chezzi had watched over them all through the night. Even though he was too weak to rise, Running Wolf's alert eyes now followed Beela-chezzi in whatever he did.

Lola Mes looked at everything inside the lodge and in the fire area where she had sung her songs the night before. She found nothing except two very faint lines in dust around the outside lodge fire. They had been stepped on many times, but following what remained, showed that they formed the edges of a spearhead that came to a point at a spot behind the lodge. She looked behind the lodge and followed in her mind where the lines would cross to form the spear point. At the point of the spearhead she found a round, black stone about the size of a man's head lying in the grass. Black with a flash of lightning chipped across the top, it sat so low in the grass it was not noticeable unless one knew where to look.

She said, "Remember this stone, Yellow Boy. In the ceremony tonight, I'll send you to it. Beela-chezzi will carry a torch for you to see it. Approach it from the east, kicking the dirt to rub out any lines leading to it. Sing the words I give you. Lift up the stone and put it one pace to the west with the lightning mark up, as you see it now. Bring me what you find under it. I'll sing so what is there can't hurt you. When this witch weapon burns, the curse will be broken, and Knows Horses and Running Wolf will know healing."

CHAPTER 16
THE SECOND WITCH WEAPON

Darkness backed away from the bright yellow and orange fire, popping and swirling, that stretched and jumped for the tree limbs over us, sending sparks high to die among the stars above the slash in the earth where we stood. Nearby, but away from the fire's searing heat, Knows Horses and Running Wolf lay, wrapped in blankets, facing the east as they'd done the night before. They had life in their eyes, but their bodies were still slow to move. The blue swelling in Knows Horses's arm had retreated enough that he could almost make a claw-like fist. I had guessed Lola Mes possessed strong medicine. I had been right.

Beela-chezzi, Moon on the Water, and I waited beside the young men in the same places we were the night before. A low, white glow from the moon appeared behind the eastern ridge of our canyon, and the camp was quiet and still. Even the insects and night peepers made no sounds. They also seemed to be waiting to see what would happen, waiting for Lola Mes to appear.

And then, as the night before, she was there, out of nowhere, like a low cloud in the early morning forming over cold creek water waiting for the first breeze down the canyon to send it away. She held a big, flat basket before her with the things she had asked me to give her for the ceremonies and other special things she might need to defeat Ojo Verde's Power. She put the basket at the young men's feet and, raising her hands, made a

138

prayer to Ussen and the spirits to help us defeat the Power Ojo Verde had used against them. After she finished her prayer, she spoke to the People watching.

"Here in the night, by light of moon and fire, I will try to break the Power of Ojo Verde. She used her Power on the young men, Knows Horses and Running Wolf, and the woman of Yellow Boy, Moon on the Water. The Power used by Ojo Verde is strong. It may kill me, but I will try to save them from it. They're good people and should live free. First, I'll sing four songs. Then I'll tell you what Ussen has shown me."

An old man sitting on the edge of the fire's circle of light began a soft rhythmic thump on a stiff piece of horsehide, and Lola Mes raised her hands and began her song in a low, flute-like tone. First she made a north-to-west circle around the boys, stopping at each cardinal point to sprinkle a pinch of yellow pollen from a small bag hanging around her neck before proceeding, and then finished the song, sprinkling three pinches of pollen, one for each victim who asked her help.

In her second song, she moved in a south-to-west circle; the third song, in the direction of the first song; and the fourth song, in the direction of the second song, all the time sprinkling pollen as she had for the first song. When she returned to the starting point of the fourth song, she lowered her arms after giving the three pinches of pollen, and the drumbeat stopped.

There was a long pause as Lola Mes stared at the boys and swayed back and forth as though in a trance. She argued with someone we could not hear or see, her Power. We heard only her words. "Yes, I know the witch's Power is great. I know it better than any other . . . But these young men will one day show their people a good way . . . and this woman desires a child for her man. She must have it. I know this is a blinding power . . . I don't care if I'm blinded by it. I must help these people overcome the witch's Power. Help me do this."

There was a time of no voices. We were all afraid to move.

Lola Mes slowly scanned the circle of watchers, looked at each man, woman, and child, and said, "To find the witch's weapon against these good people, I marked every lodge with yellow pollen where I looked and did not find it. This is the only lodge I have not marked. The witch's weapon hides behind this lodge. I have shown Yellow Boy and Beela-chezzi where it hides. I have given them words of Power to bring it to me. I will sing with them. I have given them the words to sing as they look for it in the place I have shown them."

She began to sing again, and Beela-chezzi and I sang with her,

"Hey-ya, hi, hi, hey-ya, hi, hi,

"Ussen is over all,

"Ussen's light is the sun's light.

"Hey-ya, hi, hi, hey-ya, hi, hi,

"Nothing hides from Ussen,

"Ussen knows all secrets.

"Hey-ya, hi, hi, hey-ya . . ."

Beela-chezzi held a torch high as we walked to the north and then walked a quarter-circle behind the lodge to approach from the east, singing and kicking the dirt before us, wiping out any spear-point lines of Power the witch had left pointing to the black, lightning-marked stone. When I picked up the black stone, it was not as heavy as I thought it would be. I walked one pace west and put it down, as Lola Mes had instructed, while Beela-chezzi stood by the spot with the torch held high and continued to sing.

I stepped back to where the black stone had lain, and there in the torchlight lay a smooth, polished shaft, as long as the spread of my fingers from the tip of my little finger to the tip of my thumb and about two fingers wide in diameter. Beautifully crafted, it had feathers on it of many kinds—hawk, raven, buzzard, canyon wren, and cardinal—and at the end of the handle, cut in four ways, finely worked buckskin with beautiful beadwork in the shape of yellow lightning strikes. Like the first weapon, there were four long strands of hair, two black and two white, circling it from top to bottom. Along the shaft were markings of all kinds of shapes—claws and heads of animals, the sun and moon, the face of a man, and that of a woman. I trembled inside when I glanced at it and looked away when it felt like the night was overpowering my eyes. I covered it using a piece of finely worked and beaded buckskin Lola Mes had given me. She had said it must not touch my skin and that I must not look at it except by quick glances before I looked away.

I picked it up and carried it in front of my body as Beelachezzi, with the torch held high, led me back to the front of the lodge, moving south and then around to the west. My heart pounded in my chest as though I had run a long time, and the thing wrapped in buckskin felt hot against my fingers. At the fire, I handed it to Lola Mes. She held it so the buckskin cover opened like flower petals to show the shaft, held it high, and said, "Look at it, but only for the blink of an eye! This is what made these young men lame, made Knows Horses's arm swell like a dead thing, made Running Wolf too weak to walk and sit in his own dirt." The People peered quickly and then looked away. I felt prickles on the back of my neck when I glanced at it. "Now I'll hold it to face the heat of fire." Her hand shook and wobbled, holding it like an animal struggling to get away from her. "It knows it will die. It struggles to be free. Against the blaze of the fire, it can do no harm, and its evil power begs to leave this place. I won't let it leave. The evil must die. I'll sing its four end songs and then cast it into the fire. Don't look at it, or it will blind you."

Holding the weapon upright and between herself and the fire, she sang four songs while the old man thumped on the stiff, horsehide drum. There was only the sound of the drum and the snapping of the fire as she sang. When she finished, she yelled, "Hey-ya!" and threw it hard into the fire. There was a flash of light, a loud, sharp bang, and sparks of many colors shot up into the night. Lola Mes stood with her left hand covering her left eye, the flesh of her face below that eye seared red. The edges of her hair were burned and smoking, but there was no smell of burning flesh. The crowd stared at her. The women covered their mouths in fright, and the group appeared to draw back from her.

She turned to Beela-chezzi and me and said, "The evil is almost all gone. I will heal, but I may lose sight in this eye, and my face may be marked by its rage. Bring the rock that covered the weapon, and throw it in the fire. You must approach it from the east and step around the place where it covered the witch's weapon. When it burns to powder, the evil done by Ojo Verde will be gone."

I went for the rock, and Beela-chezzi, holding his torch high, led me back behind the lodge the way we had come, both of us singing in loud voices for the spirits to hear us. I brought back the rock that had covered the witch's weapon and tossed it on the fire. Soon it, too, was burning and making much heat.

We watched it burn, almost afraid to breathe until it burned to powder. Lola Mes, keeping her left eye covered with her left hand, said, "The witch's Power over these men and your woman is gone. I sing one more song, and Ojo Verde's Power in this camp will return no more."

Her song finished, those watching arose from their places and, nodding respect to Lola Mes, left to return to their lodges. They all knew they had seen something not many ever expected to see. A few old women and an old man stopped and asked her to touch them, which she did.

After all others were gone, Lola Mes said, "I'll stay in this lodge four days to heal from the attack by Ojo Verde's Power when it was destroyed. Let no one in. You and Beela-chezzi must not come in. Let Moon and the men heal. Let Moon come to me at the rising and disappearing of the sun or if I call her. Moon and the young men will recover, even as I do, from this evil."

I wiped the water from my face made by the fire's heat and said, "So you have spoken. So it will be done." She entered the lodge still covering her eye and carrying her basket. When she was inside, she pulled down the door blanket.

After Lola Mes disappeared into the lodge, Moon on the Water and I sat on one side of Knows Horses, and Beela-chezzi sat by Running Wolf on the other side. Both young men slept, and we did not disturb them. I asked Moon on the Water how she felt. She smiled and said, "Soon I'm ready to make another baby. Lola Mes is a very powerful *di-yen*. I feared she was taking too big a chance to rid us of this last weapon, but she was right. I'll ask her to lodge with us until we return to Mescalero, and I can fill my eyes with Juanita and Maria."

"So you'll return north with us when we go?"

"I'll go. I don't know how long I can stay before the Blue Coat dreams come."

I didn't care who saw us. I put my arm around her shoulders and squeezed her as the Indah do when they are proud of their women and said, *"Enjuh!"*

CHAPTER 17
RETURN TO THE RINCONADA

Four days is a lifetime to await the return of brothers to the land of the living. Knows Horses and Running Wolf came back to us. Moon on the Water grew stronger and cooked for them and carried food and water for drinking and bathing when she went at sunrise and sunset to care for Lola Mes. On the second day after the ceremony of Lola Mes, Kitsizil Lichoo' returned and told us the cattle raid was a good one, that no one from the camp was killed or wounded and no hacendado vaquero was hurt. The hacendados would not risk the lives of good vaqueros in the canyon for a few cattle and with blood vengeance not due. The camp stayed safe another season.

Beela-chezzi and I went to help make meat and left Moon to look after the young men and Lola Mes. The cattle, driven to a nearby side canyon, were used to make dried meat and cured hides. The women worked the hides for moccasins and other needs. The dried meat would last into the Season of Earth Is Reddish Brown when more would be taken before the women finished gathering cactus fruit, herbs, wild potatoes, acorns, walnuts, juniper berries, and mescal for the Ghost Face time.

A moon passed and Knows Horses and Running Wolf, strong enough to ride the canyons, prepared for their raids as novitiates with the warriors. Moon was herself again and anxious to be with me under her blankets. Lola Mes had lost the vision in her left eye. It looked like an old one's eye, clouded over with the center white. She had scars on the left side of her face, as if

144

some big cat had clawed her. The marks were not deep and soon healed. If a man had them, the People would call them scars of war and admire them. On Lola Mes, the People called them scars of honor and respected her for her courage and the risks she took in finding and driving off the Power that had tried to kill Knows Horses and Running Wolf and had taken Moon on the Water's baby. The People showed her the same respect when she passed that they showed the greatest warriors. She spent time with Fat Old Woman, learning her Power's ceremonies and showing her some things she had learned from the Power of Ojo Verde.

One evening I smoked with Beela-chezzi in front of our lodge while Moon and Lola Mes worked leather for new moccasins. Knows Horses and Running Wolf had gone to the end of the canyons to watch for cattle the camp could take. I said, "It is nearly two moons since I brought Lola Mes to Kitsizil Lichoo's camp. My eyes would see Juanita and Hígháh. Moon, will you come with me to visit your sister, mother, and little son? Lola Mes, are you ready to return to Mescalero?" I glanced at Beela-chezzi, who smiled. Already that day, we had discussed when to leave. He was ready.

Moon glanced up from the work in her hands and, smiling, said, "I'm ready to see my family in Mescalero. I've never seen our son, and already he's three harvests and off the *tsach*. Say the day we leave. I'll be ready."

Lola Mes looked at me from across the fire, her bad eye shining white. "It's been good for me in the camp of Kitsizil Lichoo'. I have many new friends. I'll miss them, but I'm ready to return to my mother and sister in our tipi in the Rinconada. I'll be ready to travel with you, but I warn you, Ojo Verde will one day try to destroy us, even in our own tipis. Like Coyote, Ojo Verde waits."

I nodded and pulled much smoke from my cigarro to blow straight up into the cool night air, which had filled with the sounds of insects and frogs on the creek. "You speak wise words, Lola Mes. I'll speak with Kitsizil Lichoo' tonight to ask that Knows Horses and Running Wolf eat at his fire and to warn him of what you say. When the sun hides tomorrow, we'll leave and travel only at night back to Mescalero. Do you agree, Beela-chezzi?"

He nodded as he flicked an ash off his cigarro into the fire.

The first night after leaving Kitsizil Lichoo's camp I wanted to ride as far as the Animas Mountains, but we found a *Nakai-yi* army camp near the border. They had a small herd of cattle and a pack train of mules carrying supplies. Since the army had shipped Geronimo and the Chiricahuas east to the place called Florida, the Nakai-yes still fought skirmishes with the Yaquis and a few Blue Mountain Apaches. However, without Geronimo waiting to kill them, the *Nakai-yi* army had grown careless about where they camped and how they posted guards, if at all.

Beela-chezzi and I decided to stampede the little herd, make the soldiers think they were under attack, and then take what we wanted from their supplies. Just as the sun rose and the camp began to stir, I put a few shots through their tents and into their fire, while Beela-chezzi snapped a blanket among their already-nervous cattle and gave a few war whoops. The half-dressed soldiers ran from their tents, firing their pistols in any direction while they scrambled to saddle their horses. Then, leaving everything else, including mules, tents, and their supplies, they rode off toward Janos like evil spirits were after them. Beela-chezzi, the women, and I rushed into the camp, took everything, loaded it on the mules, and headed for the border before the Nakai-yes realized no one chased them. We took a hard, rocky path that most Nakai-yes couldn't track a wagon train across, much less a few mules and horses. We chanced being seen in the Animas Valley during daylight in order to make it across the playas to the mountains, where we made a camp soon after the sun passed the time of shortest shadows. Then we rested in a little canyon with an entrance that gave us a good view in the direction back toward the border.

While I kept watch, Moon, Lola Mes, and Beela-chezzi sorted through the sacks of food, pots and pans, canned goods, canvas, and ammunition loaded on the mule pack frames. We decided we should keep it all and carry it to Mescalero. One mule carried four cases of ammunition. Two of the cases had the same caliber as Rufus Pike's old buffalo rifle with which he planned to teach Hombrecito how to shoot. I told Beela-chezzi why I wanted to give a case of ammunition to Rufus, and he agreed.

The moon approached the top of its arc when we rode into the Rinconada camp four days later. The fires banked low in every tipi soon grew bright as Juanita, Carmen Rosario, Sleepy, and Falling Water welcomed us back in high, trilling voices, singing the returning warrior song. Yibá and Kah and their families rushed from their tipis when they heard the glad voices.

Para-dee-ah-tran, Kah and Deer Woman's tall and thin thirteen year-old son, who had her doe-like eyes and great running ability, helped Beela-chezzi and me unload the mules and rub down our ponies. Yibá and Kah made a great fire, and the whole band gathered around it while we gave gifts to all from the *Nakai-yi* loot and made many happy smiles.

Beela-chezzi and I told our People stories of our times in the Blue Mountains and how Lola Mes had overcome the Power of Ojo Verde. Now she wore scars on her face and had lost an eye so all would remember her courage and Power. We said that, since she had saved Knows Horses and Running Wolf from a bad death, we must call her sister. We warned that Ojo Verde might strike again one day to try to kill us all in the worst kind of way with her Power, but we would be strong and defeat her.

Moon on the Water told how with glad eyes she had returned to see her mother and Juanita. She said she would stay until her Power said it was time to return to the Blue Mountains. Kah began to sing and pound a stiff piece of hide he kept as a drum, and the camp danced until sunlight appeared on the edge of the mountains.

Two moons passed and the time was peaceful, like the old days. The Season of Large Fruit had come, and the women wandered across the reservation and down to the llano harvesting the good things to eat and save for the time of the Ghost Face and Little Eagles. The men hunted and made meat from elk and deer.

In those same days, Stottler worked the other men on the reservation hard, making them dig postholes with knives and sticks and string fence around plots of land he told them to claim as their own. He forced more and more children to go to the agency school, and there was much unhappiness for their parents and grandmothers. But the tribal police were careful to leave us alone, and we stayed out of sight of the rest of the reservation as part of Stottler's bet with me.

On a bright day, as the sun fell toward the mountains, I sat and smoked with Beela-chezzi on a blanket under the big pine tree near our tipis. I cleaned my rifle and studied the specks of yellow high on Sierra Blanca, the great Sacred Mountain, where stands of aspen trees grew, making the mountain look as if it wore a coat patched with *pesh-klitso* (literally "yellow iron," gold).

Soon it would be time for Moon and me to return to the camp of Kitsizil Lichoo'. She had dreamed of the bad times only once since we had returned. We all believed Lola Mes when she told us the Power that brought the dreams grew weaker by the day. I was tempted to stay the winter in the Rinconada, but I decided we ought to go to the camp of Kitsizil Lichoo' rather than be trapped with bad dreams by snow-filled passes in the Season of the Ghost Face. We waited for the women to finish their food gathering, so Moon and I could take a mule loaded with supplies back with us and not show up empty-handed like bad guests.

Beela-chezzi and I did not speak for a time as I worked, and we both smoked cigarros and enjoyed the sight of the great Sacred Mountain and the breeze filtering through the trees. A movement, more sensed than seen, drew my attention to the trees on the south end of the camp. Beela-chezzi had felt it, too, and stared at the same place. Two men came out of the trees and sat their horses in the shadows, studying the camp.

Knows Horses and Running Wolf had come home. Between them sat a young woman. I had seen her working around the lodge of Kitsizil Lichoo' and believed her mother was Calico Dove, his second wife. I raised my rifle and waved it back and forth for them to see, and, smiling, they rode toward us.

CHAPTER 18
YOUNG MEN COURTING

I looked at Beela-chezzi and smiled. Beela-chezzi frowned, apparently uncertain and curious why a woman was with them. I remembered the young woman. She was tall and willowy, had bright blue eyes, a true daughter of redheaded Kitsizil Lichoo', and had listened with interest at her father's lodge when we discussed Knows Horses and Running Wolf. Riding without an old one to protect her virtue meant Kitsizil Lichoo' must have given her to one of them for a wife.

They rode up to us and dismounted. The young woman and Knows Horses hanging back, Running Wolf stepped close and knelt by his father, who put his hand around the back of his neck. *"Nish'ii'* (I see you), Beela-chezzi. Knows Horses and I return as warriors from the camp of Kitsizil Lichoo', who has given me his daughter, Blue Flower, the one I desired."

Beela-chezzi smiled and motioned for the young woman and my brother to approach. He said, "My son is no longer a boy. He returns a warrior with a fine woman. My heart is glad for him. Welcome, wife of Running Wolf and daughter of Kitsizil Lichoo'." She took his hands as though she had known him and been away a long time and said, "I come to visit the lodge of my husband's father and mother." Then she turned to me and said, "My father sends his thanks for bringing him men worthy to be warriors."

I nodded and put my hand around the back of Knows Horses's neck, and he grinned but said nothing. Beela-chezzi motioned toward his tipi and said, "Come, and we'll speak with Carmen Rosario, mother of your man."

As they went to Carmen's tipi, I pulled out a cigarro while Knows Horses sat down on my blanket. We smoked, and then I said, "My brother returns from the land of the *Nakai-yes*, a warrior from the camp of Kitsizil Lichoo'. My heart is glad. Tell me of your trail."

The sunlight falling over the great Sacred Mountain bathed our faces in gold and warmth. Ussen had returned our son and brother. It was good to be alive.

Knows Horses said, "After Lola Mes saved us from the witch's weapons, Running Wolf and I grew stronger. We rode to the end of the canyons to watch for cattle while our full strength continued to return. One day, far in the distance, we saw two *Nakai-yi* vaqueros drive off cattle from the great herd. We ran to follow them as they drove the cattle north to hacendado corrals by a water tank. Two other vaqueros had a fire there and used hot irons on the cattle brands to make them look different. My work with Yibá's cattle told me these men took hacendado cattle even as we planned to do, but they took them to sell, probably across the border. They knew they took a big chance on hacendado vaqueros discovering them, because another vaquero did nothing but use *be'idest'iné* to search the llano. These vaqueros also had a fine string of ten ponies and two mules. They used the mules as pack animals and had pack frames and supplies at one side of the corrals."

Knows Horses's story sounded like a good one from the old days when we raided to live. I pulled two more cigarros from my pocket and offered Knows Horses one. It was time for a smoke just for the pleasure of it, a time of celebration. I lighted them with a big, Redhead match, and he continued.

"Running Wolf and I hid in an arroyo and watched. Running Wolf said, 'I think those vaqueros taking the cattle are *Nakai-yi* banditos. If the hacendado vaqueros caught them, they would hang them by their necks from that water wheel (windmill) or drag them across cactus on the llano. I say we kill them all and take their ponies, supplies, and cattle before the hacendado vaqueros come. Let's wait until dark when they're all close to the fire, and then take them with our rifles. We'll load the mules and drive them, the ponies, and cattle into our canyon and back to the camp of Kitsizil Lichoo'.' It was a good plan. I agreed to wait."

The sound of children playing their fighting and running games down by the running water came to my ears, and, as Knows Horses paused to blow smoke up into the breeze, I wondered if the games our children played now would prepare them for the fights and risks they would face on the reservation.

Knows Horses said, "As the sun disappeared into a blood-red horizon, a good omen, one of the vaqueros dug a small fire pit and stuck sticks in the ground to hang slices of pig meat the Anglos call bacon over the fire—brother, I have never understood how Nakai-yes and Indah eat that nasty meat."

I shook my head. "Truly, the Indah and Nakai-yes have strange taste in food."

"Since you taught me to shoot, Running Wolf asked that I take the men around the fire while he killed the guard hidden on the llano who watched for hacendado vaqueros. I agreed. Running Wolf said, when he was done with the guard, he would call like Coyote and for me to start shooting.

"Not one of the vaqueros sitting around the fire had time to shoot back before they died. We left them where they fell, loaded the pack mules with their supplies, and saddled their horses. We drove the cattle back toward the main herd so it looked like someone had returned them to the main herd and then headed them down an arroyo that led to our canyon. We had ridden well up the canyons and to the first watering place by sunrise. I changed horses and dragged some big bushes, wiping out our tracks down the canyons to the arroyo. There were almost too many animals for us to handle, but we took our time and made it back to Kitsizil Lichoo's camp in three days."

I felt pride I had not known in a long time in the great raid Knows Horses and Running Wolf had accomplished. There was no doubt they could have been warriors in the old times and now stood as men among us.

Knows Horses smiled and said, "Kitsizil Lichoo' was surprised and happy to see us and the supplies we brought back. He and his warriors wasted no time holding a council and deciding we had proved ourselves worthy warriors. He told us to stay as long as we wanted. So you see, brother, your plan to make us novitiates worked out after all, even though Ojo Verde nearly killed us, but, because Running Wolf had a wife, we rode horses back rather than run."

I did not allow my face to show my pride, but muttered, "Sometimes rabbits escape rattlesnakes." I flicked away my cigarro and asked, "How did Running Wolf come to take Blue Flower?"

"The camp had a big dance, and we gave away most of the supplies. Blue Flower tapped Running Wolf to dance with her. He decided he wanted her for his woman before the light came with the next sun. He asked if I would speak for him if she accepted him, and I agreed.

"The custom for asking for a woman in the camp of Kitsizil Lichoo' is different from ours here. The next day he washed his roan pony in the creek, brushed it smooth, and then saddled it with the best saddle and bridle we had taken on the llano. He led the pony to the lodge of Kitsizil Lichoo' and with Kitsizil Lichoo' sitting by the fire, grinning like a bear at a honey tree, Running Wolf asked him if he might speak with Blue Flower. Kitsizil Lichoo' nodded and called for her inside the lodge. She came out and smiled when she saw Running Wolf. He said so all around could hear him, 'I tie this pony for you at the corral gate. It is yours if you decide to lead it inside the corral and take off its saddle and bridle.' She nodded she understood, and I think the whole camp watched him lead the pony down the trail to the corral.

"Nothing happened to the pony the rest of the day and into the night before we slept in our lodge. The next morning the pony's saddle and bridle were lying by our lodge door, and the pony's mane had a braid made in its forelock. I've never seen Running Wolf smile so much. He was anxious for me to bathe and go make an offer of gifts to Kitsizil Lichoo'.

"Kitsizil Lichoo' didn't haggle over the bride gift of three ponies and a mule we offered. He gave his daughter a place for her lodge next to Moon's. In four days, they had their feast and then disappeared to a place Running Wolf had made ready down the creek. I think them well-matched, and I'm happy for them. Now I would ask your help."

I knew what he wanted, and I said, "Yes, I will speak with Sleepy if Lola Mes accepts your pony." I hoped he would not be disappointed.

Knows Horses laughed. "Brother, you have a good memory."

"Have you spoken with Lola Mes about how you feel?"

He looked at the blanket under our legs and slowly shook his head.

I have seen the asking for a woman by men young and old many times in my life, and it always brings a smile to my face. If the man is smart, he will find a way to speak with the woman he wants and learn if she will accept him before he ties his pony in front of her guardian's tipi. If the man has not spoken with her in private, he has a big risk of rejection and embarrassment when the camp sees she does not accept his offer.

Two days later, as the sun fell into the western mountains, Para-dee-ah-tran, young son of Kah, led the pony of Knows Horses, washed and groomed, to Sleepy's tipi, dropped the reins, and walked away.

Knows Horses had trained his pony to stand in one place for dropped reins like our father had taught me to train my pony in my novitiate years. That day all the women who could work, even the grandmothers, gathered fruits, nuts, and other good things against the time of the Ghost Face. Knows Horses told me he planned to hunt that day, but I knew that he watched Sleepy's tipi when the women returned.

Soon, in the time of long shadows, they came leading two mules loaded with sacks carrying their harvest. Near the center of the camp, they unloaded the mules and carried the sacks to their common workplace. Yibá led the mules to the corrals to feed and brush them down, and the women headed to their ti-pis. Sleepy was the oldest working woman in camp, and while she could still get around, she moved slowly, and her daughters stayed close by in case they needed to help her if she stumbled and fell. They didn't see the pony standing in the shadows until they were almost to her tipi, and when Sleepy saw it, she said something to the other two before her widowed daughter, Falling Water, helped her and followed into the tipi.

Lola Mes stared at the pony for a few breaths, and then scratched it behind its ears and ran her hand down its nose before she entered the tipi. This was very unusual. Even if the woman planned to accept the man's interest in her, she didn't show her own interest. Usually she waited nearly the entire three-day time she had to consider the offer, in order to perhaps get a higher bride gift for her parents or guardian before returning the pony to its owner. I knew somewhere back in the deep canyon shadows, my brother smiled.

Two days and two nights passed. On the morning of the third

day, Knows Horses found his pony tied and fed in front of Sons-ee-ah-ray's tipi where he slept.

Lola Mes was old for her age. She was a powerful *di-yen* and had the scars and a blind eye to prove it. From what she told me when I first spoke with her, she would accept Knows Horses if he was accepted as a warrior and no longer a boy. She had also agreed to ask Sleepy if she would adopt her as a second daughter so that, if either Knows Horses or Running Wolf asked for her, Sleepy would get the bride gift. She asked, and Sleepy gladly took her. After all, two daughters were better than one when it came to gathering and saving food.

Knows Horses wanted to give Sleepy a big bride price, six ponies. After all, Lola Mes was a *di-yen* and had been scarred and lost an eye helping him. He wanted her, he told me, like nothing else he had ever wanted, even though they had probably not spoken more than a sun's hand-width on the horizon (about an hour) in the moons since she had come to the camp. He believed she would give him strong children and, with the help of her Power, keep their entire family strong. He said that in quietly watching her, he was impressed with her kind and straight dealing with others. I gave the same advice He Watches, our grandfather, gave me when I had asked for Juanita. I told him to add an extra pony to the bride gift for Sleepy as a sign of his great respect, and that he wouldn't regret it. Knows Horses nodded with understanding and told me to make the offer.

CHAPTER 19
KNOWS HORSES MAKES A BARGAIN

It was two hands from the time of shortest shadows but cloudy, almost cold, with the smell of rain in the air. Most of the camp worked inside that day. I bathed and put on my best clothes and stood in front of Sleepy's tipi. Clearing my throat, I heard, "Coffee is on the fire. Come. You are welcome here." I pulled back the blanket and stepped into the low, flickering light from the small fire. Sleepy and her two daughters sat by the fire sorting berries and nuts to dry. Sleepy smiled when she saw me and lifted the coffee pot with eyebrows raised to ask if I wanted a cup. I nodded. As she was pouring it, she said, "Daughters, I have business to discuss with our visitor. Perhaps you will go and visit with Juanita and Moon on the Water for a while." Falling Water and Lola Mes, smiling, left without a word.

We spoke of the day and about how animal furs and the harvest of nuts said it would be a hard Ghost Face. I finished the coffee, and she poured me more. Sleepy said, "A time of new beginnings makes an old woman's heart happy, my son. Lola Mes tells me she will accept your brother, Knows Horses, as her husband if he offers her mother an acceptable bride gift."

"Knows Horses thinks Lola Mes is a fine woman and would be honored to have her. What is a suitable gift for her?"

"She is a strong woman, a woman with Power, she suffered scars and lost an eye to use her Power to help those attacked by Ojo Verde."

I took a sip from the steaming cup. "This I know, grand-

157

mother. I saw her Sings. What is a worthy gift to you for her?"

"Four ponies and a promise."

"A promise?"

"Lola Mes will be first wife, but if Falling Water is not taken by next harvest, she becomes his second wife. I will not ask more ponies for her."

I must have looked a fool, staring at her with my mouth open. Falling Water was still a nice-looking woman, but she was close to my age, nearly old enough to be Knows Horses's mother, and she had been a widow for a long time. Before Delgadito had decided to ride with Victorio, he had almost taken her. Now Sleepy offered her to my brother?

Sleepy laughed at me. "Close your mouth, Yellow Boy, or one that crawls and flies will go down your throat. What I ask makes sense. Knows Horses will need two wives if one is a strong *di-yen* and needed by the People. It will take much of her time. Lola Mes is a strong *di-yen*. In the harvests to come, many will ask her help. Falling Water is strong and has many camp skills that Lola Mes has not yet learned. Falling Water can still have children. Our people must make more children faster as the bad air takes us. Perhaps Lola Mes cannot make children. Lola Mes and Falling Water work well together, and both respect Knows Horses. Make Falling Water useful to the People and to Knows Horses. Since he will be the only man around my tipi, the horses he offers me now will still be his to use. It is a good bargain I offer. Go now and speak with him. I'll wait."

I put the cup down and said, "I hope I'm back soon."

I went to the tipi of my mother. Knows Horses sat with Sons-ee-ah-ray and cleaned his rifle. He grinned and said, "She must not have haggled for more ponies."

Sons-ee-ah-ray laughed. But then Knows Horses saw the serious expression on my face, and he frowned. "She wants more ponies? I will give all I have. Three more."

I shook my head. "Her price is four ponies and a promise."

"Four ponies! Not seven? A promise? What promise?"

Sons-ee-ah-ray shook her head and stared at her blanket. "I feared Sleepy would do this."

I said, "If Falling Water is not married in a year, you will take her as a second wife."

"That's loco! Falling Water is old and a widow. Why would I ever want her as a wife?"

I gave him all the reasons Sleepy gave me. He listened with bowed head and could not dispute anything she had said. He was quiet for a while, deep in thought.

Sons-ee-ah-ray stared at him a moment, cut her eyes to me, and made a tiny nod. She said, "Go on and make the promise, my son. If you have to keep your promise, some may shake their heads at you as they walk by, but you will be one of the happiest and richest men in the camp, with two of its best women. Who knows what the next sun brings? I will say no more."

Saying nothing, Knows Horses pulled an oak leaf and *tobaho*, made a cigarette, lit it, and we all three smoked. After tossing the last bit of *tobaho* in the fire, he looked at me and smiled. "Will two women live in one tipi?"

I laughed and said, "Only if it's a big one."

He nodded. "Tell Sleepy I'll keep my promise to take Falling Water if she is not taken by next harvest. I still want to offer seven ponies for Lola Mes. Falling Water is a good woman. Sleepy makes much sense."

Sons-ee-ah-ray and I said in one voice, *"Enjuh!"*

I don't know how they knew it, but as I walked back to Sleepy's tipi, I heard four women laughing in my tipi.

When I told Sleepy that Knows Horses would make the promise and offered her seven ponies as a bride price, she looked toward the sky and said, "Truly Ussen cares about his people."

The weather stayed good, with bright, sunny days, little wind and cold, crisp nights. The camp women took Lola Mes aside and instructed her in the best ways to serve her husband. I suspected she could have taught them a thing or two, but she played her role as a shy young woman. In four days, tipi poles were up near Sleepy's tipi, and canvas we had taken from the Nakai-yes covered it. The camp feasted on the fourth day when Knows Horses came to Sleepy's tipi for Lola Mes, who wore a fine, beaded buckskin shift. No one noticed when Lola Mes and Knows Horses disappeared during the feast. For ten suns, they stayed in a hidden place Knows Horses knew in the Rinconada. They reappeared smiling and full of life on the morning of the eleventh sun.

While Moon on the Water visited in Mescalero and had happy times with Juanita and Maria, I went twice to visit Rufus Pike and Hombrecito. Rufus had Hombrecito reading the Indah tracks on the stacks of paper they called books. I listened one night as we sat on the porch, and he read the tracks to Rufus and me. The tracks, Rufus told me, were a story from the Indah long-ago times when the Indah had no guns, only bows and arrows and spears, like the Apache grandfathers. The tracks spoke of a tribe named Greeks attacking another tribe named Trojans. The part I listened to spoke of a warrior named Ulysses, who had a Coyote mind. It was a good story.

The second time I returned, Rufus had taught Hombrecito to use the shoots-today-kills-tomorrow thunder rifle. The rifle was too heavy and powerful for Hombrecito. He had to rest it on a stump or tree limb to shoot it, but he learned fast, soon becoming a good shot. Rufus told me that unless Hombrecito, like me, had some kind of Power vision, he would not shoot as good as me with the rifle, but he shot better than nearly anyone else. He also helped Rufus pick up rocks to make fences and a house like the old one, who had lived at the entrance to Dog Canyon, built many harvests ago. Rufus called him Frenchy Rochas.

I told Hombrecito that carrying rocks for Rufus would make him strong, but he also needed to learn to let the desert feed and take care of him. I began showing him how to find water and which plants he could eat. I told him he needed to run every day to become strong in his wind and legs. This he said he would do. Before I left, I told Rufus what had happened with Moon on the Water, that I would take her back to the Blue Mountains soon, and that we would winter there. I promised Rufus and Hombrecito I would come back in the spring and teach Hombrecito more of what all Apaches knew.

I returned from Rufus's ranch to Mescalero early in the Season of Earth Is Reddish Brown. The women had made all the dried meat, berries, nuts, mesquite beans, and mescal they had collected to carry us through the Ghost Face ready for storing. This harvest, along with the few supplies sent us for our agency allotment, would be enough to feed the camp. Bad dreams had come again for Moon. Three suns after I had returned from my second visit with Rufus and Hombrecito, Moon, Juanita, Híghah, and I sat by the fire eating an evening meal.

I said, "Moon, your dreams come again. I think we must return to the Blue Mountains before the passes fill with snow. If we wait too long, we must stay here with your dreams. If we go now, I'll stay the winter with you and return to Juanita and Híghah in the Season of Little Eagles."

Moon bowed her head and looked into the fire. Juanita looked at me with a sad face, but nodded she agreed. She said, "Our

161

husband is right, sister. I'll miss having you in the tipi during the Ghost Face times, but I know his friends and brother will help us. I know that your dreams must leave you before you can stay here. Perhaps Lola Mes will find a way with her Power to help us one day. I'll speak with her about this. Go and make another son with our husband. Make a brother or sister for Híghéh. Someday you won't leave us. This I know. I see it in my dreams."

Moon on the Water raised her head and looked at Híghéh, who was nearly asleep, his eyes closed, a piece of acorn bread in his hand, then at Juanita and me, and, finally, around the tipi. She sighed and rubbed her forehead with her long fingers before saying, "My sister and husband speak wise words. Can we leave tomorrow night? I would spend one more sun with Maria."

I said, "*Enjuh*. This we will do."

I went to the tipi of Beela-chezzi, smoked with him and Carmen Rosario, told them of my plans, and asked that he and Kah look after Juanita and Híghéh. As usual, he told me he and Kah would take care of my family as if they were their own. I also spoke with Kah and Deer Woman. Kah vowed I had nothing to worry about in the care of Juanita and Híghéh. Deer Woman, now a happy mother, had two children: the boy, Para-dee-ah-tran; and a little girl, about six harvests, Red Bird Singing, a bright child, full of energy.

I made one more visit, stopping at the tipi of Running Wolf and Blue Flower before returning to Juanita and Moon. After Running Wolf and I smoked, I said, "Moon on the Water's dreams return. We'll leave for the camp of Kitsizil Lichoo' when the sun goes down tomorrow. I don't know your plans, but if you and Blue Flower wish to return to her people, then I'm glad for your company. This may be the last time before the next Season of Little Eagles that you can get past the snow on the passes or even through the canyons."

Running Wolf glanced at Blue Flower, who nodded. He said, "Blue Flower and I have spoken of this, and I've discussed it with Beela-chezzi. She is lonesome for her people, but she will stay where I say. We'll be ready to travel with you and Moon on the Water. We're proud to ride with a great warrior."

CHAPTER 20
VANISHED

We saw no one on that ride to the camp of Kitsizil Lichoo', and Blue Flower and Moon on the Water, already good friends, grew closer. Word had continued to spread of the wisdom and good leadership of Kitsizil Lichoo', and his camp had grown. He balanced with care the camp's needs against cattle he took to avoid fighting with hacendados, who understood the loss of a few cows didn't merit risking the lives of vaqueros, who were almost sure to die if they chased the raiders into the canyons.

With the turning of the seasons, every moon or two, I rode the trails from Mescalero to the camp in the Blue Mountains, from the Blue Mountains to the rancho of Rufus Pike, where I began the training of Hombrecito, and then back to Mescalero for a moon or two with Juanita and Hígháh, who showed much light behind his eyes as he grew, and I and his uncles taught him how to hunt and the ways of our People. I knew the day must come when I would have to bring Moon back to Mescalero and ask Lola Mes to help us drive away her bad dreams, but, at the time, it was good to wander the country like the Apaches did in the old times. Neither of my wives complained, and I had the pleasure of training two young boys to be true Apache men.

Two harvests passed in this way. Knows Horses and Lola Mes had a child after the first harvest of their marriage. Falling Water still had not been taken, and, true to his word, Knows Horses asked for her after Sleepy delivered Lola Mes's baby, her second grandchild. Yibá's child, Always Laughs, was her first. Sleepy told me, when, as the representative for Knows Horses, I asked for Lola Mes, that she would not expect a bride gift for Falling Water. But Knows Horses, who had come to appreciate her strength, courage, and happy face, offered four ponies for Falling Water, and Sleepy happily accepted.

Before the end of the second harvest, Falling Water's belly swelled with a new child for their family. I laughed to myself and thought, *Knows Horses must have learned something from the studs he runs in his growing herd.* Our little camp grew larger, and it was becoming harder to save enough food for the camp in the Ghost Face times.

During the time of the second harvest, Yibá, who worked with other Mescaleros and who ran cattle, learned that Agent Stottler was leaving at the beginning of the Season of Large Leaves. A new agent named Walter Luttrell would come near the end of the Season of Earth Is Reddish Brown. We hoped that, with the new agent, things would get better for our growing camp and others on the reservation.

In the harvest time the Indah called 1898, near the time for the Season of Earth Is Reddish Brown, I made ready to leave our Rinconada canyon for a winter with Moon on the Water in the Blue Mountains. One evening as Juanita, Híghá, and I ate our meal, the sun looked as if it were falling into mountains bathed with blood. The whole camp heard the pounding of a horse's hooves racing down the canyon trail toward the camp. Juanita and I looked at each other. No one came to the camp on the run unless it was important business.

I wiped my fingers and grabbed my rifle, while Juanita pulled Híghá down close to the ground. My head and shoulders were just out of the tipi when Yibá's pony, lathered even in the cool evening air from a hard run across the ridges, slid to a stop in front of me. Yibá, breathing hard as if he had run a long time, leaned over his pony's neck and said between gasps, "The great Indah *di-yen* . . . your friend at the agency . . . has gone to the happy place . . . his woman and son . . . wear the Indah cloth of the dead."

A great sadness filled me, and I stared up at the blood red mountains. Doctor Blazer, the best Indah friend I had on the reservation, had gone to the Happy Place. He and Rufus were the best Indah friends I had anywhere. I thought, *Ussen take that great* di-yen *and good man on the short trail to the Happy Place.*

Yibá, catching his breath and seeming to read my mind, said, "The Indah bury him tomorrow among their gravestones on the hillside above *La Máquina.*"

I waved my arm at him to go tell the others. I knew the ways of the Indah when they buried their dead. Their ways were not Apache ways. My people would stay away, always avoiding the dead, even though I knew Blazer's friends and family would accept us there. I decided I would honor my friend and, hidden from the Indah, watch the ceremonies from a distance using my *Shináá Cho.*

I wondered if Blazer's son, Almer, would speak to me with a straight tongue as his father had done. With the new agent Luttrell coming, we would need all the advice and help we could get.

The next day, in the cool air, I watched the Indah burial ceremony for Doctor Blazer. I waited until the sun and people at the ceremony had left before I went to the mound of fresh dirt covering the grave. With raised hands, I sang in a low, soft voice a song asking Ussen to give Doctor Blazer a good journey to the Happy Place, and I sprinkled golden pollen to the four directions as a special blessing.

★ ★ ★ ★ ★

Four days after the burial ceremony, I left Juanita and Hígháh to return to Moon on the Water. During the Ghost Face I spent with Moon on the Water, I hunted deer and bighorn sheep as they came down from the high places, and I thought much about what I had to do when I returned to Mescalero in the Season of Little Eagles.

The time had come to begin pushing Hombrecito in what I taught him about the desert and taking care of himself. Each time I visited, he had grown bigger and stronger. He was becoming a good shot with the big thunder rifle Rufus owned, but he wasn't running as hard as a boy his age must. That would change when I returned.

Most of the time, I thought of Hígháh and his training and what I might expect now that the new agent had come. I hoped he would be easier to deal with than Stottler. Perhaps he would give us increased rations because of our growing camp, and not insist our men cut their hair and wear Indah pants so we could mingle with our friends in other camps without the tribal police coming to send us away. I remembered Doctor Blazer telling me that Stottler's chiefs had praised what he had done to the Mescaleros. Perhaps the new agent, Luttrell, would try to follow Stottler's path. At least my little band was safe as long as we stayed out of sight. I knew I would learn the thinking of Luttrell soon enough when I returned to the Rinconada.

That harvest, the Ghost Face in the camp of Kitsizil Lichoo', was an easy one. I hunted often, and when I left in the Season of Little Eagles, Moon had enough to live on until I returned. I had served as Running Wolf's uncle when he was a child. I'd taught him how to hunt, make straight arrows and strong bows, and how to survive in the wilderness. He had been a good child, and I was glad my warrior brothers and I had saved him when he was a baby from destruction by the witch, Sangre del Diablo. I thought Ussen must have had a good laugh when Sangre del Diablo's own daughter saved Running Wolf from Ojo Verde's witchcraft. Now that he had grown to be a powerful warrior with a fine wife living in the same camp with Moon and me, we shared a close bond, truly like uncle and nephew. Before I left, he asked to be responsible for Moon on the Water while I stayed at Mescalero, and I gratefully agreed.

The nights on the trail from the Blue Mountains were filled with stars, quiet times, and much thinking about what would happen when I returned. Sometimes thoughts of Ojo Verde crossed my mind. But in all the harvests since she had disappeared, there had been no trace of her, and I began to think that perhaps she had died escaping the fire at Kitsizil Lichoo's camp. I thought, *Maybe I don't have to worry about Lola Mes's warning after all.*

At Rufus Pike's rancho, I spent time with Hombrecito teaching him how to hunt, disappear when he needed to, and use Apache words he must know to live in a camp. I made him start running harder to increase his strength and to do long-distance running to increase his staying power.

Rufus told me that in a moon or two, the man Hombrecito believed had paid for his father's killing would be judged for the killing in the mining village named Hillsboro in the mountains the Indah call the Black Range west of the great river. Rufus said that by Indah law, he did not believe this man would be found guilty and punished. He also told me he had heard no news from Mescalero, and that things seemed quiet on the reservation since the new agent had arrived. I left Rufus and Hombrecito for Mescalero and, as usual, on the way stopped for rest in the Jarilla Mountains.

Two suns after leaving Rufus and Hombrecito, eager to see

Juanita and Hígháh, I rode up the camp's canyon trail in the Rinconada, the sun's edge pushing over the edge of the eastern mountains. Bushtits left the brush in whirring flocks as I rode by, and ravens flew high from their mountain trees to water. Something was not right. In the low light, the trail looked little used, if at all, for a long time, and above the trees at the end of the canyon, there was no hint of smoke, light, or smell from morning fires, no thumps of women's axes for morning firewood. Nothing.

As I approached, I looked through the trees for the outlines of the tipis in the cold morning mists, but saw none. I tied my pony back in the trees by the little creek rushing by in full flow from snowmelt. Staying low, I ran forward, hiding behind a new tree at every chance. Nothing was in the camp. Not even bare tipi poles. The horse dirt in the corral showed horses had not been there during the Ghost Face, and supplies in the cache were all gone. It was as if we had never lived there.

Ripples of memory made my skin pucker as I remembered finding *Cha's* camp after Sangre del Diablo had wiped out everyone there. Had Ojo Verde come in place of Sangre del Diablo? But here I found no bodies or any traces of big fires, and this gave me hope. I thought, *They must have moved, but why and where?*

I rode over to the camp we had left for this one, hoping my People might have returned there, but it, too, stood barren. I put my pony in the corral, rubbed him down, and left him to graze on the new green grass starting to grow around the stones. At the shallow cave where we held camp councils, I made a fire and ate what was left of my trail food while I tried to decide what to do. Nearby a canyon wren called, *jeet, jeet,* and the wind rolling off the mountain and whispering through the tops of the tall pines made the place seem even more abandoned. I rested in the cave until the night came again. After considering the many possible forks in the trail forward, I decided to speak with Almer Blazer, the son of Doctor Blazer, and learn what he knew of my People.

Before dawn, from the top of the ridge above the agency, I studied the lights in the valley. Even as high as I was, I could hear the Río Tularosa, filled with snowmelt, rolling past *La Máquina*. I didn't know where Almer and his woman lived. I decided to ride down, hide near the Blazer barn, and gamble he would come early to feed the animals, giving me a chance to speak with him alone.

From where I sat in the junipers, I could see most of the valley. As the light grew, I looked from Blazer's house up the wagon road toward Fort Stanton and saw the great Indah houses for the reservation school Stottler had tried to make us use. I ground my teeth, thinking about how Stottler, even *Tata* Big Nose, and other agents had wanted to take our children away so we could see them no more until they were grown, teach them Indah ways, and turn them away from remembering their days as Apaches. The other agents had tried and failed to make all the Mescaleros give up their children. Only Stottler had gone so far as to cut off rations and put grandmothers in the jail when they refused to send their grandchildren to the Indah School.

I pulled out the *Shináá Cho* and watched the school big houses. The doors opened on the one where the children slept, and they began to march out, all the same in their uniforms, to the place where they ate meals. The short, youngest ones marched at the head of the lines, boys in one line, girls in another, each line led by an Indah adult. I could see their faces, none happy, and I was glad my son was not there. But as I watched them, I felt my heart tighten and my guts squeeze. Hígháh marched in that line of children led like horses to eat in a barn. I looked down the line and saw them all, every child

170

from my camp. Yibá's child, Always Laughs; and Kah's daughter, Red Bird Singing, marched in the girl's line. A little farther back, Kah and Deer Woman's nearly grown son, Para-dee-ah-tran, marched in what could have been a soldier's uniform with the older boys.

Stottler had kept his word for two years after our shooting bet. Now I saw his word had been broken and our children taken. This must not stand. I would kill the agent to stop it if I had to, but first I had to find Juanita and the rest of my People.

CHAPTER 21
THE SEARCH

I watched the last child march into the building where the In-dah gave them their meals. Despite the angry fire roaring in my head, I made myself think in a cold, hard way, like a true war-rior. At least I knew where the children were. Now to find my woman and People.

I swung the *Shináá Cho* toward the sound of a door slam-ming shut on the side of Blazer's house. Almer Blazer walked out toward the corral and barn followed by a vaquero. I watched and waited in the cold air as the sun sent shafts of light across the valley through the ridgetop trees. Ravens flew, cawing, down the valley along the Río Tularosa, and birds began to chatter. I saw a man who worked in Blazer's store unlock the door and go in. Soon smoke came out of the pipe that went to the *pesh biyi'kq'i* (iron stove) where fire burned to warm the store.

The vaquero rode out of the barn on a nice red pony with a white blaze on its nose and headed up the wagon road toward Fort Stanton. Almer Blazer remained in the barn. I looked all across the agency and saw no one outside. Staying low, I ran for the barn. I knew someone might see me, but I had to risk it or wait to find my family.

I slid around the edge of the barn's open door into the low yellow light from a lantern hanging on a post. As I had ap-proached the barn, I heard the clink of rings and chains that told me someone harnessed a team. Almer Blazer had his back to me, buckling the hames in place on mules to be hitched to a green wagon the store used for hauling supplies. He saw the mules' ears prick up and turned, saying, "Forget somethin', José? Wah? Yellow Boy! Thank God, you're back."

"I see little ones in Indah School. Where are the others? You speak straight to me like your father? If no, I go."

He held his hands up, palms out, and nodded. "I speak straight. I know you came to Father's funeral. I saw you up on the ridge in the junipers and the pollen on his grave the next day. He always had the highest regard for you, and I want to help you any way I can.

"Your people are spread all over the reservation. Juanita and Maria have their tipis up a canyon west of the Fort Stanton road about three miles up from here. The others are scattered in camps around the reservation. I think Yibá, your mother, and Knows Horses and his women are in No Foot's camp, and Kah and Deer Woman are with Beela-chezzi and Carmen Rosario somewhere in canyons not far from Juanita. All your people are unhurt, but their spirits are low."

I could only shake my head and wonder if Ussen had taken away all our Power. "Why did this happen? These two harvests Stottler keeps his word, and I keep mine."

Almer Blazer puffed his cheeks and blew, scratched a mule on the jaw behind his bridle, and, looking at the ground, said, "When my father was alive, he guided the new agents away from bad ideas until they learned how best to manage the agency. Stottler wouldn't listen to most of his advice, but he listened some. Luttrell, who replaced Stottler, thinks that tin-pot martinet was a great man and wants to continue his rules. He won't listen to anyone except his faraway chiefs."

The mule Almer Blazer scratched shook his head and stamped his foot. I knew he wanted to get on with pulling the wagon. The other mule just stood there as though he were asleep.

Blazer jerked the bit and said, "Whoa, son. We'll be going soon.

"Sábado told the new agent, Luttrell, the people in your camp didn't have to follow Stottler's rules because you had won a shooting bet. Luttrell got red in the face, pounded his fist on his desk, and said he didn't have any bet with you. He said for Sábado to take every policeman, surround your camp, and tell you there was no more bet because Stottler was gone. He said, if you tried to resist, to kill you and anyone else who did. He had them take all the children old enough to attend the school and tell your people that, after the men cut their hair, to come to the agency for supplies and trousers the men had to wear."

I felt weary, angry, and like I had a bad stomach. I was weary from all the days we had fought to make the Indah leave us alone. I was angry because the Indah were strong enough to steal our children and teach them they needed to be like Indah and forget that their fathers were Mescaleros, and I was sick because I didn't know how to fight them and survive. I didn't miss when I used my rifle, but after much thought in the Blue Mountains, I knew there were too many to stop them that way.

"What happened when Sábado didn't find me?"

"No one in your camp would say where you were. Sábado took all the children to the school that day, and before he left, he told the men to cut their hair and come to the agency for their trousers the next day or there would be no rations during Ghost Face. Sábado told me that when the police rode over the ridge with those children, they heard every woman in your camp outside in the wind and snow wailing, even the grandmothers. He said your warriors did nothing. It was like they were carved from stone, but he saw the fire in their eyes and was glad he and the other police left when they did. Beela-chezzi told me that if you had been there, there would have been no more tribal police, and Sábado knew it."

As Almer Blazer spoke, I could see everything he spoke of as if it were a vision, and I wondered why Ussen hid his face from us.

"The next day, everyone in your camp came to the agency. All the men had their hair cut, and they took the trousers, put them on, and demanded their supplies. The women begged the agent to let them see their children, but Luttrell wouldn't allow it. He told them to come back in a moon, and maybe they could see them then. Juanita decided to move close to the school and try to see Highah every day she could, even if she had to stand in the road to see him when the children marched to their meals. Lucky Star and Deer Woman said they would join her to see their children and decided they, too, would find places close by in the valley. The next day all your camp moved. I don't know much more than that, my friend. Please don't try to take vengeance on Luttrell. It will only get you killed and do your wives and children no good."

I shook my head. "Almer Blazer speaks straight and is a man like his father. I must think on all this and go to Juanita."

"If I can help you and your people, tell me, and I'll try."

"Almer Blazer is good friend."

I rode my pony in the tree and ridge shadows on the east side of the Fort Stanton road up the Río Tularosa and looked for the canyon on the west side where Juanita had her tipi. I rode slowly, careful to avoid being surprised. The sunlight was bright coming through the trees, and yellow flowers bloomed in meadows. The sky was bright blue, but I was in a dark place.

The road made a long curve toward the northeast and then straightened out as it climbed toward Apache Pass. A rider came down the road toward me. I paused in the shadows, not sure if I had been seen. The rider came to a stop, too. It seemed we studied each other for a long time, but it was only a breath or two. The rider, in the shadow of a big pine, sat forward on his pony's saddle, and wore a calico skirt. It was still too dark, the shadows around her making it hard for me to recognize her. Suddenly she slapped her legs against the pony to urge him on and, charging straight for me, yelled, "Yellow Boy! Yellow Boy! Husband, you come!"

We sat together by the tipi fire feeling each other's body warmth, lost in our thoughts, a blanket over our shoulders. Far up the canyon, coyotes yipped, and a light wind walked through the pines, making the boughs up high shake and sound like the murmuring of a distant stream. When Juanita had ridden up to me in the cool morning light, I'd felt the same pleasure and relief as the day I learned that she and others still lived after Sangre del Diablo had slaughtered our people, taken their scalps, and burned our camp. I felt the same fire for vengeance, but I knew it was a desire I could never satisfy, hollow and without muscle and bone. Without destroying my family and friends, I would never be able to settle the debt of vengeance I owed the Indah for taking our child to teach him Indah life and train him to never again be a Mescalero. I knew that when Híghâh grew to be a man and have children of his own, he would only know to teach them the ways of the Indah. Our own children and grandchildren would no longer know they were Mescaleros, Apaches, Shis-Indeh (People of the Woods).

Juanita sighed and, laying her head against my shoulder, said, "Híghâh will forget us in the Indah School. They won't let him speak as we do. He is allowed to use only Indah words. They've cut his hair and given him the Indah name, David. They make him walk in lines with the other children, like horses led to water, and to stand up and sit down when a bell is struck. He's no longer free. He's a slave. I've lost two children, one to bad air and one to the Indah. I can't leave this place while our mothers live. When they go to the Happy Place, then I say we should join Moon on the Water in the camp of Kitsizil Lichoo' and be done with the Indah and *Nakai-yes*. What will you do, husband? I follow you. You're all I have left in life."

I poked at the fire, sending sparks toward the stars, and turned to look in her black-flint eyes.

"I want the lives of Luttrell and Sábado and most of the tribal police, but, if I take them, the army will come again. There will only be more blood, and it will be ours. We must outsmart the Indah. Until Ussen tells us how to do this, we must live our lives with pride. Indah agents will come and go, but we will remain. We are Shis-Indeh. Maybe leaving for the Blue Mountains is the right answer. Perhaps Ussen will give us a sign. The only way I know how to fight now is to outlast the Indah and stay on our land the way we want to live.

"Perhaps Hombrecito is the answer, and the words of Geronimo and my vision were given for this time. I don't know. Only visions of the future or the time when it happens can tell us this."

"Will you also cut your hair and wear Indah trousers? The agency gives me no rations because you haven't come with your hair cut and willing to wear the trousers."

Again, I stared at the fire for a while and listened as the calls of coyotes drew closer.

"I don't like the Indah trousers, but I'll wear them over my breechcloth. I'll cut my hair a little, but leave it so it touches my shoulders. Before I go to the agency, you'll braid it so it stays on top of my head, and I'll wear a hat. My hair is my pride. The Indah won't take it. Coyote, the trickster, will help me fool the Indah. If I'm the last warrior killed because he didn't cut his hair, let it be so."

Juanita smiled at the idea of tricking the Indah agents and tribal police. "I'll braid your hair so that with your hat you look more like an Indah than an Indah. You should also know that before Stottler left, his chiefs said we can leave the reservation without agent tracks on paper. You can leave whenever you want and not worry about being caught."

"Hmmph. Maybe things will be better."

Her hand rubbed my shoulders and back, and she relaxed against me. In a while, she said, "Husband, my body can still make babies. I want another child. Give me one."

I smiled and looked in her eyes. "You're my first wife, woman of my heart, woman of my desires. We'll have another child. This one, the Indah won't take."

CHAPTER 22
PLAYA WITCH

Juanita trimmed my hair a little and then plaited a set of clever braids on top of my head that I easily kept under my old campaign hat, making me, at first glance, look like I wore my hair Indah style. I went to the agency with Juanita to collect our rations, and then we planned to try to see Híghàh when he walked between the school buildings. The clerk who issued rations knew me, saw my hair looked short below the brim of my hat, smiled, and nodded, but said nothing, gave me my trousers and our rations, and then wished us well.

Juanita and I rode up into the junipers, where I had watched the school while waiting for Almer Blazer to go to his barn. We were patient, watching with the *Shinàà Cho*, and, when the sun made no shadows, we finally saw Híghàh in a long line of uniformed boys walking to their meal. It made my stomach bad to see him there and to know what the Indah were doing to him and to us as a family.

The next sun, we rode over to the camp of Kah and Beelachezzi. We men smoked and talked while Juanita and Deer Woman visited and sorted cache supplies with Carmen Rosario and her child, an unexpected gift from Ussen, Hawú dat'éhe (Quiet Dove), who was still on the *tsach* (cradleboard). Kah, his hair short and wearing Indah trousers, looked strange. I could tell he was furious with himself, feeling foolish like a man who had lost his way but was unwilling to ask the right path from someone who knew. I was glad whiskey was so hard to find, or,

179

in his rage over his helplessness, he would have become a useless drunkard by the time we now sat and talked.

Kah said, "After we moved the tipis here, I planned to kill Sábado and Luttrell. I was halfway to the agency with my rifle before I realized I must protect my family and couldn't satisfy my need for revenge. I wished you were here so we could think this through and take back our children. I decided this challenge was like hunting. We had to be patient and watch and wait for our chance to take the game."

Beela-chezzi nodded. "I feel the same way. What will we do, my friends? Kah's oldest is nearly a man. The Indah School won't change him. Maybe he learns good things, like how to read and make the Indah tracks on paper. But Red Bird Singing still has a year or two before her *Haheh*. Only Ussen knows if, after going to Indah School, she still wants to be an Apache woman looking after her man, children, and People after her woman time comes."

Kah made a sour face. "Why can't we take our children now when it's dark and ride to the land of the *Nakai-yes*—the Blue Mountains and the camp of Kitsizil Lichoo'? I know life is not easy there, but at least we'd be free."

I blew a stream of smoke toward the top of the tipi and shook my head. "I, too, have considered this. But Almer Blazer, who speaks straight, like his father, told me that the Indah fear the children running away. They check their beds three or four times while the sun hides behind the mountains, so they know none have left. When children run, policemen go after them. If we took our children and ran with our families, we'd have less than half the night to get away and hide before Sábado and the tribal police came after us. We can't outrun them with women, children, and old ones with us. We might ambush and wipe out Sábado and the policemen following us, but then the army would chase us even into the far Blue Mountains, and the

Nakai-yes would help them. I saw this when Nantan Lupan went after Geronimo and other Apaches about fifteen harvests ago. Someone would show them our camps in the Blue Mountains, and we, as well as our friends, would die or be taken prisoners of war like the Chiricahua, or, if taken by the *Nakai-yes*, sold for slaves. This we cannot do. Maybe one or two of us might get away, but, I think, never all of us. We cannot leave the others of our band."

A dark time, like a cloud over the sun, fell over us, as we thought about what we might do to save our children and our life-way, but we knew there was nothing in our power except to wait like hunters and look for an opening. We spent the rest of the day discussing what to do through the next harvest and how to get around Luttrell and the rules he learned from Stottler.

The following sun, Juanita and I rode to the camp of No Foot to visit the Yibá and Knows Horses's families. In the Ghost Face, many harvests ago, just before our little daughter Kicking Wren went to the Happy Land, I'd killed a big cougar that had been hunting No Foot's little herd of cattle. Some, including No Foot, believed the cougar was a shape-shifting witch, and I wouldn't deny it. No Foot was happy to help people from my camp. The tribal police took Yibá and Lucky Star's child, Dawahn Dáha (Always Laughs), who was eight harvests, but Lola Mes's child, a bright little girl running and playing with much curiosity, Idlaaní (One Who Drinks), and the child of Falling Water, a little girl still on the *tsach*, brought happy times to our day.

Yibá, Knows Horses, and I smoked and made the same talk I had with the other men in our old camp. As with the others, Yibá and Knows Horses understood we had to watch and wait. There was no other way.

I spent some time with my mother, Sons-ee-ah-ray. She and

Maria had begun leaning on sticks to walk, their bodies too weak to go far or do much work, and the loss of most of their teeth meant they didn't eat much. Their anger at having their grandchildren taken gave their voices strength that didn't show in their arms and legs. I thought, *Ussen will see them in the Happy Land before I return from my next trip to the Blue Mountains.*

Before we returned to Juanita's tipi, Lola Mes asked to speak with me alone. I noticed the Power surrounding her felt even greater than it had before she used it against Ojo Verde. We sat together, saying nothing in the flickering light of her tipi fire as she rolled a cigarette with Indah *tobaho* in an oak leaf. When we finished smoking, she looked at me with her good eye from across her fire, her blind eye white and shining, and the scars on her face beside it making me even more aware of her Power. She said, "Brother of my husband and last true warrior, I have dreamed. Beware of Ojo Verde. She comes near you when you return to the Blue Mountains. She seeks her vengeance. Be ready for her strike."

I felt the hair on my neck prickle. "Sister, you're a *di-yen* of great Power and a good friend. I'll remember your words."

Early in the Season of Large Leaves, I returned to Moon on the Water. It was hard to leave Juanita and Maria with our little son imprisoned in the Indah School at the agency, but she urged me not to stay away from her sister for too long. Before I left, I helped Juanita move to another canyon closer to the camp of Beela-chezzi and Kah, so it was easier for Juanita, Deer Woman, and Carmen Rosario to meet and work together. The new camp had better water and bigger trees for shade than the first one, and anyone coming up the canyon to Juanita's tipi could be seen by those in the Beela-chezzi camp.

On the sun before I left for the Blue Mountains, I watched the Indah School for Hígháh and caught a glimpse of him doing Indah work with some of the other children. He was growing before my eyes, and the anger at the Indah for taking him from us burned in my guts like coals of a banked tipi fire deep in the night. Still, I waited.

As the sun was falling, I held Juanita close after we ate an evening meal. I told her I would be back in a moon or two and rode off for the rancho of Rufus Pike. I spent four suns with Rufus and Hombrecito, who was growing into a strong boy.

I started making him run harder and longer, even running with a swallow of water held in his mouth to test his discipline and make him breathe through his nose when he ran. I shot some with the boy and Rufus. I learned that Hombrecito was a better shot with the shoots-today-kills-tomorrow thunder gun than most men with any rifle, and he was still getting better. Before I rode on, I worked with him on how to use a sling and told him to practice across many suns with it.

Rufus, his anger nearly making him swallow the *tobaho* he chewed, told me that the council the Indah held in Hillsboro village to decide if Oliver Lee had killed Hombrecito's father decided Lee had done nothing and let him return to his rancho. The council's decision only made Hombrecito's desire for blood vengeance grow stronger with the passing of each new sun, and I thought, *Always the Indah choose to look the other way when evil comes. They won't demand their honor.*

I rode across the llano during the time of a bright, full moon and followed a trail I often used through a valley between the mountains Indah call Animas and Guadalupe. The Animas Valley ends in a great white playa that stretches across the border toward the Blue Mountains. The playa had no water then, only dust and white sand. It was near the season of rain. Soon after I began my ride down the valley, clouds began filling the night sky and making the moon a great, white fuzzy spot. Off to the south, I saw flashes between dark clouds from which walked great, thick legs of rain.

I thought of the night long ago when I saw rain coming like that from the top of the mountains named Organ where the spirits gave me my Power from Ussen and how I was grateful for all Ussen had done for me. This night, the rain legs did not walk toward me but stayed south, even though I could smell the rain in the wind when it came and stirred the sand and dust in the playa, creating great swirling clouds, making it hard to see and biting my face like hungry ants. I stayed on the east side of the playa next to the Animas Mountains and foothills in the shadows of the moon, which sometimes disappeared in the swirling dust clouds.

For a short breath, the wind paused, not blowing at all, making no sound, and I heard my name, "Yellow Boy, Yellow Boy." The voice sounded far away. I rose up in the saddle and looked all around in the low light, across the great white playa and toward the Animas Mountains, but I saw nothing. The wind began again, starting quick, like a horse in a race.

My pony snorted and stumbled to his knees. I tried to stay in the saddle and pull him up, but his strength was gone, and he continued to fall. I jumped clear, and as the wind began its fury again, he fell over on his side, kicked once, and died before my unbelieving eyes. Crawling to a jumble of boulders nearby I found cover to wait for better light.

The wind died in fits and starts, growing weaker each time it tried to come back. The clouds passing in front of the moon disappeared, and, in the moonlight, I saw an arrow buried almost to its feathers in the side of my pony near its front legs. If the arrow had been two hand-widths farther back, it would have hit me in my thigh and pinned me to him. I waited, unmoving, barely breathing, and studied everything around me, trying to find some trace of who shot the arrow.

The sun came with its fresh, early light, the sky clear and deep blue to black. As bright yellow light poured through the canyons and valleys on the western side of the Animas Mountains, I pulled out my *Shináá Cho* and studied every detail of the playa next to me within an arrow shot of my pony, but I saw nothing. I went to my pony and pulled the arrow from his side, where I knew it must have stabbed his heart. The arrow was heavier and feathered differently from Apache arrows, its point a third the length of the shaft and made of bone. I wiped the dark blood from it, thinking the point probably came from a human leg bone. The point was painted blue except for where it met the wood shaft, and there it was red. The red and blue markings looked like those Ojo Verde had painted on the witch's weapon Lola Mes had sucked from the head of Knows Horses.

The arrow had come from the direction of the playa, yet I saw no sign anywhere of tracks the shooter had made coming to or going away from where the arrow must have been shot. That meant the bowman was still hidden somewhere on the playa. I eased to the back of my dead pony, reached across and cut the saddle cinch, so the pony wouldn't burst in the hot sun. I continued to study the details across the playa in front of me and waited, standing with my rifle in the crook of my left arm, hoping to draw my attacker from his hiding place.

The sun's heat grew and water filled the bandanna around my head. The glare from the white playa was blinding. A tight squint when looking toward the wavering playa was the only way to see anything. The pony cooking in the sun's heat began to swell, and the cloud of big black birds circling above me grew thicker and closer. I could hear the flutter of their wings and croaking calls to each other. I kept still and waited.

As if in a dream, seventy-five yards out on the playa, a ripple in the dust and sand began to grow in the shimmering air. With a scream like an animal falling from high mountain cliffs, a figure rose up from under a blanket in a cloud of white dust, a man white from head to toe, except where little springs of water left trails in the dust on his body. An arrow notched on a bowstring and three more in his hand looked like the one that killed my pony. The sockets of his eyes were painted black. His head had no hair and was painted white, like a skull, in the style of Sangre del Diablo. His voice, low and moaning, called, "Yellow Boy, Yellow Boy." I felt a blazing fury grow in me.

For a moment, I thought I looked on Sangre del Diablo's ghost. But ghosts didn't shed water, and this man was no giant. His first arrow thunked into my dead pony near where I stood. He notched another arrow and came on. I kept still and waited.

Fifty yards, another arrow aimed for my heart, close but easy to dodge; thirty yards, another arrow and a miss, but I had to be quick and move, anticipating his shot. He notched his last arrow standing close enough for me to see the yellow in his eyes. He grinned and began drawing the bow, again aiming for my heart, as though I were a wooden post, while calling, "Yellow Boy, Yellow Boy, in the sun, I see you die." I was the last thing he saw as my rifle went to my shoulder. He tried to aim the arrow, but he was in too much of a hurry to beat my shot, and it flew low, thumping into the swelling horse. As he released the arrow, I took his left eye first and then his right, the spray of bright, red blood and brains flying out the back of his head making feathery streaks of red on the white of the playa, as his head jerked back. He fell backwards, his body stretched out to cook on the brilliant, fiery sand, and his ghost to wander away, blind, toward the Happy Land.

I didn't recognize him or the blanket with its strange pattern he had hidden under. I collected all the arrows and his bow, pulled some dry brush together, and, there on the great spread of white sand, under the burning sun, started a fire. I burnt the bow and arrows and the blanket, and they made loud popping noises as the fire took them. The man I killed, I left naked, lying on the sand for the big black birds that soon came for him and my pony, hunger driving them there despite my being nearby. I sat in the shade of rocks with my saddle and blanket until the sun fell into the mountains, and then began a run south for the camp of Kitsizil Lichoo'.

Lola Mes had warned me in the Season of Little Eagles that she had dreamed of Ojo Verde trying to kill me soon. Lola Mes's dreams had spoken true. I knew I had to find Ojo Verde and send her to the Happy Land before she worked more of her evil and destroyed me.

CHAPTER 23
WARNED IN A DREAM

I thought for a long time about the playa witch as I ran for the Blue Mountains. I wondered how Ojo Verde knew where the Comanche should hide and when I would pass by there. I knew she had great Power, but I didn't understand how she knew these things or her relationship to the witch I had killed on the playa. I'd have to start changing my trails each time I went back to the Blue Mountains and be very careful wherever I traveled, until I could send Ojo Verde to the Happy Land.

When I returned to the camp of Kitsizil Lichoo', Moon on the Water, with much happiness on her face, told me that another child grew in her belly and that she was sure it was a son. In a few moons, she had a strong boy early in the Season of Little Eagles in the harvest time the Indah named 1900. We decide to name him Redondo because he had been born while I traveled around between his mothers and Rufus and Hombre-cito.

When I told Juanita, she was happy for her sister and our family, but she wouldn't leave the reservation to stay with Moon even after our mothers went to the Happy Land. She said, "I want to see Hígháh every day to be sure he's well and not dying from worms (the Apaches believed tuberculosis was caused by worms) or bad air (smallpox or pneumonia)."

After Redondo had his *tsach* ceremony, done well by the second wife of Kitsizil Lichoo', Calico Dove, Running Wolf continued to help me support Moon with meat from the hunt and beef taken from the hacendados, while I stayed with Juanita through the days made hard by Agent Luttrell. I also spent some days training Hombrecito, who ran faster and faster toward manhood and his long awaited blood revenge.

Two harvests passed. Juanita and I continued trying to have another child. She knew the days when she might still bear a child were fast racing away. But she said, "I must try until Ussen takes the power of making and carrying new life from me."

Luttrell followed Stottler's lead and cut all rations to the Mescaleros, except for those too old, sick, or weak to provide for their own lives. He said the White Eye chiefs gave the Mescaleros sheep, goats, and cattle. Now they had to provide for themselves, using those animals or working to make money for supplies in return for $1.25 a day without work animals or $2.50 a day for a man and his team of horses. Luttrell was worse than Stottler in how he treated us. I thought many times of killing him, but I never tried, because I knew that in doing so things would only get worse for the People.

I hunted often and with success. Juanita and I dried the meat, and she cached it for the times when I was gone. She finished the skins from my hunts into fine leathers and furs to sell along with her beautiful baskets at the agency store. She worked a garden with Deer Woman and Carmen Rosario, and, with the other women, gathered mescal, wild potatoes, piñon nuts, mesquite pods, new yucca shoots, juniper berries, acorns, walnuts, and herbs from the desert and mountains. These things the Mescaleros had lived on since before the grandfathers. Times were hard, but we were strong and waited for Ussen to send the spirits to help us.

The chiefs at the agency Indah School let Híghah visit with us maybe once a season for two or three days. Híghah told us that, at the school, he mostly worked to help the Indah, but he had learned to read the tracks on paper and was learning how to make them. He said the Indah teachers told him he learned to make good tracks on paper much faster than the other children. I thought this making Indah tracks on paper a good thing, but I didn't like him staying at the school all the time or being taught things he would need for making a farm. He continued to believe he was an Indeh, not an Indah, which was a good thing.

The fire burned low, its smoke slowly going out the smoke hole of the lodge roof. The village of Kitsizil Lichoo' slept peacefully, and I slept in peace with my wife and baby. A dream came. I knew it was a vision, even as I dreamed.

I am an eagle flying high over the basin. I see Hombrecito run across the Organ Mountain pass Rufus Pike calls Baylor. He runs with Rufus's shoots-today-kills-tomorrow thunder rifle. He runs well. He runs hard and fast even up a mountain pass. He is strong.

Indah in big hats come from a great *hacienda casa* and ride to a big corral filled with cattle. Hombrecito shoots at an Indah wearing a big, white hat. Many harvests before, Big White Hat gave *pesh-klitso* to Bitághaa' Lichoo' to ambush and kill Hombrecito and his father. Hombrecito's shot misses. It hits only the white hat and sends it flying. Hombrecito hides and runs through the junipers that stretch back toward Baylor Pass. Big White Hat learns Rufus Pike has a shoots-today-kills-tomorrow thunder rifle. Big White Hat goes to Rufus's shack. His man beats Rufus, and takes the rifle. Big White Hat sees Hombrecito, who stirs his memory. In darkness and rain from big black clouds shooting lightning arrows, Big White Hat sends Bitághaa' Lichoo' to kill Rufus and Hombrecito. A voice from the clouds tells me, "Bitághaa' Lichoo' is a witch. You go now. You stop the witch. Use your Power to shoot out his eyes. He must wander blind in the Happy Land and do evil no more."

My eyes snapped open. I threw off my blanket and sat up. I reached up to touch my face, and I felt water like that made by the heat in the sweat lodge. Moon, still at the edge of the land, of dreams murmured, "My husband has a vision?"

"Yes, I must go now. A witch comes to kill Hombrecito."

She came to her knees and, taking my shoulders in the dark, whispered, "Be strong, husband. Your child and I wait for your return. A sack of trail food and a jug of water are next to your rifle and saddle. I made it while caching the harvest yesterday and set some aside for you in case you needed it soon. Ussen speaks to us both. Go to the stream and bathe. I'll awake the fire so you can eat and I can see your face once more before you go."

I left as the moon began falling in the south. It was not a bright moon, less than half, but it gave enough light for me to see the trails I knew to follow out of the Blue Mountains. My pony and I stopped for short times to eat and drink at water tanks and hidden springs in the desert. To rest my pony, I sometimes ran and led him.

I reached Rufus's rancho at the beginning of the third night after leaving Moon and Redondo in the Blue Mountains. The face of Rufus was bruised and cut, so I knew part of my dream had come to pass. Far to the south, I could see flashing arrows flying between clouds and the big stumpy legs of rain as Wind and Thunder Spirits walked in our direction. I told Hombrecito and Rufus what I had seen in my dream. Rufus, who understood Power, said my dreams always spoke true. We had to hide plenty quick, so we moved to a place on the cliff wall above his shack.

Since Hombrecito tells of this in his paper tracks, I'll leave most of the telling to him. That night, wind came, carrying sand stinging our faces and bringing the strong, good smell of wet creosote bushes. A sudden flash from a Thunder Spirit arrow showed riders with Bitághaa' Lichoo' sitting in their saddles before Rufus's ranch house. They yelled for Rufus to bring Hombrecito out. When no one left the house, a rider kicked in the door and went inside, shooting. No Rufus, no Hombrecito there. Male rain, much water falling plenty quick, came. Bitághaa' Lichoo' and his riders left.

We climbed down and talked after the rain walked away. We decided we must attack and kill these men who had come to kill them. Next day Rufus and Hombrecito loaded supplies on a mule and we left the rancho. First we went to a hiding place in the Jarilla Mountains and then to a place I knew on the reservation where we could stay until we found the camp of Bitághaa' Lichoo' and Big White Hat and took Hombrecito's revenge.

We camped next to a spring on a ridge near the Great Sacred Mountain (Sierra Blanca). The camp was an easy ride to Juanita's tipi. To find Big White Hat, Rufus decided to see a woman he knew in the village the Indah call Lincoln. He thought she might know where Big White Hat and Bitághaa' Lichoo' were, and might even know where the vaquero hid who rode with Big White Hat and took the shoots-today-kills-tomorrow thunder rifle.

I found Juanita when the sun had fallen halfway into the western high places. She was on her knees grinding long brown *iyah* (mesquite bean pods) she pulled from one of her big baskets. She looked up when she heard my pony snort as I approached her.

She laughed in happiness and said, "Yellow Boy returns early to his first wife. My heart soars with the eagles. All is well with my sister and our son?"

I waved my hand parallel to the ground. "All is well. I had a vision of witches finding and killing Hombrecito. I came as

soon as I awoke from my dream. I was in time to hide Hombrecito and Rufus Pike. Now they're in a camp not far from here.
Soon we'll attack those who tried to kill them. I come now to
my woman. All is well with her?"

She nodded, "All is well. I see Hígháh ten suns in this moon.
He grows and learns Indah ways, but knows he's always a Mescalero. Beela-chezzi and Kah are gone for three days to work
with cattle. Red Bird Singing also does well in school. She'll
have her *Ilaheh* the next time the People have one. Deer Woman
and Carmen Rosario go to cook for their men with the cattle. I
look after the camp while they're gone. The women grind *iyah*
we have already collected. I'll use it to make you some bread.
Come, sit and talk with me in the tipi while I cook for you."

We shared much news as the sun hid in the western mountains. Luttrell had left as the reservation agent the previous
harvest. The new agent, Carroll, treated us with respect and
worked to make many things better for us. Juanita had decided
Carroll was a man who stayed true to his word and liked him.
She also told me she liked his woman, who was chief of the Indah School. Carroll did not force the Mescaleros to live in the
cabins Stottler had made them build. Now most lived in tipis.
Big chiefs in the east said that the Mescaleros ought to sell their
pony herd and buy good draft horses for heavy work like log-
ging so they could earn more money to buy supplies and other
things they needed.

I shook my head at this. Our ponies had become our pride
and wealth. Men sometimes died during arguments over horses.
We wouldn't give up our fine ponies for big slow horses that
could only pull a wagon or a log. But I was wrong. During the
next harvest, the Mescaleros sold five hundred ponies and
bought draft horses. Pride doesn't often stand in front of a man
feeding his family. I didn't sell my pony. I didn't farm, and I
didn't need a big, slow horse.

Rumors flew that Lipans in Chihuahua who had relatives among the Mescaleros in Magoosh's band would come to the reservation. James Carroll, with the priest in Tularosa, made it happen. The reservation needed those Lipans. We thought that maybe, if the Mescaleros became too few, the Indah chiefs would try to take our reservation and give us less land. Many Mescaleros were dying from the worms the Indah called tuberculosis. The Indah *di-yens* did not know how to make the People well again from these worms and neither did our own *di-yens*. It was a long time before any *di-yen* knew how to cure tuberculosis.

I told Juanita about Moon and how Redondo did now that he was off the *tsach*. Moon, a good mother, taught him well, and I was proud of her. Juanita was glad for her sister and me and smiled, but I saw longing in her eyes for her own child.

Soon, I rode with Rufus and Hombrecito to take vengeance on Big White Hat, Bitághaa' Lichoo', and their riders in an ambush in Dog Canyon. We killed all but one of them, but we lost Rufus. Only Bitághaa' Lichoo' escaped that day. I ran him down and took off his head the next morning. After we buried Rufus, Hombrecito decided to travel with me to Kitsizil Lichoo's camp and live among the warriors there. He stayed four harvests. Hombrecito has read me his own account of how we killed those men. In his paper tracks he included my story of Bitághaa' Lichoo's end and how we later took Oliver Lee, and he decided to let him live. He also tells of his time in Kitsizil Lichoo's camp. His words were true, so I'll leave the telling of these things to him.

CHAPTER 24
TIMES OF CHANGE

Juanita gave me another son. He laughed often, and we named him Hidloh (He Laughs). They named him John at the Indah School, and he is called John Hidloh on the reservation. The Indah School had little left to teach Híghâh, who they had named David, and Juanita and I thought they would let him return to live in our tipi. Agent Carroll sent for me one day to have a talk in his office.

He said, "Yellow Boy, your son, David . . ." He saw me frown and then used his proper name. "Your son, Híghâh, has much light behind his eyes. He reads and can make tracks on paper as well as anyone his teachers have taught, and he can do sums in his head correctly without making tracks on paper. He doesn't forget anything."

I nodded. Apache children, first taught at their mother's knee, learn never to forget any detail. Agent Carroll looked in my eyes, almost to the point of insult, but then looked away. "My wife leads the teachers at the school here. She watches how Híghâh helps teach the other children these things and knows he has much light behind his eyes. She wants him to go to a faraway school where he can learn much more than we can teach him. She thinks maybe he might learn to be a teacher and come back here to the school. I think she's right. Unlike some agents, I won't send him away without your consent. I have too much respect for the Mescaleros, for you, Juanita, and Híghâh to do this. I ask you to let me send him to a school where he can learn much more than he can at Mescalero and do all the things with his mind Ussen has given him power to do, maybe even to teach other Apache children, maybe come back here to do this. Will you let him go? I know it's a hard thing for you to consider. Speak with Juanita about this and think on it. Tell me your answer by the next moon."

I looked at the floor, angry the Indah wanted to send away my oldest child, thinking I might never see him again. I wanted to tell him no, but Carroll was a good man. We had become friends, not as I had been with Blazer or Rufus, but I trusted Carroll to speak the truth and do the right thing. He was a man of honor. I looked Agent Carroll in the eye as the Indahs expected when you told them the truth. "I'll speak to Juanita. I don't like this, and neither will she."

Agent Carroll wanted to send Híghâh far away when he was twelve harvests. By that age in the old days, he would have been hunting rabbits and other small animals, training for war and raiding, learning to handle horses, and making his body strong to endure much. But he had been in the Indah School for seven harvests and had learned few things an Apache boy his age should know. My friends Kah and Beela-chezzi, and his uncle Knows Horses, could train him to hunt and use weapons and condition him physically, but that should have started soon after he was off the *tsach*. Now I doubted that he could ever become a warrior. Then I realized that, on the reservation, most of the children his age had also been in the hated reservation school. He would not be behind anyone his age. None of them would ever have the heart or skills of a true Apache warrior. It was hard to think on this, but it was true. My heart was heavy with sadness when I understood it.

Juanita didn't want him to go to a faraway school either, but she had a child on the *tsach*. She could no longer watch the reservation school to see Híghâh when he passed down the school paths. We spoke about Híghâh over evening meals or as we sat by the fire, she making her baskets or nursing Hidloh, I cleaning my rifle or making arrows to share with Hombrecito. We finally understood our days, the days when we and our People were free to live as we wanted within the reservation, were gone forever for our young and would pass soon enough forever for the old Apaches. The Indeh, our People, had to live on Indah land, our own land they had taken from us and given a little back. But it was like they had given us a grain of sand when once we owned the desert. To be free in the coming days, our People had to be better and quicker thinking than the Indah believed we were. Our children had to learn everything the Indah could and would teach them and more. They had to learn to be like Coyote, the trickster, to survive as a People in the land of the Indah.

At last, we understood why our children must go to the Indah School and learn all the Indah would teach them. We spoke with Híghâh about this and the need to go away to another Indah School. He said he was ready to learn what the Indah could teach him and that he would come back to us. I hoped he would, but no one knows the mind of Ussen except Ussen.

We let Agent Carroll carry Híghâh to the iron wagon in Tularosa for his ride to the faraway school. It would be eight harvests before we saw our first son again.

I continued to ride the moons between my wives, until the harvest time the Indah call 1906, when Moon on the Water had a dream. It was like the ones she had in Mescalero where Blue Coats watched her disappearing in the stone corral filled with horse dirt, except in this dream she didn't sink out of sight, but found her footing, stood straight, and walked out of the dirt to the Río Tularosa where she washed herself clean. Returning to the corral, she found the soldiers gone.

She told me of the dream and said, "Husband, I believe the bad dream that haunted me like a ghost is no more. I'm ready to live again in Mescalero with my sister, Juanita, and our sons Redondo and Hidloh. Take us back to Mescalero."

There was much to do before we returned to Mescalero. Moon made the things she wanted and needed to keep ready for pack animals, and gave many gifts to those in camp who had helped her while I was gone. I had to find a pack frame for our things and also a mule to carry it. I spoke with the men in camp and met with Kitsizil Lichoo', who already knew from his wives that we planned to leave. We sat by his fire as the sun hid in the west, smoked, and remembered old times. I told him we would depart his camp because Moon believed her bad Mescalero dream had left her. He was happy for her, but he said his heart was heavy to see us go.

He asked if Hombrecito was leaving, too, and hoped that he would stay. I told him we had not spoken yet, but that there was a blood-revenge debt still to be paid, and I guessed he would go. I spoke with Running Wolf and told him I owed him much for the care he had given Moon while I was gone, and that I was proud of the way he had proved himself. He had become one of Kitsizil Lichoo's best warriors. I told him I would tell Beela-chezzi his son was admired and respected in Kitsizil Lichoo's camp, and that he and Blue Flower should visit and not forget Beela-chezzi and Carmen Rosario. He promised they would always remember them and come when the time was blessed by Ussen.

I smoked and talked with Hombrecito and told him what I planned. I told him Kitsizil Lichoo' hoped he would stay, but understood his need to return with me to avenge his father if he chose to go. Hombrecito did not hesitate, but said, "It's time to settle with Oliver Lee. I'll return with you and your family."

In the Season of Large Fruit, Hombrecito, Moon, Redondo, and I left the camp of Kitsizil Lichoo' and returned to Mescalero. In the harvests when I rode alone back to Juanita, I had made four different trails between the camp and Mescalero and never used the same one two times in a row. No more Comanche witches sent by Ojo Verde tried to kill me. At least none had attacked me since I had killed the witch on the playa near the border in the Animas Valley. On many occasions, before my trips, Lola Mes would, as Juanita requested, make medicine to protect me from Ojo Verde. Still, in all that time of keeping vigilant, I knew Ojo Verde would one day try to take her revenge against me.

Hombrecito left our trail to go to Rufus's rancho when we saw the great river. As my Blue Mountains family approached our reservation home, Juanita saw us coming up the little creek that ran down the center of the canyon. She stared for the length of a breath, and then her fingers covered her lips. She spoke to Hidloh, and he turned to look at us.

Moon saw her sister and raced past me to stop her pony in the middle of the stream, slid off, and, splashing across the water, ran to Juanita, laughing. My wives, long separated sisters, hugged each other with water in their eyes. I heard Moon say in a loud, happy voice, "Sister, the dream haunts me no more!" She was loud enough that Deer Woman and Carmen Rosario, who were drying meat up the canyon, heard her and came running. Soon there were four excited women all trying to talk at the same time, while two little boys shyly studied the ground at their mothers' feet.

Juanita held up her hands and, asking for quiet, said, "Sisters of the camp, my blood sister, haunted many harvests by an evil dream, returns to stay and brings our family a new son and brother. My heart sings. Let us feast and celebrate tonight when Kah and Beela-chezzi return."

Much work preparing food happened in a short time while I unloaded the ponies and mules and rubbed them down. As the sun began hiding behind the mountains, sending long shafts of yellow light through the tops of the tall trees, Kah and Beela-chezzi returned with a deer Kah had taken.

We feasted and ate much. Kah and Beela-chezzi laughed and played with my sons and made them ready for sleep in their blankets. The women talked and shared stories by the fire in Juanita's tipi, and the men and I sat together by the fire outside. I lighted a cigarro, and we smoked to the four directions. Cool air, like water down a slow creek, washed down the canyon and made the yellow and orange light and heat from the fire feel good.

Kah said, "So Yellow Boy returns with a son and wife and rides no more to the camp of Kitsizil Lichoo'? *Enjuh.* Now our camp grows much stronger. Your children are the only ones in camp. Redondo may be forced to go to the Indah School soon, but you will still have Hidloh for a while."

Beela-chezzi shook his head and poured more coffee in his ancient *pesh* (iron) cup with many dents. "It's a sad thing to lose a child to the Indah School. The agent, Luttrell, sent the tribal police and made me send my daughter, Hawú dat'éhe (Quiet Dove), to the Indah School when she was six harvests, and that was three harvests ago. Now, in two or three harvests, she will approach the time when her *Haheh* might be given, and she is fast losing her ability to speak the words of her grandfathers."

Kah nodded. "For a boy like Para-dee-ah-tran, who was close to being a man when Luttrell made us send him to the Indah

School, a few harvests in the Indah School might be a good thing for learning to read and make the Indah tracks on paper. But he still remembers the language of the grandfathers and speaks it well. Now he works with Almer Blazer at *La Máquina* and looks over Apache girls for a good wife like a man should. But Red Bird Singing started at the school when she was about Hawú dat'éhe's age now. She is nearly seventeen harvests and will have her *Haheh* at the next gathering of the People during the Season of Large Leaves. Many men watch her when we go to the agency store. Her looks are good, but she does not have the manners of a good Apache girl and doesn't speak our words good. But at least nearly all the girls who will be in her *Haheh* have the same problems. Maybe the men won't care. I would, and I worry no man will want her for a long time. The Indah are ruining our children's futures."

Many coyotes were calling that night. I wondered if their cries were a sign of things to come. At last, Kah asked, "Did Hombrecito stay with Kitsizil Lichoo' or return with you?"

"He returned with me to claim the blood he believes Oliver Lee owes him for ordering the death of his father. When Lee is no more, Hombrecito will return to his mother. He watches and studies Lee now. Soon I'll help him catch Lee."

Chapter 25
Hombrecito Makes Choices

We took Lee in the middle of the night at the top of San Agustin Pass when he didn't expect it. By the time the sun was making the eastern mountains glow, we had him, tied to a post, at Rufus's rancho. Proud, strong, and unafraid, he watched us make the fire. I thought, *Enjuh, he'll last a long time when the fire and knife work begin.*

Hombrecito offered Lee a quick death if he spoke the truth, a very slow one if he lied. Lee asked for coffee and said he would speak what he knew. He told us Bitághaa' Lichoo' came to his ranch and asked for money because he had just killed Lee's worst enemy. Lee said he beat Bitághaa' Lichoo' for killing Albert Fountain and warned him he would kill him if he returned to his ranch, because people would believe that he, Lee, had killed Fountain and his son.

All Lee's words and their telling sounded true. Hombrecito hesitated to kill him. He asked that I watch Lee while he went to the porch on Rufus's shack—for him, a place of wisdom. There he asked Ussen to guide his thinking. I told Hombrecito Lee would stay tied to the post until he returned.

Lee watched Hombrecito walk down the trail toward Rufus's house and said, "The boy having second thoughts about killin' me, Chief?"

"He goes for wisdom. Maybe so he kills you, maybe so you live. You run, you die. That is all I have to say."

Lee made a smile with half his face, nodded he understood, and asked for more coffee. I gave it to him. Then I sat facing him with the Yellow Boy rifle cocked and ready to kill him if he tried to run.

In face-to-face fighting, always watch your opponent's eyes. Good warriors learn this from the time they can walk. I watched Lee's eyes, and he watched mine as he slurped his coffee. He was a powerful warrior, strong, and with much light behind his eyes. By and by, he looked away, puffed his cheeks and blew, and again asked for more coffee. I filled his cup and then sat down to continue watching him, with my rifle cocked and a finger on the trigger.

He said, "Chief, I've heard some powerful stories about your skill with that old Henry rifle. Where'd you learn to shoot?"

"Rufus teaches me, and Ussen speaks and sends spirits to visit me there." I pointed with my nose toward the mountain behind him, where Ussen had given me my Power in the middle of a great storm. "My rifle and I are one. Bullet goes where I look. I use my Power for the People. I'm a killer of witches. I shoot out their eyes when I kill them, so they wander blind forever in the Happy Land. Maybe I shoot out your eyes, Lee. Maybe you go to the Happy Land blind."

Lee puckered his lips in a noiseless whistle. "Don't reckon that'll be necessary. I ain't no witch, and I ain't runnin'."

Lee watched the sunlight creep down the canyon walls and said nothing. When his gaze came back to mine, he said, "Chief, you boys hid out pretty good these last four years or so. Ain't nobody I know seen either of you around these parts. Where you been? Hidin' out on Sierra Blanca?"

I shook my head. "No. Stay with Apaches in Blue Mountains."

His brow wrinkled in surprise. "You mean, twenty years after Geronimo surrendered, there are still Apaches in the Sierra Madre? I've heard tales about Apaches raidin' ranches over in the boot heel, but I always figured it was just some that sneaked off from San Carlos, or maybe Massai or Apache Kid or both."

"Many Apaches still in Blue Mountains. Hide good. Nakai-yes no find. Nakai-yes afraid to go in mountains. They meet Apaches, no come back. Apaches in mountains take hacendado cattle on llano. Sell some to *Tejanos*. Keep others for meat and hides. Hard life, but more better than one Geronimo and Chiricahuas have as prisoners at the Blue Coat fort next to Comanche and Kiowa reservation."

Lee nodded. "I hear tell they keep a pretty tight rein on the Chiricahuas over to Fort Sill. Guess they need to do that, with that old murderer Geronimo still livin'. He's the reason they ain't been turned loose yet, and won't be until he's in the ground."

"Hmmph. Maybe so."

We spoke of many things that day. I learned much from Lee about how the Indahs planned to steal reservation land as they had tried to steal his. Some of this I had already heard from stories the People told at Mescalero. He warned me to watch the reservation agents. They did what the chiefs in the east told them to do, not what they should for the Mescaleros.

As the sun was falling behind the far Florida Mountains, Hombrecito returned. Wisdom told him not to kill Oliver Lee, but he warned Lee that if he ever learned Lee was involved in the murder of his father, Lee would die and never hear the bullet that killed him. Hombrecito let Lee go, and, after listening to him, I was glad he did. In the harvests that followed, Hombrecito was never sorry he allowed Lee to live.

Hombrecito lived at Rufus's rancho through the Ghost Face and Season of Little Eagles after we let Lee loose, and then he rode to Las Cruces. He showed his mother he still lived, but he never let her tell his brothers and sisters. She convinced him he should be an Indah *di-yen* and helped him enter a *di-yen* school to learn Indah *di-yen* medicines, tools, and ceremonies. The school was far away in the west, by the big water. He told me he would be gone many harvests.

He came to the reservation in the Season of Large Fruit to leave his great black horse he called Satanas. We had taken him from the Comacho rancho in Chihuahua during the days he lived in the camp of Kitsizil-Lichoo' in the Blue Mountains, along with his saddle and bridle trimmed in *pesh-lickoyee* (silver). Hombrecito also left the shoots-today-kills-tomorrow rifle, and other things he wanted me to save for his return. We sat by the fire outside my wives' tipi and talked, while Redondo and Hid-loh played in the creek, and Juanita and Moon worked on their baskets in the tipi.

I lighted a cigarro, smoked to the four directions, and passed it to Hombrecito. The night breeze down the shadow-filled canyon was cool, and the fire felt warm and good. There was laughter from Kah's tipi as he and Deer Woman had an evening meal. Beela-chezzi and Carmen Rosario had gone to the Blue Mountains to spend time with Running Wolf and Blue Flower. In the darkness, the tipis scattered in the canyon with firelight showing around their bottoms looked like glowing oil lanterns. It was a place of peace.

I said, "So, Hombrecito, you learn Indah *di-yen* ceremonies as your mother asks. This you want to do? Or you do this to please her?"

A wolf howled as Hombrecito shook his head and said, "No, I do this to please myself. You and Rufus taught me many harvests ago that if I'm not happy with my choices, no one else will be either. If I had known *di-yen* ways, I might have saved Rufus, or my woman Rafaela, or any number of the People here on the reservation who left too soon for the Happy Land. When

I return, the Mescaleros can always expect me to help them if I can."

I smiled as Geronimo's advice about saving an Indah boy who would help our People floated across my mind. I said, "*Enjuh*. Learn much powerful medicine, Hombrecito."

I paused for a moment to listen. My sons were playing war by the creek. I had told them to be careful throwing rocks, but young ones sometimes forget the words of their fathers. Juanita stuck her head out of the tipi and called for them to come in for the night, and they came running.

"Before you leave, I think I should tell you a true story. Will you listen?"

"I will listen."

I told Hombrecito the story of my meeting with Geronimo twenty-five harvests ago, when I was an Apache Scout for Nantan Lupan and Al Sieber, who was Chief of Scouts. Geronimo told me, "A time comes you'll need to help an Indah boy who will help our people."

Hombrecito frowned and said, "Am I the Indah boy Geronimo meant?"

"I'll add another piece to the story, then you can decide for yourself."

I told him of my dream of being an eagle flying over the basin when I slept by the mountain, of my vision at the rancho of Rufus Pike, and how everything the dream showed me looked just like what I saw when Bitághaa' Lichoo' killed his father.

Hombrecito sat by the fire and stared at the flames a long time, slowly shaking his head. At last, he said, "Yellow Boy, I think I'm the child of your dream and the one Geronimo told you to help." He waved his hand parallel to the ground. "It's a good thing, and I'll help the People the rest of my days."

"*Enjuh*. Hear me well. Healing the People will mean more than just stopping their sickness. The agency chiefs bring Indah *di-yens* to the reservation to heal our sickness. Still, too many of the People go to the Happy Place before they should. If the Lipans had not come from Mexico three harvests ago, the Indah chiefs in the east would have told us we had too much land and given it away to their amigos. We need more People here. Maybe the army chiefs will let the Chiricahuas out of their prison and they will come here. Only Ussen knows if this is so. We need all the *di-yens* who will help us. Come back to us, Hombrecito. You'll help give us new life."

"This I will do, Yellow Boy. I speak straight."

We spoke about many other things long into the night before the fire burned low, and we went to our blankets.

As the sun poured gold over the canyon edges, Hombrecito and I rode in the cold mountain air down to Tularosa. At the train station, he said, "I'll see you and your family again when I can." I waved my hand parallel to the ground and said, "It will be a good harvest time when our eyes see you." He climbed on the iron wagon, and I watched its black smoke fade in the distance, carrying him away.

CHAPTER 26
A WHITE EYE DISAPPEARS

Agent James Carroll treated the People with respect, kept his word, and didn't try to force our children to live like the Indah. He reminded me of Agent Llewellyn, who the People called *Tata* Crooked Nose. In the Season of Earth Is Reddish Brown, soon after Hombrecito left on the iron wagon, James Carroll asked me to join the tribal police again, and I agreed. This happened in the harvest time the Indah call 1907.

The Ghost Face that followed came with hard cold, but little snow. Deer and elk stayed low in the good grazing country, making it a time for good hunting. I brought meat often to the fire of my wives and children. With hunting and my tribal policeman's pay, my family and I had enough to eat and warm blankets. We had all we needed.

Each time I took my women to the agency store to buy our rations, I remembered the days at Bosque Redondo when I was five harvests, and went with my mother to collect our rations of bad meat, wormy cornmeal, thin blankets, and cups and buckets for the bitter water from the *río* the Indah called Pecos. My mother told the soldier giving us those rations she needed more. The soldier said, "Take it or leave it; there ain't no more." The army wouldn't let us hunt or take mescal from the llano for more to eat. We were close to starvation when we all left Bosque Redondo one night and scattered to the four directions like seeds in the wind. My family went south to Cha's camp in the Guadalupe Mountains. Free at last, my father, on raids with

Cha's warriors, took what we needed and wanted from the Indah and *Nakai-yes*, and we lived much better. We were never hungry and had good things like rifles that could kill at much greater distances than our bows.

When the survivors of Sangre del Diablo's massacre of Cha's camp and I came to the new reservation in the mountains the Indah call Sacramento, the agents again gave us rations. These rations were better than those at Bosque Redondo, but most agents cheated us by buying poor tools and thin blankets and keeping the money they saved. They also made money by selling part of our rations to storekeepers in the Indah villages.

Tata Crooked Nose, who never cheated us, bought herds of cattle for the Mescalero and Jicarilla then on the reservation. The People ate most of the cattle rather than letting them increase to sell for money. But a few Mescaleros understood the value of making their part of the herd grow. Boys like Yibá, who married my adopted sister, Lucky Star, had learned to protect and manage their cattle herds to make money for themselves and those who helped them.

They told me they were having a good harvest time when I again became a policeman. Jamen Carroll ordered the tribal police to help protect Mescalero cattle from Indah thieves, and we did.

Since the beginning of the reservation, Indah ranchers had used good Mescalero pasture grass to fatten their cattle. For a long time, they took our grass without paying, while we made do with rations the Indah chiefs in the east gave us and with what we could harvest and hunt. A harvest came when an agent—Beela-chezzi said it was Stottler—told the ranchers they must pay to use our pastures. Some ranchers paid; some didn't. The agents weren't strong enough to make sure the ranchers didn't cheat on their agreements. They knew there would be big trouble if they asked Indah police to come on the reservation and count all the cattle, including the People's. The trouble would grow if the tribal police counted Indah rancher cattle grazing on the reservation. The People understood this. They decided that if the ranchers didn't catch them, then it was all right to take stray Indah cattle for meat as a kind of payment, as long as they weren't caught. The ranchers who didn't pay and lost a few cattle didn't complain to the agent or the Indah police. If they did complain, they knew we would catch them cheating us and make them pay. It was a game the ranchers and the Mescalero played. Both sides knew the rules very well and played the game, though the rules were never written down or spoken.

I knew the Circle H Ranch chief, Roy McLane. He was a man of his word, treated the People with respect, and told his vaqueros they must do the same. The People spoke well of Roy McLane. He used one of the biggest pastures on the reservation for his cattle, and he paid for the grass.

One day in the Ghost Face of the harvest time the Indah call 1908, I met Roy McLane on the wagon road between Fort Stanton and the Mescalero agency. The sun was near to touching the western mountains as it painted clouds in oranges, blood reds, and purple, and sent streams of bright yellow light through the tops of the trees. Cold air snapped and chewed at fingers and toes, but there was no smell of coming snow. Roy McLane rode north to his ranch house; I, south to my tipi, after carrying papers to Fort Stanton for Agent Carroll. We stopped to talk, the cold air making our breath look like steam from a cooking pot.

Roy McLane pulled his pony to a stop, waved his hand parallel to the ground, and said, "*Nish'ii*' (I see you), Yellow Boy."

I returned his hand wave. "*Nish'ii*', Roy McLane." I knew he or one of his vaqueros checked the Circle H cattle in our pasture every day or two in the time of the Ghost Face, and seeing him didn't surprise me.

Roy McLane nodded and reached in his coat for paper and *tobaho*. "Things calm down to the agency?"

He rolled the *tobaho* in a thin Indah paper and lighted the cigarette, cupping the match in his hands as a shield against the wind.

"Usual arguments and fights over monte games, usual men finding whiskey and getting drunk, but no killings. Pretty quiet, I think."

He blew his first draw of smoke toward the sky and handed the cigarette to me.

"How's your family? I ain't seen your boys in a while. Bet they're getting big."

I took a couple of puffs and handed the cigarette back.

"My wives work good together. Boys play hard. Grow strong."

"That's good. My younger brother's visiting me from Oklahoma. He's a rodeo rider, but ain't had much time to learn anything about ranchin' in this part of the country."

"Hmmph. You teach him good. You know ways of cattle."

"Well, I'm working on it." He curled his fingers into his palm and blew in the hole. "Dang, it's cold, ain't it? Best we'd be gettin' on down the road. *Adios.*"

"See you under a new sun, Roy McLane."

He touched his fingers to his hat, but before he started his pony, he said, "By the way, I was ridin' fence this afternoon and found a gate in the wire left open, and a few cows had gotten out. I'll send somebody after 'em tomorrow. Now that I think about it, I think I'll send my brother. He's still green, but he can handle it and needs to learn the country."

I nodded, *"Enjuh."*

The next sun, I spoke with Almer Blazer at the sawmill about one of the People working for him who had disappeared after a fight over a monte game. He asked me to find him. While we talked, we saw a young Indah ride over the ridge in front of us. His big roan with a Circle H brand carried him as he leaned over his saddle horn studying the frozen ground for tracks.

Almer watched him until he disappeared behind the ridge and said, "Why's that Circle H rider tracking on the reservation? I don't think I've ever seen him before."

"Last sun Roy McLane say some cows leave big Mescalero pasture. This sun, he send younger brother for cattle. Cattle must have run far. He comes back with loose cattle by and by."

Blazer shook his head. "Well, I haven't seen any loose cattle run through here since dawn. They got down here from that pasture mighty fast without being driven. They get out like that, they usually just wander around lookin' for grass. Something ain't right, but we'll see."

Blazer and I finished our talk, and I rode off to find the man I sought.

The sun was sending shafts of golden light through the trees, and mists were rising on the eastern ridges. It was so cold birds stayed close together in the trees. All the iron stoves burning wood and black rocks held hot fires in the agency *casas*. Two other policemen and I sat with James Carroll in his workplace, where he made tracks on paper and spoke of work we had done the last three suns.

Besides learning about thieves and fights over monte games, Carroll wanted to know if the old ones had enough rations for the cold weather, and if any were so sick they needed the Indah *di-yen*.

After we shook our heads, he said, "I was talking to Almer Blazer yesterday afternoon about seeing the McLane boy tracking a few cows that got out of their pasture. Any of you see him come back through yesterday evening with the Circle H's stock?"

We looked at each other and shook our heads. James Carroll frowned. "I wonder how we missed him. Surely he came back through here sometime yesterday."

I thought, *Almer Blazer spoke true. Something's not right. Those cattle wouldn't wander this far in a night. Maybe they run from a cougar, and it's taken one of them.*

We heard the agency door squeak open and slam shut, caught by the blowing wind. *Vaquero* boots came thumping down the hall toward James Carroll's office. We all turned toward the open door to see a tall, Indah vaquero, wrapped in a heavy, wool coat with a blue *rebozo* under his hat and tied around his ears and chin and another around his neck. His face was red from riding a long time in the cold air. It was Roy McLane.

Nodding and pulling off his gloves, he said, "Mr. Carroll, Officers."

James Carroll stood, and they shook hands. Then we tribal policemen stood and each pumped Roy McLane's hand.

James Carroll offered him a spare chair and said, "We were just talking about seeing your brother go over the ridge after stray cattle."

As he sat down, Roy McLane pulled off his hat and *rebozo*. He puffed his cheeks and shook his head. "He didn't make it back last night. I'm looking for him now and just stopped by to find out if you'd seen any sign of him since yesterday."

James Carroll frowned and shook his head. "I was just asking these policemen, and none of them have seen him. Have you asked Almer Blazer? I think he was probably the last one to see him go over the back ridge yesterday."

McLane nodded and puffed his cheeks again. "Yeah, I saw him a little while ago just as he was goin' to the mill. He ain't seen him either. If you don't mind, I'll thaw out here for a few minutes and then hit the trail to find him. I'm sure he made it through the night all right. Maybe this little adventure will teach him to follow his back trail. Thanks for the help."

James Carroll glanced at us, then looked at Roy McLane and said, "Sure, help yourself to the stove any time. Good luck. I'm sure you'll find he's all right." But we policemen glanced at each other and knew something bad had happened.

CHAPTER 27
MURDER ON THE HIGH MOUNTAIN

Roy McLane soon left the agency and rode over the ridge, following the same path his brother had taken. The sun hung just above the western mountains, and the cold air's bite was growing stronger when he returned alone. I was tightening the cinch on my saddle when he rode up and swung down from his pony.

He looked over his saddle at me as he loosened his cinch and said, "Damn, it's cold. I about froze my tail off today."

I nodded. "Plenty cold. You find your brother and cattle?"

He shook his head. "Nope. I ain't much good at trackin'. As soon as the shadows started gettin' long, I lost his tracks. Ground is frozen harder than a rock, and there's not much sign. I'm going back tomorrow and'll pick up the tracks where I lost 'em. Could you and maybe another tracker help me tomorrow? I'll be glad to pay whatever is fair. But I need somebody who's a better tracker than me to follow his trail over that frozen ground."

"I go where James Carroll says I go."

"Come on then. Let's go talk to James Carroll, and then I have to take care of my horse and get over to Blazer's house for a meal and some rest."

James Carroll frowned when he saw Roy McLane without his brother, and he didn't hesitate to let me go with him as a tracker the next day. I nodded and said, "Beela-chezzi good tracker, better than me. You want him also?"

McLane, standing with his back next to James Carroll's

wood-burning stove, sniffed and said, "Sure, whatever the boss says."

James Carroll nodded, "All right, Yellow Boy. You go with Mr. McLane, and ask Beela-chezzi to come with you. Roy, between those two men, you should find him. Check back here with me tomorrow when you do. You can meet here at sunrise before you leave. Does that suit you, Roy?"

"Yes, sir. That'll do just fine. See you boys in the morning."

The next day, Beela-chezzi and I rode along with Roy McLane and picked up the trail where he lost it the day before. It was a hard trail to follow, and the setting sun that day caught us still without finding the boy. The next day, we followed the pony horseshoe tracks up a ridgeline where they seemed to be leading the day before. The tracks crossed a large place of flat stone and then disappeared. We had to backtrack and circle around before we found them again. Besides the McLane boy's horseshoe tracks and those of two cows we were following, Beela-chezzi and I found another set of horse tracks—unshod horse tracks—which meant a Mescalero had to be driving the cattle up the ridge, probably to some hidden draw for slaughter and making meat. I saw sadness in Roy McLane's eyes when I told him this. We both knew what this meant.

We followed the trail winding through patches of snow and tall trees, low brush, and stone flats until near the time of no shadows, when we saw a pony nibbling on brush by the trail. Its reins tangled in the forks of a fallen tree; it stood with its tail turned to the mountain wind. Roy McLane offered it water from his hat, which it greedily drank. While Roy McLane tended the horse, Beela-chezzi and I followed the horse's back trail. Its direction and the distance between its tracks showed that it had run from a little shallow draw, which was not visible from the main ridge trail.

At the bottom of the draw, we found the frozen body of Roy McLane's brother lying on his back by the side of the trail. His eyes were wide with surprise. Under his left eye was a round bullet hole, and the backside of his skull was blown away. On the other side of the trail, a hatchet stood erect, dropped with the top of its blade buried in the frozen ground, its smooth brown handle a stake showing where the boy had fallen. I nose-pointed for Beela-chezzi to bring Roy McLane.

A little farther on from the body lay the partially butchered carcass of one of McLane's cows on its back, shot between the eyes for slaughter, its head pointing downhill and its red-haired hide pulled back enough to get at good cuts of meat. A single moccasin print showed in the frozen blood drained from the cow's slit throat. An obvious path of someone hurrying down the draw led through the brush and then disappeared on the rocks below.

Roy McLane and Beela-chezzi came quick. When Roy McLane got to the body, he stared at the face, took a deep breath, and then shook his head. "That boy just wouldn't listen. Damn it! I must have told him a hundred times never to ride up on a man butchering a cow by himself in some out-of-the-way place, because he'll kill you in self-defense and ask questions later." He saw the hatchet handle, walked down to the partially butchered cow, looked around, and then said, "Well, it's pretty clear he must have surprised an Indian making meat and got killed for it. But how in blue blazes would an Apache not have heard him coming a mile away in this brush?" He puffed his cheeks and blew warm breath into his cupped hands. The wind passing through the tops of the trees shook the branches, making a low, sorrowful clacking sound like bones shaken in a bag.

Beela-chezzi and I looked at each other. We both knew that only an Apache who had no ears would not have heard the boy coming. If the Apache had ears, he would have slipped away. The only Apache we knew who couldn't hear was Kedinchin, who had also lost an eye many years ago to a witch. We said nothing to Roy McLane about him.

"Can you boys help me wrap my brother in a blanket and tie him across his saddle? It's going to be a long, cold ride down to the agency."

"Hmmph. Bring blanket. We help. Go to James Carroll. Maybe then we hunt one who kills boy."

Roy McLane nodded and walked back up the trail soon to return, bringing a blanket from the boy's horse. The body was frozen. We had to wrap it straight and stiff and tie it sideways on his saddle.

Roy McLane walked the area once more, looking at every detail. After he finished, we had a smoke before we mounted for the ride back down to the agency.

He said again, "I don't understand it. No Apache in these parts would kill a White Eye unless he was defending himself. Somehow, that boy managed to surprise whoever was butchering the cow. How in the world could that boy have done that to an Apache? I just don't understand it."

The ride down the mountain was slow, the wind cold, steady, and cutting. Men at the sawmill saw us come in sight as we dropped down over the last ridge. They paused to stare for a few breaths and then resumed their work when Almer Blazer stepped out on his porch to watch us.

We stopped at the agency and went inside. The warmth from the stoves was welcome, even as it left our faces stinging like being struck by blowing sand as we pulled off gloves, opened coats, and followed Roy McLane to James Carroll's workplace for making tracks on paper.

James Carroll was smoking a pipe, making Indah tracks on

paper, and speaking with his wife, who oversaw and taught at the reservation school. When she saw us at the doorway, she said, "I see you have business. I'll wait outside." She stepped back and motioned us in. Carroll looked up, laid down his pipe, and said, "You still haven't found the boy?"

I saw James Carroll's wife move to the door and knew she waited in the hall so she could hear what we said. Roy McLane pulled off his hat and *rebozo* as he slumped in a chair. "Oh, we found him, all right. Cold and stiff, shot through the head, and lying close to a half-butchered cow. Apparently, he had a hatchet in his hand because we found it stuck in the ground where he must have dropped it. Looks like he surprised somebody. I've told him and told him never to do that, not in this country, but he didn't listen, and it got him killed."

I heard James Carroll's wife suck in air.

"I know the Mescaleros. Ain't a one of 'em would kill a White Eye without bein' pushed into it. But how in the devil did that kid surprise an Apache with the ground cold and hard and bushes everywhere? Somethin' about this ain't right."

James Carroll glanced over at Beela-chezzi and me while Roy McLane spoke, but we showed no sign of what we thought.

Roy McLane said, "Be that as it may, whoever killed him has to be caught and tried. It may have been an accident, but whoever did it has to pay. Killing a kid like that ain't right, and I won't abide it. What do we have to do to get the sheriff from Alamogordo or the state police on the reservation for official business to catch the man or men who did it?"

James Carroll picked up his pipe, struck a match to relight it, and puffed until he had smoke again. He leaned back in his chair, looked at Beela-chezzi and me, and crossed his arms. "What do the tracks say?"

I said, "Tracks say what Roy McLane tells you. One man, no more, surprised with cow he takes that is not his. Kills boy.

Runs away."

James Carroll blew a stream of blue smoke toward the top of the room and looked Roy McLane straight in the eye. "Roy, sounds to me like the boy started this ruckus."

Roy McLane twisted his mouth and nodded.

"Roy, if I let the sheriff come up here on the reservation with a posse and start throwin' his weight around, tryin' to find out who killed your brother, they're gonna make these people angry, and there's likely to be big trouble. Your brother might not be the only White Eye killed over a cow, and there might be a few Mescaleros dead, too. I can't let that happen. We've got first-class tribal police here on the reservation. As long as things stay on the reservation, I'm gonna let them handle it. If the killer gets off the reservation, then all bets are off, and the sheriff can bring a posse along with 'em to track the killer down. What do you say?"

Roy McLane said nothing as he pulled out his *tabaho* and papers and rolled a cigarette, lighted it, and took a deep draw to blow the smoke out through his nose. He puffed his cheeks and looked at James Carroll, then glanced at Beela-chezzi and me.

He said, "All right, we'll do it your way. But I want to ride with your policemen here on the reservation, and I'll act as an intermediary with the sheriff's posse if your boys follow the trail off the reservation. Will that work?"

Carroll nodded. "That's okay with me. You go on home with your brother and take care of the burying services. I want Yellow Boy and Beela-chezzi to go back and see if they can follow where the killer ran. Maybe we'll find him still at home. In the meantime, I'm going to make some inquiries and get a posse ready. Meet me here in the office first thing in the morning in three days, and we'll get started."

Roy McLane said, "Sounds fair. I'll be here."

He stood, reached in his pocket, and brought out a gold

piece of Indah money that he laid in front of James Carroll. "That's a ten-dollar gold piece for Yellow Boy and Beela-chezzi. I'm much obliged for their help today. That's about twice what I pay my ranch hands for a day's work, but it was rugged up on that mountain, and I'd never have found that boy without 'em." He turned and nodded to us. "Thanks, boys. You've been a big help. Now, I got some sad work to do. See you in three days." We heard him say "Ma'am" to James Carroll's wife as he passed her in the hall.

We listened to his boot steps fade down the hall, and the front door opened and closed. James Carroll took Roy McLane's money, pulled out two pieces from his money box, and gave Beela-chezzi and me one each.

He said, "Each of those pieces is worth half the money Roy McLane left for you. I'm guessing that's all right with you?"

We nodded, happy to get some money for our families.

James Carroll sat back in his chair and thought, scratching his short face hair. After a while, he said, "Magoosh is the Lipan head man, and Peso and Sans Peur are Mescalero chiefs. First thing tomorrow, I'll send someone over to Magoosh's place and ask him to find out if there's anyone missing from his people, and to come in for a meeting with the Mescalero chiefs and me first light after the next sun. I'll send another policeman out to the Mescalero chiefs and ask them to check to see if any of their people are missing. Since you know as much as anybody about what seems to have happened where that beef was butchered, and you and Beela-chezzi are going to follow the trail away from where the killer was making meat, I want you to come in, too. Beela-chezzi, I'm mighty glad for your help."

I said, "Beela-chezzi and me ride to look at killer's trail first light tomorrow."

James Carroll said, "*Enjuh.* Now go to your wives."

When Beela-chezzi and I left the agency, the night had come, and the stars were out. It had been a long two suns, and the next would be a hard sun, too.

CHAPTER 28
APACHE POSSE

Magoosh, the Lipan chief, had lived many harvests and had great respect among the People. He had seen and done much in his time. James Carroll told me once that when Magoosh was a boy, he had seen the great *Tejano* Alamo battle between the White Eyes and *Nakai-yes*. Now at James Carroll's council, Magoosh, his eyes bright, most of his hair gone, except for a little over his ears, listened with an ear cocked in James Carroll's direction so as not to miss any of his words.

Peso, near the harvests of a grandfather, but still strong enough to follow a long trail in the worst of the Ghost Face; and Sans Peur, in his prime and youngest of the three chiefs, also leaned forward to hear every word from James Carroll, who spoke softly and without emotion as he told them all he knew about the killing of the McLane boy, often stopping to ask me to confirm what he said was true.

After he finished speaking, he looked at each of the chiefs and then said, "What do you think we should do?"

Only the fire burning in the stove made any noise; the iron, red with heat, straining and groaning against its straps as the chiefs looked at each other, their mouths set in hard, straight lines. Magoosh sat back in his chair, pulling *tobaho* and a thin paper from his pocket. With sure fingers and using only one hand, he rolled a cigarette. He struck a match with his thumbnail, a vaquero trick I had learned many harvests ago, lighted it, smoked to the four directions, and passed it to Peso, who smoked and passed it to Sans Peur. Everyone sitting around James Carroll's table had smoked when it reached me. I smoked to the four directions and returned the cigarette to Magoosh, who put out the bit that was left.

Now that smoke had been made for serious business, Magoosh said in an old man's whispery, commanding voice, "An Indah lawdog posse should stay off the reservation. They do not know us. We have good men. We've shown we can make a posse and find who did this killing without the Indah. Let's choose warriors for a posse to go after the one who might yet give the Indah a reason to wipe us out."

There were grunts of approval, including my own. James Carroll, nodding his agreement, looked around the room and asked, "Does anyone here know who might have killed the McLane boy?" We all looked at each other, but shook our heads in answer to his question.

James Carroll spread the fingers of one hand to touch those of the other, making them look like the ribs of a cabin roof. He sat thinking for a few breaths before saying, "Are the tipis of any of your People empty since three suns ago?"

Magoosh slowly shook his head. "All my people are in their tipis, sitting close to their fires."

Peso and Sans Peur looked at each other.

Peso frowned and said, "I know the tipi of Kedinchin and his woman Minnie stands empty. I thought it strange they travel in the Ghost Face when they left. But Kedinchin has always been strange since he lost his eye, the one that burst from a fight he had with a witch many harvests ago. Even his ears have become as stones. For two suns, Kedinchin and Minnie are gone. All others in my camp sit by their fires. Minnie's tipi stands alone on a ridge close by. Maybe they see Yellow Boy and Beela-chezzi bring in stiff body of McLane boy gone to Happy Land. Maybe they go then."

Sans Peur shook his head and said, "All my People stay by their tipi fires. Only ones who leave are Kedinchin and Minnie. Kedinchin has no fear to take Indah beef. Ghost Face hard time. Boy fool to surprise Kedinchin when he makes meat, but Kedinchin easy to surprise. Boy probably very close when Kedinchin sees. No time to think. No time to run off. Shoots first then ask who comes. Now Kedinchin runs."

Leaning against the doorway, listening to Sans Peur, I nodded. If Kedinchin, while butchering an Indah cow, killed the McLane boy, he knew the Indah would demand that he be hanged. Beela-chezzi and I had followed his horse tracks away from where he killed the boy. They went east away from the agency. He stopped twice and dismounted to kneel behind bushes to face his tracks. He planned to ambush anyone following him. Nobody followed. When he understood the boy alone surprised him, he turned toward his tipi fire. Kedinchin might be half blind and totally deaf, but he was Apache: smart and deadly, dangerous to track.

James Carroll filled and lighted his pipe. When he had a good coal, he blew a puff toward the roof, and, tilting his chair back against the wall, said, "I thought it might be Kedinchin. I've told the boy's brother, Roy McLane, that the tribal police and our chiefs can take care of this business, and he agreed with me, but he asked to go along with the posse. Roy McLane speaks straight with the People and pays his grazing fees without cheating you. I told him he could ride with the tribal police. I told the sheriff in Alamogordo about the killing of Roy McLane's brother here on the reservation. He wanted to send a posse, but I told him we'd take care of it. He agreed, but he wants to send a deputy and a state policeman along with Roy McLane to report back what we do. If we follow Kedinchin off the reservation, then a posse of state police will join you."

There were frowns and narrowed eyes on every face around the circle.

I said, "So the Indah sheriff didn't think we would speak true about catching the killer?"

James Carroll shook his head. "I didn't think you would care if they went with you, and it would prove you speak with straight tongues." He paused and looked at all three chiefs, whose faces became masks that said nothing of their thinking. "I want Yellow Boy to go because he's a policeman, knows Kedinchin's tracks, and he's the best shot on the reservation. Sans Peur, I ask that you choose the rest of the posse and lead it. Who do you want to go?"

Sans Peur crossed his arms and looked at Magoosh and Peso before he stared at the floor a few breaths and then said, "All chiefs should go. Kedinchin and Minnie will run south, head for the Blue Mountains in Mexico, maybe hide in the foothills around Janos until the passes in the high mountains are clear of snow. We'll have a long, hard ride to catch 'em. They'll be three days ahead of us by the time we ride. I need men who have not grown soft on the reservation. My brother, Crook Neck—he tracks good, shoots good—I want. Muchacho Negro, Dana Evans, Antonio Joseph, and Caje are hard men who have known the inside of Indah jails, know all the tricks to escape, and track and shoot good—they should come. Willie Comanche, Elmer Wilson, and Sam Chino are good men and tribal police; let them come. Any other policemen you send besides them and Yellow Boy, we take."

Magoosh shook his head and stared down at James Carroll's table. When he looked up to see us all staring at him, he said with water at the edge of his eyes, "I can't go with these strong, young men. The cold makes my old bones ache and makes me too slow for a chase in the mountains and maybe across the desert into the land of the *Nakai-yes*. I've done my last chase with the young men. Let my son, Willie, go in my place." Sans Peur and Peso gazed at each other and nodded as they said, *"Enjuh."*

James Carroll looked at us all and said, *"Enjuh.* You have chosen well." He knocked the ashes out of his pipe and leaned back in his chair to say, "Roy McLane says he will keep you supplied with food wherever you go. Meet here at sunrise tomorrow. Be ready for a long, cold ride. Any questions?" He looked at each of us, and we all shook our heads. "I know you all will show us your great skill and bring Kedinchin back."

Mescaleros, including those Sans Peur wanted; the policemen James Carroll sent; Roy McLane, leading a pack mule loaded with food; a young deputy, who chewed his lip and kept rubbing his chaps with his gloved hands while he sat on his horse; and a quiet man with a big hat pulled down over his eyes, the state policeman, were at the agency ready to ride as the sun began to light the snow patches on the high ridges. James Carroll counted us and then saluted as we passed by him.

Peso led us to Minnie's tipi on a low ridge above the agency. Antonio Joseph and Muchacho Negro, the best trackers in the posse, rode a large circle around the tipi, and then, without stopping, headed down a back trail screened from the Tularosa Canyon wagon road by small ridges that ran toward Nogal Canyon, which in its lower parts near the agency, was about four hundred yards wide with good grass. It was used by many Mescaleros for the few riding ponies they had left.

Nogal Canyon began at Tularosa Canyon and worked its way south, narrowing and climbing about three thousand feet in ten or twelve miles to the top of the spine of the Sacramento Mountains near the village of Cloudcroft. There were many side canyons branching off Nogal where one might disappear. Kedinchin knew no Indah could ever find him in the rough country of the Sacramentos. He'd gambled the Apaches couldn't either.

The tracks said Kedinchin and Minnie had run to Nogal Canyon from their tipi, and that he had waited by the trail up the canyon while Minnie caught his best pony—he called him Star of the West—and another for herself before they followed the trail up Nogal Canyon. They stayed on the eastern side of the canyon away from the creek on the west side. The ground was frozen and left few signs of their passage.

Antonio Joseph and Muchacho Negro rode wide on either side of the tracks to be sure Kedinchin and Minnie didn't disappear up some side canyon. Caje ran along the trail, never faltering or doubting that it was headed south, but often having to run back, when he lost their tracks in the rocks or frozen ground, then running forward to pick up the trail again. It was slow, hard work in the brittle, cold wind sweeping down the canyon.

The rest of the posse rode up the middle of the canyon and stayed behind the trackers so the trail they followed wasn't disturbed. Kedinchin didn't push his ponies and seemed to be saving them. Sometimes Kedinchin and Minnie ran, leading their ponies. There were signs they stumbled and fell several times, but after each fall, they were up running again, never seeming to stop and rest. They kept on the winding canyon trail that climbed higher until near dark on the first day. Then he and Minnie took a branch of the canyon that swung out toward the western edge of the Sacramento Mountain cliffs and canyons and began descending slowly toward the basin. Losing the light, we made camp there near a small tank of water with a thin layer of ice, easy to break for our ponies, and ate the supplies Roy McLane brought for us.

We made no fire the first night out. Its light would make it too easy for Kedinchin or Minnie to see where we were. The cold had a strong bite there high in the mountains, and it grew worse as the sun left a slash of yellow light through the canyon wall shadows as it disappeared behind the San Andres Mountains far across the basin.

Roy McLane told Sans Peur to take all the food we needed for night and morning meals, because he planned to take the Indah policeman and stay the night with friends who had a place near Cloudcroft village. He said he and the deputy would return with more supplies the next morning and would ride on with us. Sans Peur nodded he understood, and, waving his hand toward Cloudcroft, said, "*Enjuh.* You go. We ride when good light comes."

We took our blankets and pulled a big pile of pine needles around and over us for cover so we could all eat and sleep together to share the warmth from our bodies against the Ghost Face cold. We fed our ponies the oats Roy McLane brought us. Then, shoulder-to-shoulder, we ate the jerky and canned fruit and potatoes. Some smoked, hiding the flame and glow on the cigarro tip, and talked a while before lying down next to those already sleeping and pulling the pine needle cover-up over themselves and the others.

I sat next to one of the best trackers, Muchacho Negro, and I offered him one of my cigarros as I readied to light mine. He accepted it with a nod and lighted his from the match I cupped in my hands. He said, "I'm glad you're with us. Kedinchin may be half-blind and stone deaf, but if we corner him with no escape, he'll fight and be hard to kill. Your good eyes and deadly rifle will help protect us."

"You think we catch 'em soon?"

Muchacho Negro took a deep draw on the cigarro, spat a piece of *tobaho* off his lips, and shook his head. "No. It will be a hard run. He knows we'll chase him. He runs straight and true. Tracks show he doesn't stop and look around. He knows where he goes. Kedinchin knows many deep canyons on the other side of Cloudcroft village where he can hide and slip away toward the land of the Nakai-yes or ambush us. Hard to track 'em. Many places for 'em to backtrack and get behind us. Many dangerous places. We go slow and careful. You be ready to shoot all the time past Cloudcroft." I nodded at his words. I had thought the same things.

CHAPTER 29
THE TRAIL TO HIGH ROLLS VILLAGE

The next morning we untangled ourselves from under the pine needles, broke the ice on the pool of water close by, watered and fed the ponies, and ate the rest of the provisions while we were wrapped in our blankets. We waited for the early morning shadows on the east side of the canyon to climb up the mountain enough to see trail signs.

Like dogs following a cougar, Caje, Muchacho Negro, and Antonio Joseph led us up the canyon. There weren't as many side canyons to slow us down as there had been the sun before, but the ground at the higher altitude was frozen even harder and that made it more difficult to track.

The canyon trail climbed steadily until it split, one branch headed up a steep path to the southwest, while the other went east around the ridge and was not as steep as the first. We sat on our ponies under some pines out of the wind and smoked while the trackers found Kedinchin and Minnie's trail. Antonio Joseph rode up the steeper of the two trails looking for signs. Caje took the other branch, but he had not ridden far when Antonio Joseph waved us up his trail. We waved for Caje to come back to the steeper trail.

As he turned back toward us, we saw Roy McLane behind him, leading two packhorses and followed by the Indah policemen. We waited while Caje joined Antonio Joseph, spoke for a short time with Roy McLane, and then we all followed Caje and Antonio Joseph up ahead on the steep trail. Muchacho

Negro hung back with us to check some possible side trails, but he found nothing. The trail became steeper, and the ponies worked to make the climb on the rough, icy ground. Near the top of the pass were more side canyon trails that Muchacho Negro checked, but again he found no signs of passage.

At the top of the pass, we rested the horses while the trackers again looked for trail signs in the whistling wind and bright, cold sunlight. Not far from the top of the pass, they found tracks heading down an arroyo that ended below in a big canyon that looked like a great, tree-covered slash across the mountains, leading down to the basin and white sands far below. The arroyo helped shield us from the cutting wind at the top of the pass as we rode down the ridge, but near the bottom, boulders blocked our way, as if giants had made a fence to stop us. We had to backtrack and ride our ponies up and around the boulder wall, and then back down. Antonio Joseph found the trail of Kedinchin and Minnie headed west through the canyon. I looked at the high ridges above us and thought, *This is the trail Kedinchin and Minnie will follow into the basin and then run for the land of the* Nakai-yes.

In a small clearing, near where the arroyo joined the big canyon, Muchacho Negro found the cold, black charred remains of a small, well-hidden fire, and in thawed dirt near where the fire had unlocked the frozen ground, moccasin tracks showed holes and outlines of toes. Kedinchin and Minnie were practically running barefoot.

The sun neared the horizon, and the high western side of the big canyon was already covered in heavy black shadows starting to reach over the trail. We camped for the night at the same place used by Kedinchin and Minnie. Roy McLane spoke for a short time with Sans Peur, and then he and the two Indah policemen unloaded our supplies and left for a ranch on a ride they could finish before full dark up the big canyon.

We again spread our blankets on a big pile of pine needles under some low junipers, made no fire, and sat down close together to eat. After we finished and some were pulling out their *tobaho* for a smoke, Sans Peur said in a low voice that we all could hear but wouldn't carry much farther, "We're close to the edge of the reservation on Indah maps. Tomorrow, we'll be off the reservation, and the Indah posse comes soon. Roy McLane told me the next sun he sends the deputy to tell the sheriff he can send his posse to ride with us. I think they come in two suns."

Weak light from a quarter-moon rising behind the northeast canyon wall filtered through the trees, and a lonesome wolf called from the high western ridge above us. Several of the warriors lighted their *tobaho*, me included, with match-fire cupped in their hands.

After a couple of puffs from his cigarette, Muchacho Negro said, "How do we treat this Indah posse? It's not right for them to take the man we hunt and hang him. Kedinchin is one of us. He deserves to die like a warrior, not like a dog, choked with a rope. He deserves a good death. We must kill him."

Sans Peur nodded and grunted in the dim light made by the smokers. "Hmmph. Muchacho Negro speaks true words. We won't let the Indah have him. We're Kedinchin's friends. He will die like a true warrior. Ussen will be glad to see him in the Happy Land, and Minnie will go back safe to Mescalero. Maybe she finds another man to take care of her. This is my word. It will be so."

The tips of all the smokes glowed bright in the darkness as the smokers drew deep on their *tobaho*, blew the smoke to the stars, and grunted they understood his words. When the *tobaho* was finished, we again pulled pine needles over our bodies, lying close together to share warmth. A white river of bright stars

233

ran across the sky high above the trees, and soon we slept in the cold, biting air.

After caring for our ponies and eating a meal at sunrise, we waited for the shadows from the eastern wall of the canyon to retreat enough to give the trackers the light they needed. Roy McLane came down the trail, leading two packhorses carrying supplies for another day. He said to Sans Peur, "Chief, I studied the map last night, and it shows we're off the reservation. I sent the White Eye policemen down to Alamogordo to tell the sheriff we're ready for his posse. I suspect they'll take the train up to High Rolls and wait for us there. My guess is that your man will cross the trail to Cloudcroft village some place around High Rolls or Mountain Park, and look for a hiding place in the mountains south. Or he might stay on the west side to get down into the basin, so he'n his woman can make a fast break for Mexico without being seen."

Sans Peur nodded. "We follow where the trail leads. Roy McLane thinks like a Mescalero. Catch 'em pretty quick, I think."

The ridges on either side of the canyon were high. There was no getting out of that canyon or finding a place to hide until the ridges opened up near High Rolls. The trackers and the following posse made good time. We passed a ranch house. An Indah woman and three children wrapped in blankets stood on the porch and watched us ride by. She had an old repeating rifle in her hands, and the children, wide-eyed and quiet, stood close to her. Her face relaxed from her hard-eyed squint to a smile, and she set the hammer on the rifle to safety when Roy McLane rode up and spoke to her. She shook her head at a question and then pointed to a spring on the east side of the canyon where we were welcome to water. Roy McLane tipped his hat to her in the strange way Indah do to acknowledge their women, and then rode down the trail where Sans Peur and the rest of us waited.

Roy McLane said, "The woman and the children say they haven't seen any other Apaches ride past here." He pointed with his nose toward bare boulders showing a little up the side of the canyon through the trees. "Says we're welcome to all the water we need from that spring over yonder. You had a dry camp last night. You and the animals must be thirsty."

Sans Peur nodded and led us to the spring. We broke the ice from around the spring's flow, watered our ponies, drank our fill, and filled our water jugs. We didn't stop to rest. Kedinchin and Minnie's nearly barefoot tracks were easy to see on the wagon road running along the bottom of the canyon, and we all believed we were gaining on them. They were leading their ponies, but Kedinchin's pony had developed an irregular foot placement as it ran, a sure sign it was going lame. We hurried on like a pack of wolves, the smell of its quarry's blood filling their noses.

When the sun was a hand's width higher, the mountain ridge on the canyon's east side rolled into a gentle notch before it began rising again. The wagon road split at the notch. One branch led up the side of the ridge and across the notch; the other continued down the canyon. Kedinchin and Minnie went up the trail through the notch. The tracks of one pony they led showed its lameness was getting worse.

At the top of the notch, the trail continued almost due south as it wound across mountain meadows covered with patchy snow and dark, green junipers toward the top of a distant ridgeline. Within four hundred yards of the top of the notch, over a small rise, a stream twisted and turned on its way down the mountain. About three hundred yards along the little stream, a small wash between two small hills ran into it from the south.

Even from the trail we rode, I saw tracks and bent bushes disappearing into the wash. The trackers turned down the creek toward the tracks and disappeared up the wash. I saw three wolves racing out of the wash on the far side of the hill that formed one side. Soon Caje reappeared and waved for us to join them.

Up the wash, out of sight of the main trail, Kedinchin had slaughtered his lame pony. Its carcass lay skinned in the snow. Wolves had already started feeding on it. Kedinchin and Minnie had taken choice cuts of meat and roasted some over a small fire pit hidden under nearby junipers. From the bits of meat scattered around where the hide had been dragged, it was clear it had been scrapped clean of meat and fat, and from the small pieces of leather scattered around the fire, we could tell they had made new moccasins out of the green hide before taking the meat and running on. We found their old, worn-out moccasins hidden under a juniper. After I looked at them, I had to smile. Even using a green, uncured hide, their feet had to feel much warmer than in the practically useless moccasins they had worn. Also, the meat, along with the new moccasins, would give them strength to go farther, faster. Still, they had taken significant time to take the meat and hide, and to make moccasins. We were gaining on them, but every face, from the chiefs' to the tribal policemen's, was grim. Half-blind and deaf, Kedinchin was running a good race, but he was surely losing.

We rested our ponies and ate roasted corn, nuts, hard bread, and honey from Roy McLane's supplies. Although the climb was gentle up the ridge from where we sat, it was a long one, and the wind whipping off the ridge in the bright, blinding sun was cold and it cut exposed skin like a knife. We saved our ponies and led them as we ran up the winding trail over the ridge and then across a series of small ridges until we came to the village of High Rolls.

Kedinchin's trail, now much harder to follow, with he and Minnie wearing new moccasins, led directly past the station house where the iron wagon from Alamogordo stopped for riders to climb off or get on. Roy McLane asked Sans Peur to wait while he asked for news inside the building for the iron wagon. When he returned, I heard him tell Sans Peur that the White Eye posse would be on the next iron wagon that came in about when the sun disappeared.

Sans Peur saw the sun was close to the San Andres Mountains and told Roy McLane we would camp under some pines near the iron wagon house and wait to begin tracking until the next sun. Since there was smoke from many fires in the village, we had one, too, and ate some hot meat we cooked on sticks held over the orange and yellow flames. I was glad to feel the fire's heat. It had been a long, cold three days.

CHAPTER 30
KEDINCHIN AND MINNIE

We stood with our backs to the fire, soaking in long-denied heat, and ate pieces of hot meat off our knives. The iron wagon carrying the Indah posse came to High Rolls as the sun disappeared behind the far, western ridges. Roy McLane left our fire and went to speak with the posse chief while the posse unloaded its ponies.

I thought, *Their horses look sleek and in good physical condition. They should hold up until we catch Kedinchin and Minnie.* There were also two packhorses loaded with supplies. We thought that, with Roy McLane and the Indah posse bringing supplies, we would have plenty to eat. For work in the high, cold air over frozen ground, that was a very good thing.

Roy McLane brought the Indah posse to our fire, and we went through the Indah I-see-you custom of hand-shaking, head-nodding, and telling our names. Sans Peur gave the Indah posse chief a strong, double pump when they shook hands and said, "We gain ground on killer and his woman. Sun comes, we start at first light after shadows leave trail and light strong enough to see their trail sign."

The Indah posse chief nodded and said, "That there is good news, Chief. We'll be ready. The sheriff and all us here shore appreciate the reservation police chasin' that damned, no-good Indian who killed Roy's brother. We're gonna give him a permanent neck stretch after we find him. Now we're gonna get some supper and a place to sleep at a ranch up the road here a little piece. You comin', Roy?"

Roy McLane nodded and, with a grin, tipped his hat to us and said to Sans Peur, "Be back in the mornin' with trail supplies. Don't ya'll get restless and take off without us." He joined the posse disappearing into the dark and rode up the road to a friend's *hacienda* to eat and sleep for the night.

At the fire, we finished our meat and sat and smoked. A quarter-moon came up from behind the ridges to the northeast, sending cold, soft light and deep, black shadows to our camp. We wrapped in our blankets and lay down close together near the fire. Off to the north, a wolf called to his brothers while I thought of my women and children, hoping they were safe by their fire. The words of the Indah posse chief drifted across my mind . . . *that damned, no-good Indian.* Muchacho Negro was right. We couldn't give Kedinchin over to the Indah, no matter what he'd done. As Apaches, we owed him that.

Antonio Joseph picked up Kedinchin and Minnie's trail as mists floating through the trees began to run from the sun. Trail signs showed that they had ridden Minnie's pony into High Rolls and, after crossing the wagon road to the Cloudcroft village, stopped, hidden from the road, behind a little grove of piñons. While Minnie stood waiting with her pony, Kedinchin ran back to a corral and, without being seen, took a pony.

The farmer who owned the corral had complained to the sheriff's deputy about a horse thief when he saw the posse come to High Rolls on the iron wagon. Roy McLane had sent word to Sans Peur that Kedinchin might have taken the stolen pony and told him where to find the corral. Our trackers picked up the trail at the corral, certain they had seen Kedinchin's moccasin tracks next to a pony wearing horseshoes.

The trail from the corral was narrow and winding. It led south up the ridge above High Rolls, and then up and down the sides of canyons that began near the top of the Sacramentos and dropped off in great gashes that emptied into the basin.

The trackers were slow, careful not to miss signs, their progress determining how fast the posse moved, since any riders who went ahead of the tracks might destroy trail signs and make us lose the trail. The Indah posse rode in a long winding line along the trail crossing the beginning sides of the canyons that the Mescalero trackers and posse, for the most part, followed on foot as they looked for trail signs, always pointing south toward the land of the *Nakai-yes*. Far away to the north and west, between the roll and heave of the canyon ridges, we could see the great spread of white sand at the foot of the sacred San Andres Mountains. There was a feeling among us like that on a big cat hunt. It was a sense of unseen power, deadly and strong, waiting to take us. We kept ourselves ready and watchful.

As on the north side trail we had followed above High Rolls, the frozen ground, hard and unyielding to pony or human feet, made tracking slow. South of High Rolls, rocky flats on the edges of the high canyons made it even easier to lose tracks than on the frozen ground. Many times, we had to backtrack and look for a barely visible indication of movement, while the posses waited in the cold wind for the trackers to find the trail again after seeing a stone slightly twisted in its frozen bed, a broken twig, or finding the places where the runaways had made water.

By the end of the first day out of High Rolls, we had climbed high toward the spine of the mountains and followed a long, winding canyon leading up from a ranch pasture sitting above High Rolls. When the light became too bad to track anymore, we again found a place under some junipers at the beginnings of a little side canyon leading off the one we had followed and out of the wind.

Sans Peur told the Indah posse we would make camp without a fire. The Indah posse chief decided they would ride back down a wagon road leading to a ranch, where they could sleep out of the wind and cold and have a fire and a hot meal.

Once more, we spread our blankets and pulled together a pile of pine needles. We made our cover for sleeping close together, as we had on the trail north of High Rolls, and ate again the jerky and canned food Roy McLane left for us. While we smoked after eating, we spoke of the trail we had seen during the day.

Caje surprised us all when he said, "Minnie wants us to find them."

Sans Peur stared at Caje and frowned. "Why do you say this?"

Caje reached in his vest pocket and pulled out a few small bits of cloth. We could barely see them in the drops of moonlight and shadow falling through juniper needles above us. He held them out and showed them to Sans Peur and then to the rest of us sitting close to him. They were about a thumb wide and a knuckle long. It was clear they all came from the same piece of material. I rubbed a finger over a piece. It felt like the same cloth my women used to make their skirts and shirts. I studied the edges in the dim light and looked at Caje. He nodded. An edge had been cut on one side, sewn smooth like the bottom of a skirt, the other edges torn.

I said, "Where did you find these?"

Caje looked at me with a sideways glance. "First piece is last camp north of High Rolls. Next piece is where she waited while Kedinchin took the corral pony. Other pieces were on brush at places today where we lost their trail because it split into two or three others. Tears in woman's cloth made by fingers, not brush. She leaves it so we can follow."

Sans Peur pulled his blanket up around his shoulders and made a face. "Maybe so. Maybe so she readies us for an ambush. Who knows? Don't move too fast looking for her cloth and forget Kedinchin might wait to stop us with his rifle like he did brother of Roy McLane. We watch 'em good at first light. Now we sleep."

The place where we slept close together kept the wind away. We didn't move much before we got up. The night was very cold. I wondered how Kedinchin and Minnie fared in some canyon ahead of us. I thought, *They probably have a fire to rest by, but they'll wear out their horses soon. They're growing weak if the meat is gone. When the meat is gone, we catch 'em.*

The next day, two hands before the time of shortest shadows (about ten o'clock), Antonio Joseph found the remains of a small fire hidden off the trail in a little arroyo that drained into a big canyon. He also found a bit of Minnie's cloth nearby and brought it back to show us. The posse, not understanding what we found or said, sat their ponies and watched us with curious frowns in silence. Later in the day, the trail might have gone in three or more different directions. We took the western trail where we found another bit of cloth. We all looked at the cloth. There was no doubt Minnie wanted us to find them.

It was a hard day. There was much waiting for the trackers and some hard climbs for the horses out of the big canyons. Kedinchin was no fool. He used every trick uncles teach an Apache child or that he had learned tracking game in order to make false trails.

Three more days, like that first one with the posse, followed. But each day we found hidden fire remains closer to where we rested for the night and more bits of cloth Minnie had left. We knew we were drawing closer to Kedinchin and Minnie.

The posse usually left us each day as the sun floated not far off the tops of the San Andres. They went to stay at ranches or line cabins where they knew they would have a fire and meat to eat. Each day, Roy McLane returned with cooked meat and Indah bread and beans for us to eat. On the third night, the White Eye lodges were all too far away to reach and return the next morning. They planned to stay with us, but they said it was too cold not to have a fire, so Sans Peur made them go back the way we had come and camp down in a canyon that would block the light from their fire.

On the fourth night, after the posse left, we climbed to the top and a little down the backside of a ridge near a trail leading into a canyon that emptied into the basin. Sans Peur wouldn't let us smoke. He thought we might be close enough that Kedinchin might catch a glimpse of the glow from the coals on our *tobaho* or even smell the *tobaho* smoke, and he wanted me, who had the best night eyes, to climb to the top of the ridge to look for firelight down the trail from us.

There was still a little light left from the sun passing behind the San Andres when I bedded down under some junipers on top of the ridge, pulled my *Shináá Cho,* and began to look over all the arroyos that fed into the big one running in the middle of the canyon. I didn't have to look long before I saw a faint orange glow in the shadows where the big arroyo disappeared into the main canyon leading to the basin. I thought, *Sleep good this night, Kedinchin. Tomorrow we come, and you go to the Happy Land.*

CHAPTER 31
APACHE JUSTICE

Feeling the ground with my moccasins, avoiding places that might be slick with ice, and sliding my hands along the trunks of nearly every big juniper I passed in case I started to fall, I worked my way back to the posse camp behind the ridge and told Sans Peur what I had seen. He nodded that he understood, and we waited as the moon rose to shine softly through the clouds forming over the canyons and around their ridges while he thought what to do.

When the moon was halfway to the top of its arc, he said, "You all agree that Kedinchin must not be given to the Indah posse? If they take him, they'll go to the town of Alamogordo and with much ceremony hang him."

Muchacho Negro looked around at all of us and then nodded. "We agree. Roy McLane has blood right to him, but he'll let the Indah posse have him. Let's do Roy McLane's revenge business ourselves. He's always treated us fair and with respect. We owe this to Kedinchin and to Roy McLane."

Willie Magoosh said, "I speak for my father, Magoosh, Chief of the Lipans. Muchacho Negro speaks wise words. Let us do as he says and also save Minnie. I think he forced her to come with him because he needed her eyes and ears. She has betrayed him by leaving us her bits of cloth to follow. For that, maybe she should lose the end of her nose, but I wouldn't do it. It would make James Carroll angry, and I don't think she should be punished."

244

We argued in the quiet darkness about this for a while before deciding not to kill Minnie or punish her. Sans Peur listened to us, and then told us his plan to get rid of the Indah posse and how we would take Kedinchin.

Sans Peur sent me back to my spot on top of the ridge to watch where Kedinchin and Minnie went. He believed they were short of meat. He thought Kedinchin would follow the canyon from where they camped to the basin, where he might take a range cow without anyone catching him. The place where Kedinchin and Minnie hid was west of Grapevine Canyon in the west branch of a canyon the Indah called Nigger Ed.

The morning light, pushing through low clouds over the canyons, was weak and slow to come. From my place under the junipers on the ridge above them, I had stared with the *Shináá Cho* where I knew Kedinchin and Minnie's camp was. Since before moon fall, I had seen no movement. Then in the dim light, I saw Kedinchin and Minnie leading their horses and disappearing down the winding, brown sand of the arroyo leading to the bottom of the canyon.

I retreated over the top of the ridge, found my pony, and rode up the trail below the top of the ridge to Sans Peur and our posse, where they were to meet the Indah posse for the day's tracking. By the time I found them, the trackers had already started west, along the trail of the canyon next to the one where Kedinchin and Minnie hid. The trackers acted like they followed trail sign, and the tribal police and White Eye posse, as usual, strung out behind them. I rode up beside Sans Peur, pointed to where I had come from, and shook my head to make the Indah posse behind us believe I found nothing on my back trail, while I told him in the Apache tongue that Kedinchin and Minnie had already started down their canyon.

The cold wind blew off the top of the mountains and rolled down the canyons. The posses following the trackers sat with their horses' tails to the wind and waited for the trackers to call them forward. But the trackers seemed to ride farther down the trail than usual, and then they all returned, spread out on both sides of the trail. When they got to Sans Peur at about halfway to the time of shortest shadows, Antonio Joseph, the lead tracker, rode over to us, shook his head, and said, "No good." The trackers dismounted along with the tribal police and, with their backs to the wind, made smoke and spoke among themselves with much nodding and shaking of their heads.

Sans Peur went to the Indah posse chief and told him the trackers had lost the trail and would join the rest of the tribal police while we tried to decide what to do. The Indah posse chief frowned and slowly nodded before he turned back to his men and told them the trackers had lost the trail, and the Apaches were trying to decide how to find it again. They hunched deeper into their coats, and then led their ponies behind a grove of junipers that would act as a windbreak while they waited and smoked. The tribal police and trackers talked in groups and walked up and down the trail, but they actually did nothing.

After a hand-width of the sun moving past the time of shortest shadows, Sans Peur met with the trackers and then went to the Indah posse chief. He told him the trackers would have to backtrack to pick up the trail again, and that the posse chief and his deputies with Roy McLane should follow a couple of the tribal police and a tracker on the canyon trail to the basin, looking for tracks. If none were found, then the Indah posse should go on to Alamogordo and wait until one of the tribal police came with word that the trail had been found again. The White Eye posse chief didn't want to go, but it was clear we were not making any progress, and his men needed to move out of the cold wind. He agreed to go with Roy McLane, who promised us more supplies the next day. The White Eye posse followed Crooked Neck, Sam Chino, Willie Comanche, and Caje on the winding trail out of the canyon to the basin. Of course, Caje and Willie Comanche found no more sign on the trail to the basin. Down out of the mountains, the cold Indah posse wasted no time riding for warm rooms and *cantinas* in Alamogordo, and Roy McLane rode for the closest ranch house. The Apache policemen rode back up the canyon trail to Sans Peur and the others.

After the White Eye posse left, Sans Peur asked me to take the *Shináá Cho,* and leaving my pony, run the rim of the canyon Kedinchin and Minnie descended, and find them. When they stopped, I was to come back to tell him where they were. We knew that for Kedinchin and Minnie to lead their ponies down the rough canyon bottom filled with brush and boulders to its washout in the basin might take two or three days. Sans Peur guessed they wouldn't get much farther from where the east and west branches of the canyon joined before dark, and with Kedinchin's bad eye, they would stop for Minnie to make a small fire and cook while they rested.

I ran down the trail the White Eye posse had taken until I thought I was close to where the two branches of Kedinchin and Minnie's canyon joined, and then I followed a small arroyo over to the rim of the canyon. I was just above where the two canyon branches joined and could see almost all the way back to their last camp to the north, but the twists and turns of the main canyon beyond where the two branches joined made it hard to see much of the trail below.

I moved carefully down the ridge until I found a place where I could see and scanned the bottom of the canyon. I didn't see them and wondered how they had got down the canyon so fast, as rough as the trail was. I focused the *Shináá Cho* on the sand in the arroyo and could tell horses had passed over it and carefully followed the trail until it appeared to stop in brush where the arroyo had washed out the sand and small rocks from under a big overhang of rocks casting a black shadow on the trail. I soon saw their horses, tied in the brush in the shadows. Just behind the horses was Minnie, preparing to make a small fire in a hole she had dug. Kedinchin appeared carrying a blanket and, spreading it out, he sat down close by to watch her. I smiled. They would go no farther that day.

I backed off the ridge and went down its far side to a small arroyo that emptied into the big canyon below where Kedinchin and Minnie camped. Following the arroyo all the way down and then turning back up the canyon would be an easy way to reach them when the shadows grew long and darkness came.

I told Sans Peur what I had seen. Gathering us all together, he said, "We're near the end of Kedinchin's trail. He makes camp deep in the canyon where the only escape is along the bottom of the canyon. To climb the sides in the dark will be too slow and dangerous. Caje, I want you to take half the men and go up the ridge toward their last camp and then follow Kedinchin's trail into the canyon. Wait until the moon rises before you start down the trail toward his new camp. Be careful and ready if Kedinchin runs. Shoot only if you have clear sights. Save Minnie if you can. I'll take the other half of our warriors and go down the ridge in the way Yellow Boy says is close to Kedinchin's camp. Yellow Boy, Muchacho Negro, and Antonio Joseph, I want you with me. Before the moon rises over the ridges, we'll go up the canyon toward Kedinchin's camp and wait for a chance to take him. The other policemen will wait where we start up the canyon in case Kedinchin and Minnie get past us. They'll shoot also only if they have clear sights."

After Caje's group disappeared up the ridge, Sans Peur had me lead his warriors to the shallow arroyo that drained into the canyon. Daylight was still good as he led us toward the canyon bottom. The shadows were deep and the sun nearly gone when we reached our destination, and we waited for full darkness. Sans Peur had told us in a voice only we could hear, "I want Muchacho Negro, Yellow Boy, and Antonio Joseph to go first and the others to spread out, in case Kedinchin somehow sees us and starts shooting. Try not to shoot Minnie, but don't let her get you killed. Don't shoot up the canyon from where your brothers come. Now go, and do what must be done." We began working our way toward Kedinchin's new camp.

We spread out and moved up the canyon. Around the first bend, we saw the glow from Minnie's little fire. When we had left Mescalero, the moon was bright and full, but in the canyon now, it showed less than a quarter, and its light was weak. As the moon rose above the high ridges, the smell of cooking meat, its fat dripping in the fire, drifted toward us and made our empty stomachs howl with long-denied want. I was on the east side of the canyon, Muchacho Negro in the middle, and Antonio Joseph on the west side. It was warmer in the canyon than on the ridges, but still so cold we had to keep flexing our fingers to be sure they didn't get so stiff they would be slow to move when we needed to shoot. When we were within the shadows, a few paces from the fire, we saw Kedinchin sitting cross-legged with his rifle across his knees. Leaning back against a canyon boulder under the overhang, his hat tipped back, he stared up the west canyon side, studying the scattered juniper shadows with his good eye.

Muchacho Negro spoke in a low, calm voice from the brush near the fire as Minnie bent over to rotate the meat on her sticks. He said, "Minnie, show no sign you hear me. We have seen your bits of cloth and know you want to be free. Take the meat to Kedinchin and then step to the other side of the fire and don't move. We won't hurt you if we can avoid it."

Minnie never showed any sign she heard Muchacho Negro. She lifted and twisted the meat on the stick, letting the last fat sizzle and drip in the fire as we pulled the hammers back on our rifles. Minnie carried the meat to Kedinchin and held it out to him. He looked down from the shadows on the canyon side, smiled, and nodded. He took the stick with the meat from her, and, breathing deep, smelled it, raised his brows in pleasure, and smiled again. Minnie walked back to the other side of the fire where her small piece of meat also cooked on a stick. She took it and slowly backed away from the fire and into the shadows. Kedinchin, blowing on the meat to cool it a little, never noticed her step away.

I aimed for his heart. We all fired at about the same time. The roar of our rifles echoed through the canyon. Kedinchin jerked back as our bullets hit him, a smile formed on his lips, his head tilted forward, and he fell over sideways, leaving streaks of blood on the boulder where he had rested his back. I had a hard time hearing for a little while as the others came up. Minnie stood, staring at him as if she didn't believe her eyes that he was gone. Her hands flew to her mouth as if to stop a scream, but she never moved, standing there as if frozen in the cold darkness.

Their horses, which were tied to junipers in the circle of the fire's light, rolled their eyes in surprise and fear, snorting and jerking on their tie ropes before calming and settling while Sans Peur and the others ran forward. Antonio Joseph walked up, kneeled beside Kedinchin, and looked close at his face. "Kedinchin goes to the Happy Land. He goes smiling, like a true warrior."

CHAPTER 32
RETURN TO MESCALERO

We wrapped Kedinchin in a blanket, tied him over the pony he had stolen, and, with Minnie leading her pony, climbed to the top of the ridge where we made a fire to warm ourselves. Sans Peur rode on to let Caje know we had taken Kedinchin. Minnie sat by our big fire wrapped in a blanket and stared into the twisting orange and yellow flames. We offered her food, but she wouldn't take it and looked many times at the blanket bundle that was once Kedinchin.

The sun came, and the wind died. Sans Peur decided to take Kedinchin to Alamogordo for the Indah posse chief to see that we did as we said, and then to Mescalero to put Kedinchin's body in a place where a di-yen would make a good ceremony for him. We made ready to go and decided to take the easy Grapevine Canyon trail rather than the hard one full of steep falloffs and tight turns the Indah posse had followed to the basin.

From the Grapevine Canyon trail, Roy McLane saw our fire smoke reaching high into the early morning sky and came galloping up to catch us before we left. He frowned when he saw Minnie wrapped in her blanket and sitting astride her pony. Looking at all the men saddling their ponies, he said, "Where's Kedinchin?"

Minnie raised her eyes and nose and pointed to the blanket bundle on the pony nearby. "There."

He rode over to the bundle, lifted one end of the blanket

enough to see under it, and said in a low voice, "I'll be damned."

He turned to Sans Peur, who had ridden up. "I figured when we got to the basin yesterday that you wanted some privacy to take care of business. The posse rode on to Alamogordo and is waiting for you to call them back. I owe you boys a big vote of thanks for tracking down my brother's killer. Ain't nobody in the world could have found this man up here except you." He nodded, leaned forward, and, resting his forearm on his saddle horn, said, "Come on with me to Alamogordo. I want that railroad town to see what real law officers look like. You're due a big meal, and I'm buying."

Sans Peur nodded. "We come."

Roy McLane and the Mescalero police riding behind him caused a stir among the people on the street when, as the shadows grew long, we rode into Alamogordo and up to the Indah posse chief's lodge with Kedinchin's body. The Indah posse chief said he would have an Indah *di-yen* make tracks on a paper to prove to all other Indah that Kedinchin had gone to the Happy Land, that it would be ready by the next sun, and then we could take the body and go.

Roy McLane led us to a place where anyone who pays can eat. The Mescaleros do not have such places. You come to our tipi, and you can eat what is in our pot. He had us sit at tables like the Indah do, told the one who cooks that he will pay, and said to feed us all the beef, potatoes, bread, and coffee we wanted. He said to Sans Peur, "You boys are the best posse I ever saw. You did without fire on mighty cold nights, put up with fogs and sleet, and didn't have much to eat. Now I want you to eat all you want of the best beef we can offer 'cause I'm mighty grateful for what you done."

After we ate all we could, it was dark and very cold outside. Roy McLane asked, and the Indah posse chief let us inside a big lodge the Indah called Courthouse. It looked a little like the agency lodge at Mescalero. It had many fires burning in iron stoves like those at the agency, and it was warm. We brought in our blankets and slept there on the floor.

At sunrise, Roy McLane brought his chief to meet us. His name was E.S. Ward, and he and Roy McLane brought us big pots of coffee and much bread. While we ate, Ward, who owned the ranch where Roy McLane was chief, thanked us and gave each of us a twenty-dollar gold coin, more money at one time than most of us had seen before.

The Indah posse chief brought a team and wagon hauling a long basket with Kedinchin inside and said we could take him back to Mescalero. Minnie, who'd said nothing the whole time we rode back from Grapevine Canyon and had eaten and slept in Alamogordo, went out, sat on the wagon seat, and waited.

Sans Peur turned to Roy McLane and E.S. Ward and said, "We go." They nodded and used the Indah hand motion for signing *adios*.

The ride to Mescalero was long and cold, but we had eaten much, and we had twenty-dollar gold pieces in our pockets. Somehow, the cold didn't cut as deep as it did before. The shadows off the ridges were long when we came to Mescalero, and Sans Peur went into the agency lodge to bring James Carroll to see we had returned with Kedinchin and Minnie.

Soon James Carroll and Sans Peur were out the agency door. James Carroll looked at all of us and nodded. Then he walked over to the wagon, lifted the lid on the basket holding Kedinchin's body, and peered in, nodding, before he lowered the lid. He came back to the front of the wagon and looked up at Minnie, who sat with her blanket covering the top of her bowed head. James Carroll, a good man who understood the People, said to her, "Your man went to the Happy Land like a true warrior. They know him there. You helped him, like all good women help their men. *Enjuh.* Sleep here at the agency tonight where it's warm. When the next sun comes, we'll find a place for him. Come." He motioned for her to get off the wagon. She climbed down and followed him inside.

We took the wagon to the stables, parked it outside, unhitched the horses, rubbed them down, and gave them a ration of oats. We lifted the basket off the wagon, carried it inside, and left it in an empty stable. By the time we finished, it was dark, and most of the posse had disappeared. I had a smoke with Muchacho Negro, Antonio Joseph, and Sans Peur. Then I rode up the wagon trail to my wives and little boys sitting by a fire in our tipi under the tall pines pointing to the stars.

I felt like I had been gone from their warm fire and company for many moons, even though it had only been about ten suns. In my blankets, listening to the sleeping sounds of my family, I asked Ussen that I never again have to chase another Mescalero to kill him.

CHAPTER 33
DAKLUGIE COMES

A harvest passed, and Ghost Face drifted toward the Season of Little Eagles. There had been much talk in the reservation lodges about what had happened to Kedinchin. Even the tracks in the Indah newspapers had spoken of it. James Carroll read us what they had to say. Most of what they said was true, but some of their words were lies. The Apache posse members wanted to speak to the newspaper track maker and get the words changed, but James Carroll said it would do no good. So, as with many Indah things, we looked the other way and said nothing.

After she returned with the body of Kedinchin, Minnie saved her things and then burned their tipi and all his belongings, as is right and proper, to keep his ghost from coming back. When the Season of Many Leaves came, she again put up a tipi after the tribal police cut her some new lodge poles and James Carroll gave her some canvas.

Minnie placed her tipi high above the green strip of Tularosa Canyon on a ridge running north out of the mountains. From her camp, she could see most of the canyon. It was near a natural tank that collected water from a small spring in a grove of junipers that gave her plenty of wood for fires. Minnie lived by herself, and James Carroll told the tribal police to check on her often and to let him know if she needed any support.

The tribal police had little trouble to handle that year. When the Ghost Face came again, we spent most of our time at the agency or with our families, rather than trying to ride through deep snow to camps all over the reservation.

One morning in the middle of Ghost Face, I walked by James Carroll's workplace and saw him talking to a young Apache man, his hair short and his face round, his body big and muscular. He was well dressed, even for an Indah. James Carroll saw me and motioned for me to come in and join them.

After I sat down, James Carroll, motioning to the young man, said, "Yellow Boy, this gentleman says he knows you. Do you remember him?"

I frowned and shook my head. His face and the way he carried himself were familiar, but I didn't remember ever meeting him.

He smiled and stuck out his hand for a shake the way the White Eyes do. We pumped hands twice, and he said, "I'm Asa Daklugie, youngest son of Juh. I doubt you remember me, but I remember you when you shot the gourd off the running slave child's head in my father's stronghold. I was a small boy then with a toy bow and thought your shot was unbelievable until my father told us Ussen had empowered you to shoot your Yellow Boy rifle with great skill."

"You look very much like your father, who I remember well, but I don't remember your face as a small boy. I'm happy to see Asa Daklugie, son of Juh. Why have you come to Mescalero?"

"Like my uncle, Geronimo, I'm a prisoner of war for the past twenty-three years. The White Eyes sent me to the Carlisle school to learn to read and write and to learn a trade while they moved my uncle and our People from Florida to Alabama to Fort Sill, Oklahoma. I learned cattle husbandry at Carlisle. When I left Carlisle, I moved back with my People at Fort Sill. Now, I'm in charge of our cattle herd."

James Carroll, his pipe clamped tight in his teeth, crossed his arms and leaned back in his chair as the hot stove creaked and groaned.

Daklugie continued, "All the great leaders who were in captivity, Chihuahua, Loco, Nana, Mangas, and many others have gone to the happy place. Geronimo still lives, but I think the Indah will give us our freedom soon. The army once said it would give us Fort Sill land and the Comanche and Kiowa agreed. Now the army says it may decide to stay. Where will we go? I have a pass to look at Mescalero and to ask your leaders if they will accept us as brothers. In a few days, I'll talk with them about this, but first I wish to see the reservation lands and learn if and how it can support us all. I know John and Sam Chino, who live here. Somehow, we're related. I expected to ask them to ride with me over the reservation, but someone in John's family just left for the Happy Land, and he grieves. I won't disturb him. Perhaps, if James Carroll agrees, you'll show me your land?"

I glanced at James Carroll, who raised his brows, stuck out his jaw, and gave a little nod. I said, "I'm a tribal policeman. I do whatever James Carroll tells me to do. If he says go, I go. I'll do it with a good heart. I knew your father. He helped me find the witch I hunted, Sangre del Diablo. The Mescaleros need more people for our reservation to keep the Indah away. I hope your People come."

James Carroll said, "Good. I'm sure we can make Yellow Boy available to guide you around the reservation. When you're ready to meet with the chiefs, let me know, and I'll call them together."

Asa Daklugie nodded and said, *"Enjuh."*

Asa Daklugie, three others, and I rode all over the reservation. We hunted every day. Deer were in good shape, down from the mountains and grazing in the canyons. He liked everything he saw and was especially happy to see many areas where the grama grass was plentiful, dead for the season, but still capable of providing food for cattle.

The night before we returned to the agency, we sat smoking by a fire after filling ourselves with fresh, roasted meat, Indah bread, potatoes, and beans. I said, "Asa Daklugie, what do you think of our reservation? If our chiefs accept you, will Geronimo's People come?"

Daklugie grinned and said, "Mountains in which to pray, wood, water, grass, much game—and no White Eyes to watch our every move! Best of all, we'll be among our own people and worship Ussen as our grandfathers did. The Indah religion tells the story of the Hebrew tribe Ussen led to a place they called the Promised Land. This is the Promised Land for the Chiricahua and the others who are with us in captivity. I pray to Ussen that your chiefs will accept us as their brothers."

I liked Daklugie and thought he gave a powerful answer. "*Enjuh*. I think the chiefs will welcome you. But we'll see."

He nodded. "Yes, we'll see."

A few days later, Daklugie and the chiefs met. Daklugie said much of what he had told us by that fire. When he asked them if they would accept his group, they said, as if with one voice, "Come to us."

The next day, I rode with Daklugie to the iron wagon station in Tularosa for him to return to Fort Sill. We didn't shake hands as the Indah do, but we waved our hands parallel to the ground. I said, "Bring us your people."

He nodded. "When the White Eyes let us go, it will be so."

I watched him get on the train and expected to see him with his people soon. They came four harvests later. The White Eye chiefs in the east think and act very slowly.

CHAPTER 34
OJO VERDE COMES

Less than a moon after Daklugie left, the sun was high and the wind, still. I rode to the agency to help other policemen with stacking hay at the barn and rounding up ponies that had found a way out of the corral. Near the end of the day, our work done, we sat in the agency building beside a stove filled with fire, and, smoking and drinking strong coffee with much sugar, we told our stories of the old days.

James Carroll came from his place in the building where he studied Indah tracks on paper and sat listening to us. I told my story of shooting the rattlesnake before it struck Tzoe. This happened when Nantan Lupan's scouts ran for the Blue Mountains to find Geronimo and other great chiefs like Chihuahua, Loco, Nana, and Juh. The policemen all laughed that Tzoe had changed his mind about needing to do his personal business in the brush after I shot the snake.

James Carroll laughed with us and then said, "That reminds me. You fellows might be interested in knowing that Geronimo went to the Happy Land six days ago."

We stopped laughing and stared at him. Caje said, "Who killed him?"

James Carroll shook his head and said, "Nobody killed him. He had pneumonia." He patted his chest and added, "You know, breathing sickness—we have it here at Mescalero sometimes. They say he grew sick after sleeping out in a cold rain at Fort Sill."

I thought, *The great warrior and* di-yen *Geronimo is sent to the Happy Land by the same sickness as my little daughter, Kicking Wren. This sickness respects no one. I wonder if my son, Hombrecito, will learn at the* di-yen *school by the big water a ceremony to defeat it.*

Someone on the other side of the stove cocked his head to one side and said, "Why would he sleep in the rain? He was an old man. Someone must have witched him. That's the way witches work if they're trying to kill you."

James Carroll shook his head. "No, no witch killed him. They say he got a hold of a bottle of whiskey and sat out all night drinking. Some relation—I don't remember if the story said who was with him—took him to the Apache hospital at Fort Sill after he heard Geronimo's bad cough and could feel he had a high fever."

The room was quiet except for the fire hissing and popping inside the stove. We all sat and looked at each other and thought about the *di-yen* warrior who brought so much grief to the Chiricahua through his broken promises to the Indah. I remembered hearing a story about Geronimo's children being sick all the time at Fort Sill, and he believed a witch might be after them. He brought in a *di-yen*, a friend named Lot Eyelash, to do a Sing and identify who was casting the spells. After three or four songs, Lot Eyelash stopped and, pointing at Geronimo, said he was the one, that he wanted his Power to take his children instead of him to the Happy Land. The man who told the story said Geronimo looked at the ground, shook his head, and with sad eyes said the Power Lot Eyelash heard wasn't from Ussen. Who can know the will of another's Power? I think Ussen makes a trail straight for everyone, but few have the strength to walk it.

Geronimo had spoken straight when he told me in the Blue Mountains to take care of a young boy in the desert when I found him. I was glad I did. Hombrecito had grown into a good man, half Indah, half Mexican, all Mescalero. Perhaps, just as Geronimo said, he would help us someday when he returned from the Indah *di-yen* school.

I finished my coffee and started out the door to return to my family and a good evening meal, when I heard Caje say to James Carroll, "As you asked, I stopped by Minnie's tipi yesterday. She is good. A woman I haven't seen before stays with her, but Minnie said the woman plans to move on in a day or two."

James Carroll nodded. "Good. I'm glad she has company to help her during the Ghost Face. How is the woman called?"

Caje made a face. "I didn't ask and Minnie didn't say. But she is easy to remember. She's tall and has a brown eye and a green one."

I thought, *So, Ojo Verde, at last you come. Now I will find satisfaction in ending your evil.*

I hurried to the barn and saddled my pony. I rode to Minnie's tipi, intending to kill the witch as fast as I could. I didn't care if James Carroll put me in the Indah calaboose a long time for killing this witch. I had to do it. I knew if I waited, she would probably get away. Then my wives, children, and Beela-chezzi's and Knows Horses's families would be at risk.

The stars were beginning to show through the black velvet of the sky when I tied my pony to a juniper and crept up the trail like a hunting cat to get up close to Minnie's tipi, listen for voices, and watch for shadows against the firelight inside. But once there, I saw only one shadow sitting up, and the only voice I heard was Minnie singing some child's song to herself. I waited and looked in the shadows of the cold night air with my rifle cocked and ready, but there was no one outside.

I moved in silence to the tipi entrance and cleared my throat.

From inside I heard Minnie. "Wah? Who stands at my tipi?"

I said, "I'm Yellow Boy. I come to talk with you."

I heard the strain in her voice relax as she said, "Come and be welcomed. My coffee is hot."

I pulled back the blanket and stepped inside. She sat on the opposite side of the fire with a long knife in her lap. She smiled and motioned for me to sit. She poured coffee in an old blue speckled cup and waited for me to drink it. We spoke of the Ghost Face and how good the deer hunts had been lately. She asked after my family and if they were in good health. After a long pause in our talk, she offered me more coffee, which I politely refused. She said, "Yellow Boy comes late in the night to the tipi of Minnie, and his rifle is cocked. Is it men or animals you seek?"

"I seek the woman Caje says was with you yesterday. She's a witch. She killed the first child Moon on the Water carried and tried to kill Moon, my brother Knows Horses, and his friend Running Wolf, son of Beela-chezzi, many harvests ago. She failed. Now I believe she comes to try again."

Minnie's eyes grew large, and she shook her head. "She's not here. She left this morning, riding her big black pony. She said she was returning east to her people, the Comanches. I gave her food, and she thanked me. She said I was a good person and left me a gift in this little basket. I haven't even looked at it yet."

I leaned back from her when she held it out to me. "Don't open it. It will make you sick. I'll make a fire outside, and then we must burn it. It's an evil thing."

Minnie nodded. "I believe you. Build the fire."

I went to the fire pit in front of her tipi and soon had a nice fire with good, high, orange and yellow flames. I called to Minnie to bring out the witch's gift. Her hand trembled as she came outside holding the basket, still unopened.

"Throw it on the fire and step back here close to me."

Minnie tossed it on the fire. The basket, made of grass stems, burned fast and left what was inside exposed and barely scorched. It was a big, carved rattlesnake head, its jaws open wide with its fangs down, ready to bite. It was covered with beautiful beadwork, and its eyes were made from two round, clear stones that seemed to bulge from the sockets. There were streamers of feathers of many colors coming out of its mouth and beadwork on top and at the back of its head. It hurt my eyes just to look at it. I reached my arm around Minnie's shoulders, and we backed up more, staring at it, as the flames began to take it. There was a loud bang, and the thing disappeared in a ball of fire that rolled up into the stars. I felt Minnie trembling.

"It's all right now. The evil has been destroyed, and it can't hurt you."

"What would have happened if I had opened it and touched that thing?"

"You would have become sick and died in a lot of misery and pain. Are you sure you don't know where the witch went?"

She shook her head. "No, I don't know. If I did, I'd go after her with my knife. She only said she was taking the road east."

"I must get to my own family now. I'll check on you in a few days."

She smiled and nodded. *"Enjuh."*

I pushed my pony hard to get to the canyon where Juanita and Moon kept our tipi. I feared Ojo Verde might get there ahead of me. But all was calm and peaceful, and they had the evening meal waiting for me.

As we sat and ate by our fire, I told Juanita and Moon that Ojo Verde had stayed a day or two with Minnie, and that they must watch themselves and the children while I made a fast ride to the camp of Knows Horses to warn him and his wives, Lola Mes and Falling Water.

Juanita had heard the stories Moon and I had told about Ojo

Verde, but she'd never seen the witch. Juanita said, "I'll keep my sling and stones close to my hand. If she comes near, I'll put a stone in her head. She'll be no more. What will you do now?"

I glanced at my sons and saw they listened with wide eyes and open mouths. Redondo said, "Father, we saw someone up on the ridge watching us today while we played. He sat on a big pony, and then turned down behind the ridge. We saw him no more after that."

"What color was the pony?"

Redondo grinned. "It was a big black one, like the one you keep for Hombrecito. There was no white on it anywhere. I wished I had a fine pony like that one, even if I'm too small to ride it alone."

My belly felt like I was falling from a high place. "I must go to the camp of Knows Horses tonight and warn them. I hope I can beat the witch there. If I make it in time, I'll speak with Lola Mes to hear her counsel and ask her to make a ceremony to protect us from Ojo Verde's Power. Then I'll find Ojo Verde and shoot out her eyes before she can attack us. I must be careful, or James Carroll will learn I did it and send me to the Indah jail for unjust killing. I won't let that happen. I have good wives and children to support."

Moon and Juanita nodded, their fingers over their mouths. Moon said, "Hurry, husband. Ojo Verde is far in front of you."

CHAPTER 35
WATERFALL OF FIRE

Early, before the sun lighted the snow on the high ridges, I rode into the canyon where Lola Mes's tipi stood. Even without the wind carrying it to me, I smelled burning leather and meat, and saw a smoke cloud hanging low to the ground. My heart raced and my belly churned with sickness and bitter bile.

The place where Lola Mes had her tipi was now a black, burned circle in the surrounding snow with a few charred lodge poles standing over it. If only I had come sooner. All my grown life I thought often, *If only I had reached the village of Cha sooner, I could have stopped Sangre del Diablo from killing and scalping those he caught there.* Now it seemed I was too late again, and his incestuous woman had taken my brother and his wives. I wanted to scream and yell in rage, but waited for the light, now coming fast, to learn what had happened and decide how to catch and kill the witch.

Lola Mes's tipi had stood in a grove of junipers on a little rise above the floor of the canyon and close to the cliffs in its southern wall. As the light came, I could see burned brush and black marks along the cliff face made by what must have been a waterfall of fire. At the bottom of the cliffs, there was a round place where the snow had melted, and bushes had burned not far from the tipi fire. It looked as though fire had come down the cliffs, set fire to brush where it first hit the canyon bottom, and then jumped from that place to the tipi. I made myself look and poke around in the tipi ashes and puffed my cheeks with relief to find no charred bones.

In cold, brittle, early morning light, where every breath looked like the clouds that come from a pot of boiling water, I saw moccasin tracks, two distinct sets, in long running strides across the snow leading up the canyon. I felt a little fire of hope grow in my chest as I followed them. I knew without question where they were going. Lola Mes and Falling Water had a food cache in a small cave about twenty feet up the cliff wall and three hundred yards up the canyon from the tipi. I smiled when I saw a blanket, the glow of a fire shining through it, hanging over the opening and not the usual brush standing before it.

I climbed up beside the blanket and stood to one side of the cave entrance out of the way of rifle fire that might come through the blanket. I cleared my throat and waited. I heard shuffles of moving moccasins and the hammer on a rifle pulled to full cock before the barrel pushed the blanket cover back. Leaning back, Lola Mes looked from side to side with her good eye, trying to see who had called. I moved my head to where she could see it and said, "Don't shoot. It's Yellow Boy." Smiling, she put the rifle hammer on safety and waved me inside. Lola Mes and Falling Water moved back to the fire and, kneeling down, rearranged the blankets over their shoulders before resuming their cooking. They looked up at me, their cheeks sagging with relief.

Falling Water said, "How did you know to come? Without our having Lola Mes's Power, you would have found our bodies in the tipi ashes. Do you know who did it? Lola Mes thinks she does."

I squatted by the flickering orange and gold of the fire and held out my numb fingers to its warmth. I nodded. "Yes, I know. It was Ojo Verde. I learned last sun that she lived with Minnie, the woman of the man we had to kill last Ghost Face. I went to kill Ojo Verde, but she was already gone and had left Minnie a gift that, had she opened it, would have killed her. I told Juanita and Moon what I had learned and to be watchful. I came here as fast as I could, but I see it was not fast enough. What happened? Where is Knows Horses?"

Lola Mes looked at me with bright eyes, her good one glowing with her Power. "Knows Horses hunts elk up on the great mountain with Beela-chezzi." A soft sigh, sounding like wind through tall grass, came from her lips. "So she comes after all these harvests. Some troubles never die until burned. I knew one sun she must come."

Falling Water covered her mouth with her fingers, staring first at me and then at Lola Mes. "This is the witch who tried to kill our man? Now she comes to kill us all? Are the children safe at that school? Where will we go to get away from her?"

I nodded. "Yes this witch comes to kill us all. I killed the great witch, Sangre del Diablo, many harvests ago. He was her brother and her lover. She comes for blood. The agency school is well protected by tribal police, and I doubt she knows the children are there. Wherever we go, she'll come. We must be ready to kill her on our own ground before she kills us. Tell me how you escaped her fire. Ussen must have helped you."

Falling Water smiled as though I spoke the truth and turned a stick with meat hanging over the fire, its grease dropping into the flames to smoke and snap and pop as it filled the little cave with the fine smell of good eating to come. My belly growled and my mouth watered.

Lola Mes said, "My ears and Power saved us. We were in the tipi eating our evening meal. I heard a faraway roar like a big wind, and a voice said to me, 'Leave the tipi now. Go to the cache cave, and you'll be safe.' It was very dark, but we ran hard for the cave. I heard the roar get louder and looked back at the tipi. A great, orange ball suddenly appeared on top of the cliff behind our tipi. It flew off the top as if it had wings and bounced down the cliff like a waterfall of fire, scattering fire everywhere, but little to nothing burned where it landed. The snow protected everything. The fireball hit the bottom of the cliff, bounced off some bushes, setting them on fire, and roared on into the tipi, which exploded into flames. If we had been inside, it would have burned us to ashes before we could have made the first move to get outside."

Falling Water said, "Yes, we barely escaped, but as we ran, I kept thanking Ussen that our children weren't here." Their children, Idlaaní (One Who Drinks), the first child of Lola Mes, and Na'ilín Súl (Flute Girl), the first child of Falling Water, were both living at the reservation school.

The two women offered me a piece of the meat that had been hanging over the fire. I ate it greedily. My belly quit grumbling and was happy. It had been a long, cold ride, filled with bad visions of what the witch might have done in Knows Horses's canyon.

I waited the proper time after I finished and then announced my business. "Although I came to warn and protect you from Ojo Verde, I also desire the help and wisdom of Lola Mes as a *di-yen.*"

Falling Water raised her brows and looked at Lola Mes as if to ask should she stay. Lola nodded. "My sister and I have no secrets. How can I help our brother?"

I pulled a cigarro from my coat pocket, lit it with a twig from the fire, and we smoked to the four directions before I pitched the end of the cigarro in the fire and said, "Do you want to disappear while I hunt Ojo Verde?"

Lola Mes shook her head. "We won't run from her. Her days must end here. I don't think Minnie knows us, but somehow she found out where we were. I haven't seen her for a long time, and I don't think she yet knows of the children. Otherwise, they would already be sick." She looked at me, her eyes narrow and angry. "You must take Ojo Verde quick, before she kills us all to satisfy her Power and takes blood revenge for Sangre del Diablo."

"Can you to do a Sing that will protect us and give me advice about how to find and kill her? If I find and shoot Ojo Verde face-to-face or kill her with a long shot, James Carroll will somehow learn who did it and send me to the place of *pesh* bars or maybe hang me, because he'll think I broke the law of the Indah. She'll use witch weapons to kill us all like she tried in the camp of Kitsizii Lichoo'. I know I must be very careful when I take her."

Lola Mes thought for a while, saying nothing as she stared into the fire. Falling Water took the coffee pot sitting hot by the edge of the fire, went outside to dump the syrupy brew, returned with it full of nearly melted snow, and made a fresh pot. By the time Falling Water handed me a fresh cup of coffee, it was hot and had the taste of ground piñon nuts, which was like the taste of bitter chocolate sold at the agency store. I took a long swallow and nodded my head in appreciation. Lola Mes looked up from the flames.

"I'll do a Sing and ask for protection for us all from Ojo Verde's Power. I'll do this in a special place after this sun hides behind the mountains, and I'll call on a special Power to come help us.

"You ask my opinion, Brother. I'll give it. My Power says that when the snow on the ridges disappears in the Season of Little Eagles, Ojo Verde will come out and roam to find you when the sun hides behind the mountains. She has waited a long time to kill you. She'll try to put out your eyes as you die for killing Sangre del Diablo and the Comanche you killed in the playa by the mountains the Indah call Animas. This is your advantage. She can't use a rifle or a pistol as you do. She'll have to take your eyes with her knife. It will fill her with pleasure to do this.

Beware of ambushes when you're alone. Find her first or trick her into coming to you if you can."

She saw me frown in confusion and smiled. "If she thinks you're too weak to fight her, she'll come. Ambush her before she tries to ambush you. That is all I have to say."

I nodded and drank more coffee as I thought on what Lola Mes had told me.

I finished my coffee and told the women I would return to cut them new lodge poles after I looked at the top of the canyon where the fire had first appeared. It took a while to find a path to the top of the canyon, but I knew it was the right spot when I found a big empty can of lamp oil and an empty bucket of the type of grease used on wagon axles. Juniper branches cut off the surrounding trees and the bits of rope lying about said the branches had been tied together in a big bundle. A big melted spot in the snow that led to the cliff edge, and places on the bare ground where the snow had melted, showed splashes of lamp oil and grease drippings. I understood then how the fireball had been made by tying juniper limbs together, smearing axle grease on the branches, soaking the ball of greasy branches with lamp oil, lighting it, and when in full flame, pushing it over the cliff edge with a long lodge pole to land on the tipi. That wind Lola Mes heard just before the fire came was from the flames roaring up from the ball.

I had expected something like that to make the fireball, and what I saw did not surprise me. The tracks from five ponies and four different sets of boot tracks and one of moccasin tracks were surprising. The tracks led away from the canyon and up toward the great mountain. I followed them, but they soon split into different directions, impossible to follow. At least this told me that there were four others with Ojo Verde. Truly, as Lola

Mes had told me, I had to watch for an ambush and stay close to home in order to protect my family.

After I returned from the top of the canyon cliffs, I spent the rest of the day cutting new tipi lodge poles and dragged some up to a site Lola Mes showed me near the burned tipi. As the light was falling, Knows Horses returned to the canyon leading a packhorse loaded with fresh meat and an elk hide. Knows Horses saw me and waved his recognition, but when he looked through the trees and saw the place of the burned tipi, his expression went from surprise, to rage, to fear. He rode up and said, "My women? They're good?"

I nodded. "They're good. They barely escaped before fire fell on the tipi. They're in the cache cave with a hot meal waiting for us. I've cut new lodge poles for you. They're anxious for you. Bring your meat and come."

We rode up to the cache cave, the air filled with the good smell of cooking meat and acorn bread. Knows Horses called to them, and they came running to his pony. They took the meat and hide inside the cave, where they could cut the meat up for meals and caching and begin work on curing the hide.

After Lola Mes and Falling Water gave us a meal and we talked of fixing and replenishing a new tipi, Knows Horses and I spoke long into the night about the best way to kill the witch and her riders. I finally slept after two days without rest. I could tell I was getting old. I badly needed to sleep.

As the first light made the black of night gray, I ate from Lola Mes and Falling Water's stewpot, made my belly warm with their coffee, and, after saddling my pony, began the ride back to Mescalero.

CHAPTER 36
THE ATTACK

On the ride back to Mescalero, I thought a long time about where Ojo Verde might hide and how she and her followers might try to ambush me. I thought of the lessons my father taught me. One of the best was that the safest place to hide from an enemy was right in front of his eyes—his camp or in places where he would least expect to find you.

I let my mind range over the canyon where Juanita and Moon had their tipi and decided there was no place there or on the ridges above it where she might hide for more than a sun or two. I thought of Mescalero and places there, but anyone new, especially a woman with one brown eye and one green eye, would be noticed quickly. Gossip would fly, unless she lived away from the People, maybe on a ridge or in a canyon by herself, so no one would know who she was. I decided that she would likely set up a tipi like Minnie's on a close ridge where she could watch the valley and wait for her chance to kill me.

The sun was nearing the time of shortest shadows when I returned to my family. They had seen nothing since I had left. Juanita and Moon had taken half-night turns guarding the camp and had been ready to do battle if Ojo Verde tried to attack, but all was quiet.

While eating from a gourd filled with hot venison stew and chilies, I spoke of what had happened to Lola Mes and Falling Water. Juanita, the skin on her face growing tight with fury, her teeth clenched, said, "You must kill that evil one, or she'll use her Power to take us all. Knows Horses and his women must make their camp with us until someone kills or drives that witch away. With the women of Knows Horses here, there will be four of us to help protect the camp while the men are away, and Lola Mes has the power of a *di-yen* to help us if we have to fight the witch alone."

Moon on the Water, who sat on the other side of me, nodded her agreement. "My sister speaks wise words. Bring Knows Horses and his women here. There is plenty to eat. Knows Horses can find young men to watch his ponies and cattle in the far pastures while he's here."

Even if I was against the idea, which I wasn't, I knew Juanita would find a way to make it happen, regardless of what I thought. I rested that night and returned the next day to bring Knows Horses and his women to camp in our canyon.

The Season of Little Eagles passed into the Season of Many Leaves. Knows Horses rode across our canyon and up on the ridge edges every sun, looking for signs that someone watched the camp, but found none. I studied the ridges around Mescalero every day, looking for a new tipi, but saw none. Every two or three days, Knows Horses rode to the pastures he used for his horses and cattle, stayed a day or two looking after them with Mescalero boys he paid as his helpers, and then returned to help keep watch over our camp. We all knew Ojo Verde was waiting, waiting with the patience of Coyote the trickster, to wipe us out. I believed that Lola Mes's ceremony asking for our protection from the Power of Ojo Verde had worked.

When I said as much one night when we ate together, Lola Mes said, "Maybe so," as she hunched her shoulders and raised her hands. "But a powerful witch like Ojo Verde will find a way around it. She believes she has to avenge her brother, and she won't stop until she has killed you or she is sent to the Happy Land."

One day, in the Season of Many Leaves soon after the time of shortest shadows, dark clouds formed over the high ridges, and a powerful wind blew down the canyons, raising dust in the dry places and making the tall trees sway. When the wind came, the women carried their work inside their tipis and moved the flap poles to cover the tops to keep out the coming rain.

I was at our camp that day making a new pack frame for Juanita's pony and other things I had promised to do. Knows Horses had once more gone to check on his cattle and horses. When the wind came, I was sitting under the trees, shaping a bow strong enough for Redondo to use for hunting. I, too, moved my work inside the tipi. Juanita and Moon asked Lola Mes and Falling Water to join us, and just as they entered, there was a flash of light, an arrow from the Thunder People, followed by the rumble of their voices.

As Juanita was closing the tipi door cover, Redondo, who sat looking out the doorway watching the trees shake in the wind on the far side of the canyon, said, "Look! There!" Juanita glanced out the open crack of light before she tied the door closed.

She said, "I saw nothing, my son. What did you see?"

"There was a rider on a horse up on the ridge looking this way. I know I saw one. Didn't you see one, Mother?"

Juanita glanced at me as she said, "No, son, I saw no one, but that doesn't mean you didn't."

Redondo made a face, crossed his arms, and stared at the ground while I pulled my rifle from its scabbard, dropped extra cartridges in my vest pocket, and slid my knife in its sheath behind my belt. As the rain began to fall, I lifted the edge of the tipi cover on the side opposite the door and crawled under it into the rain and shadows. I heard Redondo ask where I was going, and Juanita say, "Keep silence!"

I crawled through the brush along the canyon edge of the side with the tipis, staying out of sight of the other side of the canyon. It was raining so hard, no one on the far ridge could have seen me anyway. I reached trees growing up the slope and across the end wall of the canyon, and crossed to the other side while climbing to the ridge top. The rain moved away down the big canyon toward Mescalero. Already the Thunder People with their lightning arrows had left.

Steam rose like smoke from the ground as I reached the top of the ridge, but it was clear enough to look down the canyon and see the two tipis far below in the trees on the other side. I moved along the top of the ridge toward the place where Redondo had pointed. Water dripped off the trees, and the little rushes of water rolling and tumbling down the hill toward the creek at the bottom made the only sounds in the canyon. Heavy clouds still hid the sun, making the light seem like it was near the end of the day.

Down the ridge on the backside of the spot where Redondo had pointed, I saw a black pony tied to a bush out of sight of the tipis. I cocked my rifle and moved like a shadow toward the pony. It was hard to do. The leaves of every bush were loaded with water waiting to shake and fall. I had to move slowly and very carefully to avoid nudging the brush and announcing my progress to whoever owned the black pony.

I crept to within fifty yards of the pony, but saw no sign of its rider. *The rider must still be watching our tipi, but from where?* A slight breeze was in my face. The pony couldn't smell me and, at that distance, couldn't hear me as he grazed on the surrounding brush. I paused, listening for a while, but heard only the thumping of my heart before edging forward. The clouds were passing, and the sunlight began sending shafts of bright white light through the branches and steam rising off the ground.

At twenty-five yards from the pony, I still saw nothing. I looked for track signs around him and saw none. I sniffed the air but smelled only him. *Maybe this is a trap.* I paused again but saw nothing in the low light of dark clouds and tree shadows. My growing curiosity moved me on. I edged closer; twenty, fifteen, ten yards from the pony, whose ears lifted. He turned toward me when my weight on the wet juniper needles made a low squeaky sound. I sighted down the rifle barrel, pointing to places where I thought the rider might be hiding, looking for the least movement of anything, but saw no one.

Suddenly the brush on the ground between me and the pony and just behind and to my right and left seemed to explode, hurling sticks, small bushes, and pine needles into the air. I saw a face painted in black above the nose and in white below. I shot an eye. I levered a new cartridge as my rifle swung in a fast arc to find a clear shot at the figure on my right. But before I could shoot, two rawhide reata loops whipped over me from behind and to my left and were jerked tight around my legs and neck. With sharp, quick pulls they threw me to the ground. I landed hard on my back, and breath left me. My rifle was jerked out of my hands and disappeared. The loop around my neck tightened as I grabbed my knife and slashed left and right while I struggled to stand. I couldn't breathe and felt my body being stretched beyond its length. I saw a club raised, a flash of bright light, and darkness filled my eyes.

Light returned. I hung by my wrists from the limb of a tall pine growing on a little flat on the ridge below the black pony. My mind began to clear as if awakening from a dream. I felt a reata burn circling my neck, the pull of my shoulder joints against the reata where I dangled, a dull pounding ache across my forehead, and the crinkle of stuff on my face that I knew must be drying blood.

I looked down and saw that my moccasins dangled just above a pile of brush. My knees were lashed together, my upper arms tied above my head with tight, solid knots. I hung like a side of beef ready for butchering. As I came back from the darkness, I realized the People burned witches this way. Ojo Verde planned to burn me like a witch. Of course! The thought of burning someone who was not a witch as a witch must fill her mind as the best possible revenge.

As my eyes began to focus, I saw Ojo Verde sitting a few feet away with her legs crossed and my rifle lying in her lap. She had black paint around her eye sockets in the same way her brother had painted his, and there were vertical streaks the color of blue stone from her forehead to her jaw running down her face. Her hair hung in braids woven from her black and white-streaked hair. When she saw my eyes opening, she bared her teeth, stained the color of blood, in a snarling grin.

A man sat on each side of her, and up on the ridgeline were two more, who, looking young enough to be on their first raid, watched where the tipis stood. They all looked like reservation vaqueros, except, unlike Mescaleros, they had long, tight hair braids and wore holstered revolvers. I had never seen any vaqueros like them around Mescalero or the ranchos nearby. They rolled and smoked cigarettes, holding them between two fingers or letting them dangle from the corners of their mouths in the way Indah vaqueros smoked.

An old man, his gray hair falling from under his ancient, wide-brimmed, sweat-stained hat, sat on the right side of Ojo Verde and leaned back on an elbow, smoking as he studied me with narrowed eyes and a twisted grin. The young man on her left side sat cross-legged carving a long, sharp point on a stick the size of his thumb. I didn't doubt the worst of tortures were coming, but I was determined to never shame my family or grandfathers with a sound of agony that might satisfy these people.

Ojo Verde, despite the way her face was painted, still looked like a woman Comanche men would want to take to the dark bushes in the heat of a big dance. She cocked her head to one side when she saw my eyes open. "So, Killer of Witches, we haven't killed you after all? That's good. That is very good. It will increase my pleasure to see you screaming in a fire. How do you like the reata skills of my friends from Quanah Parker's rancho? Are they not *excelente*?"

I croaked, my voice slow to return after being choked by the reata around my neck. "I think maybe there is one less vaquero for Quanah Parker's rancho. For Comanche vaqueros, it's probably the best they can do. Bring them to Mescalero, and Apaches will teach them better."

The old vaquero's thumb flipped a pebble he curled in a forefinger that hit me on the forehead and stung. "Soon we'll teach you to scream with a begging tongue, if you still have one, Apache."

After staring at me for a time, Ojo Verde slowly shook her head. "I don't understand how you managed to kill my man. You are so weak and small. He was big and strong, a mighty warrior, and yet you shot out his eyes. I've heard the story told around campfires all over Chihuahua and in the Blue Mountains. I would have avenged him long ago if his girl from a slave woman hadn't run off and then come to save you and your boys and woman in the Blue Mountains. No matter. I'll have my revenge and taste its sweetness on my tongue as I slaughter her and your women and children, drink their blood, and, with my own hands, send you blind, on fire and screaming, to the Happy Land. All of Mescalero and Chihuahua will know the Power of Ojo Verde, woman of Sangre del Diablo, and they will fear me.

They'll see with their own eyes what I did to you and how I sent you to wander the Happy Land for all time burned, with no man parts and, like my brother, with no eyes."

The old vaquero who stretched out beside her, grinning and nodding, finished his smoke, mashed its ashes in the ground, pulled my knife from its sheath to test its blade with his thumb, and, nodding that its sharpness was satisfactory, slid it back. I struggled against the rawhide ropes that bound me, but I couldn't even twist my wrists as the prickles from no circulation started growing on my arms and legs.

Ojo Verde, showing her red-dyed teeth again in a snarl, continued. "It does no good to try to wiggle off the reata, little man. Before you go to the Happy Land, you'll see your women forced many times and then gutted by my vaqueros, and your children hung by their necks next to you to strangle and kick against their last breaths. We'll make your brother last a long time, upside down, while his head roasts over a fire. He'll die like the *brujos* killed by the People in the long-ago times. I'll take your mind with suffering before you go to the Happy Land, Killer of Witches. No more will you ever know the pleasure of having killed my man, even in the Happy Land."

She turned to the old vaquero. "Take the women and boys in the tipi. Send two of your *hombres* to watch on either side of the canyon entrance for Knows Horses so he doesn't surprise you. Then we begin."

He grunted and stood up. "Soon we return. My vaqueros will be eager for the women. They can have them then?"

She sneered, "*Sí*, bring them for us all to watch while you mount them. Perhaps, for the greatest stud among you, I myself will give a little extra reward, eh?"

His smile broadened, and he nodded. He waved the other men to follow him across the ridge. "*Muchachos! Vamos!*" ("Boys! We go!")

CHAPTER 37
A WITCH'S FIRE

After the vaqueros disappeared up the ridgeline to the path into the canyon, following nearly the same dim path I had followed to their trap, Ojo Verde reached over and picked up the stick with the sharp point the vaquero had been carving. Squinting at me, she caressed the long point with her long, smooth fingers and grinned. "Something to fit in your eye sockets before you leave us, eh, Yellow Boy? Especially after your rifle shoots off your man parts." She giggled in the way of old women. "After your women are done and gone, you'll have no need of them." She paused to stare up into the treetops and then, turning her gaze back to me, giggled again. "No, wait. Maybe I won't use this old rifle to take your man parts. I'll use my knife instead and use them to make strong medicine. That way, part of you'll still be around after you're gone. Maybe I do you a favor and do that if you beg hard enough. How do you like that, Killer of Witches?"

I stared at the evil in front of me and said nothing, wanting only to rid the land of her.

She opened a bag she carried around her neck and pulled out a sliver of bone about half a hand-width long. It looked the same length as the witch's weapon Lola Mes had sucked from Knows Horses's forehead many harvests ago. She pulled her knife, felt its sharpness with her thumb, and began to carefully scrape and shape the bone sliver into a tiny arrow. The sun descended a hand-width against the horizon, and the shadows grew longer.

My arms had become numb, but I could still feel the rawhide reata slowly cutting into my wrists and little streams of blood begin trickling down my arms. She finished her work, dropped the bone sliver back into her bag, and, with the back of her hand, swept the bone scrapings off her shirt. She looked at me and showed her red teeth again. "The vaqueros will be taking your women and children soon. This will be fun to watch. Too bad you can't see it. Ha, but I can."

She laid my rifle to one side and climbed up the ridge to stand concealed behind a big pine where she could watch the ti-pis. I heard her say, "Ha! Good. Two vaqueros are going into the trees and brush on either side of the canyon as I told them to do. The other two go to the tipi to take your women and sons. Soon, we pleasure ourselves with them." She looked back over her shoulder at me and grinned as she turned back to watch the action below.

While she watched the tipi, I struggled in desperation to get free, but the reata knots held as I jerked and tried to break the reata. The blood streams from my wrists run down my arms, and I could feel my strength fading. She continued talking aloud to herself, or maybe she wanted me to hear and imagine what was happening as I struggled to get free.

"Old Quick Rope pulls his *pistola* and cocks it. He slowly pulls back the door blanket. Easy, Quick Rope. You don't want to make them slide under the back cover for Blue Hand to catch or shoot. I hope they come easy, so he does not kill them all on their blankets . . . Easy, that's right. Let them see your *pistola* first . . . Speak easy . . . Ease your head through the door and let them know you will have them or kill them."

The snapping low thunder from a rifle echoed down the canyon. Her mouth dropped open in surprise, and she ran a few steps to the right for a better view, moving her head in all directions to find a hole in the brush she could see through. *So your vaqueros rape and kill my women and hang my sons, Ojo Verde? Maybe you put out my eyes and burn me, but taking my women with Comanche vaqueros won't happen. My women are Apaches.*

The echoes from the rifle shot were barely gone before there was another shot, and in the space of a quick breath, another, filling the canyon with echoes. Ojo Verde turned toward me, her teeth clenched, her face dark with rage. She screamed, "Coyotes, tricksters, have killed my vaqueros, but I will have my revenge!"

She stopped at her blanket, spread a few rifle lengths from the brush pile where I dangled and where she had worked on the arrow carving. She bent over the blanket, and the sharpened stick filled her hand ready to stab me. She stood up straight, looking at it and then me. She started toward me, her arm raising the stick toward my eyes, but she stopped and turned, looked at the rifle for the space of several breaths, thinking, and then laughed. "No, Killer of Witches, this won't be so easy for you. First, I start the fire, and then use the rifle to take your man parts. Ha! The same weapon that took Sangre del Diablo's eyes will take your man parts. When the grease begins falling from your flaming body, then your eyes will go while you scream. It's a revenge Sangre del Diablo would want. I will tear the guts from your coyote women after I send you to wander blind and burned with no man parts in the Happy Land."

She disappeared down the ridge into the brush where the vaqueros had tied their ponies and returned with a brown whiskey jug. She bared her red teeth to bite into its stopper like an apple, jerked it free, spat it away, and walked around the brush pile under me pouring the whiskey over it all. The whiskey's sweet, strong smell made my mouth water, but I knew I would never taste whiskey again. *You whore witch, Ussen will take you after I'm gone. I can only hope you die by the hands of my women.*

She pulled a big, Redhead match from the bag around her neck and struck it, using the butt end of the knife she carried. A smile filled her face, and she said as she tossed the match toward the brush pile, "This is for you, my brother, wherever you are."

In a quiet swoosh, blue flames followed the whiskey paths she had thrown on the brush under me. I could smell the smoke as the first flash from the flames quieted, and the little fires that had caught sputtered to grow in the damp brush. Ojo Verde waited, still and quiet, like a hunter waiting for deer to come down a game trail. As she watched the flames slowly grow, she mumbled, "Burn him, burn him."

The smoke choked my lungs and burned my eyes, and then began to clear, filling my chest with air that grew warmer with each breath. Small sputtering flames scattered in the brush began to leisurely spread and rise, gaining strength to send me to the Happy Land. *At least the women survived. Knows Horses will have more wives than he knows what to do with. Ussen give me strength to face the growing fire and the bullets from the rifle you made part of me to use as a gift of Power. May my women escape the evil of this Comanche witch.*

Ojo Verde sat down on the blanket, rested her elbows on her knees, and sighted the rifle on my man parts as I slowly twisted above the growing fire. "At last, my brother, you will have your revenge." She pulled the hammer back. "Just a little longer, Yellow Boy, let us give the fire time to grow and start burning you. Then will your own rifle take your man parts like a cougar tearing meat with sharp claws. You must feel the fire, feel it like witches, my good sisters, when they're sent to the Happy Land. I promise, your women will see what's left of your bones swinging at the end of that reata before I take them."

Time seemed to slow, and, like watching a far scene through the *Shináá Cho*, I clearly saw her finger curling around the rifle's trigger to blow away my man parts. Then I heard a thump, a sound like a fist striking an overripe melon. Ojo Verde's face froze, and her eyes rolled back in her head. The rifle slid out of her hands as she fell over on her right side, blood oozing from the hair on the side of her head. I looked up the ridge path and saw Juanita running for me with her sling in one hand and her knife in the other.

She ran past the still body of Ojo Verde to the tree where the reata holding me over the growing flames was tied and, in a swooping slash, cut the reata so I fell into the brush pile. Running into the scattered flames, she reached around my chest and dragged me out of the fire, scattering burning twigs and limbs on damp pine needles and brush. She pulled me into a little hollow behind the tree from which I'd hung and slapped out the little burn spots that had begun on my pants and shirt, saying between puffs, "I . . . can't . . . run as I did . . . when I was a girl. I was . . . almost not here in time . . . and even then I had to use the sling while I ran . . . not very accurate using a sling when you run . . . but I think I got her."

I coughed more suffocating smoke out of my chest and croaked, "*Ish-tia-neh,* you came before she pulled that trigger, and then you pulled me off the fire before it could take me. That's soon enough."

She smiled, her eyes wide with relief, and pulling her knife, began cutting the ropes that held my hands, arms, legs, and feet. Feeling began to return to my arms and shoulders as she helped me to a sitting position and slapped and kneaded my muscles to get the circulation back.

My rifled spoke, and bark and splinters flew off the tree trunk a forearm length above my head. Ojo Verde, one side of her face turning blue and her hair matted in blood, sat up and, again, tried to rest her elbows on her knees for rifle support. The end of the rifle waved back and forth as she attempted to sight on us with eyes that still refused to focus while she mumbled,

"These must die. These must die, my brother."

The burning twigs and limbs Juanita had scattered while pulling me off the fire had found dry tinder beneath the damp pine needles, and a wall of fire and smoke grew, concealing us from Ojo Verde trying to shoot my rifle.

Juanita grabbed my shirt and pulled me over on my side, out of sight behind the tree, when we heard Ojo Verde cursing and struggling to lever another cartridge into the Yellow Boy. It fired a second time, grazing a tree just behind us. Ojo Verde's voice grew louder and stronger, "Die, Killer of Witches. I will see you die." The flames and smoke blocked our sight of her.

Juanita raised up on her knees, out of sight behind the tree, and pulled a smooth, brown, river stone from a sack tied to her belt, mounting it in her sling. Then, moving so she had a shot at Ojo Verde, she twirled the sling just fast enough for the stone to stay in its pouch. We waited. I feared the fire would spread and burn the trees off the ridge and us along with them, but it did not. The powerful rain, making everything lying near the top of the ground wet, saved us.

We heard no more from Ojo Verde. I tried to draw her fire by slowly raising my head above the depression where we'd taken cover. Juanita waited, whirling her sling so hard the straps hummed and swished through the air like a cloud of angry bees. Juanita was ready to loose the stone that would end Ojo Verde's life in that little window of time when she levered another bullet to fire.

The rifle never spoke. Looking through the fire and smoke I saw that Ojo Verde had taken the Yellow Boy and gone. She had stolen my Power. My stomach felt like I had eaten bad meat and my head hung in despair, my mind confused and enraged. A witch had stolen my Power. How could that be? How could Ussen let her do such a thing? I had to reclaim my Power.

Juanita pulled me to my feet and I staggered down the ridge

following Ojo Verde's trail, Juanita behind me ready with her sling. We came to the place where Ojo Verde's vaqueros had tied their horses. The body of the Comanche I had killed in their ambush was wrapped in a blanket nearby. Three horses still stood there with their saddle cinches loose and watched us with their ears up. Tracks showed Ojo Verde had taken two ponies and ridden off down the canyon. After she reached the wagon road between Fort Stanton and Mescalero, her tracks would disappear as they mixed with all the others. My rifle, my Power from Ussen, was gone. I had to find Ojo Verde to get my Power back again.

Juanita left me with the ponies and climbed back up the ridge to bring the big, black pony Ojo Verde had left. When Juanita returned, I tightened the cinch on one of the vaquero ponies and mounting, my arms and body sore and stiff, we rode down the big canyon to our camp.

CHAPTER 38
LOLA MES DISAPPEARS

I was close to falling off my pony by the time Juanita and I reached the camp. The other women had used a horse to drag the Comanche vaquero bodies to the corral where they could be burned. The women and boys were happy to see us and took our horses to care for them. I made it inside the tipi and fell on my blankets with no strength left. The women, singing, made a big cooking fire and started to work on an evening meal to celebrate our victory. Only Juanita understood that I had lost my Power.

Moon kept the boys outside to eat and play in the growing dusk while Juanita brought me a savory meal of venison, wild potatoes, acorn bread, roasted tips of yucca, and slices of steamed mescal. She watched me closely as I ate, studying the burned places on my neck and body from the reatas and fire. She shook her head. "Considering all you went through today, you're very lucky you're not hurt any worse than you are. When you finish eating, Moon and I will make medicine for your burned places, and we'll get Lola Mes to do a Sing for you. Maybe she can advise you on how to find Ojo Verde and regain your Power."

The pleasure of the good meal filled me, and hearing the wise words of my first woman made me smile. Setting the empty eating gourd down, I was finally able to flex my fingers and move my arm joints. "So, *Ish-tia-neh,* once more your sling has saved us from disaster like it did against the Chiricahua soldier

287

scout Soldado Fiero many harvests ago. I'm proud my woman is a strong warrior. I place great value on her as first wife. Tell me what happened here at our lodges."

She looked at me and puffed her cheeks. "Lola Mes saved us. As soon as you left, she said she had dreamed all this the night after her tipi was burned. Her dream showed a black horse standing high above her. Ojo Verde had already taken you, and had you floating high in the air at her command. She saw the four Comanches from clouds come to take us."

Juanita lifted her chin with pride and smiled. "We decided to ambush the Comanches when they came for us. Lola Mes crawled under the back edge of our tipi in the same place you did, and then went back to her tipi. She took the rifle and some cartridges Knows Horses had left for her. Then she eased out and crawled through the brush until she found a place to sit where she had a clear shot at the blankets over the doors of the tipis. Moon, Falling Water, our sons, and I slipped out the back, and, staying low, ran to the little cave where we cache meat and supplies. I gave Moon your *pistola* and some cartridges and told her to use them if the Comanches came."

I held up my hand for her to stop and pulling a cigarro from my shirt said, "Your story will be told around the fires for many harvests. I would smoke to honor it." We smoked to the four directions. "Go on," I said. "Now my ears will always remember your words."

"By that time, the rain had stopped. I was running toward the trail you had taken up the ridge. True to Lola Mes's vision, I saw four Comanches coming down the ridge trail and running toward the tipis. I hid, let them pass, and then followed them back down to the tipis. I saw the old man with gray hair send two to watch the canyon entrance and one around to the back of my tipi. While they waited for the two running for the canyon entrance, I moved down the trail toward the tipis, got within sling range of the one behind the tipi, and dropped him, never to rise again, where he crouched.

"When the old Comanche with gray hair pulled back the door blanket and waved his pistol for us to come out, Lola Mes killed him where he stood at the tipi door. When the others came running, she killed them, too. Then I ran back for the top of this ridge and the place where Redondo had seen the black pony. The rest you know."

My chest swelled with pride enough to break my shirt buttons. I waved my hand parallel to the ground. "I have great pride in my women and my brother's wives. Today you saved us all from a great evil that has been around a long time."

She smiled. "Rest now. Soon Moon and I will put poultices on your burns."

Before I slept, Moon and Juanita packed poultices on me like Rufus had used on Hombrecito's cut face when he ran from his father's killers. Just as Moon and Juanita were leaving, Lola Mes appeared at the tipi door to do a Sing for my quick healing.

I waved her in and thanked her for coming. She wrinkled her nose at the stink of the poultice, but smiled and sat near my pallet, making the sign with her palm that all was well. "You will heal fast. I'm happy to do a Sing for you. I want you to heal quickly so you can search for your Power and send Ojo Verde blind to the Happy Land. I'll help you any way I can."

Her eye with the milky white center glittered as if it had sight like the other one flashing in the firelight. The scars that had appeared when she had been blinded during the ceremony to destroy Ojo Verde's big witch weapon were hidden by her long hair falling over her face.

I nodded and made a smile on one side of my face. "Your good shooting saved us all much sorrow. I'm very grateful. I don't know where to find the witch who has stolen my Power. Can you do another ceremony to help me find her?"

She folded her hands over her belly and stared at the flames for a while. "Yes, I can do a Sing to help you find Ojo Verde, but you won't need it. My dream vision that saw this day said that soon Ussen shows you the way. You'll see. Now I'll do you a healing ceremony."

I slept much during the next three days, and my burns healed much faster than I thought they would. Juanita told me Knows Horses had returned the day after the attack. Great anger had come on him, and he wanted to burn the bodies of the Comanches and immediately start the search for Ojo Verde, but Lola Mes convinced him the bodies ought to go to the tribal police for burial, so the police knew Ojo Verde had attacked us and would be ready to help find her. He loaded the stinking Comanche vaquero bodies on a couple of ponies and took them to the tribal police, who buried them. Then they began a search with Knows Horses all over the reservation, but they never found any trace of Ojo Verde.

On the fourth day after the attack, I staggered, sore and torn, out of the tipi to sit on a blanket. A shaft of sunlight falling through the tall pine branches warmed my face, and it was good to hear the little animals scrambling in the pine needles, the twitter of congregations of bushtits in the brush, and the *Jeet! Jeet!* of a canyon wren. The women and boys had already left to find trees with acorns and to search for berries. *Soon Ussen will give me strength to begin my search for my lost Power.*

I lighted a cigarro and, before beginning work on new long arrows for my bow, I prayed to Ussen, asking a blessing to make them shoot straight with great power. Their wood I had split from a nice piece of cedar I had found and set aside after Knows

Horses had first moved his camp to have his tipi near ours. The sun rose above the canyon rim and headed for the top of the sky while I made the once-rough shafts smooth and straight. As I worked, I thought of the many places Ojo Verde might be, and, sick in my spirit, wondered if I would live long enough to find her and take back my Power.

Near the time of shortest shadows, the breeze paused in the tall trees, and I thought I heard a distant yell over on the far side of the big canyon ridge. I stopped and, holding my hand to my ear, listened, but heard nothing else as the breeze came again. *It's probably just children playing,* I thought.

The sound of horses running up the canyon came after I had smoothed six straight shafts and sat cutting notches for their arrowheads I had made out of barrel hoop iron like those in the days many harvests ago. The women and boys were returning from their gathering hunt. When I looked up as they splashed water in great rainbows galloping through the creek into our camp, I saw terror in their faces. Only three of the four women who had left that morning returned.

Juanita slid off her pony and ran to me as I pushed myself up to stand. "Lola Mes has disappeared!"

I felt my guts grow tight. I knew Ojo Verde would return and that this must be her doing. We could only hope we would find Lola Mes before Ojo Verde sent her to the Happy Land. "Tell me."

Juanita, still gasping for air, took a deep breath and puffed her cheeks to gain control of her worry. "We separated to look for stands of juniper and other berries and then planned to come back together when the sun was two hands after the time of shortest shadows. She didn't come back. We waited over a hand-width against the sun and then looked for her."

The breeze through the tops of the pines sounded like a sigh, and high above, ravens returned from the mountains to the Río

Tularosa and their night trees.

"We found a place where the brush was bent down like someone had stomped it, but we found no tracks, only this." She handed me a shiny blue stone. I knew it was the one Lola Mes always carried in a pocket in her skirt.

"Moon and Falling Water, stay here with the boys and guard the camp. Juanita, bring your sling and come with me." All my wounds and internal soreness were forgotten as I went to the tipi, got my old revolver, saddle, and bridle, and then went to the corral to saddle my pony. Knows Horses was still out with the tribal police. I could only hope I caught Ojo Verde before she used her Power on Lola Mes.

The shadows from the falling sun were growing long when Juanita showed me where she had found the blue stone. The broken and bent brush told its story. Lola Mes had not been taken without a fight. I studied the scene, looking for signs. I saw where three men and a woman hiding in the brush had watched her for a while. The faint tracks I found in the brush showed the woman had watched the men take Lola Mes in a big struggle, and that one had carried her away. The tracks led to a cliff edge and then disappeared. I studied the rocks and boulders in the shadows below, but saw nothing. It was nearing full darkness when Juanita and I returned to camp.

Over a meal, I told the women what I had seen and why I thought Ojo Verde and three others, probably all Comanches, had taken Lola Mes. My sons listened with big round eyes, probably thinking they were lucky Ojo Verde hadn't taken them. Moon and Falling Water listened with bowed heads. When I finished speaking, Falling Water looked at me with sad eyes, "Will they kill my sister?"

I shook my head. "Not if I can find her in time, but I don't know where they've taken her. I'll search again tomorrow. Maybe I'll learn then where they go."

CHAPTER 39
A SPIRIT SPEAKS

In the darkness far across and high above a distant llano, Thunder Spirits sent lightning arrows between black, angry clouds. Wind danced and sang. In the flashing light from the lightning arrows, the llano approached endless towering cliffs. Two great eyes, one brown, one green, crossed the llano and floated together high into the darkness above the cliffs there to see a woman floating above a great shiny mirror and, above her, a bright yellow flame. The mirror was surrounded and protected by balls of green fire. The Thunder Spirits came closer, sending rain on great swollen legs and lightning arrows, speaking their anger. The big eyes turned from the woman and came for me. I ran toward the Thunder Spirits and Wind, calling on Ussen to help me, but the great eyes followed. I ran faster. The eyes drew closer.

My eyes snapped open, and, looking up the through the hub of crossed tipi poles, I saw many points of white light in the smooth blackness of the night sky. A few orange coals dusted with gray ashes still glowed in the fire pit, and my women and children slept peacefully. I used my shirtsleeve to wipe the water from my face as my breathing and pounding heart slowed. *Thank you, Ussen. I know you have shown me the way back to Ojo Verde, Lola Mes, and the gift of Power you gave me.*

I sat up, eager to ride. At almost the same time, Moon and Juanita awoke and sat up in their blankets. Moon whispered, "Our husband dreams? He has visions?"

"Ussen has shown me the way to Lola Mes and the witch who took her. I must go."

Juanita was out of her blankets and through the tipi door. Moon used twigs to bring flames from the orange coals, and then she, too, was out the door. Soon Juanita returned with firewood in her arms. As she placed it over the twig flames, Moon came in with a piece of venison and a sack of trail food.

While Moon and Juanita cooked, I carried my saddle, blanket, bow, and quiver of arrows to the corral and made my pony ready to ride. The moon was falling into the black mountain outline against the stars on the southwest horizon when I saw the glow of a fire in Falling Water's tipi. I met her as she threw back the tipi door blanket, and told her I had dreamed. I asked her to come share a meal with us before I left to face Ojo Verde and take back Lola Mes and my Power.

My sons slept through our meal. While I ate, I told my women and Falling Water of my dream. They listened with bowed heads and ears turned toward me. When I finished, Juanita nodded. "So they have taken your Power and Lola Mes to an old Cha camp in the Guadalupe Mountains where we lived in our young days?"

The fingers of Moon and Falling Water flew to their lips, and I heard Falling Water whisper, "Of course. That's the place."

I nodded. "I think my dreams say it is so."

Juanita drew her blanket tighter around her, as if she shivered with the cold night air. "Those camps are at least a hard three-, maybe four-day ride. Be strong, husband, and don't leave us widows. I hope you make it in time."

"We'll probably return in ten suns. Look for us then. Falling Water, tell Knows Horses what I have told you, and tell him I said to wait here."

Falling Water nodded. Juanita followed me to my pony. I mounted, and, looking down at her, said, "Soon we return."

Her hand rested lightly on my knee. "Your family is here."

I rode off down the canyon as the long-ago warriors went to war, quiet, ready.

I rode along the wagon road to Tularosa and followed a little-used trail south through the creosote and mesquite on the west side of the Sacramento Mountains until I passed west of Alamogordo. Then I pointed my pony southwest toward the little canyon in the Jarillas I had used many times as the first resting place out of Mescalero on my way to the Blue Mountains or to the rancho Rufus Pike had left Hombrecito. My pony was weary, and I was, too. Given the Indah way of considering distance, their maps would show we had covered over sixty miles that day.

The little spring that always ran there was in full flow, and the natural water tank at the end of the canyon was full. I carried grain for my pony and, after rubbing him down, fed him well. He needed to be strong and able to run for a long time on this witch-hunt. I ate my trail food without a fire, smoked a cigarro, and, taking my blanket, climbed up the canyon wall to a shelf we used to watch over the camp where I could see the llano between the Jarilla and Organ mountains in soft moonlight and the black shadows cast by tall yuccas, mesquite thickets, and many scattered creosotes, gourds, and weeds. I wondered as I drifted into the land of dreams if, after facing Ojo Verde and her Comanches, I would be alive to see this land again.

I left the Jarillas when the moon was not long above the western mountains. By the time the sun was halfway to the time of shortest shadows, I had followed a great arroyo up to flat land that stretched south. The Guadalupe Mountains—the place where I grew to be a warrior and my dream said Ojo Verde hid—rose high in the gray distance, rugged and waiting, filled with life or death for anyone who chose to enter them.

As the shadows grew long and the great Guadalupe cliffs grew bright from the fast falling sun, I crossed the sand dunes on the northern end of the great salt flats. Many points of light in the darkening sky had begun appearing when I found a water wheel keeping a cattle tank full and stopped to rest my pony.

I left the cattle tank when the moon rose above the Guadalupes and rode through the foothills around the mountains until I came to the canyon in the cliffs my People under Chief Cha used to access the llano south to the Davis Mountains, where other Apache bands camped. A flood of memories filled me, and I thought of the many good times my friends and I had as we grew to manhood and became warriors. I looked up the cliffs. The white stone bathed in moonlight near their tops high above me hid the shelf and shallow cave where I had spent many days with my adopted grandfather, He Watches, searching the San Antonio to El Paso road for the dust raised by freight wagons or that of approaching Blue Coat horse columns.

Those good bright days became black when Sangre del Diablo and his warriors and pistoleros came looking for scalps while Cha and most of his warriors were off raiding in Mexico. I was in the Organ Mountains with Rufus Pike learning to shoot and, in a mighty storm from the Thunder and Wind Spirits, received my Power to kill witches from Ussen.

I entered the canyon we used to take off the llano for Cha's camp. After a short ride, I caught the scent of smoke in the cold, black air. I looked up the canyon walls but saw no signs of firelight anywhere. Soon the moon would fall behind the mountains to the southwest and dawn would come. I rode on, needing to find a hiding place for my pony while I looked for Ojo Verde and her Comanches.

The smell of smoke brought back the memory of the long-ago time when I rode into the Cha camp of burned lodges. As my pony strained to climb up the steep trail toward a high meadow where I could hobble him to graze unseen, my mind strained to understand why Ussen had let Ojo Verde take my rifle, my Power.

Why did my Power leave? Now I'm facing a mighty witch, and all I have for weapons are a bow and arrows, and a knife. How can I save Lola Mes or protect myself without my Power and only a bow and arrows against evil men with rifles? I know I probably won't leave this place alive. Yet somehow, the circle of death and revenge feels complete here. Whatever happens, my fight with a witch's evil began here, and it will end here. Perhaps Ussen will speak to me before I go to the Happy Place.

I hobbled my pony in the shadows of the cliffs in the first meadow nearly halfway to the top of the mountain. There I slept, hidden under junipers in the cool canyon air, until the sun had fallen halfway from the time of no shadows to the west side of the canyon. I crawled from my sleeping place and drank long and deep from the spring dribbling into a small stream nearby. Then, taking my weapons, as I had when I was a boy in training, I ran up the trail to the high meadow where Cha's camp had been.

Somehow, the trail didn't seem nearly as long or steep as when I was a boy. By the time I reached the meadow at the top, I had seen many signs of someone using the trail a few days earlier and knew I had come to the right place. I took care not to be seen as I worked my way through the grama grass and junipers toward Cha's camp.

It seemed natural to see six ponies grazing in the meadow as other horses had in the long-ago days. I hid in the grass and weeds and watched them for a while. Their mixed brands and iron shoes told me they probably had been stolen.

As the shadows began to grow long, I slipped closer to the juniper grove where Cha tipis and wickiups once stood. The smell of piñon wood smoke grew stronger. I neared a grove of great, ancient piñons and let my head float above the weeds and grass to see a thin column of smoke rising above the trees. I crawled into the dark shadows and splashes of yellow light under the piñons to rest and wait for the coming darkness, when I could move without danger of being seen.

The air was still and hot. Bees and butterflies buzzed and floated around the blossoms on the weeds and yucca nearby, and slow-moving sap oozing from the bark of the piñons gave the air a tart, sweet smell.

CHAPTER 40
THE SPIRITS COME

Far to the west, the sky was a blaze of changing colors—purples, reds, oranges, and yellows—on thick, heavy clouds that foretold rain to the south as darkness like a soft blanket settled over the high meadow. I stood unseen in the shadows. I saw firelight flickering against the tree branches. In the lengthening shadows, I moved toward the light.

As I drew closer, I heard chanting and a slow, rhythmic beat made on a stiff dry hide. Looking through the trees, I saw the bare backs of three warriors ready for war, wearing only breechcloths, their hair in tightly woven braids and, on top of their heads, two or three eagle feathers that showed they were battle-seasoned Comanche warriors who had counted coup. Streaks of blue and white paint looking like lightning arrows ran the length of their arms and the sides of their legs, and someone had painted symbols in white and red I didn't recognize on their backs. They kept time, pounding on the hide with a hoop stick in one hand while holding a repeating rifle in the other.

I heard ceremony singing in high-pitched words in a language I didn't understand from the barking mouth of Ojo Verde, as she sang with her arms held out straight from her sides. Her face still showed blue and yellow bruises from Juanita's stone, and the side of her head was swollen. She stood between a big fire crackling behind her and, a few yards away, to her front the edge of a shiny circle surrounded by large balls of brush made by tying juniper limbs together. Something shiny was on the juniper limbs that gleamed in the firelight. At the center of the circle stood a tall, shiny pole perhaps half a forearm in diameter. Lola Mes was lashed to it. Tied at the top was a beautifully beaded leather sack that held my Power, my rifle, pointing straight up toward the milk river made by points of light filling the smooth, black sky. Many different kinds of fetishes and feathers hung from the leather. I knew it must contain a witch weapon, and I would have to be careful if I got the chance to handle it.

The face of Lola Mes was purple and yellow from bruises, but she stood there, her good eye nearly swollen shut, her bad eye gleaming in the firelight, her jaw lifted in defiance, waiting without fear the evil Ojo Verde would surely bring her. Beyond the fire, I saw many of the same kinds of buckets of lamp oil and wagon grease I had seen on the cliffs above the tipis of Lola Mes and Falling Water when the ball of burning juniper limbs went over the cliff edge.

So, Ojo Verde had everything around Lola Mes soaked in lamp oil, and wagon grease was on the balls of juniper limbs around the edge of the puddle of oil. The shiny pool in which Lola Mes stood would become a great fireball, burning her to nothing but dusty ashes, and my rifle into useless iron fit for nothing when fire touched the oil.

From where I watched, I knew I was fast enough with my bow to put arrows in the backs of all three warriors before one could turn to fire his rifle, and, if none of them in their dying alerted Ojo Verde, I might be able to put an arrow in her head to stop her from casting fire into the oil. The closer I got to the warriors, the better chance I had to stop Ojo Verde.

I knew this ceremony would probably go on deep into the night before fire touched the oil. Ojo Verde had to pray to all her spirits, making sure she hadn't left a single malevolent one out. And she didn't want the ghost of Lola Mes to come back for her, or to protect my family and me when she returned to Mescalero.

I eased forward to find the best place from which to attack the witch and her warriors. As I moved, a cool rolling wind came from the dark clouds off to the south, and there was a low rumble of thunder with lightning arrows flying between the clouds or going to the earth. The wind came, shaking all the trees like an angry giant, and whipped the fire into a greater blaze carrying burning sparks high into the sky before they burned out. I feared the wind-scattered fire might set the circle of oil and the juniper balls on fire, but Ojo Verde and her warriors paid it no mind. I waited.

Lightning flashed many times in the coming clouds, and the occasional lightning arrow striking the earth lighted the great legs of rain falling from them. The Thunder and Wind Spirits grew stronger. The sharp, pleasant smell of rain-soaked creosotes came sweeping up the cliffs from the llano far below. Soon great drops of rain fell, rattling the leaves and branches in the trees and exploding in sprays of small drops when they hit something hard. Ojo Verde held out her arms and repeated the same few words in each direction as she quickly turned and then motioned her warriors to follow her to a shelter in the junipers I had seen on the far side of the meadow.

Then the rain, so thick I could barely see the pole where Lola Mes stood, came on us, pouring down like a waterfall from a sky river. I ran for the pole, taking care not to slide in the pool of oil. Lola Mes stood with her head bowed, the pouring rain splashing and running off her head and down her soaked hair in little gushing streams. I heard her chanting a prayer for courage in the trials to come.

I splashed up to her, and, pulling my knife, in two strokes of my blade, slashed the reata lines holding her. Raising her head, she opened her mouth for a swallow of water and then yelled,

"Yellow Boy! I knew Ussen would send you. The pole is covered with grease. It's too slick for you to climb for your rifle. I can support you. Stand on my shoulders, and you can reach it. Don't touch that leather fetish with your hands."

I nodded, and she laced her fingers together for me to step up in order for my feet to reach her shoulders.

A great arrow of lightning flashed in the clouds nearby and the Thunder Spirits roared and crackled in the air as the rain poured over us. I balanced myself on her shoulders. Her body didn't seem to shake at all from my weight. She was as strong as any warrior.

I ran a hand up the side of the pole. She was right. It was too slick with grease and oil to climb. I could just reach the rifle barrel without touching the leather fetish holding it. I grabbed the barrel with one hand and, fighting to keep my balance, slashed the leather with my knife and pulled the rifle free. As soon as I had it, I jumped backwards from her shoulders. I landed on my feet but slid backwards and fell with a great splash in the oil floating on the pool of water collecting around the pole. Lola Mes helped me stand. I pointed in the direction of the trail He Watches and I had used many harvests ago to get to the cliff tops and yelled, "Run!"

She was fast and dashed off, leaving me behind, but I caught up with her when we were nearly to the tree line.

The rain slowed as we ran, but the lightning arrows continued to fly between the clouds, and the Thunder Spirits continued to rumble. I felt my hair standing up even in the rain, and I saw Lola Mes's hair standing out as if pulled by some great wind.

The darkness suddenly disappeared in a blinding blaze of light brighter than the sun. A great lightning arrow struck the pole where my rifle and Lola Mes had been tied, sending its wood flying into flaming splinters, and Thunder spoke in the greatest, bellowing, unknowable, angry words I had ever heard.

The oil and balls of juniper exploded in a roar of blue and orange flames, making a great cloud of water and smoke rising straight up into the rain, and lighting the night as no fire I had seen in my life.

I glanced toward the shelter on the far side of the meadow and saw Ojo Verde and her Comanches staring toward us as we disappeared into the junipers. I could hear her, between the growls of Thunder, screaming that her Power would find us. We would pay. The light from the fire was enough for me to find the old path up the ridge to the cliffs as a new downpour began.

Soon rain and darkness hid the remains of the old path He Watches and I used. I had to stop and wait several times for a flash of lightning to show me the old path up the ridge. At the top of the cliffs off the ridge facing south toward the llano, I led Lola Mes along until I found the little path, nearly gone, down to the bench with the shallow, cave-like overhang where He Watches and I sat to watch the San Antonio Road. In the hard rain, we climbed down to the little shelf in front of the overhang and then sat back out of the rain. The rain would wash away our tracks up on the ridge and the path down to our hiding place. It would take Ojo Verde and her Comanches a while to find us, and by that time, we could decide how to rub them out.

I suddenly felt very weak, and my hand holding the rifle's barrel felt locked in place. I started tilting backwards, but Lola Mes grabbed my shirt and helped me as I slowly sat down.

She stared at me through her swollen, good eye. "You touched the leather fetish?"

I shook my head. "No. I grabbed the rifle barrel and slashed it free of the bag with my knife."

She grabbed my wrist and pulled the rifle barrel toward her so she could see the barrel in the next lightning flash. As we waited, I felt weaker, and the skin on my fingers locked in place around the barrel began to feel hot. At last a flash came. Lola Mes said, "Ahh. Ojo Verde is clever. Give me your knife."

I handed her my knife. She laid it aside and pulled off one of her moccasins and, folding it, placed it next to my side where I held the rifle.

"Listen to me. There is a witch weapon in the barrel of your rifle. I saw some of the string that goes with it lying in the barrel when Ussen gave us light. I need to twist your hand holding the barrel, and we have to pound the barrel's end against my moccasin to make the weapon slide down toward the end so I can pick it out with your knife. Your hand may burn some before I can get it. Are you ready?"

"I'm ready. Do what you need."

Holding my wrist and singing a prayer to Ussen, Lola Mes turned the rifle so it pointed toward the moccasin. We bumped it hard three times against the moccasin, and then she took my knife, and pointing the barrel so that, if light came, she could see down its end, we waited. A flash came. She pushed the knifepoint at an angle into the end of the barrel and slowly raised it. Another flash, and we saw a finger-length of a witch's weapon sticking out the end of the barrel. She continued to raise the knife higher until another flash showed it had cleared the barrel and was pinned to the point of my knife. I felt my fingers relax around the barrel, and the skin on my hand and fingers grow cool. The rain had slowed, and the clouds were passing.

She handed me the knife. "Hold this while I put my moccasin back on, and then I'll put it where it can be destroyed, and you'll get stronger."

Her moccasin back on, she lifted her hands and sang four songs to Ussen. Then she took the knife still stabbing the witch weapon and left the overhang for the top of the cliffs. When she returned, she gave me back my knife and sat down. I started to ask her what she could do about my weakness, but she shook her head and, raising a finger, said, "Wait."

We waited as the rain picked up again, and then slowed. There was a burst of light as a lightning arrow struck very near us, and then Thunder and Wind were gone. I felt my strength returning. I could tell I was getting stronger with every breath. I said, "What did you do with the witch's weapon?"

"For you to get better, it had to be destroyed. We couldn't start a fire, so I left it on a boulder at the top of the cliffs and prayed to Ussen to destroy it, which he just did with a lightning arrow. You're already getting stronger. I need to drive away any of its remaining Power. Hold on to your rifle and lie down here to face the rising sun."

I did as she said. She ran her hand along the inside edge of her left moccasin until she found a small beaded possibles bag. She pulled it open and poured three blue stones in her hand, dusted with a small amount of yellow pollen. She placed one blue stone at the top of my head and the other two by my ears, all the time singing a song to Ussen. With the yellow pollen, she made signs on my forehead, cheeks, and a lightning arrow down the middle of my chest to the center of my belly. Each time she made a sign with the pollen, she sang a new song. Thunder and lightning arrows and wind were disappearing, and the rain slowed to nothing. Somewhere above us, a great lightning arrow struck with Thunder so loud, it hurt our ears. I could feel my strength returning as though being raised out of a deep pool of water, and my Power with the Yellow Boy rifle being renewed. I closed my eyes and thanked the great god, Ussen, for returning my gift of Power to me.

The storm growled and rolled northeast across the great llano. Water fell from the cliff tops in great spewing falls down steep canyons, carrying the runoff from the storm. Soon, like the clouds, the runoff was gone, too, and the sun was showing its light in a soft, blue sky on the far horizon.

CHAPTER 41
DEATH OF A WITCH

Clouds, thin and wispy, rolled up from the llano far below us where the rain had passed. I knew the cliff tops above us would be bathed in clouds as the mountaintop ridges dried out. We moved to the back of the overhang and sat, leaning against the back wall. I ran my fingers over my rifle, reconnecting with my Power. Just feeling the cool iron and wood under my fingertips made me feel better. I pulled the lever down and heard the familiar satisfying clicks as the loading gate dropped.

As I'd guessed, there were no bullets left to load, and the loading platform was empty. I held the breech up to the light and looked down the end of the barrel. The dim light showed the rifling spiral clean and unscratched, as it should be for the rifle to shoot straight and true. I closed the lever and laid the rifle across my knees. I asked Lola Mes to hand me the quiver of arrows and, pulling all the arrows out, handed them to her as she watched with a frown of curiosity. I turned the quiver upside down with my hand over its mouth and gave a little shake. A buckskin bag dropped in my hand and then a second, much smaller, one fell on top of it.

Lola Mes giggled like a young girl. "Not only is Yellow Boy a powerful warrior, he is very clever, too."

I grinned and, handing the bigger bag to her, took the arrows and slid them back in the quiver. I pulled the small bag open and pulled a shiny cartridge out to show her, put the cartridge on the loading platform, closed the lever, then pulled the load-

308

ing spring button up and twisted the end of the barrel break aside to open the loading tube under the barrel. She watched with interest as I let cartridge after cartridge slide backwards down the tube. The loading tube held thirteen cartridges and that, with the one I had put on the loading platform, was the number in the little buckskin bag, then empty, which I slid back into the quiver.

"Open that bag of food, and let's eat. Maybe the witch comes soon."

She opened the big bag that had fallen out of the quiver and poured the mix of nuts, dried berries, mesquite beans, and pounded venison jerky into my cupped palm and then filled her palm. We ate half the bag of trail rations, drank more water from the little tank just outside the overhang entrance, and then sat back in the darkness against the back wall of the little cave looking out over the great llano far below us, beginning to grow in the light. I didn't like where we hid. Ojo Verde knew we had run to the top of the ridge and were probably hiding up here somewhere. Unless we moved before the clouds cleared the ridge, we were trapped and would have to fight our way out against the witch and her Comanches. I told this to Lola Mes.

She said, "If we leave here, where else can we hide and still expect to take Ojo Verde?"

"We could hide in the brush and ambush her and the Comanches when they gathered their ponies. But we couldn't pick them off one at time. It would be us two against the four of them in an open field. The chances of winning that battle are with them."

Lola Mes shook her head. "You are a true Apache warrior and will fight well anywhere, anytime. This witch, this Ojo Verde, has been a burden all my life. It must end. I would kill her in a face-to-face fight so I can see the light go out of her eyes and know that never again must I think of her. Let us stay here. Let me finish it here."

I nodded. "It will be so. Here we fight and end Ojo Verde and her Comanches."

As the sun rose toward the time of shortest shadows, the air hot and wet, I asked Lola Mes to tell me what the witch had done after taking her. She said Ojo Verde had promised to set her free if she would betray me, but this she had refused to do, even after Ojo Verde beat her and promised the worst kinds of tortures Sangre del Diablo used. The warriors were fearful of Lola Mes's Power, fearful she knew how to use the Power of Sangre del Diablo on them, after Ojo Verde told them who she was and offered her to them. They would not touch her, even after Ojo Verde offered to let them to take her as often as they wanted and block any Power she might have from Sangre del Diablo.

"The warriors were wise to leave me alone. I would have killed them, every one, if they had taken me. Now that you have your Power back, can I use your bow to fight the witch?"

I pulled the fine mulberry wood bow out of its case, slid the string of sinew up to the end notch to string it, and handed it to her along with an arrow.

"Are you strong enough to pull the bow back to the full length of your arm?"

She took the arrow and smiled. Sitting cross-legged, she laid the arrow nock against the sinew and, holding the bow out with her left hand, easily pulled the arrow back on the sinew until her fingers were just under her right earlobe, the arrow pointed out toward the cliff edge ready for release. She knew what to do with a bow as well as any man.

I nodded and handed her the quiver and bow case made from cougar hide. "I'm glad for the help and company of another warrior. We'll send Ojo Verde to the Happy Land from this place."

Lola Mes's eyes narrowed as she nodded; then she pulled three more arrows to hold with the bow while keeping the one she had drawn to full length relaxed and ready against the sinew. "She comes soon, Killer of Witches."

I pulled the hammer on the rifle to half cock. We waited.

As the sun reached the place of shortest shadows, we heard the Comanche warriors coming closer, whistling back and forth and making occasional barking howls as they signaled to each other while they looked for signs of us along the cliff tops. A whistle and a bark sounded just above us. We heard the shuffle of moccasins in the brush and pebbles sliding on stone along the narrow path down to our hiding place.

Lola Mes looked at me and began to draw the bow. I shook my head and signaled silence before crabbing over to the place where the path came around a big vertical boulder before entering the bench. I waited, listening, near where a warrior would come around the edge of the boulder.

The warrior must have been afraid of heights. He moved down the path carefully, sliding his feet forward, close to the vertical stone on the path's cliff side, and kept a hand on the cliff side as he came toward me. Then I heard his breathing, hurried and fearful, puffing like a man running. His hand slid around the boulder where I waited out of sight. His foot reached the bench, and I heard a sigh of relief as he saw he was nearly off the narrow path. He eased around the boulder, and his eyes grew wide when he saw me suddenly appear out of the shadow.

He started to raise his rifle, but I pushed hard against his chest to make him stumble backwards, and making him fall into nothing but the bright clear air. He screamed, "Hiiiiiiii! Yeeee!" Tumbling end over end, he crashed against the boulders in the canyon far below us, his body bouncing and rolling until it disappeared under some junipers on one side.

We heard the other two warriors shouting at each other in a

language I didn't understand, but guessed was Comanche, as they ran toward the path from what must have been at least a hundred yards away. I looked over my shoulder at Lola Mes. She motioned me to come back to her. In four quick steps, I was beside her. Soon the warriors arrived above us. We waited while they paced and looked over the edge, calling back and forth to each other.

Lola Mes whispered, "They heard him yell but didn't see him fall. They don't see him anywhere below. They're trying to decide where he is. I have a plan. Maybe I can lure Ojo Verde to come down here to us. Do you want to try it?"

I nodded, and she moaned loud enough for the ones above us to hear her and called out to them in their language, making her voice sound like a man's growling in pain. "Ohhh, aiiii. My leg is broken. I see bones punching out my skin. There is a big snake down here. Be careful. Help me. Help me. My suffering is great. Maybe the snake comes. Help me. Hurry before I go to the Happy Land. Ohhhh."

A voice above us yelled, "Ho! We bring Ojo Verde. Watch out for the snake."

Lola Mes nodded and spoke in a low voice. "She will come by herself. The other two fear snakes. That's how she controls them. She will bring her snake medicine and maybe a weapon to use against it."

"Lola Mes, the sun shines inside your head."

"I will put an arrow into her evil body before you send her blind to the Happy Land. I have suffered her evil for too many harvests. Now she must pay."

I shrugged. "Shoot straight, Lola Mes. It's your revenge to take."

In the space of a hand-width of the sun moving across the sky, we heard Ojo Verde begin a ceremony above us. With a long chant, she called on her Power to help her protect the warrior lying broken below her. A light breeze brought the smell of the sage she burned. Her chant called on the spirits in each major direction to come and assist her. We could hear the other two warriors keeping the rhythm of her ceremony as they beat on a stiff hide they must have used in the ceremony to burn Lola Mes.

The sun, heading for the western mountains, was sending dark shadows to our hiding place and making the clouds blood-red and purple. There was a long pause before Ojo Verde began a new song, but the drum of the warriors was silent. Lola Mes mounted an arrow on the bow, rose up on her knees, and mouthed, "She comes."

I brought my rifle to full cock and sighted where she would appear from around the boulder. We waited.

Ojo Verde called from near the boulder that guarded the shelf in front of us, "Grandson, do you still live?"

Lola Mes moaned, "Ahhhh. Help me. Help me. The snake is near."

"The spirits will protect you. I'm coming."

"Ahhhh. Help me."

Something was not right. A few small pebbles rolled off the top of the overhang and bounced off the shelf to sail rattling down the steep canyon wall below us. The warriors were quiet, but the falling pebbles said they were right above us. Ojo Verde must have decided we were waiting in ambush. I tapped Lola with the end of my rifle to get her attention and pointed above us. She nodded.

In two or three breaths, we saw the long tip of a Comanche spear pass the boulder where I had waited for the warrior. Ojo Verde walked around the boulder edge holding the long spear in one hand and her knife in the other. She stared into the dim light of the overhang where we waited and, as her eyes became

313

familiar with the dark shadows, saw us. "Aiyee! Now I have you, bastard daughter."

Ojo Verde, a sneer of triumph on her face, didn't hesitate. She charged Lola Mes with the long spear. Before she could complete the first step, the sinew bowstring hummed.

The arrow hit Ojo Verde high in the chest, nearly in the same spot where I had shot Sangre del Diablo in the Río Grande. Her charge, with the spear held at waist height, carried her forward. Lola Mes fell flat, and the tip of the spear missed her head by a hand-width and jammed tight into a crack in the stone at the back of the overhang. The shock of the arrow and spear's impact sent Ojo Verde staggering backwards. Her Comanche warriors, their heads painted white with black eye sockets like Sangre del Diablo, screaming their courage, clinging to reatas with one hand and holding revolvers with the other, swung on to the bench from the top of the overhang.

Roaring and showing her red teeth in a snarl like some wounded animal, Ojo Verde grabbed the spear shaft quivering beside her to stop her backward stagger while raising her knife.

The Comanches landed hard and, stumbling toward the back of the overhang, fired their revolvers. Their shots were wild, but I felt the spatter of the rock dust on my back and legs from their bullets ricocheting off the wall and bench floor to sail out into the canyon. As they swung into the overhang, their shots had come blindingly fast. They were fast to cock their revolvers to shoot again, but Ussen made me faster as I shot an eye of each one, sending them staggering backwards into a red cloud of blood and brains that floated them off the edge of the bench, twisting and turning, as they crashed into the canyon wall and slid a distance down the wall, leaving blood streaks on the canyon stone.

I swung my rife to aim for Ojo Verde's green eye, but Lola Mes, holding the middle of an arrow in her hand like a knife, had jumped to her feet and charged the witch.

It all seemed to happen faster than the flight of an arrow to a close target. Ojo Verde screamed, "Die, dog's daughter," and, pulling forward on the spear shaft, made a great, arching swing of her knife for Lola Mes that sliced through the front of her shirt but missed her belly. Lola Mes, her hand a striking rattlesnake, grabbed Ojo Verde's wrist as the knife hand slashed back in an upper cut, and stabbed her arrow into Ojo Verde's right breast. Ojo Verde let go of the spear shaft and grabbed Lola Mes by her shirt as she stumbled toward the bench edge. Lola Mes jerked and pulled at Ojo Verde's hand to rip her shirt out of Ojo Verde's grasp, but didn't dare let go of Ojo Verde's hand holding her knife as she fought to drive the blade into Lola Mes's belly.

Ojo Verde, mumbling "Kill her, brother. We must kill her," continued her backward stagger, dragging Lola Mes toward the bench edge. Lola Mes worked to stop their struggle toward the long fall by bracing her legs and leaning back, while still trying to tear her shirt out of Ojo Verde's hand and holding on to the wrist of her knife hand. Ojo Verde was bigger and stronger, even with two arrows in her chest, and they fought to within an arm's length of the long fall to the Happy Land the warriors had just taken.

I didn't hesitate. I shot the fist holding Lola Mes's shirt. Lola Mes, blinded by the spray of flesh and bone and blood, let go of both the wrist behind what was left of the bloody powerless hand, and Ojo Verde's knife hand. She fell backwards into the overhang. Ojo Verde, staring at what was left of the hand stump pumping blood in squirts, staggered a step back to the bench edge, mumbling, "I don't understand, brother. I don't understand how these little people killed us."

My Power took her green eye and then her brown one, the sound of the shots echoing across the cliffs and filling the overhang with the crack of deafening thunder, as she sailed back through the spray of her own blood and brains. We ran forward to see her falling, falling, and time seemed to slow down, making her fall appear as if she were a dead leaf drifting to the ground in the Ghost Face. In the quiet late afternoon stillness, she sailed past her warriors on the floor of the steep canyon and smashed against a boulder.

Her body lay stretched like a skin over the big boulder, her sightless eyes staring at the darkening sky, black streams of blood rolling in tiny rivulets down the sides of what was left of her face. Lola Mes used her sleeve to wipe the gore from her own face and said, "Let us find water to wash away the filth from these witches. Then we must burn her and her warriors, or their evil will return."

I nodded. "I know. I need to think up a way to burn them without climbing down to where they landed. Come. There are places near their camp where we can wash."

We walked down the ridge to Cha's old campsite where Ojo Verde had planned to burn Lola Mes. There was a great black circle where the lightning had struck the pole in the center of the oil pool. Everything in that circle had been burned to ashes. The only thing left of the pole was the hole in which it stood.

Well off to the side, I found the oil buckets I remembered seeing when I had watched Ojo Verde singing her ceremony before the great lightning arrow came. Each bucket still had a little oil left, and when I divided it among three buckets, each one held about half a bucket of oil. I gathered a few short pieces of rope left from when the Comanches tied the juniper limbs together, took the buckets, and led Lola Mes to a nearby water tank where I let her wash in privacy. I went to another tank to wash and think about the best way to get the oil down to burn the bodies of the witch and her warriors. If I had to climb down to the bodies I would, but I thought there must be an easier, better way.

By the time we returned to the overhang, it was too dark to see the bodies of Ojo Verde and her warriors. Even when the moon was up, the shadows in the canyon hid the boulder where Ojo Verde landed, making us rest and listen to the growing yips of coyotes until the sun gave us light.

When the dawn came and we could finally see Ojo Verde and her warriors, coyotes were creeping down the canyon sides, and great black birds were already spiraling down the face of the cliffs toward the canyon. I could hit the warriors and the boulder where Ojo Verde's body lay by throwing stones, and decided I could hit them with the half buckets of oil.

I tried to heave the first bucket on nearly the same arc the falling body of Ojo Verde had taken. It landed close enough that when most of the oil flew out of the bucket, it splashed on her body. The oil buckets for the warriors I tossed so they landed just above them and the oil ran onto their bodies.

We had soaked a few of the rope pieces in the oil and tied them to arrows at their points. I strung the bow and mounted an arrow. Lola Mes struck a match and lighted the oil-soaked rope piece. I shot it, flaming and smoking, on a long blazing arc to land in the body of Ojo Verde within a forearm's length of the other two arrows. There was a sudden burst of flame, and her body caught fire, sending a column of black smoke high in the still air. We did the same to the warrior bodies except to send a burning arrow sliding into the oil above their heads so the flames rushed down on them. Soon three black columns of smoke were rising straight up. The coyotes began creeping away, and black birds found the wind to carry them high above the llano to watch the destruction of a morning meal.

Lola Mes and I sat down on the edge of the bench, let our

317

legs dangle over the edge, and watched the flames take the evil that had pursued us for so many harvests. The loud bangs we expected sounded down the canyon, and the fires flashed up briefly and then slowly died. Only ashes and charred bones cooled by the canyon breeze and a few black streaks left by her blood remained on the boulder.

Lola Mes and I spent the rest of the morning in the lower meadow finding and catching our ponies. By the time of shortest shadows, we began the long ride back to Mescalero. Lola Mes, the daughter of Sangre del Diablo, and I had destroyed the last evil of Sangre del Diablo, his sister and lover, with fire. Neither ghost would return. Ussen had returned my Power to protect us from the evil of their spirits.

CHAPTER 42
CHIRICAHUAS COME TO MESCALERO

It was a happy time when we returned to our tipis at Mescalero. My women and Falling Water made a great feast and invited many friends to come to our fire and hear our story. When the feasting was done, I returned to the tribal police, and Knows Horses decided to return to a canyon with Lola Mes and Falling Water, where they could live close to his horses and cattle. As Juanita said, life became smooth again.

A moon after Ojo Verde went to the Happy Land, James Carroll sent for me. When I stood at his door, he looked up from the tracks he read on paper and motioned me to come sit by his worktable.

He said, "Remember in the Ghost Face of last year how you and three others showed Asa Daklugie, Geronimo's nephew, and a prisoner of war from Fort Sill around the reservation? It was less than a moon afterwards that we learned Geronimo had gone to the Happy Land."

I nodded, wondering where this talk was leading.

"My chiefs in the east have sent word that since Geronimo has gone to the Happy Land and the great chiefs like Loco, Nana, and Chihuahua have been gone even longer, they've been thinking about releasing the Chiricahuas as prisoners of war and finding them other places to live away from Fort Sill, which the army has decided it wants for an artillery range."

I smiled. Daklugie had said he thought the captivity of Geronimo's People would end soon, but I didn't think he anticipated that it would come because of Geronimo's death.

"Our friend Daklugie must have gone home and told the tribal elders what a fine place Mescalero is, and that it would be a good place to live when they're free. Some of Geronimo's People told army representatives they might like to come to Mescalero, if the Mescaleros accept them. I hope they do. White Eyes such as President Roosevelt look at your reservation land and want to make it a national park because it has so few people. As I told you and Daklugie, if we could get Geronimo's People to join us, there'd be no question that we'd need every acre we have and more. I've spoken with Magoosh, Peso, and Sans Peur about this, and they reminded me they told Daklugie to come.

"The big chiefs in Washington have agreed to let the Chiricahuas and the Mimbreños send some of their educated young men to visit and see the reservation and what's left of Ojo Caliente reservation land to determine if they should come here or stay where they are with much less land at Fort Sill. Five are coming, counting an army officer, escorting them, and they'll be here in four days. I'd like you and the others who showed Daklugie the reservation to show this group the same areas and any other places here they want to see."

I nodded and said, "It will be done."

The Apaches from Fort Sill included Eugene Chihuahua and Goody, the grandson of Loco, who represented the Chiricahua, and Kaywaykla and Toclanny, who represented the Mimbreños. We rode over the same areas Daklugie saw in the Ghost Face season. These visitors came in the Season of Many Leaves, so it was much greener and easier to see without patches of snow hiding the ground.

Our last night out as we smoked by the fire, Eugene Chihuahua said, without my asking, "Your land is better than Daklugie described to us. It's like the mountains at Turkey Creek near

Fort Apache that the army forced us to leave. There's much game here, big and small, all the wood we could ever need, and the grama grass is tall in many pastures. It stands dry in the Season of the Ghost Face so the livestock can graze in all seasons. There are nuts, wild fruits, and vegetables the women will be eager to collect. This is a fine land. Goody and I agree. We'll tell our People what we've seen. They'll want to come."

I nodded. "*Enjuh.* I'll tell James Carroll what you say. I know he'll help you any way he can."

They waved their hands parallel to the ground.

I learned later that the Mimbreños, Kaywaykla and Toclanny, were disappointed at what they found when the group visited Ojo Caliente. Only a few sections that Indah settlers had not bought still existed. What remained of good fertile land had washed away in a big storm. There was not enough land available to support them. When the Mimbreños learned this, they decided to continue living at Fort Sill.

The next three harvests were good. There was little trouble on the reservation. Beela-chezzi and Carmen Rosario's daughter, Hawú dat'éhe; and Idlaaní and Na'ilin Súl, the daughters of Lola Mes, Falling Water, and Knows Horses, all had their *Haheh* the same year. As their uncle, I helped with the ceremony preparations, and Juanita and Moon spent much time preparing food for the feasts given during the *Haheh* days.

Red Bird Singing, daughter of Kah and Deer Woman, married a young man from Peso's camp. We Mescaleros called him Bitl'ól Dáhále (His Fast Rope), but the Indah insisted on calling him Charlie Rope. They had an Indah-style wedding, and, refusing to live in a tipi, they built a house close by the tipi of Kah and Deer Woman. Kah thought the Indah School at the agency had taken all their sense about how to live, but he said nothing and decided to let them learn by experience which was better—house or tipi. Charlie Rope worked cattle for Yibá whose daughter, Dawahn Dáha, had married two harvests earlier and already had a child. The man she married was not a good choice. He was lazy and didn't provide for them. She left him and went back to Yibá and Lucky Star. Her husband was so afraid of Yibá, he didn't even ask for the bride gift back.

Beela-chezzi, Kah, and I taught Redondo and Hidloh when they came from the Indah School to be strong, good hunters in the way we trained as boys in the old days. I wanted my sons known in the Mescalero camps as good men who did the right thing.

Four harvests after Daklugie had come to the reservation and soon after a former helper for James Carroll, C.R. Jefferis, had become our agent, word came that Geronimo's People had been released from captivity. They were coming to Mescalero on an iron wagon to Tularosa during a sun the Indah named April 4, 1913. C.R. Jefferis asked several tribal policemen, including me, to accompany him and Ted Sutherland, the new reservation livestock superintendent, to the Tularosa iron wagon station to meet the iron wagon carrying the Chiricahuas. We were to help unload their animals and possessions and guide them to Mescalero.

C.R. Jefferis led us from the agency down the wagon road to Tularosa in the early light of the coming day. The breath from our horses and our own mouths looked like steam from the iron wagon bringing the Fort Sill people to Tularosa. The sky was a soft, turquoise blue when we stopped to look at the distant San Andres Mountains and the bright, white spread of sand at their base, which in the early morning light looked like a white cloud lying close to the ground. I had seen the white cloud many times, but I never tired of seeing it.

The wagon road, looking like two fuzzy, brown pieces of twine in the distance, tracked southwest around Tularosa in the early morning shadows off the mountains as it went toward the iron road on the west side of the village. Farmers already in their fields plowed ground or planted rows of seed. Dogs barked, roosters crowed, and doves in the trees along the field edges announced our coming, but the villagers with their big straw hats and bare feet just smiled and waved as we rode by. Many harvests had passed since my People and those of the village had fought one another.

At the station, we unsaddled our ponies and hobbled them to graze on thin grass and scattered brush in a dusty pasture nearby. We sat on the rough board ends marking the porch edge of the station and smoked while C.R. Jefferis talked to an old Indah with white hair and a face holding many wrinkles. He was chief of the place of iron wagons in Tularosa and told C.R. Jefferis the iron wagons carrying the Fort Sill people would come soon. He said they came with iron wagons carrying their horses, wagons, farm tools, and personal belongings.

The Indah feared their cattle and dogs might bring "Texas Fever" from Fort Sill. Their army *di-yen* said it was a sickness carried by ticks, and it killed cattle. The army had made the Fort Sill People sell all their cattle and leave their dogs behind to keep Texas Fever out of New Mexico. *Too bad,* I thought. *We Apaches like our dogs.*

We were laughing and telling stories from the old days when someone looking down the tracks said, "They come!"

The iron road curved away to the southeast, and we had to step out from the station porch to look down the tracks. Far down the rails disappearing into the dark green creosotes, light green mesquite, and turquoise-colored salt weed, a black smudge just above the brush was turning into a cloud. It wasn't long before we heard the low, moaning call the iron wagons make as they approach places where they stop and saw the black engine racing toward us like an angry bull.

We stepped back on the station platform, and C.R. Jefferis and Ted Sutherland went to stand where the station chief said the Fort Sill people would get off the iron wagon. Soon we heard the puffing engine slow down enough, with squeals and shrieks of iron pushed against iron, to begin a walking roll to its stop.

The iron wagons carrying people were first behind the engine. We could see women and children looking out the half-opened windows, trying to see this land to which some of the older adults were returning but that their children had never seen before.

Daklugie, Goody, and Eugene Chihuahua were off the iron wagons first. Following the custom of the Indah, they smiled, pumped hands with C.R. Jefferis and Ted Sutherland, and said their names.

Chihuahua nodded, "I remember you, C.R. Jefferis, from our trip four harvests ago. You helped James Carroll, but I don't think I ever met Ted Sutherland."

Ted Sutherland was a young man who looked and dressed like a vaquero. He grinned. "Well, your memory is reliable. I wasn't here then."

C.R. Jefferis said with a big smile, "We're all glad to have you and your people come to Mescalero. The Mescalero women wait for us at the agency with a big feast ready, and the Mescalero chiefs are there to welcome you. How can we help you unload?"

Daklugie took charge and said, "We should get the ponies and workhorses off first and get them watered. Then we can unload and hitch up the wagons—nearly every family has a wagon—and load what we brought with us. For the few who don't have a wagon, there will be room on the others. There are enough Chiricahua men and boys to unload and hitch, but it would be a great help if you would help us keep the free ponies together and drive them to Mescalero."

C.R. Jefferis nodded. "Ted and some of these tribal policemen will help you with the ponies. When the wagons are ready, line them up on the road over yonder, and we'll form a wagon train to go up to the agency."

Daklugie, Eugene Chihuahua, and Goody all grinned, nodded, and said, *"Enjuh."*

Men left the iron wagon and gathered in a group around Daklugie, Chihuahua, and Goody, who told them the plan to unload the iron wagon and form a line of their wagons to go to the agency. The men walked down the tracks with Ted Sutherland to the iron wagon carrying their ponies and workhorses. When Sutherland drew close to the first door on the iron wagon carrying horses and ponies, he cocked his ear to one side, listened a few moments, and frowned. He nodded for a station worker to pull the lever to slide open the door.

As soon as the door opened, a flood of dogs—collies, hounds, tame wolves, and little ones of breeds I had never seen before; black ones, brown ones, spotted ones, dogs of every size, shape, and color—burst through the horses' legs and jumped out the open door, barking and yapping, twisting and turning, happy to be out of the iron wagon. Most of them ran up the iron road to where the women and children were climbing down from their iron wagons. The solemn faces of the Fort Sill men broke into grins and laughs as some dogs, barking and their tails wagging, ran up to sniff their masters' hands.

Daklugie, shrugging his shoulders, turned to Ted Sutherland and said, "We didn't know the dogs were on the train. We hated to leave them. Maybe the train crew put them in the cars with the horses. Can we keep them, or must we kill them?"

Ted Sutherland shook his head. "There're no cattle here now.

Get any ticks off them. You have medicine for that. We ought to be all right. Just know that if Texas Fever shows up in any of your livestock, they'll all have to be put down, sick or not. It'll be your loss."

Daklugie crossed his arms and nodded. "We'll live by the rules you require. We've lived with the White Eyes for twenty-seven years now and know we must do this."

Ted Sutherland grinned. "*Enjuh*. Now let's get you folks unloaded and on the road to Mescalero."

There were nearly forty men in the hundred eighty-seven Fort Sill people to help with the unloading of their animals, farm equipment, and possessions. Women and children who were able also did their part. It was a good time for the People, and the work went fast. Before the time of shortest shadows, the line of wagons from Fort Sill wound its way past Tularosa and up the road to the agency.

CHAPTER 43
NEW LIVES, OLD SOULS AT MESCALERO

As the Chiricahuas drove past the agency to their camping spot, they saw Mescalero women working around cooking fires to welcome them. The Chiricahuas set up their tents on a flat place a little way above the agency where Mescalero families had their tipis and were waiting to greet and help them. The Chiricahua tents were big flat-sided ones like the army used, and from the top of a ridge above the agency, the ground where they stood looked like scattered patches of snow left from the Ghost Face in the Season of Little Eagles.

When the Chiricahuas arrived and began setting up their tents, our People had many happy reunions among family members separated a long time. We feasted and visited for five or six suns until Daklugie and Eugene Chihuahua asked C.R. Jefferis if the Chiricahuas could have a place of their own on the reservation. James Carroll had taught C.R. Jefferis how to treat and deal with the People in a good way. C.R. Jefferis told Daklugie and the others to ride across the reservation and find a place where they wanted to live. He said he would make it their place if there were no other claims on it. After looking for three days, they decided to settle at White Tail, about twenty miles from the agency, where big meadows waved with tall grama grass, especially good for raising cattle, and high ridges kept down the wind.

Only Chato, still very bitter that the White Eyes had forced him to go to Florida after he served them well as a scout, chose to live by himself. He did this because the Chiricahuas said he was a traitor to his own people and would have nothing to do with him. Those stories made the Mescaleros keep their distance, too.

Chato decided to live at the top of Apache Pass on the road to Ruidoso, about ten miles from the agency. His place had no flowing water, and he had to haul a week's supply from near the agency in barrels on his wagon. I remembered him with the Apaches we brought back to San Carlos after Nantan Lupan's campaign in the Sierra Madre. Chato had wanted to be a chief with the Mimbreños, but my old friend Nana told me that Kaytennae was his *Segundo* because he and the other elders did not want Chato to lead their people. The stories about him said he was a good warrior, but he had no manners in dealing with his elders, spoke out of turn at councils, and invited himself to councils where he wasn't wanted.

The Chiricahuas moved to White Tail, set up their tents with iron stoves inside, cut and stacked wood to keep snow away from the doors, and put earth around their tent walls to help keep out the Ghost Face cold and to help keep them cool in the Season of Large Leaves. The money made from the sale of their Fort Sill cattle and the fencing, which they had put up and then had to leave, came to C.R. Jefferis with a list of each Chiricahua's share. They asked C.R. Jefferis to spend it to buy them cattle for starting a new herd. Ted Sutherland, a good young man, always speaking straight and doing the right thing for the Apaches without fear of any man, went to ranches he knew had good breeding cattle and bought two thousand young breeding cows. He also bought eighty bulls from the Cox Ranch, over by the Organ Mountains, the place where Hombrecito tried to kill the man named Stone who had helped kill his father.

Ted Sutherland drove the cattle into Elk Canyon, where they branded and turned them loose for the winter. The young cows liked those Cox Ranch bulls. Nearly every cow had a calf. After the calf branding in the next Season of Little Eagles, Daklugie learned that Ted Sutherland, always honest, was a man who kept his word. He and Ted Sutherland became and stayed good friends over many harvests.

One day in the Season of the Earth Is Reddish Brown, I was at the agency and heard Daklugie asking C.R. Jefferis when they could expect building supplies so they could get their houses built at White Tail and not have to live in tents. C.R. Jefferis told him he would send the request to his chiefs in the east and thought maybe they could get permission to build the houses by the next Season of Little Eagles.

Later that day, Daklugie came into the trading post where I sat smoking a cigarro and drinking coffee by the iron stove in the middle of the room. He gave his supply order list to the clerk and came to sit down beside me. We talked while the clerk did his work.

He opened his coat and tipped back his hat, poured some coffee into a blue speckled cup, and said, "Is it often this cold on the reservation for this time of year?"

I shrugged. "Sometimes colder, sometimes warmer. Why?"

He shook his head and said, "I'm used to the damp wind off the plains at Fort Sill. Here it is not as windy, but the cold is dry and feels worse than at Fort Sill. Maybe it just takes getting used to."

I grinned. Getting used to mountain winters took the passage of a few harvests. "Maybe so. I would ask you a personal question."

"Speak. I will answer."

"I heard you ask C.R. Jefferis about when your people will get houses. What's wrong with your tents? My two wives, two boys, and I live in a tipi just fine. Stottler tried to make all Mescaleros live in cabins about fifteen harvests ago, but most returned to tipis when he and the agent who followed him left. The women claimed the cabins seemed to make dirt no matter how much they cleaned. I have never lived in an Indah house. Why do you want a house? It seems unmanly. You can't take it with you when you need to move, and inside, it seems like you're living in a cave."

Daklugie smiled, nodded, and blew the steam from across the top of his cup before he took a slurp and smacked his lips. "You have to remember that we Chiricahuas were forced to live with the Indah for twenty-seven years. We didn't have any choice. We lived where the Indah lived and ate what the Indah ate. We had gardens and cattle and cut hay to keep the cattle alive during the Ghost Face. Anything left over, we sold to the Indah. I went to school at Carlisle and learned to read, write, and speak the Indah language and to raise cattle. Raising cattle is about as close as we can get to what our fathers did in the old days. We like the taste of beef even better than venison. Indah houses are one of their customs we liked and adopted. They are warm in the Ghost Face and comfortable and convenient for storing things all the year. An iron stove makes it easier for your women to cook and save food than an open fire in a tipi, and windows let you see out without opening the door, so you have time to think before you let in one who comes. If you have to move, you just find another house someone has left, or build a new one. But here on the reservation, we don't have to move much, if at all. When is the last time you moved? Houses are good. We want them."

Daklugie's words on houses gave me much to think about. Juanita and Moon and I spoke about a house that night, but they weren't ready to live in a house, and I didn't know if I wanted one, either. I remembered Kah thinking that his daughter, Red Bird Singing, and son-in-law, Charlie Rope, wanting a house instead of a tipi was foolishness. I didn't think I was ready to be foolish with my family.

One sun in the Season of Little Eagles, during the harvest time the Indah call 1914, C.R. Jefferis called me to his workplace in the agency. When I came to his door, he motioned me in and picked up a talking-wire paper lying on his worktable. He said, "Yellow Boy, I have some good news for you. This telegram says that your son Híghâh, the one we call David, will finish school in June, what you call the Season of Many Leaves, and will be coming back to Mescalero. I know you must be very proud."

It had been eight harvests since Híghâh had gone to the big school in the east. James Carroll asked the school often to send word of his health and how he did learning Indah ways and customs and making tracks on paper. The stories they sent back all said he learned well and was strong in his body as well as his mind. When C.R. Jefferis told me he was returning, I wondered if he would remember his family, if the White Eye school had taken all that was Mescalero out of him, and if he remembered anything about hunting and war I had taught him when he was a child. I wondered about many things that might make him think he was no longer my son or an Apache. My thoughts made my guts feel like I had eaten bad meat.

A sun came in the Season of Many Leaves when C.R. Jefferis told me that in three suns Híghâh would come on an iron wagon to the place the Indah called a station in Tularosa, when the sun was three hand-widths above the horizon (about nine o'clock). When the sun came for Híghâh to come on the iron wagon, I borrowed a wagon and team from the agency and left early to meet my son. The cold early-morning air made my fingers stiff, and the breath of the horses and me looked like steam from a kettle. The sky, the color of light turquoise, and the white sands at the foot of the far mountains made me glad I had lived to see the day.

I came early to the Tularosa iron wagon station and sat on the edge of the porch to smoke a cigarro in a blessing to the four directions, and to think of what I should say and how I should act around Hígháh. I smoked and looked down the shiny *pesh* (iron) road that disappeared west into dark green, feather-leaved creosotes; delicate, green mesquite thickets, standing like islands in a great lake of creosote bushes; and yucca with stems rising high, like the stick the Indah used to hold up their cloth flags. After a while, I saw a black smudge in the distance above the brush along the tracks and knew an iron wagon was coming.

Only one rider got off the iron wagon. He was tall for an Apache. His hair was short behind his neck, but longer than normal over his ears. He wore a big, flat-brimmed, black hat, pulled down in front to shade his eyes, and a long, black coat like the ones I saw Indah *di-yens* wear. He looked my way, and I was startled at how much he looked like his mother, Juanita. My knees were weak when I slid off the edge of the porch and walked toward him. A big grin filled his face when he saw me, and he dropped his case and stood straight for me.

I reached him and looked over his face. I liked the good man I saw there. I said in the tongue of the Indah words I had practiced many times, "My son has returned to the land of his father and family. We're glad you come."

He put his hands on my shoulders and said in perfect Apache, "Father, I've come home, come to you and my family, come to help the People."

My heart soared, flying high like a bird.

CHAPTER 44
HOMECOMING

During the wagon ride back to Mescalero, Híghấh told me of his harvests in the Indah School and how he had learned many things, including what he had learned to do with numbers and what the stories meant that the Indah told about the earth, moon, and stars. I said, "*Enjuh.* To know these things will help our people understand and know the Indah and grow strong again. Has Ussen sent you your Power yet?"

He looked away at the mountains to the south, then to his feet, and slowly shook his head. "Ussen won't come to me, Father. I've become a Christian. Perhaps the Christian god and Ussen are the same spirit. I don't know. Maybe I'll learn the truth when I'm back among the People."

I puffed my cheeks and blew in sadness. The Indah School had done what I had feared. It had separated Híghấh's heart from his people and his family. I hoped he would find his way back to us. Only Ussen could make it so.

He asked me what had happened during the harvests he was gone. I spoke of his mothers' lives and of his brothers' growth, of the chase and killing of Kedinchin, of Ojo Verde's attack, how Juanita had saved me from her, and how Lola Mes and I had killed her Comanches and sent her blind to the Happy Land. I told him of the Chiricahua's coming to Mescalero and how we had already learned much from them about raising cattle, the need to educate our young, and how to deal with the Indah for what we were due.

He asked me something that made me smile. "What of Beela-chezzi's daughter, Quiet Dove? Has she had her *Haheh*? Has a man taken her yet?"

I laughed aloud. "So this is the reason you return to Mescalero? Yes, she had her *Haheh*. No man has taken her."

"Why has she not been taken? Did she become ugly or develop nasty habits?"

I laughed again. "No, not ugly, and Carmen Rosario taught her to have manners and be a clean woman in all things. She is very good for the eyes, but she has turned down many offers. Beela-chezzi and Carmen Rosario are not happy with her. They want grandchildren here on the reservation, not just in the Blue Mountains, where their son Running Wolf lives with Blue Flower, the daughter of Kitsizil Lichoo'. They already have a young child. I think they call him Little Wolf. Be careful. If Beela-chezzi thinks you are interested, he'll make her take you."

Hígháh laughed. "I must see this woman who gives Beela-chezzi a hard time. I won't watch her with a straight eye and make her think that I, too, am interested."

"Are you? Are you interested in her for a wife?"

"No, Father. I'm just curious how this girl, who was my little friend when I left, turned out. I have nothing yet to offer anyone for a bride gift or a way to support a wife."

I smiled. I thought, *My son, the* Indah *might have taught you many things, but they didn't teach you to tell good lies.*

My women and sons sang happy songs welcoming Hígháh back. Juanita kept saying he had left a child and returned a good man. Moon showed him their basketwork, and he said good things about how excellent and useful they looked, and how the Indah would want them as trophies to show their friends. He said this in the Mescalero tongue and spoke it well. I was glad and proud when I learned this. The Indah had not taken the language of his fathers from him.

His younger brothers asked him many questions about the Indah world they studied at the agency school. He told them things about the numbers of Indah that lived in the east, how long it took to cross the big water to the east or west, the Indah stories about how the moon and stars came to be, about places that made things exactly alike over and over, about how the Indah kept all the things they knew in books that all could read, so others could learn the same things. I found all this hard to believe, but I knew he spoke the truth.

That night, we feasted on beef and venison, mescal, potatoes, juniper berries, piñon nuts, tips of yucca leaves, and acorn and mesquite breads. He told us more stories about what he had learned in the Indah School, how strong the Indah were, and of the great war between their tribes across the big water. His stories left much to consider, and did not bring us comfort.

My women and youngest sons had set up a tipi next to ours for him. There he could stay until he decided where he would live and what he would do, and there he slept that night.

The next night, Juanita and Moon had a big feast to celebrate Higháh's return. They invited our friends and brothers who had known him before he went far away to the Indah School. Beelachezzi and Carmen Rosario came with Quiet Dove; and there were Kah and Deer Woman; their daughter, Red Bird Singing, and her husband, Charlie Rope; Yibá and Lucky Star and their daughter, Always Laughs, and her child; and Knows Horses with Lola Mes and Falling Water and their children, Idlaaní and Na'ilín Súl, who were both near seventeen harvests and nearly grown. Na'ilín Súl had had her *Haheh* three years earlier and already had offers of marriage, which she'd turned down, saying she wasn't ready to take a man.

The big feast fire burned bright and, like the sun, showed gold and orange light on our canyon's walls during this happy time. All the women brought good things to eat and helped Juanita and Moon. The younger children played with my sons in the fringes of the shadows made by the fire, and Hígháh sat with the old men and me and spoke again of what he had learned at the Indah School.

The talk paused in the men's circle as we smoked and thought on what Hígháh told us. Beela-chezzi waited a respectful time before he said, "You have learned much, my son. We have great pride in you. What you will do now? The Indah have taught you many of their secrets?"

Hígháh frowned and shook his head. "I don't know, Grandfather. There's still much for me to learn. I'll never know it all. I've learned only a little. But I know that, despite all the evil many Indah have done to my People over many harvests, we now depend on them for our survival. We must learn to be better, stronger, and smarter than the Indah around us. We must learn to use their ways to help ourselves. I'll stay here on the reservation to help the People. I'll find work that I've learned to do. I can teach in the school, clerk in the trading post, even help the tribal police and the agent, or, after calluses grow on my hands, herd cattle or cut timber. Whatever I do, I'll stay on the reservation and be a Mescalero. This my father planted in my heart when I was very young."

All the men smiled and shook their fists and said, *"Enjuh!"*

There were three unmarried young women and a young divorced woman at our feast. I saw them all taking the measure of Hígháh with many side glances as he smoked and visited with their families, but Hígháh's eyes followed only Quiet Dove. Beela-chezzi and I looked at each other and smiled in the pleasure of the moment. The great wheel of life was coming full circle once more. Perhaps one day our families would share a grandchild.

★ ★ ★ ★ ★

Four days after the welcoming feast, Híghâh rode to the agency with me to meet C.R. Jefferis. When we appeared at his door, a big smile filled his face. He stood and, motioning us in to his office, offered us chairs, as he stuck out his hand and said, "There's no doubt you're David Híghâh. Your face reminds me of the features of both your mother and your father. You have her eyes and his nose and mouth. Sit down, sit down."

They shook hands like two Indah, and we sat down. They spoke of many things, such as Híghâh's school and how he did well with the Indah numbers and stories, what the chiefs in the east were trying to do to Indians, and what Híghâh wanted or planned to do. After a while, I left them to do my work as a tribal policeman, so they could speak alone.

That night, over our family's evening meal, Híghâh told us that C.R. Jefferis offered him a job to help with the tracks on paper that he had to send to the chiefs in the east and told him that he might be asked to teach some in the school. He'd also said there was a room at the school where he could live. He said C.R. Jefferis told him the work was much like what he, Jefferis, had done for James A. Carroll and would help another man already doing what he called clerk's work. Híghâh told us he had agreed to take the clerk's job and the room at the school until he found or built his own house.

I said, "Why not just live in your tipi?"

He smiled. "I don't have the strength you do, Father."

Híghâh moved to the room C.R. Jefferis offered him and started his clerk's job. He promised to come often to visit his family. Moons passed, and he was true to his word, coming three or four times in a moon to our tipi and telling us stories he read in the Indah paper about the Indah war in the land east of the big water. He told us the Indah were fighting each other from long holes, like *acequias,* on top of the ground. They shot rifles and shoots-many-times guns and used big, shoots-far guns with barrels bigger than my upper leg they called canons. This war was killing many men and using weapons I had never heard of, such as poison air and aeroplanes. I was glad the war was far away for us, too far to go fight.

The Ghost Face, a hard, cold one, passed, and the Season of Little Eagles came with the warm winds called Chinook blowing across the passes. It was not long after that when Beelachezzi, a big smile filling his face and eyes twinkling, told me that Hígháh had come to visit Quiet Dove. We both laughed and slapped each other on the shoulders.

One evening in the Season of Many Leaves, as Juanita and Moon finished cooking the evening meal, I sat by the tipi door smoking while the boys played in the big pine shadows. I looked down the canyon and saw an Indah standing at my corral fence offering fruit to Hombrecito's great black stallion, Satanas. I had kept the horse and sometimes ridden it for nearly six harvests, waiting for Hombrecito to return from the Indah *di-yen* school. I went to see this Indah and realized as I approached him that he was Hombrecito. My heart took wings.

Hombrecito stayed with us five suns before he mounted Satanas, took his rifle, and returned first to Rufus's ranch, where he would keep Satanas, and then to comfort his mother, who had lived many harvests and was nearing her time to leave for the Happy Land. Moon had known him well when we lived in the Blue Mountains, and Juanita had come to know him when we returned from the Blue Mountains to take Oliver Lee. They were both happy he had returned and had finished the *di-yen* school by the big water in the west. Redondo and Hidloh also thought of him as an older brother and asked him many questions about the Indah *di-yen* school and the western big water and how it was different from the big water in the east near where Hígháh had gone to school. When Hombrecito left, he promised to return soon.

CHAPTER 45
PAYING A DEBT TO PANCHO VILLA

Three moons passed after Hombrecito's first visit. During that time, he sent word to me by C.R. Jefferis on the talking wire that his mother would soon go to the Happy Land. He said he would stay close to her until she left, and in a moon, she was gone.

One morning, near the Season of Earth Is Reddish Brown, C.R. Jefferis motioned me into his place at the agency. "A telegram came in last night from your friend in Las Cruces, Doctor Grace. He asks if I'll let you go on an important trip with him into Mexico. Things are quiet, with the people busy preparing for Ghost Face. I'm glad to help the good doctor if you want to go. Just don't stay away too long."

I couldn't imagine what made Hombrecito want to go to Mexico. Much fighting passed there between the *Nakai-yes*. Their land was a deadly place. Word came from Running Wolf that some of Kitsizil Lichoo's families had left his camp to live at San Carlos. They believed the fighting between the two sides in the *Nakai-yi* war might catch them if they stayed in the Blue Mountains. Other warriors were drifting farther south and west, with little left to raid in Chihuahua and fast becoming so in Sonora. If Hombrecito went to Mexico, I wanted to go, regardless of the reason. I said, "I go. Return in a moon, I think."

C.R. Jefferis smiled and knowingly shook his head. "Your job will be here when you return."

I told Hígháh at his workplace that I was leaving for Mexico with Hombrecito, and that I would be grateful if he kept an eye on his mothers and brothers while I was gone. He smiled and said, "They're safe with me, Father. Mexico is a dangerous place. The Mexicans who have no money and own no land fight for their share against those who hold it all. Watch yourself. All will be well here." I felt lucky that, despite living with the Indah for so long, Hígháh was a fine young man I could be proud of and trust to do what was right.

While I saddled my pony and made my weapons ready, Juanita and Moon prepared supplies for eating on the trail. I told my family I would see them again and rode off down the wagon road to Tularosa and then across the llano to the Jarilla Mountains and those called Organ, where, at Rufus's ranch, I saddled Satanas, eager to be on the trail again, and brought him to the town of Las Cruces for Hombrecito.

The moon was about to rise when Hombrecito found me waiting in his office. He told me Doroteo Arango, whom we had once known in the camp of Kitsizil Ichoo', now said his name was Pancho Villa, and he was a big chief in the land the Nakai-yes called Chihuahua. Villa had unknowingly sent his request asking us to come to him by Camisa Roja, who had killed Rafaela, Hombrecito's woman, ten harvests earlier—a story Hombrecito tells in his own paper tracks. Roja, now a Dorado, a "Golden One," one of Villa's best warriors who always guarded him, was to guide us to a meeting with him near the border in Mexico. When Camisa Roja first came to his door, Hombrecito had not recognized him as the man who'd killed his woman. It was only after he left that Hombrecito remembered Camisa Roja. Hombrecito still wanted to kill him, but I stopped them from fighting, and Camisa Roja led us to Villa's camp below the border.

I was glad to hear that Villa wanted to see us. He had fought to save Hombrecito and me from being killed by a *Nakai-yi* cavalry charge when we escaped the hacendado Comachos after rescuing Hombrecito's woman, Sac, and her little brother. We owed Villa our lives for this and other battles we fought, even one with a bear. It was good to pay this debt and be free of him.

That ride was the beginning of a long trail of much suffering. I met Big Star Pershing, the American chief, who led a big army chasing Villa in Mexico in that time. Along with Hombrecito and a reporter named Quentin Peach, I watched Villa's army prepare for battle at Agua Prieta, nearly starving and wearing thin, ragged clothes as the Ghost Face season approached. I also saw many cut down quickly in their charges toward the barbed wire and trenches and shoots-many-times guns at Agua Prieta, but I tell little of this, for Hombrecito tells of our time there in his own paper tracks.

After the battle at Agua Prieta, Villa said Hombrecito and I had done much for *División del Norte*. He would release us from his service if we wanted to go. Hombrecito told Villa that he would stay to help the men in *División del Norte*, and Villa was grateful.

General Pancho Villa then looked at me, but I shook my head. After watching Villa slaughter his warriors, I knew he was a bad chief, and I was returning to Mescalero. I said, "I go, *Jefe*. There's no honor riding against *hombres* hiding in holes with shoot-many-times guns. Better to wait until they come out of their holes. Better to fight when they no expect you. You lose too many warriors when your *soldados* attack enemies who fight while they hide in holes behind *pesh* ropes filled with thorns. I go." I stared hard at Villa for a few breaths, sensing that his thoughts flew in many crooked directions, like bats out of a dark cave. The cool morning was as still as the death all around us. "I come back if you shoot Hombrecito. It will take a long time for you to die. *Comprende,* General Pancho Villa?"

Villa stared back unblinking, slowly nodding. *"Sí,* I understand. You're a great friend, *Muchacho Amarillo. Muchas gracias* for all you've done for *División del Norte."*

Five suns later, I entered the canyon where my women kept their tipi and my sons grew to men. It had been a long, hard trail, and they were all happy I had returned. For two days, I rested, and then went to see C.R. Jefferis. He was glad I had returned, and I took my place as a policeman again. Then soon, Hombrecito came to the reservation and told me of Villa losing his mind and betraying him, and we decided to ride back to the land of the *Nakai-yes,* where he planned to kill Villa and his enemy, Camisa Roja.

It was a boy, Jesús, one we had saved from the American Army in Chihuahua, who changed his mind, but these stories I'll leave for him to tell.

CHAPTER 46
YELLOW BOY'S HOUSE

When I returned from the land of the Nakai-yes and Villa this second time, two moons had passed since I had known the comfort of my women and seen my sons. When Juanita first saw me at her tipi door, she laughed in relief and surprise. "Husband your trail has been long, and I can see, by your eyes, very hard. Come and eat and tell us of your ride."

I sat down by her fire, and she took my rifle and blanket roll and laid them on her blanket. She gave me a gourd bowl filled from the pot on her fire, and then stood in the doorway to call Moon on the Water and my sons.

I rested a few days with my family and then went to the agency to see my son Híghán, and to tell C.R. Jefferis I had returned. I had been gone much longer than I had expected and didn't know if C.R. Jefferis still wanted me for a tribal policeman. I tied my pony near the agency door as the coming sun lighted the mountain edges, making a fan of golden shafts of light across the ridgeline. Inside the agency, I heard the coffee pot clank against the iron stove after someone poured a cup.

My amigos were glad to see me back, but laughed at how thin and hollow-eyed I looked after two moons in the land of the *Nakai-yes*. I had just finished my second cup of coffee when C.R. Jefferis stuck his head in the door to let the policemen know he had arrived. He saw me and shook his head with a grin. "Is that you, Yellow Boy? Returned from Mexico and ready to be a policeman again?"

I nodded and stood to pump his hand twice, as the Indah like to do.

"Ho, C.R. Jefferis. I return from Mexico in two moons, not one. You still want me for a policeman?"

He laughed. "Ho, Yellow Boy. Of course, we want you back. You look like you need to put some meat on your bones and some sleep in your eyes. Did you finish your trail in Mexico?"

"Hmmph. We finish and come back, and we're not shot. The trail is good."

He nodded. "Glad to see you back. If you want to start work today, I'm sure the chief of police has much work for us to do. I saw Híghah in the records office if you want to visit. When you have time, stop by my office and tell me about your days in Mexico."

I swung my palm parallel to the floor to show all was well and said, "This I will do, C.R. Jefferis."

I spoke with the chief of police, who asked me ride to Tule Canyon and settle a dispute over a pony. Before I left, I found Híghah working with a big stack of papers covered with many tracks in long lines. He smiled when he saw me walk through the door and stood to welcome me.

"Father, you return. It makes my eyes happy to see you safe. My mothers, brothers, and I were ready to leave Mescalero and search for you. You look like you've traveled far. All is well?"

"All is well, my son." I told him a little of my trials in Mexico, and then said, "Your mother says soon I must go to Beela-chezzi to speak with him and Carmen Rosario about an important matter. This is true?"

Híghah's face grew red. I knew what Juanita believed was true. He nodded. "I have visited the tipi of Beela-chezzi and Carmen Rosario a few times and walked with Quiet Dove and Carmen Rosario as they picked berries, while Beela-chezzi hunted. Perhaps before the next Ghost Face, I will ask you to dress your best and speak with them."

My eyes saw the circle of life completing again as Beela-chezzi and I had hoped, and my heart beat with gladness. "This I will do. I think you chose a good woman and her family. Your mothers ask that you come for a meal tonight."

He smiled and said, "I'll be there before the sun's light is gone."

A moon after I returned, Híghâh and I sat on a blanket under a tall pine tree and told stories to Redondo and Hidloh about the long-ago days. Moon and Juanita sat by the fire nearby, working their magic on fine baskets that were always in demand by In-dah who stopped at the trading post to see "wild" Apaches.

In the low light, as the insects and tree peepers sang, we saw a rider come up the canyon on a big black horse. I couldn't recognize the rider's face in the growing darkness, but I knew the horse. Hombrecito had come. It was his first visit since we had returned from the land of the *Nakai-yes.*

I motioned for him to come to us. He waved, but pointed toward the corral and first unsaddled and rubbed down Sata-nas. Redondo and Hidloh ran to help him. They thought of him as a brother, and in our family's mind, that's what he was. Moon saw him and went into the tipi to get him a bowl of the good things we had eaten that evening.

I had told Híghâh many stories about Hombrecito, but this was the first time they had met. We stood as Hombrecito walked up to us out of the darkness. I said, "At last my oldest sons meet. This is a good day."

Híghâh took the hand Hombrecito offered, and they shook easily, like Indah do, and then, still shaking hands, they wrapped their free arms around each other in a hug, another Indah custom long-parted friends and brothers do. Híghâh said, "I have often wondered when I might meet Hombrecito, Doctor Henry Grace. Welcome, Brother."

Hombrecito's smile filled his face. "I owe much to Yellow Boy and his family. At last I meet Híghâh and know all my brothers."

My women came to join us. Moon gave Hombrecito his bowl and said he reminded her of the long-ago times in the camp of Kitsizil Lichoo'. We sat and spoke with him, remembering our times in the land of the Nakai-yes as the stars turned far into the night. My women listened and told their stories for a long while, and then went to their blankets. I made Hidloh go with them, but Redondo, not many harvests from manhood, I let stay and listen to the talk between Híghâh, Hombrecito, and me.

I lighted a cigarro and we smoked. Now, we were ready for serious council.

I said, "So, Hombrecito, all is well with you?"

"Yes, all is well. I came to speak with you about something that has been on my heart since my last harvest in the Indah *di-yen* school. Shall I speak?"

"Speak, my son. We listen."

Hombrecito pulled out his pipe, filled it with *tobaho,* lighted it, and blew the smoke up into the trees toward the black sky filled with bright stars. Holding his pipe between his long, strong fingers, he thought for a moment before he began.

"I know how much you enjoy life in your tipi. You have lived in one since you and your family left Bosque Redondo, but now I want you and the rest of your family to have a house, a good house, one that keeps you warm in the Ghost Face and cool in the Season of Big Leaves. I owe you my life in many ways, and I will always come to Mescalero when you need me. Rufus left me money. I know you don't care about money, but I want to use it to make you comfortable and make less work for Juanita and Moon. I want to help you build a house. Will you have one?"

I looked at Hígháh, who sat between us looking at me, his arms crossed, his head nodding. "Hombrecito speaks wise words. You know the Chiricahua at White Tail have pushed to get houses ever since they came to the reservation. It's been four harvests and many tracks on paper of Mr. Jefferis asking the chiefs in the east to give him the money to pay for them. He decided to go on and give them their houses without money from the east by selling some reservation timber to the sawmill, just as Stottler did for the log cabins he made the Mescaleros build. Daklugie told me the Chiricahuas had to live with the White Eyes for twenty-seven years, and they learned that houses are good things, much better than Stottler's log cabins. I'll work with my brother, Hombrecito, if you agree to let us build it."

I looked at them, knowing they had good hearts in this, but such a change is a hard thing. My mind, as mountain water tumbling across big rocks, made many thoughts, crossed many memories. Living in a house meant that we couldn't move where and when we wanted. It meant more of our freedom and independence was gone, because we must always camp in one place. It meant we would never again be as close to the land as when we touched the earth every sun when we sat by our fires or lay down to sleep every night with our bodies. It meant we became more like Indah and less like Apaches. Where we once roamed and raided free, now we lived inside lines drawn on a map, inside lines made with boards on a house.

I knew, like the seasons, life changes. Like the earth, all things change, as when flowers bloom and grass grows green in the Season of Many leaves and then pass away in the Season of the Earth Is Reddish Brown, when the winds blow cold and ice comes in the Ghost Face, but life returns in the Season of Little Eagles. In the seasons of my life, I was happy first with one wife, and then two. It took us a long time to have children, and, for their own reasons, each wife had to live for many harvests in separate camps, but we had stayed together, and our family had grown. Powerful witches had tried to destroy us, but now they were no more. *Maybe,* I thought, *a new season comes.*

As women often do, Juanita and Moon, rather than going to their blankets while we talked, sat just inside the tipi door and listened to the men. While I thought about what we should do, they came outside and sat with us. Juanita, pulling her blanket over her shoulders, said, "Husband we have listened to our sons. I would speak that you might know what is in the heart of your women."

"Speak *Ish-tia-neh*. I will listen."

Juanita looked at her folded hands for a moment and then, raising her eyes, said, "My sister and I are becoming old women. My days to have children have passed. Perhaps, this is also true with your second wife. Since I became first wife, we have lived in these mountain canyons on a reservation the Indah said was our People's land.

"Stottler tried to make us become like the Indah and live in log houses. The People did not want them and only lived in them until Stottler and the man who followed him left. Then we went back to our tipis. The log houses were no good. They became nasty. They were hard to clean, and Stottler would not let us cook on open fires as we did in a tipi. After we moved back into our tipis, we used the log houses to store supplies and tools, and, for that, they were good things.

"I've seen the Chiricahua houses at White Tail. They're much better than the log houses. They're easier to clean, warmer in winter than my tipi, and some have open fires so women can cook that way if they want. I like them. If our grown sons want to help us build one, then I think we should build it. That is all I have to say."

I looked at Moon and raised my brows to ask if she wanted to speak, but she shook her head.

I thought of all that had been said and the things that had floated through my mind. Most of all, I saw Hombrecito's face and realized he wanted only the best for us.

"What does the mind of Hombrecito say about this house?"

"I think the house you need should be like Rufus's house, except it would be built better and would look like three of his houses built side by side, but with only one porch, and big enough with sleeping places for you, your wives, and your children. I think you should have a barn with a corral for your animals, and we can run water to the barn and the house so your women and sons don't have to carry it every day bucket by bucket. If Juanita and Moon want an open fire, that can be done, but I also want you to have an iron stove like Rufus had."

When Hombrecito finished speaking, Juanita and Moon smiled and nodded. I liked what he said, too. Redondo sat looking from face to face, in wonder at all the sudden talk about a house. I waved my hand parallel to the ground. "My sons are good men to offer our family a house. We'll try this thing you say, Hombrecito. I may stay in the tipi a while until I learn how to use this house. If we like it after a harvest, we'll stay. If not, we'll go back to the tipi. How will you build this house? I have no understanding of making houses."

Híghán said, "I'll speak with C.R. Jefferis, make certain he won't be required to stop us, and explain to him that Doctor Henry Grace in Las Cruces helps with the house."

Hombrecito nodded. "That we need to do. I'll find some carpenters who'll help build the house and decide how much and the kinds of lumber we need, and then bring them here so they understand the site where we want to build. If we all work together on this, you can live in the house before Ghost Face comes."

CHAPTER 47
WAR BEYOND THE EASTERN BIG WATER

Within a moon, work started on the house Hombrecito wanted to build for us. White Eye carpenters who had seen Rufus's house and knew how to build houses did most of the work for framing its shape with heavy timbers. I told Redondo and Hidloh to learn what they could from watching and helping them, and I watched and helped, too, when work was slow with the tribal police.

One sun at the time of shortest shadows, Híghâh drove a wagon with building supplies to the house. With him was the new *inashood dilhil'n* (Catholic priest), who lived on the reservation in the little house next to the gathering house for ceremonies he performed every seven suns. The Indah schools insisted on teaching our children their stories of the Indah god who let his enemies hang him on a post to show his Power would not let his enemies kill him. I saw nothing wrong with this, but I still believed the Apache stories of Ussen were better for my People, who had remembered and told them since before the grandfathers. I think the Apache stories and beliefs about Ussen and the spirits he sends gave the People the Power they needed in this land better than those of the Indah god.

Before Híghâh could introduce us, the *inashood* (missionary) was off the wagon and had walked up to me with his hand out for a shake. "The People have pointed you out to me, and I'm honored to meet the great marksman and warrior, Yellow Boy. I'm Father Braun. Híghâh has done me a great favor in bring-

351

ing me to you. He's a fine young man. I know you're proud of him." I took his hand, looked in his face, and saw nothing in his eyes but truth. We pumped hands twice.

Father Braun said, "Hígháh tells me your adopted son is a doctor in Las Cruces and is helping you build your house. It looks like it will be a fine, big one. I have some skill with carpentry tools. I'll be glad to help you."

"I know you come to do *inashood* ceremonies for the People who want them, and that's a good thing. I've seen you many places on the reservation. I should have greeted you then as a friend to the Mescalero."

"Insignificant! I've wanted to meet everyone on the reservation and help them all I can. I knew you were busy with your work as a policeman. It's a good thing we meet now."

"We're glad when you can come and help us here, but you have much to do for all the People, and the suns move fast."

"Insignificant! I have skills you can use. Many hands make quick work. I think we can finish before the Ghost Face comes, and I won't neglect the People."

I know I must have looked surprised when he spoke of the Ghost Face, and he laughed.

"Eric Tortilla has just returned from the Carlisle school and is trying to teach me your customs and words and ways of saying them. I pay him a little money to translate my words into Mescalero when I speak with your People who do not know the Indah tongue."

"*Enjuh.* Come. We sit in the shade of the tall trees and have a smoke."

He said, "That's a good thing to do with new friends who speak straight."

It was a good smoke, and we talked of many things. He asked questions about the People and how we did things. I told him about our feasts and big ceremonies, such as the *Haheh* for girls becoming women, and how Stottler had once forbidden them. I expected him to tell me that such things were wrong when the Apaches followed Ussen instead of *inashood dilhil'n* ceremonies. But he nodded and said, "Yes, Eric told me of these ceremonies. These are good things for the People to do. It shows their love and respect for each other and for God. It teaches your People always to do the right things. Stottler was wrong to forbid them."

From that time, I always had a good heart for Father Braun.

Father Braun was right. Many hands made for fast work, and the Indah Hombrecito brought to build the house were good, hard workers. We finished the house early in the season of the Earth Is Reddish Brown. It was built much better and three times bigger than the house of Rufus, as Hombrecito said. Hombrecito brought a big iron stove like Rufus used to cook on, and there was a great stone fireplace to warm the big room and to use for cooking when Juanita and Moon wanted an open fire. He also brought a table and chairs to use for working, cooking, and eating. The front door faced east, so the sun came first to our windows, and we had only to step out on the porch for Ussen to hear our prayers.

A wood trough sealed with tar carried water from the spring in the canyon down to the house and to a watering tank in the corral. The Indah builders started a barn, but hadn't finished it when cold winds began to blow and the mountaintops turned white with the first snows. The men building the barn said they would return in the Season of Little Eagles to finish. They thought it was too cold to work outside building a barn as the Ghost Face neared.

After the house was finished, we still slept in the tipi. The women wanted to get used to being in the house and to learn how to cook on the big iron stove before they left the tipi. It was not easy for us to use the furniture Hombrecito brought us.

It didn't feel right to sit up high off the ground. All of us sat on the wood floor by the fireplace rather than in the chairs when we ate inside. The floors were hard to sleep on, and sometimes the fire in the fireplace or iron stove made the rooms too hot for good sleep. I did not rest well, and neither did my women. However, our young sons didn't mind the hard floors and thought it a big adventure to sleep inside a house like an Indah. We let them do this when they wanted. Despite the cold air and winds, we slept in the tipi because it was never too hot, and blankets on the ground gave us better rest.

After a couple of moons, I thought, *We can sometimes sleep in the house for Hombrecito, but it will be a long time before I'll sleep in it every night.*

Ghost Face was passing, and the Season of Little Eagles neared. Snow had begun melting in the canyons, and already a Chinook had blown across the mountains. The Ghost Face had not been too hard for us that harvest.

We had used the tipi most of that winter, only sleeping on the hard floors of the house when the tipi and a good fire with many blankets over us still left us a little cold. Hombrecito laughed with us that we still wanted to stay in the tipi. He said to live in the house when we wanted. When Híghah came for a visit, he slept in the house and told me straight it was a better place for us all, but he respected our not changing our life-way until I was ready.

One day, the sun was fast falling into the white tops of the western mountains when Hombrecito and Híghah came to visit us. From the tipi fire, Juanita and Moon gave us a fine meal of venison I had taken a sun before. I could tell from their faces that Hombrecito and Híghah had news, but I waited to ask them until we finished the meal and smoked. Then Hombrecito said, "We have news. Will you listen?"

"Speak. I will listen."

"Quentin Peach, our friend, the reporter in El Paso, and I used the talking wire a few days ago. While we were in Mexico looking for Villa, the war across the big water to the east grew worse. Big Chief Woodrow Wilson, who you know betrayed Villa last year, has shown all Americans tracks on a paper sent to the Nakai-yes by the Germans, the Indah tribe who showed Obregón how to fight Villa from holes with shoots-many-times guns, and who our friends fight across the big water. The tracks on the paper say the Germans will help the Nakai-yes attack the Americans in a much bigger way than Villa's attack on Columbus, and, if the *Americanos* are driven off the land, will help the Nakai-yes keep it. Americans are very angry about this paper and want war against the Germans, even though the Nakai-yes did not try to start a war. Big Chief Woodrow Wilson hears many little chiefs saying the Americans must help our friends across the big water by sending them an army and stopping the Nakai-yes from even thinking about attacking us."

A feeling of dark shadows falling on us filled my mind as Hombrecito continued.

"Unless something unexpected happens, Peach says his sources tell him the Americans will join our friends to fight across the big water within a moon or two. Big Star Pershing led his army out of Mexico during the Ghost Face. The big chief for Pershing, General Funston, who you remember was at Douglas for Villa's attack on Agua Prieta, has gone to the Happy Land. Peach thinks Big Star Pershing will be made the big chief for the army going across the big water."

Hombrecito reached in his shirt pocket and held up a paper with many tracks on it. "Big Star Pershing sent me a letter asking if I will help him watch over *di-yen* healing ceremonies across the big water for men hurt in the fighting. I've thought much on it, and decided I'll go. There's also this. The big war chiefs in

the east must send many to fight across the big water. Many Indah now say the little chiefs will give citizenship to Puerto
Ricans who fight in the war."

He saw me frown. I didn't know this tribe called Puerto
Rican. He said, "Puerto Ricans look like *Nakai-yes,* but live on
a little land the *Americanos* hold in the big water to the south.
Peach says the little chiefs will do this. He thinks Indians who
fight in this war across the big water will also be offered citizenship."

I frowned and shook my head. "You mean the Mescalero
who go to fight in the big Indah war can use the same laws as
Indah? Why would I want to use the same laws as the Indah? I
want to use the same laws as Mescalero. They're better than the
Indah ones, but the Indah don't let us use all of them as we
want."

Híghǎh leaned forward, resting his elbow on his knee. He
said in a calm voice above the snap and pop of the fire, "Father,
we live on this little piece of land the Indah gave us from the
great range we once freely roamed. They gave us the land, but
not the rights we need to stand as a nation of free men. I love
all this country, from big water in the east to big water in the
west. If you ride an iron wagon going faster than the fastest
pony three days and nights without stopping, you will not yet
see the big water in the east, but you'll see many towns and villages, many farms, many machines, and unending numbers of
Indah in great buildings made of wood, adobe mud, clay bricks,
and stone. You let me go to school far away when I was young
to learn all I could. I learned well. I learned much. I know more
about the Indah than most Indah know about themselves."

He made a wide sweeping motion with his arm and hand, his
eyes glittering in the firelight. "This is our land. The land beyond
the reservation border is Indah land. If we have Indah law, it
can be our land, too. I want that land. As an Indah, I can have

land anywhere, any time, without a big chief for the reservation in the east saying he must think about it for a while, which means we must wait one, two, maybe four or five years. My heart has a big feeling for all the land here on the reservation and the land all around it. I believe Peach speaks true. I, too, will join the Indah who fight the Germans across the big water. No American land will become *Nakai-yi* land, and I expect to have Indah rights after I return."

My heart filled with a strange mixture of pride and sadness that Hombrecito and my oldest son were going across the big water to fight the German Indah: pride that they were fighters, sadness that they might die. I had seen how the German Indah fought from holes in the ground when Hombrecito and I helped Pancho Villa. This was not a war of men fighting men. It was a war with men using machines that did nothing but kill as many men as possible as fast as possible, without courage or honor.

Still, Hombrecito and Híghán, grown men, had a right to choose. Hombrecito, a powerful warrior, had walked through the fire. He knew what it meant in a fight to kill or be killed. Híghán had not yet learned the ways of Indah war, but I knew the Indah would teach him well.

I stared in the fire while they watched me, wanting to know what I thought. I looked at Juanita and Moon, who sat with bowed heads as they, too, stared at the fire. I looked Hombrecito and Híghán in the eyes, as the Indah wanted when you spoke the truth, nodded, and waved my palm parallel to the ground. "The choice is yours to make, my sons. I won't speak against you. Do as you must."

They spoke together, *"Enjuh."*

It was quiet for a little while in the tipi. Only the fire with its crackle and pop of burning wood made any sound while we watched the flames.

Then Híghán said, "Father, I need your help."

I said, "I won't fight the Indah across the big water to be an Indah, my son."

He grinned. "It's not help I need in fighting Indah across the big water. I need help in marrying. I want Quiet Dove for my wife. In the way of the Indah, I have asked her to be my woman, and she has agreed. I can't leave a pony for her to return fed and watered to show that she accepts me. Still, I want to give Beela-chezzi and Carmen Rosario a bride gift. Will you speak for me? Father Braun has said he will marry us in the Catholic way whenever we want, and I'll do any Mescalero ceremony Beela-chezzi and Carmen Rosario want."

I laughed. My women covered their mouths as they laughed, too. It was a time of dark clouds in the distance and bright sunshine on our faces, a time of worry and a time of hope. I looked at Hombrecito and raised my brows, but he grinned and shrugged his shoulders. He had no one to whom I needed to speak for a bride gift.

I nodded toward Hígháh. "Does Quiet Dove understand you plan to go to the White Eye war across the big water?"

"She does. We have talked about this many times during the Ghost Face. She wants to marry before I go."

"*Enjuh*. What will you offer as a bride gift?"

"A house that I will build next to the one I build for Quiet Dove and me. Working for C.R. Jefferis, I know how to do this now that the Chiricahuas are getting their houses, and I have some money I have saved that will help with furniture and a stove when they leave their tipi. I know they may not want to leave their tipi for a long time, even as you do not want to leave yours, but the house will be there when they are ready for it. I want my wife's people and mine to live easy before they go to the Happy Land."

"Hígháh has learned wisdom. I will speak to Beela-chezzi with the next sun."

CHAPTER 48
INDAH MARRIAGE AND WAR

One morning, a moon after I spoke to Beela-chezzi, Hígháh and Quiet Dove were given an Indah Christian marriage ceremony by Father Braun at his place of ceremonies. People who had lived in our little camp in the Rinconada came to watch and to celebrate that a son of Yellow Boy and Juanita had taken a daughter of Beela-chezzi and Carmen Rosario.

Hombrecito was part of the ceremony, but I did not understand why Hígháh needed him to stand with him and the *inashood dilhil'n*. After the ceremony, we all gathered at the tipi of Beela-chezzi and Carmen Rosario and feasted, sang, and danced. The day was warm, and the breeze was light. We spoke with all who had come and remembered the good days in the long-ago times when we camped in the Rinconada, and later when we spread out across the reservation.

As the sun was falling into the western mountains, I noticed Hígháh and Quiet Dove had disappeared. They were gone seven days, and when they returned, I had never seen a man and his woman happier, unless it had been Juanita and me. I told Hígháh and Quiet Dove they should stay in our house until theirs was built, but Quiet Dove smiled and said she admired and appreciated my generosity, but a tipi Carmen Rosario, Juanita, Moon, and others had made for them was enough for her and Hígháh until their house, soon starting, was built. Then one would be built for Beela-chezzi and Carmen Rosario nearby.

★ ★ ★ ★ ★

Quentin Peach had strong medicine. Nearly everything he told Hombrecito to expect came true. Early in the Season of Many Leaves, Big Chief Woodrow Wilson told the little chiefs that the Americans must fight the German Indah, and they agreed. The little chiefs made tracks on a paper that said all young American men, unless they were unable to fight, must learn to be soldiers. Big Chief Woodrow Wilson made Big Star Pershing the big chief for the army. Instead of wearing one big star, as he had in the land of the *Nakai-yes,* now he wore four stars, and we called him Four Stars Pershing.

When that news came, Hombrecito brought Satanas and his rifle and saddle for me to keep again and said he would send letters to me about his work and adventures across the big water. Redondo and Hidloh had been to the reservation school for five or six harvests and could read the White Eye tracks on paper. They could translate to their mothers and me what the tracks meant that Hombrecito sent. I thought, *Maybe the reservation school is useful after all.* Hombrecito left two suns after he brought Satanas to my corral, and we did not see him again for over two harvests.

After Hombrecito left, Hígháh told C.R. Jefferis he would join the army in two moons. C.R. Jefferis tried to talk him out of it, saying that he had just married and that, as an Indian, he didn't have to join, and that he ought to stay and help him help the People. Hígháh wouldn't change his mind. He didn't want the Nakai-yes crossing the border to attack us if the Indah Germans won the war across the big water, and he wanted the citizenship rights this would give him, his woman, and his children. C.R. Jefferis said he was proud of Hígháh, that he was a man with a great vision, and that his job would be waiting for him when he returned.

★ ★ ★ ★ ★

Early one morning in the Season of Many Leaves, I rode to Tularosa with Hígháh when he took an iron wagon to *El Paso del Norte*, where he would take another iron wagon to an army training camp. There was a very clear, bright, blue sky that morning, the sun rising just above the Sacramento Mountains, when we stopped our horses halfway down the trail to Tularosa. In that place, we could see clearly far across the basin the stretch of white sand lying against the foot of the sacred mountains called San Andres. As we had seen many times from this place, early in the day, the sand often looked like a great white cloud resting on the ground. The mountains, usually gray in the shimmering distance, stood out brown and green, and even some canyon entrances stood out in shadows etched in the yellow light.

Hígháh stared into the distance, his face calm and peaceful. "Father, all my life I have learned what the Indah had to tell or show me. I've never been close to being the warrior you are. Now I let the Indah, rather than my father and his People, teach me how to be a warrior. If I'm their warrior, one day I'll be acknowledged as a man with Indah rights, but always I'll be Mescalero. Wherever I am, whether I am man or spirit, Indah or Mescalero, you, my mothers, my brothers, my woman, the sacred mountains and the cloud made of sand against the San Andres, and the great White Mountain beyond our homes are with me and I with you."

Hígháh spoke from his heart, but the sound of his words filled me with worry. I wondered what he meant, but I knew he would tell me when he was ready.

"*Idiists'ag nih shiye'* (I hear you, my son). Your family, the sacred mountains, and the white sand will be here when you return."

He smiled, nodding, and turned his pony toward Tularosa.

At the Tularosa Station, several young men from the reservation were also leaving to become soldiers. Before he climbed on the iron wagon, I took Híghá's shoulders in my hands and said, "Be a strong warrior. Kill many German Indah. Then come home."

He looked far away over my shoulder. "My father is a great warrior. He'll know I'm his son."

I watched the iron wagon roll down the iron road until I could no longer see even its smoke on the horizon. Then I mounted my pony and led Híghá's mount back to Beela-chezzi's corral.

Two suns after Híghá climbed on the iron wagon, I met Father Braun riding to visit the Shantas, a family who had helped him often and well. We stopped to talk and smoke in the shade of tall pines by the wagon road.

He said, "I understand Híghá and the other men going to fight overseas left two days ago."

"I went with him to Tularosa Station, where he and others from Mescalero climbed on the iron wagon that would take them to a training place for Indah soldiers. He has never known war before."

"Insignificant! Híghá and the others are fine young men. They're strong and Apache and will do well. I thank God every day for their courage and patriotism. They make the United States the great country it is. When they leave the Indah army training, they'll be ready to fight the Germans."

"What means this thing you call patriotism?"

He frowned, thinking for a little time, took a long draw from his pipe, and said, "I guess everyone has their own idea of what patriotism means. For me, it means you want the best for your country and your people, and you put their safety and needs of the country above your own."

"Hmmph. So this means that Nana and Victorio and the Chiricahua and Mescalero chiefs had patriotism?"

He blew a puff of smoke from his pipe and nodded. "Yes, sir, I guess it does. Truly, they were Apache patriots. Híghah and those others even more so, because they're fighting for Apaches and the Indah. It shames me that they have gone to the war and I haven't. I ought to be helping them find God's Power where they fight in a time of great trial. That's why I've asked my superiors to let me go as soldier *di-yen* to help these brave boys."

He laughed when he saw the expression on my face. "You ask your chief to go over the big water to fight the Indah Germans? Why you do this?"

"I don't go over the big water to fight Germans. I go to help our boys remember God and ask for his Power in hard times. God is easy to forget when you're trying to kill someone, but you call on him when you're bleeding because the other side has nearly killed you."

"Apaches don't call on Ussen when they suffer. That is weakness. We're strong."

"Yes, you are. But when a soldier thinks he might be headed for the Happy Land, it's good for a *di-yen* to help him think of God."

I thought on these words as the wind blew through the tops of the trees and ravens flying across the ridges spoke to each other.

"Hmmph. If this is true, then Ussen will give you Power to do this."

He nodded, "Yes, that's all I ask. I have to get on up the trail to the Shantas. We'll speak again, my friend."

"Yes, we'll speak again. I'll think on all you say."

We did speak two or three more times before his chiefs let

him go to the war across the big water. I was glad when Father Braun returned. His mind was quick, and his heart was good.

Hombrecito's letters said that Quentin Peach and he worked together in the long holes where the soldiers fought the German Indah, and that they were helping Four Stars Pershing inform the other chiefs about the war.

Híghâh wrote of what he learned in the army training camp. By the time he went across the big water, he wore three stripes on his sleeve. Híghâh was a sergeant, a little chief soldier. I was proud of both my grown sons.

One evening in the Season of Large Fruit, as we ate an evening meal, I noticed my women avoided my glance, cut their eyes toward each other, and smiled.

"News!" I said, "What news have you learned from Carmen Rosario and Quiet Dove?"

Juanita said, "Why do you think we've learned any news from them?"

"Because your faces say news, and you were out gathering fruit and nuts with them today."

Juanita looked at Moon, and they laughed. Juanita said, "Our man does well to be a tribal policeman. He knows who knows, but not who is guilty."

I didn't get the joke or the riddle. "Speak sense, woman."

"In the Season of Little Eagles, you will be a grandfather."

I felt my face cracking with a smile. "Quiet Dove carries Híghâh's child? Does he know?"

They nodded. "She wanted him to know first, before she told Carmen Rosario and Beela-chezzi. A letter came yesterday, telling her how happy he was. Now they all sing happy songs, and we can, too." I stared across the tipi and in my mind saw still another circle of life beginning.

In the Season of Little Eagles, about the same time Hígháh went across the big water to fight the Indah Germans, Quiet Dove had Hígháh's first child, a boy who had Hígháh's nose and mouth and Quiet Dove's eyes. His hand from his first days could grip my finger with the strength of a steel trap, and he didn't know what it was to cry. He was a true Apache child.

Quiet Dove, waiting until Hígháh returned to name him, called him *Ish-kay-neh* (Boy). I smiled when I heard this, for that had been my name until my father, Caballo Negro, named me Nah-kah-yen (Keen Sighted) just before my trial to show I was ready to serve warriors as novitiate. I hoped my grandson would not wait as long as I had to have his own name. My grandson filled me with pride.

Before *Ish-kay-neh* was born, Hígháh had made tracks in a letter to Quiet Dove suggesting Juanita make the child's *tsach* (cradleboard). Juanita laughed, honored and happy, when Quiet Dove asked her to make the *tsach* and gave her a new knife, *hod-dentin* (sacred pollen), and a fine iron pot to make it. As I had done for Sons-ee-ah-ray many harvests before when she made a *tsach* for the first child of Juanita and me, I roamed across the reservation finding the right kinds of red cedar, black locust, oak, and arrowwood to make the child's *tsach*. Juanita spent many hours making the buckskin that she used for it soft as cloth.

Many from the old Rinconada camp came for the sunrise *tsach* ceremony, and then gathered later for a baby's water-on-the-head ceremony by the *inastood* who did ceremonies for Father Braun until he returned from across the big water. There was a fine feast after the water-on-the-head ceremony, and Beela-chezzi and I celebrated the rare event of living long enough to see our grandchildren.

CHAPTER 49
A TIME TO DIE AND A TIME TO LIVE

The letters from Hombrecito and Hígháh where they were fighting the German Indah slowed to one or two in a moon. Redondo and Hidloh continued going to the Indah School, but
returned to their mothers' tipi every five days and stayed two.
One of the first things they always asked when they returned
was if a new letter had come from their brothers. They took
turns reading them to us as we sat around the tipi cooking fire.

The letters told us how our sons and brothers were helping
the French and English Indah fight the German Indah from
holes in the ground, and how bad life was in the blood-soaked
mud around them. One letter even spoke of the German Indah
trying to poison their air to blind, maim, and kill them, but the
wind usually carried the bad air away. The letters always ended
with them telling us not to worry and that they would return
from the war soon.

Their stories told me I had never seen any war like it, even
when Hombrecito and I helped Pancho Villa fight Carranza in
Mexico. Hígháh and Hombrecito knew, saw, and heard a much
bigger war that killed many more than I would ever know. They
proved their courage as the strongest and best warriors, as the
old Apache did when making war in the long-ago times.

Juanita and Moon worked hard, as they always did, through
the days of Large Leaves and Large Fruit, but they didn't laugh
often after the letters were read. Working around the fire in the
evenings for several days afterward, they said little. I was glad of

this. I had no desire for words about the war. Thoughts of Híghâh and Hombrecito fighting the German Indah squeezed my guts and made me wake up in the night wet from the water of evil dreams.

C.R. Jefferis read the Albuquerque newspaper stories to the tribal police about the fighting across the big water. The words from the newspaper sounded like neither side was winning. Then in the Season of Large Fruit with a soldier tribe named Marines, Four Stars Pershing started winning big battles. In the Season of Earth Is Reddish Brown, a great battle, fought at Meuse-Argonne, began that lasted nearly two moons. Many on both sides went to the Happy Place, but it sounded like Four Stars Pershing's army was winning.

A couple of days after C.R. Jefferis read us the story of what was happening in one of the Meuse-Argonne battles, a letter came from Híghâh. A night later, Redondo read it to us as we sat around the fire. Its tracks said:

". . . The fighting in these woods has been the worst I've seen. Many of our men have gone to the Happy Place; more have been killed and done more acts of bravery than I can count. Yesterday one of my men killed a German Indah as he was about to bayonet me in the back. Not more than two hours later he was blown to pieces by a grenade in a new attack. The German Indah are brave too. They are strong fighters and make us fight hard for every yard of ground we take from them.

"I have spoken of this kind of fighting in letters before, and I write of it again, so you understand the price I'm willing to pay so *Ish-kay-neh* will soon have the same rights and privileges as the Indah, but can still also stand straight and tall as a Mescalero. The country the White Eyes took from us will one day again be our country too. No price or hardship is too great to have this power for my wife, *Ish-kay-neh,* and the sons and daughters who will one day be ours. I have no doubt you will see it is so. My children will be able to use all the power of the Indah. Maybe they will even go to great Indah schools like the one by the western big water that my brother Hombrecito attended. My children will live in two lands. They will dance in the ceremonies of our people and sing the songs of the Indah. When I return from this land of death, mud, and blood, I want to teach the children of my People the power of the Indah that we might grow strong from it.

"My father, I remember the stories you told me of the agent Stottler back in the bad times for our People. When we have the power of the Indah upon us, the power of men like Stottler over us will be gone forever. Please make my brothers Redondo and Hidloh understand this and learn all they can at the Indah School so they can also help our People . . ."

Híghán said other things in that letter, but those words stayed in my mind a long time. I thought of them often and wondered how I, too, would get the power of the Indah when I couldn't even read the tracks they made on the white paper. The things Híghán wrote also made Redondo and Hidloh think about what he said about learning Indah power at their school, and we talked about that sometimes when they came home to our tipi.

It had been a warm sun for the season, and, as long golden light spears passed through the tops of the trees, casting shadows toward the eastern ridges, I sat on a blanket smoking and talking with Beela-chezzi under some pines next to my wives' tipi. Juanita, Moon, Beela-chezzi's woman Carmen Rosario, and Quiet Dove laughed and played with *Ish-kay-neh* as a meal we would soon eat bubbled in the big iron pot hanging from a tripod in the tipi. It was a time that made old age worthwhile.

In the low light, I heard water splash and the click of rocks on the trail. I saw the black outline of a rider slowly jogging up our canyon. I thought, *I wonder who comes to visit us.* It wasn't long before I recognized Sábado in his police sergeant's uniform and smiled as I remembered the time when I shot holes in his hat and those of his backup men to warn them away from our village in the Rinconada. I glanced at Beela-chezzi and saw he smiled too, probably remembering the same time in the Rinconada as me.

The women saw Sábado riding toward us, grew quiet until they recognized him, and then began playing with the baby and talking again. I waved him over to us. He dismounted and tied his pony near our blankets.

I said, "Ho, Sábado! The cooking pot bubbles. Come have a smoke with Beela-chezzi and me before we eat."

He shook his head. Even in the fading light, I saw the frown on his face and knew there was trouble.

He said, "I cannot stay. Agent Jefferis sent me with this paper holding tracks from the talking wire that just came for Quiet Dove."

He stepped over to the blanket and handed her a sealed telegram. She, too, saw the trouble in his face and, with trembling fingers, pulled the talking paper out of its paper bag and squinting in the low light read it to us.

RECEIVED AT MESCALERO AGENCY, OTERO COUNTY, NEW MEXICO

WASHINGTON DC 4 32PM NOV 3 1918

MRS QUIET DOVE HIGHAH

DEEPLY REGRET TO INFORM YOU THAT SERGEANT HIGHAH YELLOW BOY

INFANTRY IS OFFICIALLY REPORTED AS KILLED IN ACTION EIGHTEEN

OCTOBER

HARRIS ACTING THE ADJUTANT GENERAL 4 55PM

All the women but Quiet Dove stared at the blanket and then buried their faces in their hands, and there was the sound of grief, a sigh as of wind moaning high in the trees. Quiet Dove, saying nothing, stared at the paper trembling in her fingers. Then she squared her shoulders and, carefully folding the paper, put it in her dress, scooped up *Ish-kay-neh* and, settling him on his *tsach*, began lacing its cover over him.

She said to Juanita and Moon, who were on their knees to help her with the baby, "My medicine says *Ish-kay-neh* and I must go. My belly will not hold food in this bad time. Will my father and mother walk with me and *Ish-kay-neh* to my house?"

Sábado tugged at his hat and said, "If you would ride my pony, I would be proud to lead it to your house."

Quiet Dove shook her head. "Officer Sábado, you are very kind, and I thank you. But I need time with myself and my family and prefer to walk with my mother and father."

Sábado nodded. "I understand. It's a hard time. Please tell me or any other policeman if you or your family needs help. I'll see you again." Giving us a little hand salute off his hat, he mounted his pony and trotted off down the creek.

Carmen Rosario helped Quiet Dove lift the *tsach* to her shoulders. I felt Beela-chezzi's warm hand squeeze my shoulder as he stood and said, "We're ready, daughter." Tottering on his old legs, a wandering spirit on arthritic knees, his face unmoving, as if chipped from stone, he followed his women and grandson and vanished in the shadows of the night.

I found myself as if awakening from a dream, staring into the darkness, feeling water in my eyes and trying to swallow a ball of thorns in my throat. I had not felt this way since the long-ago time when I had found my father killed and scalped among the bodies in our Guadalupe Mountains village that had been burned to nothing but ashes.

I felt my spirit sinking inside me, falling like a leaf in darkness drifting to the ground. Time seemed to slow, like the times when I had to shoot fast and straight. From high on a canyon ridge, Wolf again howled to his brothers. I wanted to join him and howl in my misery.

My women folded their blanket and, without words, went to the tipi, moonlight shining in the water on their faces. I sat in the cold night air a long time to smoke and think of old times and feel the loss of Híghâh cutting my spirit.

Off in the darkness down the canyon, I heard a woman wail, almost a scream of pain, like I remembered from the long-ago days in the Blue Mountains when the Chiricahuas caught a *Nakai-yi* and burned him, setting him on fire with lighted splinters stuck in his skin.

Beela-chezzi appeared out of the moonlight shadows. I said nothing and motioned for him to join me. He dropped down beside me on the blanket, looked in my face and then at the blanket, shaking his head. I pulled a cigarro from my shirt pocket, lighted it, and we smoked to the four directions, the light from its burning tip marking our faces with deep black shadows in its soft orange glow. After we finished, I ground out the cigarro's fire, and Beela-chezzi stared off into the darkness saying nothing.

I looked into the face of Beela-chezzi and said, "So, the father of our grandson goes to the Happy Place a warrior. I never knew him as a warrior. I know he will be welcomed. I have great pride in him. When he was a small child, the Indah took him and tried to make him forget the People. He didn't forget us. He came back to us. He gave us his wisdom. Now the Indah have taken him again, and he won't come back. My heart is heavy, but I know he's in a good place. Will Quiet Dove and *Ish-kay-neh* stay with you?"

Beela-chezzi shook his head. "I don't know. She asked to be

by herself for a while. Now she wails, and so does her mother. She has the house and knows Carmen Rosario and I want her and *Ish-kay-neh* close by us. She knows you and your family want them here, too. I know that if she stays, she will not live in the tipi with us. She said Hígháh told her a house was a better lodge than a tipi, and the People would change when they saw it was true. They both believed in the Indah *Ussen*, so the house won't have to be destroyed, and she can continue to live there for as long as she wants."

We sat together for a while in the silence of men who are friends and brothers sharing a black time in their groaning spirits. After a while Beela-chezzi stirred and said, "I've left my women to grieve alone long enough. I return to them. I know you want to speak with Juanita and Moon in their sorrow."

"I have a wise friend. I'll try to learn how the father of our grandson died in battle and tell you when I know. There's not much light on this the blackest of nights. Choose your steps carefully."

"This I will do. Soon I see you."

"*Enjuh.*"

Beela-chezzi crawled to his feet with a groan and disappeared into the dark.

I felt the chill of the night air on my skin and darkness in my spirit as I let my mind wander among the stars. Then I called to Moon and Juanita to come sit with me.

They came with their shawls over their shoulders and sat on the blanket by my sides, each giving me of her warmth. I lighted a new cigarro, and we smoked with no words passing between us, only looks of helpless sorrow. When our smoke was finished, Juanita said, "What does Beela-chezzi tell you? Tell us."

"He says Quiet Dove wants to be alone for a while. She and Hígháh both believed in the White Eye Ussen so their house won't be burned. He'll tell us more when he knows it."

We pulled the ground blanket around us and sat together saying nothing as the moon fell across the stars from the top of its arc. Most of that time, Juanita sat silent and rocking back and forth in her misery. Moon sat staring at her hands in her lap. As the moon began to fall, Juanita reached behind her belt and pulled out her sharp, shiny knife with the long blade she used for cooking, gathering the food, and making baskets. Moon also pulled her knife.

Their knives reflected the moonlight and filled their sad faces with shadows. Juanita said, "Our son is gone to the Happy Place. I know he respects the ways of our fathers. I cut my hair to mourn him."

Moon nodded, "As do I."

I had fought Tata Loco's demand for cutting my hair and still wore it so it touched my shoulders. Now I pulled my knife and held it up with those of my women and said, "We take our hair in grief and pray to Ussen to speed our son's journey to the Happy Place and to recognize a true warrior comes to him, one who deserves his acceptance."

Soon our cut hair lay in a sack that I tied shut. Our heads were cold as we went to our bed with most of our hair gone. The last thing I remember of that night was Juanita's long sigh. The water in her eyes was no more.

The next morning I took the sack of hair and rode down the trail I had taken with Hígháh to Tularosa when he took the iron wagon to war. I stopped at the place where we had looked at the white sand lying like a cloud far away, stretched along the foot of the San Andres Mountains. For a long time I sat on a big rock, thinking, with my rifle across my knees; thinking and staring at the white cloud of sand. After a while I opened the sack and threw our hair to the cold wind. I watched our hair carried away in the wind shaking the creosotes, junipers, and mesquites and tall, dry yucca stalks around me. At the foot of the distant mountains, the wind twisted and raised fuzzy puffs of white sand. They looked like the wispy clouds in the gray, rumpled sky. I stood on the rock and, raising my arms, sang a prayer to Ussen from deep in my guts. I sang it to each of the four directions.

"Ussen, maker of all things,
Our son comes to you in the Happy Place
Our son is a great warrior.
Make him welcome.
Ussen, maker of all things,
Give our son greater joy than he had in the land
     of the living.
Give him your Power in the Happy Place.
Our son is a great warrior.
Make him welcome."

I finished my prayer staring at the far mountains and white swirling clouds of sand below them and thinking of Híghâh's last letter and its words.

I thought of the time Ussen brought the Wind and Thunder Spirits to give me my Power, and all the times Ussen had helped me face evil with my Yellow Boy rifle, a weapon made by the Indah, one that Ussen had given me and connected to me as part of my Power.

As I sat there, I came to see that my connection with the rifle was the same kind of Power my son had written that he wanted for his son and all Mescaleros. He wanted to stay a Mescalero, but stand strong among the Indah, using their knowledge and tools, their gifts from Ussen. They were what Ussen gave the Indah as their Power. I saw then that my son was wise beyond his

374

years, wiser than I had been. I mounted my pony and rode back to my women.

I put my pony in the corral, walked to the tipi, and stuck my head in the door. There by the fire were my women in their short ragged hair of mourning, the mothers of my children. They were truly a gift from Ussen. They kept us together, rather than being scattered like seeds before the wind.

Juanita looked up when I pulled the door blanket back. She said, "The sun is still above the mountains, but our hearts are in the valley. You've cast our offering for our son to Ussen on the wind and prayed?"

I nodded as she motioned me inside.

Moon on the Water said, "If you have hunger, we'll find you something to eat."

I shook my head and sat down between them. I smelled their stew bubbling in the pot with the good smells of onions, chilies, wild potatoes, and beef, and my mouth watered, but I would wait to eat. I told them what I had done that day, sang my prayer to Ussen for them, and then told them how I had come to understand what our son had said in his last letter about being Mescalero but with the same powers as the Indah.

"Our son was born Mescalero, but was taught many things about Indah Power he wanted us to know and understand. He understood there are some things we must change from the old ways and use Indah knowledge and tools to help us live in the future time. He knew we must do this, or soon all Mescalero life-ways would be gone forever, forgotten by *Ish-kay-neh* or his sons and never to return. Today, we will make the first change using his wisdom."

Moon and Juanita looked at each other and back to me. Juanita narrowed her eyes. "Today? The day is nearly gone. What will we do today?"

"Today we begin living in a house. The house our blood son Hígháh and our adopted son Hombrecito gave us. Today we begin making the strengths of the Indah our own. Today we make our fire there, and live there as Mescaleros using the Indah Power Ussen has given us. That is all I have to say."

EPILOGUE

We moved from the tipi to the house that afternoon. The house was warm in winter. It was easier on my women to cook and do other work in it than in the tipi. We have lived in the house since the day Ussen opened my eyes and gave me understanding of Híghäh's wisdom.

A moon after the talking wire letter came telling us Híghäh had gone to the Happy Place, C.R. Jefferis received a letter from Híghäh's chief, asking that it be sent to Quiet Dove. A few suns later, she read it to Beela-chezzi, Carmen Rosario, Juanita, Moon, and me. The letter tracks said Híghäh was killed in a place called Argonne Forest while he was protecting soldiers with a shoots-many-times gun. His soldiers got away from Indah Germans who had surrounded them.

The letter said Híghäh was very brave, and his chiefs and the men he saved would never forget him. His chief had asked that he be remembered with the Medal of Honor. Truly, as I knew, my son was a great warrior, and my spirit grew when I heard these words.

In the next harvest after we moved from the tipi, the big chiefs in the east made a law that Indians who fought in the war across the big water and their families had the same rights as the Indah. Híghäh had won the reward for which he fought. Five harvests later, all Indians were given those rights.

Hombrecito survived the big Indah war and came back to us, but his memories of that war were ghosts that haunted him for a long time. He rarely spoke of those ghosts, but one afternoon in the harvest the Indah named 1919, he told me a few of his stories while the women gathered acorns in the grove of oak trees down the trail. He spoke of battles he had endured in the long deep cuts like irrigation ditches in the earth from which most of that war was fought. I often shook my head in awe at the death and destruction of which he spoke.

That day I sat at the porch steps with my back against a post listening to him and looking down the small stream toward the entrance to our canyon. In the bright golden light and black shadows, the sun no more than three hand-widths off the western horizon, I saw a pony come jogging up the trail by the stream toward our house. Its coming unexpected, I glanced toward my Henry rifle to be sure it was in easy reach.

Hombrecito saw me squinting down the canyon and turned to see what I saw. Soon the pony was close enough for us to see a woman riding bareback and holding an Indian child of maybe three or four harvests in front of her. I smiled to realize the woman was my *amiga, di-yen,* and sister-in-law, Lola Mes, but I didn't recognize the child. Lola Mes rode to the porch and, before Hombrecito could reach up to take the child, Lola Mes had easily slid off the pony and come to the porch steps where we sat.

The look on her face held power, both her one good eye and the blind one the color of milk looked in mine. In the old times her stare would have been an insult, but now her look told me she had serious business to discuss. The scar on the side of her face where the witch weapon had attacked and blinded her many harvests before stood out red and angry.

She spoke without the usual preliminary comments about family and friends that were good manners before the point of her coming was discussed. "Ho! Yellow Boy! Brother of my man and good amigo." She motioned toward Hombrecito. "Is this man the famous *di-yen,* Hombrecito?"

Hombrecito nodded and held out his arms to take the child, who showed no fear of him and sat calmly on his knees. Like any good *di-yen,* he began to look her over for problems his medicine might fix. I saw him frown when he found bruises on her arms and legs and what looked like a place where a bullet might have grazed her leg that was healing under a wrapped poultice I was certain Lola Mes had made.

"Ho! Lola Mes! Hombrecito has returned from the war between the Indah tribes across the great water to the east. Come. Sit with us. Tell us why you come, if not to look on our fine faces. Who is the child? I have no memory of it."

"You shouldn't. She is from the camp of Kitsizil Lichoo' and a reason I come to you."

Saying nothing, I motioned her to sit between us on the porch steps and then reached inside my vest pocket to pull out one of my little black *Nakai-yi* cigarros. I used my thumbnail to light a Redhead match for the *tobaho,* and we all smoked to the four directions.

When I finished the cigarro, I said, "Speak, Lola Mes. We will listen."

She folded her hands in her lap, made a little thoughtful frown, and stared off into the dark tree shadows. She said, "Knows Horses and I have had no word from Running Wolf and his wife Blue Flower for over a harvest. They are good amigos. We have been through much together. I know Beela-chezzi has spoken of not hearing from them in many moons either, and had planned to visit the camp of Kitsizil Lichoo' for a time with his son and his family. But with the passing of his son-in-law to the Happy Land, he and Carmen Rosario have stayed close to Quiet Dove and their grandson.

"Knows Horses and I decided in the fullness of the last moon to visit the camp of Kitsizil Lichoo'. We wanted to see the faces of Running Wolf and Blue Flower, hear their words and stories, and return here to tell Beela-chezzi and Carmen Rosario all was well with their son and daughter-in-law."

I thought of the time three harvests ago when Hombrecito and I had stayed in the camp of Kitsizil Lichoo' nearly two moons, waiting for word from Kitsizil Lichoo's scouts about where Pancho Villa hid so we could go there and kill him. Kitsizil Lichoo's camp lay deep in a canyon that connected to other canyons that eventually wound out of the Sierras to the cattle herds on the llano, where the Apaches took a few head for food, and the hacendados would not risk their men to get them back. But when we were there, cattle had become scarce because of the *revolución,* and half the warriors and their families in the camp of Kitsizil Lichoo' had left to live at San Carlos or even Mescalero. Hombrecito liked the widow, Lupe, a *di-yen* who helped him with his medicine for the camp people while we waited, and I knew she was the source of interest in his eyes as Lola Mes spoke.

"Knows Horses and I loaded a packhorse with presents for the camp of Kitsizil Lichoo' and rode south. We only rode at night to avoid the fighting still going on in the land of the Nakai-yes between Pancho Villa and Obregón. Using the usual trail up the Bonito River Canyon, we rode up to the ridge above the camp of Kitsizil Lichoo', but there was no sentry and no warning bell the sentry could ring. The bell was gone. The camp was empty; all the horses and mules and Ghost Face supplies were gone from their usual caves. I felt fear there. We saw tracks of ten or twelve ponies around the camp wearing *pesh líí'beshkee'é* (iron horseshoes). Some *wickiups* had been destroyed—it looked like horses had been ridden through them—but none were burned. We found no bodies, until we heard movement in the brush and found a very hungry child trying to wake a dead woman in a shallow cave in the creek bank by the camp."

I pointed at the child sitting on Hombrecito's knees, and Lola Mes nodded.

Hombrecito said, "How did the woman die?"

Lola Mes said, "She was shot twice, but the blood and mashed down brush in the cave showed she took a long time to go to the Happy Place. I think whoever killed her shot her while she was running with the child in her arms. Somehow she got away and hid, so they didn't find her. You saw the wound on the child where I have put a poultice on it. I don't think whoever shot her intended to shoot the child."

I felt anger boiling in my guts, and I thought, *Who is evil enough to shoot a woman running with a child?*

Lola Mes said, "We found and followed the tracks of unshod ponies out of the corral and down the creek before they crossed a ridge south, and then west toward Río Bavispe before we lost their trail. There were no horses with iron shoes following them. Knows Horses and I thought you and Beela-chezzi would want to know this."

I nodded. "What do you think happened?"

"We believe Kitsizil Lichoo' somehow learned Nakai-yes were coming and took the camp to a safer place, but we have no idea where, or why the woman and child were there. We think, if they're not found soon, we may never be able to find them. Cattle are few and game is in short supply, as more miners and timber cutters go in the mountains. The camp's food supplies are probably nearly gone, and judging from the tracks we saw around the camp, enemies may be hunting them. Ghost Face is already showing in the high places. We must find and help them plenty quick, or it may truly be the Ghost Face for them."

I thought, *Wise woman is Lola Mes.* I glanced at Hombrecito. He was leaning forward listening, his eyes glittering, looking like those of an eager racing pony at the starting line. "Do you plan to keep this child?"

She smiled and nodded. "Our daughters have their own families. My sister and Knows Horses's number-two wife Falling Water and I will raise this child. What will you do?"

I knew Kitsizil Lichoo's band must be in trouble. I had to find them *pronto* and offer help, but I had to think of what it would mean for my family if I rode into the land of the *Nakai-yes*. I looked at Hombrecito, and he nodded.

I said, "I'm old and stiff. Still, I can sit a pony for a long ride and shoot straight with the Power Ussen gave me. I know Hombrecito must think of Lupe, the *di-yen* he knew, and left there with his medicines three harvests ago. I think he will come. Beela-chezzi is an old man, and his joints swell in the cold. It's too far and too hard for him to ride. Knows Horses has many cattle and vaqueros he must oversee, and he has already been gone a long time. Maybe Beela-chezzi and Knows Horses will look after my family while Hombrecito and I go to the Blue Mountains. Kitsizil Lichoo' and his people have helped me much. If my son Hombrecito agrees, we'll ride in a few days to find and help our old friends who have vanished."

Lola Mes and I looked at Hombrecito, who smiled and nodded.

Lola Mes said, "*Enjuh*. Truly, you are Yellow Boy, Killer of Witches, the last warrior."

ADDITIONAL READING

Ball, Eve, Lynda A. Sánchez, and Nora Henn, *Indeh: An Apache Odyssey*, University of Oklahoma Press, Norman, OK, 1988.

Ball, Eve, *In the Days of Victorio: Recollections of a Warm Springs Apache*, University of Arizona Press, Tucson, AZ, 1970.

Blazer, Almer N., *Santana: War Chief of the Mescalero Apache*, Dog Soldier Press, Taos, NM, 2000.

Bourke, John G., *An Apache Campaign in the Sierra Madre*, University of Nebraska Press, Lincoln, NE, 1987. Reprinted from the 1886 edition published by Charles Scribner and Sons.

Bray, Dorothy, editor, *Western Apache–English Dictionary: A Community-Generated Bilingual Dictionary*, Bilingual Press/ Editorial Bilingue, Tempe, AZ, 1998.

Goodwin, Grenville, *The Social Organization of the Western Apache*, original edition, copyright 1942 by the Department of Anthropology, University of Chicago, Century Collection edition by the University of Arizona Press, Tucson, AZ, 2016.

Goodwin, Grenville, Edited by Keith H. Basso, *Western Apache Raiding and Warfare*, University of Arizona Press, Tucson, AZ, 1971.

Goodwin, Grenville, and Neil Goodwin, *The Apache Diaries, A Father-Son Journey*, University of Nebraska Press, Lincoln, NE, 2000.

Haley, James L., *Apaches: A History and Culture Portrait*,

University of Oklahoma Press, Norman, OK, 1981.

Mails, Thomas E., *The People Called Apache*, BDD Illustrated Books, New York, NY, 1993.

Opler, Morris, E., *Apache Odyssey: A Journey Between Two Worlds*, University of Nebraska Press, Lincoln, NE, 2002.

Opler, Morris Edward, *An Apache Life-Way: The Economic, Social, & Religious Institutions of the Chiricahua Indians*, University of Nebraska Press, Lincoln, NE, 1996.

Robinson, Sherry, *Apache Voices: Their Stories of Survival as Told to Eve Ball*, University of New Mexico Press, Albuquerque, NM, 2003.

Sánchez, Lynda A., *Apache Legends and Lore of Southern New Mexico: From the Sacred Mountain*, The History Press, Charleston, SC, 2014.

Sonnichsen, C.L., *The Mescalero Apaches*, University of Oklahoma Press, Norman, OK, 1958.

Thrapp, Dan L., *The Conquest of Apacheria*, University of Oklahoma Press, Norman, OK, 1967.

Thrapp, Dan L., *Al Sieber: Chief of Scouts*, University of Oklahoma Press, Norman, OK, 1964.

Worchester, Donald E., *The Apaches: Eagles of the Southwest*, University of Oklahoma Press, Norman, OK, 1992.

ABOUT THE AUTHOR

W. Michael Farmer, a member of the Western Writers of America, learned about the rich mosaic of historic figures depicted in his books while living in Las Cruces, New Mexico, for fifteen years. He has a Ph.D. in physics and has conducted atmospheric research with laser-based instruments he developed. He has published short stories in anthologies, won awards for essays, and published essays in magazines. His first novel, *Hombrecito's War*, won a Western Writers of America Spur Finalist Award for Best First Novel in 2006, and was a New Mexico Book Award Finalist for Historical Fiction in 2007.

His other novels include: *Conspiracy: The Trial of Oliver Lee and James Gililland; Killer of Witches, The Life and Times of Yellow Boy, Mescalero Apache, Book 1; Blood of the Devil, The Life and Times of Yellow Boy, Mescalero Apache, Book 2; Mariana's Knight, The Revenge of Henry Fountain, Legends of the Desert, Book 1* (which won the 2017 New Mexico-Arizona Book Award for Historical Fiction and was a finalist in Adventure-Drama); *Knight's Odyssey, the Return of Henry Fountain* (released in 2018); and *Knight of the Tiger, The Betrayals of Henry Fountain* (released in 2018). *Killer of Witches, The Life and Times of Yellow Boy, Mescalero Apache, Book 1* won a 2016 Will Rogers Medallion Award and was a 2016 New Mexico-Arizona Book Award Finalist in the Historical Fiction and Adventure-Drama categories. In 2017, *Blood of the Devil, The Life and Times of Yellow Boy, Mescalero Apache, Book 2* was a Finalist in the 2017

New Mexico-Arizona Book Awards for Historical Fiction and in Adventure-Drama.

The employees of Five Star Publishing hope you have enjoyed this book.

Our Five Star novels explore little-known chapters from America's history, stories told from unique perspectives that will entertain a broad range of readers.

Other Five Star books are available at your local library, bookstore, all major book distributors, and directly from Five Star/Gale.

Connect with Five Star Publishing

Visit us on Facebook:
   https://www.facebook.com/FiveStarCengage

Email:
   FiveStar@cengage.com

Five Star Publishing books are available through all major wholesalers and distributors.

To share your comments, write to us:
   Five Star Publishing
   Attn: Publisher
   10 Water St., Suite 310
   Waterville, ME 04901